False *Flag*

A Black Watch Security Novel

Kristen Casey

EST 2016

GALLANT FOX
PRESS

Content Guidance

I always want readers to feel comfortable picking up a Kristen Casey romance, but as an avid reader myself, I know how important it is to have the tools to make informed decisions regarding our reading.

At this time, none of my titles are categorized as dark or taboo romance. However, I recognize that certain topics and scenarios may be challenging for individuals to encounter when reading for pleasure.

Therefore, if you would like detailed content information for any of my titles, please scan the QR code or click on the link below, and you will be directed to a dedicated page on my website that lists this information.

In addition, if you ever encounter a situation in any of my titles that is not listed (but you believe should be), I encourage you to reach out to me at *KristenCasey.com* to recommend adding it.

Thank you.

https://www.kristencasey.com/content-guidance

The Black Watch Security Series

About This Book

Beau Gaines has always been the man who knows what to do when life goes sideways. It was probably why his squad dubbed him "Buck" years ago—because the buck unfailingly stopped with him.

Then a rescue mission gone wrong gets splashed all over the media by a person he shouldn't have gotten close to, and Buck and his team are drawn into a full-blown inquiry that could end their SEAL team careers. He no longer has the luxury of dealing with the fallout in his own way.

Instead, he must call in reinforcements, from the only outfit he can trust now. Thanks to Black Watch Security, he's not just a man with a plan anymore—he's an IED primed for vengeance.

The one obstacle between him and his goal is Peyton, the beautiful professor he meets unexpectedly and falls hard and fast for. She doesn't know a thing about his past, and the timing of her arrival in his life must be a coincidence.

Or is it? Does Peyton know more about the outcome of that ill-fated mission than she's letting on?

It's possible that Buck has more than brothers-in-arms to avenge. More than a public record to set straight. Because of Peyton, he must also decide if this is love—or a setup.

Again.

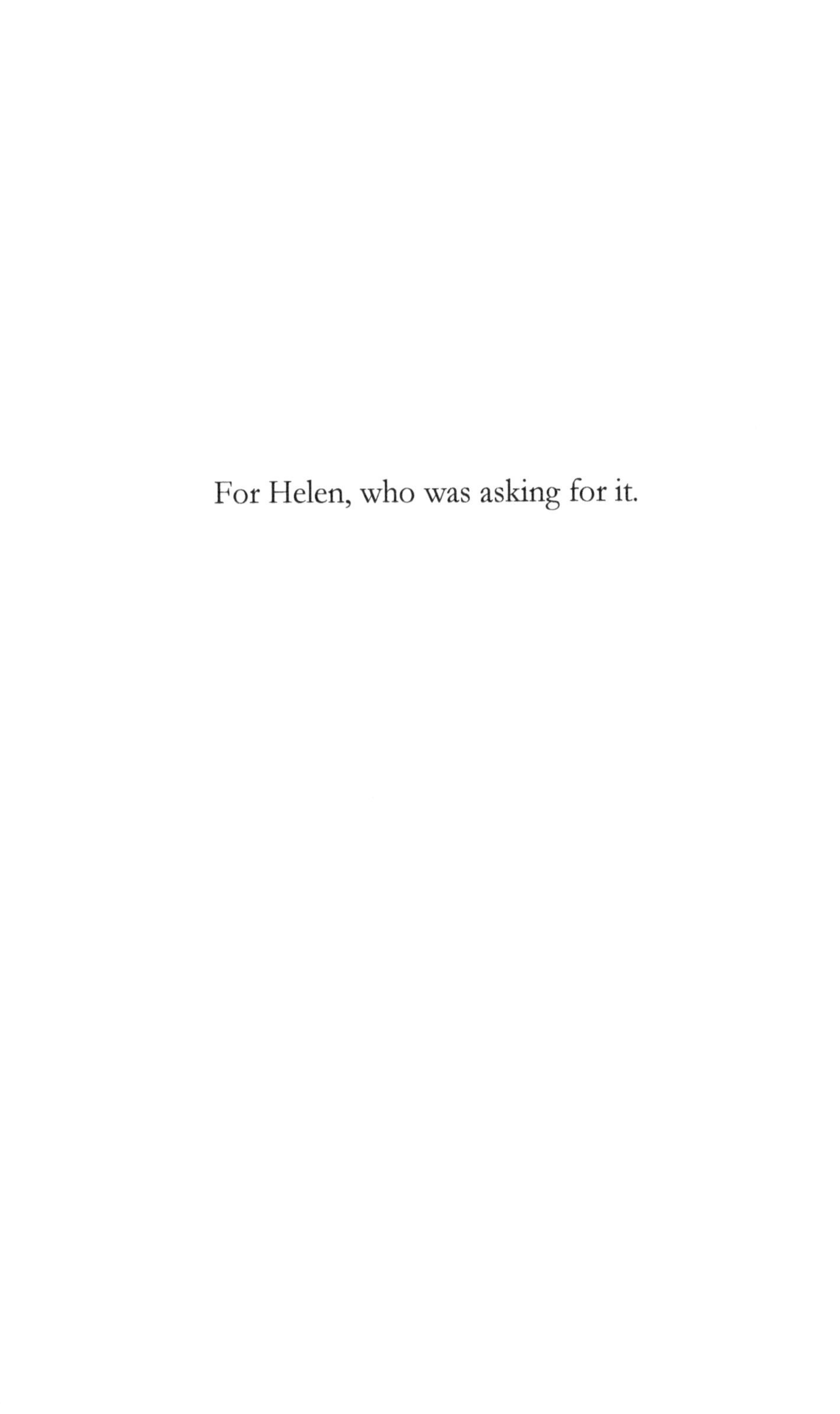

For Helen, who was asking for it.

"False Flag"

1) an attack or other hostile action that obscures the identity of the participants carrying out the action while implicating another group or nation as the perpetrator.

2) a misrepresentation of affiliation or motivation or a false equivalence deliberately put forth to manipulate the context, perception, or frame of an action, object, or argument.

Prologue

Tate

TATE MONROE HUNG up the phone in his home office and let out a heavy breath. In the next room, his wife was getting ready for bed. He had an early meeting in the morning and ought to be in there doing the same thing, but he couldn't seem to make his feet move.

Anyone would need a few extra minutes to collect themself after the conversation he'd just had. He shouldn't feel guilty.

Tate's efforts to feign calm were completely blown to hell once he breached the bedroom door, however. Lyla took one look at his face and immediately demanded, "What's wrong?"

He didn't bother pretending. Tate told her, "A call came in. Guy looking to hire us."

She frowned, adorable as ever in her glasses and messy bun. "That's…good, I thought."

"Yeah, except this job reeks like an onion," he explained, "And probably has just as many layers."

"Putting aside that scurrilous vegetable slander, I have to wonder why that's unusual. Aren't complications why people call you to begin with? Because their situations are too hairy to figure out themselves?"

"That, or because they don't want to get their own hands dirty."

As a company, Black Watch was still in its infancy, and Tate had spent the last several months building up staff and capital so they could take on bigger jobs, and more of them, but he'd been a little floored by the gamut of sticky problems that had found their way to him already.

Especially this one.

"Is that what you think this is? Someone trying to shift their mess onto you?"

"I'm…not sure," he said, considering Lieutenant Gaines's words again. "I don't think so. I think this guy's just at the end of his rope. He doesn't know who to believe or where else to turn."

Tate paused, but there was no getting around it. He had to tell her this next part, too. The most important part, in all likelihood.

"There's something else, Slick."

Lyla stood firm in her flowered pajama pants and gestured impatiently for him to go on.

With a heavy sigh, he admitted, "I might be way too close to this dude's problem. Because the guy who called me…" He stopped and raked his fingers over his scalp, already suspecting what Lyla would say.

She came and stood in front of him, hands on her hips. "Tate. What's going on? Who called you tonight?"

Hell, it wasn't like he wanted to keep it from her, not exactly. It just felt big and unwieldy in his throat, like he'd swallowed a grenade that was cutting off all his air.

"*Tate*," she warned.

Tate looked into his wife's face, so pretty and so worried. She must've had her doubts about him starting Black Watch right after what they'd gone through, but she'd never once voiced them to him. Lyla had had his back from the beginning, and he was so grateful for that.

For her, he swallowed down the lump and forced the words through numb lips. "The guy who called is part of the SEAL squad that went in after Tank and the guys."

Lyla sagged onto the mattress next to him, all her concern replaced by a shock that mirrored his own. "*Whoa.* The guys who've been all over the news? With the Congressional inquiry?"

Tate turned to her, and her eyes were wide behind her cute tortoiseshell glasses. He understood her dismay—he could hardly believe it himself.

"Sounds like the Navy's looking into them, too."

"Small world," she murmured.

"Yep. And it gets worse. My man sounds like he has a serious ax to grind about the way that mission went down. Can't say I blame him, either."

"So he's definitely not thrilled about the inquiries," she muttered.

"Would you be?" Tate wondered, then shook his head, thinking about the whole convoluted tangle. "They wouldn't let them in until after the shit hit the fan, and then a slimy politician turned around and stabbed them in the back for their efforts." He winced in sympathy. "I knew that story stank to high heaven. The second I heard about it."

"Can you be sure he's the wronged party?" Lyla wondered. "Maybe he's the villain in all this, exactly like they're painting him."

"It's possible," Tate acknowledged, "But I don't think so. I'm going to reach out to some of my contacts in Coronado, just in case, though. Make sure he's the real deal."

His wife scowled comically at him. "Since when do you have *contacts in Coronado?*"

Even as troubled as he was, Tate couldn't help himself. He winked at her and said, "Never you mind, pretty girl."

Lyla groaned and smacked his arm, harder than necessary as usual. She gave him a moment to laugh and recover, then put a gentler hand on his thigh. "Tate…babe, is this a good idea? You're awfully close to this situation. Maybe you shouldn't get involved."

He'd wondered the same thing. If he hadn't been laid up with a TBI for months—if he'd been there to help his old team when they'd needed him—maybe that mission wouldn't have been their last one. Tank and the others might not be six feet under right now.

What's more, those poor girls and their teachers might be safe, studying and learning all the ways they could make this world a better place if someone would just give them the chance.

"True," he admitted, because facts were facts. "But it doesn't necessarily have to be *me*, specifically, that works with him. It's Black Watch he's looking to hire, and maybe…maybe we *are* the best company for the job. Maybe I owe it to Tank, and to everyone else, to use my resources to avenge them."

Lyla blew out a long breath, squinting at him like she was trying to gauge his mood. Tate understood her trepidation. His survivor's guilt was something he and his therapist touched on regularly.

On the one hand, he still felt like he'd let his teammates down—like things might've gone differently if he'd been there beside them instead of sidelined with an injury that took forever to heal.

On the other hand, however, cooling his heels on the DL had led Tate straight to his wife, and to starting Black Watch. Though his marriage was new and his company, too, Tate could no longer fathom an existence that didn't include them.

"Correct me if I'm wrong," Lyla said, "but Black Watch doesn't include personal vendettas on its list of services. Unless this is what you intended all along—to set up something that would let you hunt down that warlord guy yourself?"

"Of course not," Tate reassured her. "And that's not necessarily what Lieutenant Gaines wants. But if he *did* want to go after Kadir, and I had the means to help, would I be remiss in passing up the chance to bury that bastard?"

She stared at him with a frown. "Tate, what are you saying? You can't possibly think it's okay to raise a posse and play vigilante."

"I don't. And Gaines seems to be focused on why that ambush went the way it did, and why he and his men are taking the fall for it. He doesn't trust the chain of command right now, and based on what I've heard, that's probably smart."

Beside him, his wife took another deep breath and gazed at him steadily. "All right. So…what did you tell him? Did you accept the job?"

Tate snorted, wondering for the hundredth time if he'd gone around the bend for good this time. Except…he had a feeling about this thing. He couldn't leave it be.

He told her, "I did him one better."

Lyla knew him too well. She flopped back on the bed with a groan. "Oh, lord. What have you done now, you crazy man?"

Tate grinned, despite it all. "I offered him a job."

Chapter One

Buck

H E'D RUN TOO far on too little sleep. That'd been his first mistake. He'd also overhydrated, so by the time Buck decided to pack it in and circle back around to his parents' house, he desperately needed to hit the head. Undoubtedly, that was why he forgot all about the new alarm system his folks had installed last month on the advice of their real estate agent.

Supposedly, it would increase the resell value of what was already a very nice home. The system did absolutely nothing for Buck's heart rate, though. It waited to emit its shrill, out-of-nowhere klaxon until he was already through the door and halfway to the guest bathroom down the hall, spiking his elevated pulse clear through the roof.

Buck spun and lunged back to the panel mounted next to the entrance, stabbing buttons at random while he tried to remember the passcode amidst all the chaos.

The wailing cut off as abruptly as it started, and he swung back to take that critical leak at last—and realized three steps too late that he'd probably pulled his groin with the sudden pivot.

Sweaty, limping, heart still thundering like a racehorse, Buck made it to the bathroom and took care of business, but his gym shorts were still down around his thighs when his cell started pinging with an incoming call.

From the console in the foyer.

Buck washed his hands and shuffled as fast as he could toward the chirping, cursing a blue streak the entire way. He fumbled his phone free of the pouch he carried it in when he was running and saw Bennett's name flashing on the screen. He groaned, already knowing what it had to be about.

Buck understood the guy's anxiety—*all* of their collective anxiety—but he wondered if they really needed these daily check-ins.

Shit was out of his hands for the time being. He had nothing left to tell them.

He sighed, staring at Ben's name. God, he was so freaking tired. From the sleepless night that had preceded his ill-advised run, sure—but also from everything that had happened in the last few months.

Buck had embroiled them in this mess with only a few heedless minutes of letting his dick do the thinking, and while he owned that mistake, it didn't make this less exhausting.

Especially since he had no idea if his Hail Mary play was going to work.

He couldn't leave his brother hanging, though, so he tapped the screen to connect the call, and said, "Hey."

"What up, what up," came Bennett's low drawl.

Buck didn't have the energy for a whole song and dance. He needed a hot shower and a liter of coffee, some breakfast, and some sleep. He was too tangled up in his own head to work out which had to come first, so he barked, "What do you need?"

"Just, you know—did you talk to the guy?"

Of course. Buck had promised to debrief them last night, after he placed the call they were all hanging their hats on.

He hadn't. He'd been too stymied by the unexpected turn of events and had wanted to get his thoughts straight before he had to explain it to the rest of the team.

Should've guessed they wouldn't wait patiently, dipshit.

Buck told him, "I got him last night. Took a little effort to reach the dude I wanted, but…yeah."

Bennett's response was quick and antsy, "But did you tell him about the thing?"

Buck pressed his hand to his thigh as he hobbled toward the kitchen. Maybe it wasn't a full-on groin pull. Maybe it was only a little strain that he could ice and be done with.

"Buck?"

He sighed. "Did I talk to the guy about the thing?"

"Yeah."

"What are we? Wiseguys, now?"

Ben paused. "Sorry. Yeah, that sounded dumb. We just—"

"Listen," Buck interjected, "I know. I get it. But shit got complicated right quick last night and I don't want to hash it out over the phone."

Assuming it was even possible to pull off what they were planning, they couldn't afford to get busted. But Buck also had no idea how to explain to his buddies what Tate Monroe had offered him.

He'd heard from everyone he'd talked to that the owner of Black Watch Security was as solid as they came, but…he needed more intel before he could be absolutely sure.

There was no room in this clusterfuck to be anything other than sure.

"Understood," Bennett said, disappointed. "So when are you getting back?"

They'd covered this ground already, too. With the team benched anyway, Buck had taken leave to help his parents sell their house and move to their new retirement condo on the Eastern Shore. It was as good a cover as any for the calls he'd had to make and, with any luck, the meetings he hoped to have.

He hadn't anticipated how the other guys would be climbing the walls of their temporary digs at Little Creek without him, however. Despite being the most capable people he'd ever met, they'd done nothing but whine like overtired schoolkids since he'd left.

"I told you—couple more weeks. I'm going to finish helping my folks get their place ready, and then I'll be back."

Buck rooted through the freezer, selected one of the big ice packs his mom used with her picnic cooler, and pressed it against his aching thigh.

"Right, but what if—"

"Look, we all know those assholes are going to take their own sweet time with this thing. None of us are going anywhere for a while. You guys need to sit tight."

"They could try to pull something with you gone."

"They could," Buck agreed. The last few months had certainly made it clear that paranoia wasn't misplaced, so with that in mind, he added, "But if something crops up, I can be back there in two hours, easy. Probably less."

Buck scanned the counters, and his morale dropped to subterranean levels when he remembered that his parents had already taken their coffee maker to the new place on Tilghman Island. If he wanted caffeine, he was going to have to go out and forage for some.

Bennett was quiet for a minute, no doubt recognizing that this brick wall wasn't going to budge any time soon. "Roger that," he said eventually. "Let us know if you hear anything. Or if we can do something from here."

"Will do. Hang in there."

"You too, bud."

The line went dead. Buck tossed his phone on the granite counter and the cooler pack in the sink. The A/C was turning his sweat-dampened shirt cold and clammy, and his head was beginning to ache.

Hot shower first, he decided, followed by some ibuprofen and a quick trip to the nearest coffee shop for an IV of the good stuff. By then, he would almost certainly have come up with an executable mission plan.

He owed it to Bennett, and to Wyatt and Joe. He owed it to the soldiers they hadn't been able to save, and to those poor girls at that obliterated school. *No pressure, though.*

Buck's eyes watered a bit as he hit the stairs, the pain in his groin kicking into higher gear on the climb. For a brief minute, he let himself dwell on Joely, wondering which poor soul's life she was ruining this week.

One of the stupidest things Buck had done with his adulthood was let her wide blue eyes distract him from the venom in her veins. He'd thought he was fucking a SEAL Team groupie—scratching a quick itch before he disappeared into the ether, never to be heard from again.

Instead…well. Joely had carried them all to hell in her designer handbasket.

At the time, he'd had no idea that his team would get roped into rescuing some Army platoon days after he met her, or that the documentary she'd been filming would turn into a tale of hotheaded egomaniacs, viciously critical of special operators in general—and his four-man fire team most of all.

Even with the benefit of hindsight, there was no justifying getting involved with someone like her, no reason why Buck should've run his mouth, trying to impress the literal pants off her. Joely had been an expert at stroking his ego, if nothing else—but he still ought to have known better.

She and her shitty exposé had unleashed a metric ton of unwelcome attention on what was already an epic disaster. His mission gone wrong had ended up plastered across every news channel from D.C. to Coronado within the month, and Buck and his men had been put on ice indefinitely, sent east to testify before the Congressional committee Senator Doggett had convened to investigate matters.

Not to be outdone—or under pressure from the pols, he wasn't sure which—the HQS at Dam Neck had opened its own board of inquiry, as well.

Buck wasn't *too* worried about himself. He'd already been toying with not re-upping, but he hated the thought of the other guys losing their careers over his sinkhole of suckitude.

He worried, too, about the dilemma posed by the most mysterious source Joely had cited in her film. In the months since the project had gone apeshit, they'd been characterized as a foreign affairs blogger, a high-level academic supposedly sidelined by mainstream media for their less-than-patriotic views.

In the post-9/11 world, there weren't many people who would readily criticize the special operator community, but Joely's blogger seemed to be one of them. Buck had no idea who the person was, though, or where they'd gotten their information. What Buck did know was that Joely had made a career out of hatchet jobs like this one. Was infamous for them, actually.

Maybe she'd conjured her secretive blogger out of thin air, but if she hadn't...

He stepped under the scalding shower spray, wondering for the umpteenth time whether he'd come face to face with the person here in Maryland, and not even known it. The only thing he'd been able to uncover about them was that they were based close to his parents.

Whoever they were, they were clearly a pedantic asshole with no real-world knowledge of the things they wrote about, and Buck very much wanted to have a few words with them.

Call it a bonus item on the list he'd put together for Black Watch.

He rinsed off and grabbed a towel off the hook. His groin muscle seemed a little looser on the trip to the sink, but Buck popped a few ibuprofen anyway. He could stop at the pharmacy after the coffee shop, to snag a heating pad in case it started aching again later.

Staring at his face in the big mirror over the counter, Buck cataloged the dark shadows under his eyes and the fresh scar on his chin. As he did, his mind drifted once more to his conversation with Tate Monroe last night.

Buck had been told that Black Watch was the place to go when you ran into something you couldn't fix yourself. Word was, they had the chops to fix shit, new as they were.

He hoped like hell that the whispers were true because Buck had an unsettling feeling that his backchannel investigation was going to hook some big damn fish.

He only hoped he wouldn't be one of them.

Chapter Two

Peyton

T HE COMMENTS HAD been bad enough, but Peyton was coming to realize they were probably only going to be the tip of the iceberg. As she sat at her little desk in the bedroom and stared at the screen of her laptop, she reflected on the night she'd posted her infamous article—on how freaking *insightful* she'd felt.

At first, she'd been thrilled to see her views racking up. People had found her tiny foreign affairs blog! She was finally getting some actual engagement!

But then, the trolls arrived. She'd read the comments unspooling under her stupid post, pointing out all of the ways she was a terrible human in an unending stream of poor grammar and keyboard vitriol.

In the days to come, they found her other posts, too, some going back to her college years. Peyton's elation had rapidly turned to horror when she'd seen what the vast majority had to say.

So many commenters had claimed to be military, accusing her of being an ungrateful citizen who didn't have their back in return. Some, too, seemed to be conspiracy theory yahoos, out there prepping for a zombie apocalypse while they scoured the internet for things a corrupt government didn't want them to know.

Peyton hadn't wasted a minute worrying about whether her parents had witnessed her crash and burn—they were both far too busy for that. Her brother had noticed, though, all the way from his office at the World Bank in London. He'd texted her the very next morning, wondering what the hell was going on.

Confused by the suddenness of it all, Peyton had reluctantly turned off the comments feature until she could figure out what had gone wrong. It sure hadn't been an unfortunate use of keywords, or less-than-savvy search engine optimization.

What had really happened was something else entirely. A violation of the first order.

The emails had shown up next, of course, and were still arriving with alarming regularity. Peyton had spotted 250 of them this morning alone, nearly three months after she'd first hit "publish."

She hadn't turned on her tv in ages. The rampant speculation about her identity had made her blood run cold, and she couldn't stand it anymore.

Could nasty phone calls be far behind? Or confrontations on her lawn? How soon before the hackers out in cyberspace connected Peyton's anonymous blog to her real name, to her real address—to her job at Midatlantic Community College?

How long before Peyton was out of that job and out on her ass?

It wasn't like opining about international relations in the wee hours of the morning put one on a fast track to tenure at some big-name university. Quite the opposite—when she'd talked about her blog during her interview at MCC, they'd strongly suggested she shut it down.

When they'd hired her, they'd gone on to insist that she operate it anonymously, and even made her sign a waiver saying they could fire her at will if *Global Lens* ever blew up and brought them the wrong kind of notoriety. They were fresh out of a grading scandal and weren't taking any chances.

Peyton had laughed it off at the time. She had rent and school loans to pay, and her wish to enter the foreign service had gone absolutely nowhere. She'd been thrilled to get a position even tangentially related to her field—and her blog was so obscure as to be nonexistent.

It would be funny now if it weren't so awful.

She bit her lip as she stared at *Global Lens*'s home page on her screen. She could shut the whole thing down, she supposed, in the hopes that she—and her part in the fiasco that was now national news—would eventually fade into obscurity once more.

Or…she could hang in there and wait for saner voices to prevail. Pray that her connection to the blog would remain undiscovered.

Neither option held much appeal, and the whole shitshow was just so *unfair*. Like a game of telephone gone wildly awry, her original words had been twisted ridiculously out of proportion by every media outlet in the country, making her sound like an ignorant, SEAL-hating buffoon. To this day, she had no idea how, or why, it had happened.

Despite it all, Peyton loved *Global Lens*. She might never be a diplomat like her mother, spending years at a time in foreign capitals, or a policy wonk like her dad, whose Asian affairs expertise had been sought after by two different presidential administrations—but she could do something they could not. Peyton could take the complicated history that underpinned most current events, and examine it in terms that even a school kid could understand.

Present situation excepted, naturally. She'd screwed that lesson up royally.

She'd only managed to snare a position at the local community college—*so far*, she reminded herself—but that didn't mean she couldn't do more someday. She could write books. She could teach at a higher level. She hoped, one day, to leverage her blog into something *more*.

To show her parents and herself, once and for all, that she wasn't a disappointment to her accomplished family.

Peyton refused to give that up over what felt like a gigantic misunderstanding.

And so, instead of deleting anything, she archived the problematic post and left her other articles intact. Then she snapped her laptop shut and stretched in her chair, trying to find the willpower to get on with her day.

Somewhere in the world, there was a filmmaker named Joely Spitz. For some unknown reason, she'd chosen Peyton's article, out of all the other resources at her disposal, to bolster her exposé of the special forces operating in the Middle East. Peyton wondered what she was doing right now.

Drinking tea, eating eggs, destroying the life of some other hapless bystander?

Peyton's landline began ringing—too loud and jangling her out of her morose thoughts. She jumped and peered at the caller ID, but it looked like another spam call.

Had there been more of them lately? *Possibly.* It was too early in the morning to decide for sure and she had an eleven a.m. "Middle Eastern Perspectives" class to get ready to teach today.

Ironic, that.

Peyton got to her feet with a sigh. Who was she kidding? The calls had definitely been increasing. She had to get out of here before they drove her crazy.

She gathered her stuff for the day, wondering if Devon would be on campus yet. Maybe she could meet him for coffee, so she wouldn't have to be alone.

On her desk, the voicemail clicked on, then clicked off again. In seconds, that same number called once more.

A chill snaked down her spine, and she rushed to the front door, deciding to text her friend and fellow professor on the way to school. As she left the townhouse, she was flustered and spooked, juggling her laptop and her lunch, her purse, a sweater, and a tumbler of cold brew to hold her until she could meet

Devon. She had to tuck her cell into her bra because *god forbid* women get functional pockets in their clothes.

With all of that going on, who could say what made her look across the street as she was trying to get her passenger door unlocked? It could've been a sound or a reflection of light—or it could've been sheer preservation instinct.

In any case, when Peyton did look, she found herself staring right into the eyes of a stranger, a man nearly hidden by the shadow between two blocks of townhouses and aiming his telephoto lens right at her.

She froze, arms locked around her possessions like a bad cartoon. Even in the shade, she could tell that the guy looked an awful lot like the person she'd seen near her car after work last week.

He also looked much like the man who'd been watching her from further down the bar when she and Devon had met for drinks and street tacos two nights ago.

Peyton panicked, there was no other word for it. One minute she was stuck in place, and the next she was in fight-or-flight mode—dumping everything she was carrying into the car, dashing around the trunk for the drivers' side door, and tearing out of the development like a bat out of hell.

She had no idea if the cameraman had run or held his ground, but it was impossible to pretend this was anything other than the worst-case scenario.

They'd found her. *Oh god.*

Would he try to get into her house while she was gone?

Peyton was halfway to school, stopped at a light, and trying to calm herself enough to call Devon on speakerphone when she reached for her coffee and realized it had never made it into the cupholder. Instead, it was laying on its side, its lid popped free and cold brew seeping into her cardigan and the seat upholstery in a spreading muddy-brown stain.

Crap.

She fought back crazy tears as the light flicked to green. Once again, she'd slept like shit last night, on top of the scare just now. She could not face the rest of this day without caffeine and a hit of something sweet, and she couldn't wait for Devon. He might not even be available, anyway.

Peyton was going to have to detour to the coffee shop on the way to school.

She tapped the speech-to-text icon on her dashboard and sent a message to Devon, asking if he wanted her to pick up something for him. His reply came through minutes later, right as she was turning into the shopping center lot.

> Classes were canceled this morning, remember? For that pest control thing.

Peyton parked, dropped her head against the steering wheel, and groaned. No, she had not remembered, as shaken and jumpy as she'd been. A few tears leaked out, dripping onto her hands as she thought about going home and crawling back under the covers.

But she couldn't do that, could she?

There might be a creeper in her house right now. If she stayed here for a bit, she could have some breakfast and get her feet under her in a nice, safe public environment. And then, once she was thinking clearly, she could come up with what to do next.

Chapter Three

Buck

WHEN BUCK STEPPED into the coffee shop, he didn't know whether to fall to his knees to worship whoever had created such an incredible aroma—or to whip out his knife so he could fight his way to the front of the long, disorderly line.

He waded into the throng, but he didn't notice the woman near the window until he'd finished ordering and paying at the register. However, two steps later he turned to survey the seating area, searching for candidates likely to be leaving soon, and there she was.

Softly pretty in the autumn sun filtering through the big windows, almost prim in her flowery printed top and business-casual pants, the woman looked about as challenging as a first-grade teacher.

She did not look anything like Joely, or the women Buck normally gravitated to back in Coronado. He couldn't say why, exactly, she'd drawn his eye, or why she was holding his attention so easily, but the longer he looked, the more he liked what he saw.

He'd been avoiding entanglements of the female persuasion ever since his life had gone FUBAR, but there was something about this woman that felt…*right*.

Buck wasn't the only male afflicted in the place, either. In seconds, he counted no fewer than four other dudes trying to catch her eye.

The sharks were circling, all right, not that she appeared to notice. She was too busy minding her own business to be concerned about her effect on others. Sublimely self-assured.

Women like that had always knocked him for a loop, but it'd been a while since he'd met one with this particular level of "don't give a damn." Even Joely, who liked to feign a worldly, nonchalant persona for the masses, had turned sycophantic once she'd learned why Buck was playing in the same sandbox as her.

This woman wasn't Joely, though, and the likelihood of him digging on two psychos in a row had to be incredibly slim—same as a lightning strike or an act of god.

Right?

Buck had been a SEAL for ten years now, a decade in which special operators had taken on an almost celebrity status within certain sectors of the civilian population. Word certainly seemed to get around San Diego about who was and wasn't on the Teams—and there were times when he wasn't sure if he was only a feather in some girl's cap or a guy she genuinely liked.

But this woman—this woman looked like she wouldn't care one whit about all that.

The thought was incredibly enticing. *Full steam ahead.*

Every signal in his system clicked into high alert.

Buck didn't think she'd spotted him yet, engrossed as she was in the textbook she was holding, and dwarfed by the oversized leather armchair. He took the time to flip through opening gambits in his head, trying to decide on one that might fit.

Then, in a lucky break almost too good to be true, the guy reading a newspaper across from her suddenly checked his phone, bolted up, and rushed out. Buck jostled past a couple of moms with strollers and beelined over, pulled muscle be damned.

The vulture in the suit was closer, though, and as he put his hand on the back of the vacated seat, he looked smug. Like the world owed him this conquest.

Oh, hell no.

It was packed in the shop, but Buck had bullied his way through worse conditions to get what he wanted. It was no effort at all to push past GQ and his shiny fucking loafers and drop into the seat with an exaggerated sigh.

He aimed a smile of greeting at the woman, then leveled GQ with an expression of innocent interest along the lines of, *Whatever troubles you, my good man?*

Fucker wasn't buying it. Hell, he'd probably pulled the same stunt a time or two himself.

The guy rolled his eyes and huffed, "Seriously?"

Buck looked curiously between him and the woman. "What?"

GQ turned to her, as affronted as only a man like him could be. "*He's* who you were waiting for? Really?" he demanded.

The disgust was a bit much, but Buck gave himself a quick once-over anyway, in case he'd managed to turn vile in the last few minutes without noticing.

Nope. *Still right and tight.*

The woman didn't dignify GQ's aggression with an explanation. She simply lowered her book and blinked tepidly back at him.

Buck grinned. *Legend.*

Her lack of concern infuriated the suit, but much like many guys, he was all bark and no bite, and she had given him absolutely nothing to work with.

In the end, he could only shake his head and stomp off, the heels of his dress shoes cracking against the shop's dusty wood floor like the pop of mortar fire.

Buck and the woman sat in silence, holding their collective breath while they waited for GQ to get well and truly gone. She continued blithely ignoring the other jerkoffs who'd been orbiting her and took a long sip of coffee.

"So—" Buck began, then stopped when a second vulture stepped into his line of sight two feet behind the woman's shoulder.

The guy looked to be about twenty years old and judging by his sculpted biceps and top-of-the-line athletic wear was probably a trainer at the gym next door. He was also way too young for Buck's new friend.

Trainer Boy scowled at Buck with his best "I was here first" look, but it wasn't terribly threatening coming from such a baby-faced dickhead. He could tell at a glance that the dude might have roid rage going for him, but that would be about the extent of it. He had no idea what to do with all those muscles, except pose.

Buck gazed back, supremely confident that he'd already won this pissing match.

Sure as shit, Gym Bro folded like an umbrella, executing a twitchy half-shrug that evolved into a peek at his smartwatch, then lumbered away.

To head off any further interruptions, Buck figured he'd better dispense with the remaining contenders now, but there were no other challenges brewing. Only two doughy-looking office types, who easily comprehended the two essential facts relevant to this stand-off.

One, the woman in the armchair was way out of their league. And two, a much bigger predator had taken the field.

Buck watched as they grabbed their cups from the counter, cast wistful glances at lovely Miss Bookworm, and left without a backward glance.

He turned back and smiled at her once more, and this time she smiled back.

All his, now.

He took a moment to enjoy the sense of anticipation. What would her voice be like? In this part of Maryland, you never could tell—a person could just as easily have a northern accent as a southern one. Hell, as diverse as the area was, she could hail from Ukraine, and no one would bat an eye.

Would she be sweet, or sarcastic? Buck hoped for the latter. He tended to like women smart and tart. Give him a sassy brainiac with soft hair and long legs, and he was a goner every time.

As he geared up to speak, he sifted through his conversational options one final time, but realized she'd already handed him all he needed to get started.

"Did you really tell that guy you were waiting for someone?"

Her eyes lit up like stars. "*Yes*. And then, like magic, you arrived. Thanks for the save."

Yup. Buck loved her voice. She sounded sexy, like she'd put you in your place using words you didn't know, then make you beg for the honor of fucking her. For once, appearances hadn't been deceiving.

"Happy to oblige," he told her, leaning forward and sticking out his hand. "I'm Beau, by the way. Beau Gaines."

No rank. No nickname. Not today. There'd be time enough to clue her in later, if all went well.

Besides, explaining how he'd ended up "Buck" wasn't that easy. He could hardly remember anymore how the moniker had first begun, or why it'd stuck as it had. There'd been that warrant officer in BUD/S with a thing for Buck Owens, then dollar pitcher nights at bars in Coronado. His teammates had started calling those "Buck Night" for the way girls had flocked to him and his hair, turning prematurely silver even then and apparently acting as an aphrodisiac to many horny humans.

Later, their monthly poker get-together had also come to be known as "Buck Night," after a six-month winning streak had landed Buck with more one-dollar bills than any grown man ought to have. For a while, he'd felt like a kid hoarding his allowance, until he'd broken down and exchanged them all at one of the banks on base.

His dorky nickname had morphed into something else now, though. At some point in the intervening years, he'd grown up and matured, and had turned into the squad's finisher. The clean-up man. The sting people got when they poked the wrong hornet's nest. The "buck," as it were, always seemed to stop with him.

Fuck, he was tired.

Buck took a long draw from his to-go cup, letting the scalding combination of espresso and steamed milk work its magic on his system. He didn't even mind the way it seared the skin on the tip of his tongue. Stupid injuries were a dime a dozen today, but they hadn't felled him yet.

A small sound from across the table wrenched his attention back to his new companion. The cute woman. *Shit.*

"Sorry," Buck said, "Zoned out for a minute there. What was your name, again?"

"Peyton," she told him. "Page."

"Hey, Peyton Page," he drawled, enjoying the way her name felt in his mouth, the way it teased a little of his childhood accent from wherever it'd been hidden. "Nice to meet you."

The Navy had largely drilled any traces of his hometown of Roanoke, Virginia, from his voice, but apparently, the slight twang had only been lurking under the surface, waiting for a moment when he needed to be extra charming.

With any luck, it would still work as well as it used to.

Peyton's focused gaze was traveling over him, taking in Buck's ballcap and face, tracing over his shoulders and chest, and tracking down to his sneakers. He wondered what she was thinking.

He supposed she could be estimating whether she could fend off a man of his size with whatever self-defense techniques she'd learned at her gym, but maybe—hopefully—she was measuring whether Buck had the goods to rock her world.

It was hard to tell, but when she smiled wider and told him, "You too," he figured it was a good sign.

Before they could get much farther, one of the baristas plunked his backup coffee on the counter, belted out his name, and summoned Buck over with an all-business jerk of their chin.

Peyton's eyebrows rose. "Who's that one for?"

"Me," Buck snorted. He was abruptly glad for the shitty start to his day—and the commensurate order of two of the largest caffeine delivery models they had here—because it meant he'd have a good excuse to linger longer with this woman.

Maybe long enough to get her number and a date.

"Sad to say, it's a two-fisted kind of morning," he explained, getting to his feet and finishing off the first cup. "I'm going to need both these beauties and then some if I'm going to make it to four o'clock."

She shook her head grimly. "I hear that."

Buck gave her another grin, then tried not to limp too badly on his way to the counter.

He took a look at the barista as he grabbed his cup. The poor kid looked like she was having an even worse morning than he was, and he did not want to be the one she eviscerated when she eventually snapped.

He pulled out his wallet and dropped a five in the tip jar. "Hang in there," he murmured.

When Buck turned to reclaim his hard-won seat, however, a previously unmarked contender was already attempting to unseat him. Where had that bastard come from?

When the guy pushed his hand through too-slick hair as he made Peyton's acquaintance, Buck clocked the glint of a wedding band on his finger. His eyes narrowed, but he needn't have worried. Peyton Page had it covered. She shook her head at the interloper and pointed decisively at Buck.

Buck hopped to it, hurrying over to shoulder the new guy aside and park his ass in the contested seat.

He told Peyton, "Thanks, babe," like they'd known each other forever, and didn't bother watching the new guy move boots.

It felt good enough that she'd saved his seat for him. At the very minimum, it meant she thought he was the least of all the evils in this joint.

Everything was progressing swimmingly.

Buck fussed with the plastic lid on his cup, prying it free so the molten lava inside would cool faster. As he did, he scooted his chair, and the small table between them, closer to Peyton.

If she noticed, she gave no sign of it. She only leaned in and murmured, "Where'd he come from," like they were coconspirators already.

Chapter Four

Peyton

PEYTON FLIRTED WITH the gorgeous guy—who'd appeared in the middle of the familiar coffee shop like an incongruous action hero—for so long that the morning rush thinned out and the early risers and businesspeople were replaced by knots of moms with babies and work-from-home types.

By the time the midday crowd started filling the place up again, Beau had confessed that he was getting hungry, and convinced Peyton to head over to the pizza joint a few doors down for lunch.

It was hard enough to wrap her head around a man like him showing up in her life at all, much less making such a concerted effort to charm her. But the fact that Beau had upped the ante with a meal invite so readily was nearly impossible to comprehend.

Random connections with beautiful strangers never happened to her. And yet, here Peyton was, halfway through her pepperoni-and-mushroom and chatting with Beau as easily as if they'd been dating for years. It was wild—a "meet-cute" fit for a romance novel.

Her original thought pushed its way to the front of her brain again, and she paused.

Hmm.

This kind of thing *didn't* happen to her, and the coincidence of Beau turning up on the same morning that weirdo had been taking her picture was…was probably not kismet.

Damn. Once that occurred to her, it felt as if their lunch date was unspooling on two different, parallel planes.

On one, Peyton tossed her hair and delivered her quips and compliments like she was born to flirt with just this man. Devon would've been proud of her—*she* was proud of her. What's more, Beau was eating up her banter faster than his pizza, and reflecting it right back at her.

Another part of Peyton, however, was operating on a whole different level. That side was living in a spy thriller, not a rom-com, and felt like a paranoid mess inside.

Peyton had lived long enough to recognize that if Beau Gaines seemed too good to be true, then he probably was. But if that was the case, what was his real agenda?

Could this gorgeous, magnetic man be one of the vicious people who'd hated her blog post so much that they thought Peyton herself should suffer for it? Had her life really become that cruel?

She sighed and looked the man over for the hundredth time. *Facts, not fear,* she told herself. What were the facts that she'd learned so far?

Beau had been a total gentleman from the beginning, handily fending off those smarmy guys at the coffee shop, holding doors and chairs for her, and removing his hat when they sat down to eat.

He had a handsome face and the kind of tall, buff frame that Peyton loved. He had extraordinary silver hair, a sexy, teasing voice, and an exceptionally quick wit.

He was also a grown man in casual clothes, spending hours getting coffee and lunch in the middle of a workday. Plenty of vocations allowed for that possibility she supposed, including hers, but Beau had yet to tell her what he did for a living.

He'd only explained that he lived in California and was in town helping his parents move houses. That might explain his tan and easy-going demeanor, but not much else. For all the talking they'd done, Peyton was woefully short on details.

She didn't want Beau to be a bad guy and heaven knew she could use something nice in her life after the last few months of angst, but she didn't have the luxury of wishful thinking. Peyton needed to find out more about him for safety's sake if nothing else.

At the next break in the conversation, she asked, "So, Beau— what do you do for work?"

He set down his soda and hesitated, long enough to make her wonder why it was a tricky question. Soon, his easy grin was back, though, and he was telling her, "I'm in the Navy, actually."

Her lungs seized up in panic, but Peyton managed to choke out a semi-normal sounding, "Ah."

She nearly got up and left right then, however, and wondered if she could take a roundabout route home so Beau couldn't follow her.

That seemed silly. An overreaction born of weeks of uncertainty.

Beau had been an open book all morning, willing to tell her whatever she wanted to know about him. That could mean he was lying through his teeth and really good at it—or that he was telling the truth and she simply hadn't asked the right questions.

Besides, Peyton should've guessed Beau was in the military. His hair was a little shaggy right now, but the way he held himself was Navy all the way. His clothes, his shoes...even his nails were too meticulously maintained to belong to anything other than an active-duty soldier.

Sailor. *Whatever.*

The question was whether Beau knew who *she* was. No one had been angrier about Peyton's article than the people claiming to support special operators, after all. They were the people Peyton was most afraid would find her in real life, and they were the ones she'd been most upset about hurting—unintentional though that hurt might have been.

But a person who meant her harm would want to preserve their anonymity, right? They wouldn't want to blow their cover and be seen in public with her, where witnesses and security cameras abounded. They'd lurk in shadows, like the man from that morning.

Peyton considered Beau anew. Could it be possible…that the universe had sent her an apology for its prior bad behavior, in the form of a protector? He was only here temporarily, and when his leave was up, he'd undoubtedly return to California—but maybe Beau would stick around long enough to scare off any bad guys.

As she studied him across the little square table, he sipped his fresh-squeezed lemonade and politely summoned the waiter to order another.

He didn't seem nefarious at all. She probably needed to chill the hell out.

Beau picked a piece of sausage off his pizza and popped it in his mouth, leaning in to ask her earnestly, "What about you? What do you do?" His eyes were alight, like he couldn't wait to hear her answer.

Peyton shook off her doubts and her reflexive cringe at the question. This guy wasn't one of her parents and he wouldn't try to embarrass her about her job. The position was a good one and she was good at it—regardless of where her future led her.

She told him, "I'm a professor," and left it at that.

Beau sat back with a big grin. "Really? That's so cool. What do you teach?"

"Political science. International relations, that kind of thing." She squared her shoulders and added, "I work at MCC," with the kind of pride she deserved to feel.

"That's down the street, right? Nice campus."

"It is."

Peyton was supposed to teach another class on that campus that afternoon. She checked her watch and gasped. *"Shoot.* How is it so late already?"

Beau raised his brows. "Got somewhere to be?"

"Yes, unfortunately. I have a 101 class in an hour. I'm sorry— I have to get going."

"Totally understand," he smiled, wiping his mouth and waving the waiter back over. "I'm happy that I got as much time with you as I did."

The waiter boxed up Peyton's last slice of pizza and gave Beau a plastic cup for his second lemonade. Beau refused her offer to split the bill and insisted on walking her to her car.

Peyton felt a last shiver of doubt as she watched him examine the make and model of her hybrid coupe, then stare at her license plate, too. Was he memorizing them? To what end?

She thought back to the coffee shop that morning, when the skeezy guy in the suit had demanded to know, *"Who? Who are you waiting for?"* like he'd been entitled to the information.

Even though she'd told him, *"None of your business,"* Peyton had been quaking inside.

A smile could turn to a snarl so fast on some men, and she'd needed the reminder that morning least of all. Was it any wonder that she'd segued into her conversation with Beau with a supersized dose of suspicion?

The more she got to know him, though, the more it appeared that he was a far rarer specimen of male. Beau seemed to be Superman—or some less-leotardy version of him, anyway.

He was polite without being aloof. Mannerly without acting like a prig. Big and brawny, but not a meathead. Smart without being pedantic, funny without sinking to crude…and now that she thought about it, he hadn't tried to mansplain her once.

This man, Peyton realized, was a freaking unicorn. He was also holding out his hand and asking her to hand over her phone. Apparently, she'd missed the lead-up to exchanging contact information.

She blinked and navigated to the right screen, so he could enter his number—then mutely complied when Beau asked her to text him so he'd have her details, too.

"Listen," he said, "I'm only in town for a couple more weeks. But feel free to hit me up if you need anything, okay?"

"Yeah, I will." *She probably wouldn't.* "Thanks."

"You were a happy surprise today, Peyton Page," he said. "I had a great time talking to you."

"You too, Beau. Thanks again for lunch."

He waved that off, hesitated, then announced with a sigh, "You may as well call me Buck. It's a stupid nickname, I know, but I've been saddled with it for a long-ass time. Hearing you call me Beau sort of feels like I'm in detention."

Peyton laughed. "Oh my god—but that's what you told me to call you! Why didn't you tell me sooner?"

"Long story," he grinned back. "I thought I'd enjoy hearing my real name for once. More than I did, as it turns out. Which is…odd. Anyway, don't be shy, okay? Call me anytime."

Peyton rolled her eyes. "You, too."

This was ridiculous. Neither of them was going to call the other one. Beau—*Buck*—was only visiting for a couple of weeks, and he lived clear across the country. There was no way he was interested in anything other than a one- or two-night stand, and if he'd wanted that he wouldn't have bothered with the pizza date. He would've skipped straight to drinks after work.

As Peyton watched him turn away, she was bemused by the entire interlude. He didn't get more than a couple of feet before he stopped in his tracks, though, putting his hands on his hips and hanging his head on a loud exhale. Then Buck wheeled around, cursed under his breath, and strode back over.

"Okay, here's the deal," he declared. "I don't have enough time to fuck around hoping you'll call. The truth is, I like you. A lot. And I would love to see you again."

Peyton blinked at his urgency, but she couldn't argue with the message. "Great," she said.

"Tonight," Buck clarified, "If you're available, let me take you to dinner tonight."

She paused, running through her schedule for the rest of the day in her head, trying to determine if she could swing it with the class she had to teach, and the Poly Sci papers she still had to grade.

That seemed to take more time than Buck had to spare, though, because two seconds later he was begging, *"Please, Peyton."*

She liked this guy. He was decent, and she was definitely attracted to him. He could prove useful, as well—it couldn't hurt to be seen with someone so obviously ready to rumble, given her current circumstances. Maybe by the time Buck had to leave again, strange people would stop showing up wherever she was.

"Okay. Yeah. That sounds good," Peyton agreed.

"Cool. I'll try to find somewhere that can take us on short notice. If you text me your address later, I'm happy to pick you up."

Good sense dictated that she should meet him at the restaurant, at least until she knew Buck better. But if her frightening shadow from this morning was still hanging around later, Peyton wanted him to see her get into this man's car. Let the weirdo worry.

That image was tarnished a bit when Buck ambled over to unlock the door of an ugly, beat-up junker, four spots from her hybrid.

It didn't exactly scream *testosterone to spare*, but she'd have to make do.

Buck glanced over, noticed her expression, and laughed. "Don't worry," he told her. "It's only a loaner from the car dealership. I brought my dad's car in for an airbag recall yesterday, but I'll have it back before dinner, I promise."

Peyton chuckled, too. "That's a relief. You didn't strike me as a burgundy sedan kind of guy. I was starting to reevaluate."

"Professor Page, that is very elitist of you."

She ducked her head in chagrin, but he rushed to assure her, "I'm just teasing. But you would think a car dealer would maintain their loaners better. This thing handles like a bumper car. I feel like a clown in it."

Peyton cocked her head, curious now at what a man like him considered an acceptable ride. "What do you usually drive?"

"SUV. Big, black, tricked out bro-mobile," he grinned, darting a sly glance at her car. "How does that change your calculations?"

"Hmm… handy in a move but I hope you've found other ways to neutralize your carbon footprint. The fact that you recognize it's a bro-mobile gives you a slight edge, I'll give you that."

Buck tossed back his head and laughed. "Get out of here, you giant nerd, or you're going to be late for work. I'll check in with you later to make sure you're cool with the restaurant."

* * *

PEYTON SMILED LIKE a loon the entire way to campus. For once, she found a shady parking spot in the lot near her building, her laptop hooked up to the classroom A/V system without any hiccups, and by the time the students started filing in, she was in the zone and ready to get her lecture underway.

The sooner she finished, the sooner she could go home and get ready for her date with Beau. *Buck*, she corrected herself with a private little grin. He was picking her up for dinner in approximately five hours. Later, he might even kiss her.

She bit her lip. *Damn it.* Thoughts like that were not going to get this over with faster.

Peyton pulled herself together and scanned the room, and decided enough people had arrived to start talking. Soon, she was explaining her points as clearly and concisely as she'd ever done.

For half an hour, everything went smoothly, too, until the moment she looked into the upper rows to make sure the people in the back were following her, and locked eyes with a guy she hadn't noticed before.

His stare was intense, unnerving even. Where had he come from? Peyton had been certain she was alone when she'd unlocked the classroom, and he hadn't walked past her at the start of the lecture. Had he been hiding in those seats, waiting for her to arrive? Or did he find a way to slip in the locked door at the back?

It was too late in the semester for new students—by this point, people were starting to flake out, not buckle down. So why was he here, and why was Peyton so sure she'd seen him somewhere before?

She had to be losing her mind. The guy wasn't pointing a camera at her, but he also didn't have a computer or paper to take notes. He was simply sitting there, dark-haired and fair-skinned, with a scruff of whiskers shadowing his jaw. He didn't look angry, exactly, just…focused.

Much like the man from this morning had. With a start, Peyton realized that he *was* the man from this morning, and all the other times, too.

She swallowed hard.

She knew today's lecture topic like the back of her hand, but now she faltered, the familiar words jamming up in her throat like marbles. She attempted to cover her panic by looking down at her laptop screen, telling the class, "Sorry. Give me one second to call up the next slide."

Peyton's fingers trembled as she pretended to tap things on her keyboard, but she couldn't seem to find her equilibrium. Her class had no such issue, seizing on the pause like they'd been waiting for it, hands shooting up with questions ranging from asinine to insightful.

She scrambled to keep up with the rapid shifts in direction, attempting to stay on topic, but that face in the back had thrown her completely off-kilter. He knew where she lived. He knew where she worked. Did he know she'd spent the morning with Buck, too?

By the time she called it quits, her lecture had gotten so far off track that Peyton gave up trying to reel it in.

"Look for an email from me tonight," she called into the hubbub. "I'm going to give you guys some reading, so we can stay on schedule for next week."

When the crowd cleared and the classroom emptied, the stranger was gone.

Peyton grabbed her stuff and got out of there as fast as she could.

She spent the drive home wondering what Buck would say if she asked him to meet her at her house and do a sweep for intruders before she went in. He'd probably do it in a heartbeat, but then she'd be obliged to tell him what was going on with *Global Lens* and the internet bullies, and she just couldn't bring herself to.

Buck was in the Navy. He'd probably hate her as much as everyone else did, once he knew what she'd done.

Her fear grew, daunting enough by the time Peyton parked in her driveway that she considered simply leaving again—finding somewhere to hang out for the next couple of hours and going to dinner in what she'd been wearing all day.

Except, she was already drooping from her sleepless night and the day's ups and downs, and she desperately needed a shower to perk her up before meeting Buck.

She took a deep breath before throwing open the car door, then grabbed the heavy metal flashlight from her trunk. She combed through her townhouse with the flashlight in her hand and her heart in her throat—feeling more like a cop on tv than someone who could do an intruder real harm.

Peyton was too scared to look behind the boxes her brother had stacked in the basement, waiting for his eventual return from London, even though that door would have been the easiest for someone to jimmy open.

Instead, she locked her bedroom door—and the bathroom, too—while she got ready, then sprinted downstairs at the appointed time to hover anxiously by the entrance for Buck to arrive.

Chapter Five

Buck

AFTER PEYTON PULLED away, Buck headed to the pharmacy to get the heating pad he was more and more certain he was going to need, then drove to the car dealership to wait for his dad's car to be finished.

To kill time, he looked up restaurants on his phone, eventually settling on a nice Peruvian place that had hundreds of glowing reviews and looked suitably date-worthy. Buck texted a link to Peyton to make sure it was something she'd like and tried not to feel disappointed when she didn't answer right away.

For fuck's sake, she'd already spent hours with him today—and she was supposed to be at work now, teaching her class. It made sense that she didn't immediately fire back a response.

Buck spent a couple of minutes picturing her expounding on current affairs in front of a room full of teenagers, sounding smart and sexy and making all the pimple-faced boys blush, but he didn't get far before the service manager was barking his name and handing over the keys.

He'd have to save the teacher fantasies for another time.

It was a relief to get back behind the wheel of a vehicle that had some decent horsepower under the hood, and to know he wouldn't have to pick Peyton up in the beater he'd been using for the last few days, so Buck drove around for a bit, enjoying the nice weather and familiarizing himself with the route to the restaurant.

He eventually made his way home to do more packing for his folks, but he only lasted an hour before hauling boxes turned the ache in his thigh into something too painful to ignore.

Buck gave up and dragged himself upstairs to down a few more ibuprofen, kicked back on the bed with his new heating pad, and tried not to think about how much it would probably hurt if he was called upon to do the dirty with Peyton later that night.

That was both a best- and a worst-case scenario, and he couldn't imagine how it might work. Besides, he was exhausted and his parents' guest room bed was very comfortable. Buck fell out in minutes.

The rest did him good. When he awoke sometime later and ambled into the bathroom to shower, his leg felt better and he was more than ready to grab up lovely Ms. Page so they could devour ceviche together.

Buck was standing at the counter shaving when a sound out in the bedroom caught his attention. He shut off the fan and wandered over to the bureau, and sure as shit, his phone was buzzing again.

Again.

Bennett was calling *again*. Buck tightened the towel around his waist and connected the call, and didn't bother with anything other than, "Dude, what the fuck. I thought we'd—"

"Shut up, dude. You seeing what we're seeing?"

"Ben, I'm 125 miles away. What are you seeing?"

"Turn on the goddamn news."

Something in his tone made Buck wheel around and lunge for the remote on the nightstand, stumbling a bit when his screwed-up groin muscle screamed out a sudden *Not Today, Motherfucker*.

He clicked over to channel four, where a plastic-looking blonde was speaking earnestly into the camera, video footage rolling on the split-screen beside her.

Buck's heart started knocking around in its cage when he recognized himself and Bennett in their uniforms, exiting the Congressional hearing last week surrounded by brass and lawyers on the day Senator Doggett had given testimony.

That bastard. Buck should've left him to rot in the carnage of that girls' school and never looked back.

The newscaster said, "*Fresh evidence has emerged in the story of the rogue SEAL team gripping the nation this month. The pattern of misconduct profiled by reporters this spring was on full and indisputable display last week as well, outside the very committee investigating whether men such as these are fit to serve in our country's armed forces.*"

"I'll show you fit," Buck muttered darkly.

"Shut up and listen," Bennett fired back.

"*Reporters on the scene captured this exchange between the leader of the disgraced unit and his second-in-command.*"

The footage transitioned to full-screen, zooming in on Bennett ducking his head and growling, "*I'm gonna kill that asshole someday soon. With my bare hands. Wait and see.*"

To which Buck replied, "*Get in line.*"

Lest any viewers misunderstand, the station had helpfully provided captions at the bottom of the screen, set in clear, bold-faced type.

The screen reverted to the newscaster again, blathering about transparency and whether special ops had a place in a modern military at all. Buck groaned and shut off the tv, then went to sit gingerly on the bed.

Any sense of wellbeing he'd cobbled together from his catnap and his time with Peyton had evaporated into thin air.

"Are you fucking kidding me?" he cried after stewing for a bit. "A hot mic that close to us? How many more ways can this shitshow possibly go tits up?"

"Doggett apparently gave a statement. Said that while our words were shocking, they were hardly surprising. But good news, he has no real concerns about his welfare, so there's that."

Buck snorted. Senator Doggett had been just as clueless when they'd threatened the man to his face, back on that extraction helo. "Half the village was in flames under his feet, and he asks for a souvenir hat. What kind of idiot thinks of shit like that in the middle of an op?"

"The kind that turns around and stabs you in the back with a government inquiry right after you've saved his bacon," Bennett replied drily. "Anyway, we just wanted to make sure you had a heads-up because odds are good the brass is gonna want to talk about this."

Buck dropped his head into his hand and massaged his forehead. *Fuck.* Ben was right.

What were the chances the call from HQS would come in the middle of his date tonight? With the way his life was going these days, he had to think they were pretty high.

Buck mumbled, "This is…just…the absolute fucking…"

"Dude, I get it. But we all talked about it here. Figured we may as well come up and lend a hand at your folks' place until the heat dies down. Out of sight, out of mind, right? And with all of us working, the place will be ready in no time and we can head back down here together for the verdict. Easier to present a united front if we're all in the same place, I say."

Buck clutched at the towel spread over his thighs, thinking about Peyton and the way he'd hoped these next couple of weeks would go. Against all odds, he'd managed to meet a woman who was nothing like Joely, and nothing like the Team groupies that littered the bars and beaches of Coronado. He had a scant couple of weeks to get to know her better before real life intruded once more.

How the hell was he supposed to do that with three overgrown cock-blockers dogging his steps every hour of the day?

"No way," Buck said. "I'm trying to get this place cleaned out. Not turn it into a frat house."

"Hear me out," Bennett insisted. "We can—"

"*We* are not doing anything," Buck told him. I appreciate the offer, but I got this covered."

Ben let out an exasperated breath. "Don't be a dick. You don't actually believe we'd trash your parents' house."

"Just stay put and try to keep Wyatt and Joe out of trouble. I know they're bored, but we can't afford a single whiff of questionable behavior right now."

"Said the man trying to—"

"*Ben.*"

His friend went silent, then murmured a contrite, "Sorry."

"Listen, I have to run out for a bit. I'll check in tomorrow, okay?"

"Roger that."

Buck disconnected the call and sat there for another few minutes. It was okay. This was going to be okay. This was just another publicity stunt from a career politician trying to make a name for himself in a rowdy election season.

Doggett was almost certainly dirty, but it wasn't like there was a larger conspiracy playing out here. Black Watch would simply help them get to the bottom of the senator's antics and figure out how Joely and her craptastic blogger fit into the picture. If Buck could find the blogger himself while he was here in Maryland, so much the better.

Then, once they'd dealt with the good senator from Texas, all this ridiculous shit would go away, and Buck and his squad could finally get back to work.

* * *

WHEN BUCK PICKED up Peyton for their date, she stepped out of her door and looked around warily, her eyes immediately darting past him to stare at the gleaming hotrod in her driveway like it was a polished poison apple.

He could hardly blame her. Understated, it was not.

She then looked nervously up and down her quiet street, undoubtedly because his dad's muscle car was an even worse red flag for doucheness than Buck's truck would've been. If the neighbors saw her riding around in it, he could only guess what they'd say.

He chuckled as he unlocked the car and held open her door, but Peyton was rooted to the spot, stunned into silence by all the chrome and shiny red paint. Eventually, though, she turned to him, her eyebrows at full mast and an amused tilt to her lips.

She jerked her chin at the car. "Bit young for a mid-life crisis, aren't you?"

Buck grinned. "At this point, I feel like I've earned about five mid-life crises. But no, as promised, this is my dad's car."

True, he'd earned at least one of those crises when the commander had called to tear him a new one about today's newsreels on the way over here, but since he'd had the good fortune to get it over with before he got to Peyton's, Buck was willing to rate it chaotic neutral.

"I don't believe it," she said.

Buck held up a hand. "God's honest truth. Dad bought it last year—said the whole point of retirement was to have fun for once. I picked it up from the shop this afternoon."

He waved her over, handed her into the soft leather bucket seat, then rounded the hood to get behind the wheel.

As Peyton looked around the space-age interior, her disdain morphed into mystification. "How old did you say your parents are?"

"I don't think I did say," Buck laughed, shifting into reverse, and tossing an arm behind her headrest so he could twist around and scan behind them. "In any case, my dad is seventy. Mom's sixty-eight."

Peyton let out a breathy little laugh when he put it in drive, hit the gas—and the car growled under them. Buck couldn't lie. He liked the sound of that laugh. *A lot.*

"What on earth did your mother say when your dad brought this beast home?"

"That woman," Buck grinned, "is a little rebel. She loves it. I'm convinced she spreads out her errands so she has an excuse to drive it longer. Makes my dad nuts when she readjusts the seat."

Peyton shook her head, looking around with wide eyes again. "If they love it so much, why didn't they take it with them? Why leave it with you?"

"Airbag recall, remember? Besides, I'll have you know I've been an admirable babysitter. Haven't drag-raced once."

"I don't believe that, either." She ran her hands across her seat, and Buck tried very hard to concentrate on the road and not on how those gentle fingers might feel on him. "And it makes me want to confirm again what kind of truck you drive. Please don't say monster."

"Not monster. Very ordinary and respectable Ford."

Peyton narrowed her eyes, glaring at his profile and demanding, "And you swear it's not metallic purple or something? No flames on the front?"

He glanced at her and chuckled. "Plain black. I promise."

She relaxed into her seat, watching him handle the wheel and the gear shaft as he navigated the happy-hour traffic on the way to the restaurant. Out of the corner of his eye, Buck noted the way Peyton stroked the dash, and he knew—he *knew*—what she was going to admit next.

"I can't believe I'm going to…" she murmured weakly.

"Babe, I know."

"I shouldn't be saying this."

"Trust me, I understand."

"But it's really great, isn't it?"

"It really is."

She sniffed like she was exasperated with the both of them. "Is it fun to drive?"

"Yup. Very."

"We should have the radio on," she announced, reaching for the dial.

In the second before she got there, Buck remembered what he'd been listening to on the way to her house, recalled the volume at which he'd been playing it, and tried to stop her with a desperate, last-ditch, "Wait!"

He was too late. The classic metal tune he'd been blasting, the one he'd turned off when he'd entered her neighborhood—without turning down the volume first—roared from the speakers.

All of the speakers, in deafening surround sound.

Buck's face went fever-hot as Peyton reflexively ducked for cover. "Sorry! I'm sorry," he hollered over the din.

Her hand darted out, preventing him from turning the sound system down too far. "Oh, no you don't," she said, banging her head to the chorus, then launching into the next verse with a perfect recitation of forty-year-old lyrics.

He was seventeen again. Buck felt like he was seventeen years old, driving his brother's car with the hottest girl in school in the passenger seat, and he had no idea how the time warp had happened.

He stole peeks at Peyton as often as he could without crashing into something, loving to see her lit up and carefree like this. He was…*shit*, he was done for. She was so fucking cute.

They turned a corner, heading west into the setting sun. Peyton flipped down the shade and immediately noticed the CDs his dad kept in a sleeve up there, since the man hadn't quite figured out how to sync his phone to the car yet.

As the metal song wound down, Peyton slipped a disk free and held it out to him.

"Creedence?" she crowed in delight. "Come *on*." She ejected AC/DC and fed her new find into the dashboard slot.

"I guess I should be grateful you didn't spot the Simon and Garfunkel," Buck told her.

"You should definitely be thankful. Are these yours?"

"Nope. All dad's," he smiled, checking the nav on the dash and realizing he'd missed a turn.

It was probably best that his parents had left Peyton plenty of music to amuse herself with. Her distraction with the stereo gave him time to turn around and get back on track before she realized that they were very nearly lost. Buck had to focus if they were going to make it to the restaurant in time for their reservation.

He might not be able to take his eyes off the woman, but that wasn't going to get him far if she starved before he had a chance to kiss her.

Buck rolled his eyes. He was the worst kind of cliché right now—a stereotypical tough guy with a bright beauty riding shotgun, the curve of her cheek and her elegant neck filling him with filthy, filthy thoughts when he really ought to know better.

It'd be embarrassing if it weren't so goddamn fun. Buck took another wrong turn on purpose, just to draw it out a few minutes longer.

"You look gorgeous, by the way," he told her, "Ten out of ten. I didn't have a chance to tell you before."

Peyton turned a little pink and grinned, "You, too. But keep your eyes on the road, Cupid. You missed the turn again."

Chapter Six

Peyton

S O, TELL ME," Buck said, "What do you do for fun?"

The question shouldn't have taken her by surprise—it was standard first date fare, after all. If anything, Peyton should only have been startled that he hadn't asked it sooner.

And yet, the moment those words exited Buck's mouth, she choked on her *papas ala Huancaina* and tried to fix it with a pisco sour chaser that went down the wrong way too.

"You okay over there?" he laughed.

"Fine," Peyton gasped, once she stopped coughing long enough to breathe.

"Touchy subject?"

She stalled another second to wipe away the tears staining her cheeks. "Not touchy—just aspirated a cheesy potato."

"As one does," he commented drily.

"Exactly. As for fun…I'm pretty lame, I guess." *I certainly don't write an infamous I.R. blog that's reviled by half the country.* "I do prep work for my lectures and grade a lot of assignments in my off-hours, and I read newspapers from around the world to keep up on current events." She shrugged, hoping that was specific enough. "When we can swing it, my friend Devon and I like to try new restaurants and catch movies together."

"What kind of movies?"

"Dev loves comic books and graphic novels, so he usually drags me to all the superhero ones." Peyton thought for a minute and decided that wasn't fair. "I shouldn't say *drag*. I enjoy them, too."

"They're great," Buck agreed easily. "Exotic settings, intrigue, action. Got something for everyone, pretty much. How do you know Devon?"

"We work together. He teaches in my department." She took a careful sip of her drink, still uncomfortable with how close they kept dancing to her true—and off-limits—interests. "My family moved around a lot when I was a kid, so I don't have a lot of friends in the area outside of work. Like I said, lame."

That only piqued Buck's interest more, though. "Were your parents military?"

Of course. He was an active-duty sailor—that would be the first thing he assumed. "No, my mom is a diplomat, and my dad is an expert in Asian affairs. We ended up somewhere new every few years." Which had mostly sucked, especially once she and Josh had hit their teens.

What she wouldn't have given for one run-of-the-mill prom like the ones in teen movies.

Buck didn't see the problem with such a childhood, however. He told her, "That's so cool. You probably saw some awesome stuff."

"We did," Peyton conceded. "Museums and libraries were our things. My brother and I always found the good ones, wherever we went."

"I knew it," Buck smiled. "You're not lame at all."

Peyton thought about admitting how much she liked to read, which usually served to underscore her assertion—but then he'd want to know *what* she read, and experience had taught her that was yet another topic best left for later.

Instead, she asked Buck the obvious. "How about you? What do you do when you're not sailing the world or packing up houses?"

Buck sat back and stared off into space for a minute. "I'm like you, I guess. When I'm not deployed, I mostly hang out with the guys in my squad. We work out, hit the shooting range, watch sports—that kind of thing. There's good hiking not too far away and a couple of bars we like, but otherwise…"

He trailed off, but Peyton could already picture him perfectly. Buck running shirtless along the beach in the bright California sun. Buck laughing with his buddies at some local hangout, secure amongst all the tanned, carefree women trying to catch his eye.

He cleared his throat, pulling her attention back to him. "I know it sounds like it, but I'm not a total meathead, I swear. When I'm overseas, I like to explore the local restaurants and markets when I have the chance. I like to read, too. Mostly historical nonfiction, but some current stuff when the mood strikes."

Inwardly, Peyton wanted to groan. *Another inconvenient bullseye.*

Buck was obviously trying to show her they had compatible interests, but surely there were other, less dangerous things they could discuss? With each passing moment, she let her guard down a little more, and she was terrified she was going to blurt out something that clued Buck into her recent woes.

"I read romance," she declared, reversing course and dragging out a truth about herself that had turned many a former date into a dolt.

Fortunately for her, however, reading romance, in most men's minds, was as antithetical to international relations blogging as it could possibly be. "Mostly paranormal," she clarified. "Give me witches or a steamy dragon shifter and I'm happy as a clam."

Buck blinked at her in surprise for a second or two, and then his mouth took on a sly tilt. "You don't say."

Peyton glared at him. "Say something misogynistic. I dare you."

"Wouldn't dream of it," he laughed, holding up his hands. "But trust me when I say, I'm looking forward to hearing a lot more about this topic someday soon."

"Be careful what you wish for," Peyton warned. "I've been reading romance since I was twelve years old and I have plenty to say. More than you're expecting, for sure. But go ahead and read a few current titles—then we'll talk."

To his credit, Buck didn't back down from the challenge. "I'm in. You want me to find the books myself, or do you want to assign specific titles?"

It was tempting, but Peyton grinned and shook her head. "Go out there and find what moves you. That's going to teach you more than I ever could."

Like that, Buck whipped out his phone and typed himself a reminder, and Peyton wondered if he'd really follow through.

He might. At every turn today, Buck had been a pleasant surprise.

Maybe, despite what he did for a living, he would also not disappoint her by jumping to conclusions regarding the *Global Lens* fiasco.

Peyton already hated feeling like she had to keep half her personality under lock and key with him. If she could tell Buck everything she was going through, it would make things so much easier.

She'd been lugging her questions and worries around like a millstone for months. Even Devon didn't know she had some strange man following her now. How much longer could Peyton exist this way?

If she went public and tried to defend herself, she'd lose her job and any protection her anonymity still provided her.

But if she stayed silent, she'd have to continue guarding every word and action with everyone she knew, in case the wrong person discovered something damning. She was even afraid to contact the police about her new stalker—what if her inquiry became public record and word got out somehow?

It wasn't like there was much the cops could do, anyway. The cameraman hadn't threatened her. He hadn't said a word to her. He'd only watched from afar.

She was scared, nonetheless.

Peyton watched Buck pull out his wallet to pay the dinner tab and her eyes fell on his military ID, staring up at her with a timely—and irrefutable—reminder of what was at stake.

Buck had been nice so far, she reminded herself, but she'd only known him for one day. She couldn't trust him with the truth yet. He could so easily turn on her or tell others about her identity and whereabouts.

She'd have to tread carefully for a while longer, until she knew for certain whether she should break things off or take Buck into her confidence.

It seemed like an impossible choice, but Peyton had made it this far. As long as she stepped carefully, she was bound to find a path through.

* * *

WHEN BUCK PULLED into her driveway later that evening, Peyton was both nervous and relieved. She wouldn't have to worry about spilling the beans for much longer, but a quick mental calculation made her wonder, rather abruptly, whether dinner had counted as date one, or date three.

A case could be made for either, but the two options held different expectations in her mind. Or *sexpectations*, as it were.

Buck seemed unconcerned as he shut off the ignition and hopped out, so Peyton reached down to grab her bag off the floor. It didn't matter which date he thought this was. They were consenting adults, and either they were both comfortable with a little physical intimacy, or they weren't.

While she'd been occupied with her purse and her seatbelt, Buck had trotted over to open her door for her. As Peyton swiveled in her seat and put her feet on the ground, she was grateful for his hand to help her up and out of the low riding car.

But maybe "hoist" was the better word. She hadn't exactly eaten lightly at dinner, and her exit was something less than graceful.

"Oof. This car," she smiled ruefully, releasing his hand. "So many hidden challenges."

"That's the truth."

Buck strolled beside her up the walk, then hung back and let her scale the steps to her door before he followed. At the top, he slipped his hand in hers.

His palm felt large and warm against her own, and Peyton remembered how he'd exercised every excuse in the book to put it on her that night.

Not that she was complaining—right now, she didn't want to let it go. His hand was an anchor in a complicated world, keeping her from spinning off into the night.

Her heart was thumping hard in her chest, and even though she worried that her creepy stalker might be out there in the shadows watching, she didn't unlock her door. Not yet.

Buck faced her, eyes warm and a slight smile ticking up his lips. His thumb stroked her wrist.

"I had a nice time tonight," Peyton told him. "Today, too. All of it."

He grinned at that. If he'd decided she was a goofball tonight, he seemed inclined to overlook it. "Me too." He pulled her hand up to his mouth and softly brushed his lips across her knuckles, eyes on hers.

Peyton swallowed against the odd eroticism of the gesture, and his gaze dropped to her mouth. When he spoke, she felt his lips move against her skin.

"I'd love to kiss you good night," Buck murmured, then waited silently for her go-ahead.

The lump in her throat got bigger, blocking any bold words from coming out. But Peyton could still nod, so she did.

He didn't hesitate. In a heartbeat, he'd dropped her hand and wrapped his arms around her, and then his lips were on hers. A breath later his tongue was there, too, stroking along hers with hunger and desire.

If it was possible to both melt and combust at once, Peyton did. Buck sensed it, pulling her more tightly into his embrace and making a deep sound in his throat that sent another hot flare through her.

Now Peyton *knew* she shouldn't unlock the door. She could not invite this man in—if she did, they wouldn't make it past the foyer before she was offering herself up for the taking.

There was a time and a place for nights like that, but Peyton knew she couldn't handle one now. She needed to wait with Buck. And, if a side effect of that was drawing out this exquisite blade of anticipation, well…when the time did come, they would enjoy the inevitable explosion that much more.

The kiss went on and on, developing into a dance of burning stars and molten desire. Buck cupped the back of her head and pulled her against him with more urgency.

He didn't overwhelm her—he just made it clear what kind of bonfire they could light together, given half the chance. Peyton believed every single thing he was telling her with his tongue and promised him all kinds of things back.

Door. Lock. Wait.

Shit. Buck was good. He was better than good.

He made it hard to remember the boundaries she'd set for herself tonight—hard to remember why they were so important.

Lost in his arms, Peyton didn't think about blogs or reporters, stalkers in the night, or cameras in the day. Buck's kiss made her forget all of it, and that probably should have worried her more than it did.

Chapter Seven

Buck

WHEN BUCK WAS finally able to convince himself to come up for air, he couldn't have said whether the high-voltage current zinging through his veins was the result of the espresso he'd gotten with dessert or his newfound infatuation with Peyton Page.

He sincerely hoped she was digging him as much as he was digging her because an invasion of her demilitarized zone was climbing further up his list of priorities by the second.

But then her eyes drifted to his hair, and a small smile teased the edges of her lips. She'd done the same when he'd taken off his hat for the first time during lunch, and again when they were seated at dinner. She hadn't stopped talking to remark on it, but there'd been a pause.

There was always that pause. Buck's swooping heart dropped back to earth like a stone.

Each time Peyton's gaze had returned to his odd hair, he'd seen the question floating across her expression. She hadn't said anything so far, though, and he'd begun to hope that he was in the clear.

Except then she raised a hand and brushed through the strands above his right ear, smiling wider. Buck waited for the inevitable old man joke and inside his chest, his giddy optimism shriveled a little more.

He could see the moment Peyton decided to bite the bullet and go for it.

She opened her mouth, closed it, tried again.

He deflected, saying, "I know. I need a haircut," before she could get a word out.

Her fingers felt good against his skull. Buck wished he could just enjoy that, without dreading that she was going to ruin it by making fun of him.

"No, it's not that," she told him, pulling her hand away. "And I'm probably going to sound like a giant nerd, but I have to say—"

Buck sighed. It was always the same. "The color, right?"

For years, women had been demanding to see his ID, making him prove he was the age he claimed to be, then giving him crap anyway.

And while Peyton was great—*really* great—he wasn't sure he wanted to be with someone who was going to make a big deal out of something he had little control over.

"*Yes*," she enthused. "I'm sorry, I know you must hear it all the time but it's *gorgeous*. I felt like I had to say something so you wouldn't think I was staring for a bad reason."

Buck's hand froze halfway to his head, and he had a wild moment of panic wondering if he was about to poke himself in the eye with one of his fingers.

Peyton's awe seemed genuine, however. She didn't utter a word about his age or ask why he didn't dye his hair, so he'd look younger. And she wasn't done, either.

"Someone upstairs must really like you," she told him. "Between these muscles and that hair you are not hurting for divine favors." She squeezed his arms in emphasis.

A stunned laugh escaped Buck, and Peyton turned as pink as the flowers in the planter next to her feet.

He'd certainly had plenty of occasions to wonder if his prematurely gray hair was a curse, rather than a blessing, but standing here with the taste of this fascinating, tempting woman still on his lips, he was leaning toward the latter.

"You're serious, aren't you?"

Peyton examined him again and nodded, the same way she might if he'd offered her a delicious delicacy. Buck blinked and tried to absorb this unexpected development.

Eventually, he managed to murmur, "Why thank you, Peyton Page."

She smiled, and her eyes, expression, and body language were all clear and open. No obfuscation to be seen. No agenda.

As different from Joely Spitz as a woman could be.

"How long has it been like that?" Peyton wondered.

For one of the only times in his life, Buck didn't mind the question. "It started turning gray when I was about nineteen. It was probably fully white by…twenty-five or so?"

Peyton shook her head, fascinated. "What color was it before?"

Buck shrugged. "Light brown." A very normal, very unremarkable brown. As far as he could remember, not one person had ever commented on it, good or bad.

Peyton looked mesmerized, gazing at his skull like there was a pile of crown jewels up there instead of some overgrown hair. "You must have to beat them off with a stick."

"Who?"

"The hordes of people who have undoubtedly been hitting on you for your whole adult life," she snarked.

Buck thought back to those early days when he'd finally finished growing but hadn't filled out yet. When stress and beer and crappy eating had kept zits on his face well past his teens. When his cockiness had far exceeded any actual experience with women.

All he could do was laugh helplessly and ask her, "Peyton, are you saying you think my hair is *hot*?"

"Uh," she murmured, the pink on her cheeks turning to crimson. "Yeah. I am. Definitely. How the hell are you single?"

Buck wasn't going to touch that with a ten-foot pole, but he could return the compliment. "I think your hair is hot, too," he grinned. "And if you keep being so nice to me, I might grab a nice handful of it the next time I kiss the daylights out of you."

"That's a bit forward," she said, recovering some of her normal sass.

"Does it smell good? It looks like it smells good," he prodded.

Peyton arched a brow. "I guess you'll have to find out."

Oh, Buck was going to find out, that much was clear. He was going to find out everything there was to know about her, as soon as humanly possible.

He touched her cheek gently, then grazed her lip with his thumb before slowly leaning in again. When Peyton opened readily for him, he grabbed her hip and yanked her closer, threading his other hand into that soft hair of hers and fighting the lunatic urge to press her up against the door with his body.

It was too soon for that. If he pushed his luck now, he might not get another date, and he wanted to see her again more than he wanted some immediate hip-on-hip action.

Buck pulled back and took her hands in his. He wanted to kiss her some more. By the look on Peyton's face, she wanted it too. And in that moment of sublime anticipation, Buck had a flash of clarity.

This, *this* was why he'd done it. Any of it, all of it. The deprivations and the struggles, the terrifying bursts of violence, and the interminable stretches of waiting. All of the smug victories and anguishing failures lined up in symmetry, sensical in the light of this day. These kisses.

Buck had willingly done all that he'd been asked to do in his years of being a special operator. All that he'd been capable of doing. He'd done some things without question, and others with a troubled heart.

But through the doing of them, he hoped he'd made it just a little bit easier for people everywhere to experience what he was right now—this ability to stand safely on a beautiful person's stoop on a balmy evening with the cicadas humming all around, and to have that person look back with a yes in their eyes and longing in their heart.

It was these transformative moments—where the world was quiet, but everything teetered on the cusp of change—that felt worth fighting for. Buck wanted everyone to have them. The hope, the glimpse of love, the belief in the good of the world. All mixed into a goodnight kiss.

When he leaned down to Peyton this time, he felt contentment wash through him. This woman was a gift, as unexpected as she was welcome. She'd spent the entire day looking past his veneer to find the man beneath as easily as if he'd given her a roadmap. He had to figure out a way to keep her around.

Plus, the way Peyton kissed made his head swim.

Buck lifted his lips a bare millimeter off hers, taking in air. Without any real thought, three stupid words slipped out of his mouth.

"I want you." He winced but supposed he was lucky it hadn't been three *other* little words.

Peyton's breath hitched, and she inched back a little more. She looked as dazed as he felt, but her voice was strong when she told him, "Not tonight."

Buck was too crazy about her to feel a lick of disappointment. He just shook his head and agreed, "No, not tonight." But he still moved in with one last kiss, laden, he hoped, with intent. "But hopefully soon."

Peyton sucked in a breath like she was trying to steel herself against temptation, but she also nodded as she disentangled herself and fished her keys out of her purse.

He backed up and gripped the railing, wanting her to know he wouldn't lunge once she had the door unlocked.

He wanted to. But a no was a no, damn it.

Peyton stepped into her entryway and turned back to him.

He asked her, "Can I see you again?" and hoped he didn't sound as desperate as he felt. There was something about her that deactivated every ounce of chill he'd managed to develop over the years.

"I'd like that," she smiled. The flush on her face was even more obvious in the bright light of her front hall, and Buck fought back a smug grin.

Oh, yeah. This woman was in just as deep as he was.

"How's tomorrow?" he tried, going for broke.

"Umm." Peyton tilted her head, thinking for a bit like he wasn't standing here holding his breath, hanging on her answer. "I could do…sometime after six or so?"

"Is that what you want?"

More certainty this time. "Yes."

"Great. Then how about I pick you up and make you dinner at my place?" His parents had a great kitchen and an even better backyard, even if the operation was running on the bare minimum at this point. Buck would make do.

"Sounds perfect." Peyton was positively sparkling at him now. The promise of good food or a good time hardly signified in the face of it.

When had he ever had such an ideal day?

Buck stepped closer and gave her one last peck before he forced his feet down the stairs and away. He sat behind the wheel of his father's preposterous muscle car when every bone in his body wanted to stay, and stay, and *stay.*

Peyton gave him a little wave, then shut her door. Buck started the engine and backed onto the sleepy street, and had to readjust himself three times to make room for the erection that wouldn't subside.

He'd spent nearly the entire day getting acquainted with the way Peyton felt beside him, with the way her eyes carried her expressions and the way her mouth moved with her thoughts. He'd learned how her hair brushed his arm and her fingertips flirted with his skin. Brief, tantalizing touches that hinted at so much more.

Buck already loved Peyton's voice and her soft, subtle scent. She had a pervasive feeling of rightness about her. Like they were meant to be.

But all that was nothing compared to how she tasted. After spending hours in a warm, hazy state of half-arousal, Buck had been entirely unprepared for her kiss—the shock to his system when her tongue slid along his.

When her body had melted against him, all that buildup had snapped to attention, stringing him tight as a bow.

He blew the stop sign at the end of her street, startling a deer from the shrubs on the side. Buck shook his head at his recklessness. *Party's over, dumbass. Time to focus.*

As he drove, he thought back to Bennett's call and the news coverage his friend had brought to his attention. It'd been simmering in the back of his mind all evening, something more than the obvious bothering him about the whole thing.

All at once, it came to him. Buck hung a quick left into a gas station, grateful for the car's excellent handling, and parked in front of the minimart. He snatched his cell out of the console and rung up Bennett.

"Yo, yo," Ben said by way of greeting.

"Listen, that whole hot mic thing."

"Yup."

"How far away were those reporters?"

Bennett chuckled. "You saw the footage. Several yards, at least."

"That's what I thought."

He didn't have to explain. His buddy knew exactly where he was going with this. Still, Bennett assured him, "That's pretty much where we're at, too."

"So, who was it? Who did it?"

"What an excellent question. If only you had someone you could call for answers," Ben drawled.

"Yeah. I'll catch you later."

"You'd better."

Buck disconnected and stared at the industrial ice machine for another minute or two, then went into his contacts and sent a text to the secure number Tate Monroe had given him days ago.

Not ten seconds later, his phone lit up with an incoming call from an unknown number. "Gaines, here."

"Lieutenant, you might have warned me what kind of hours you were going to be keeping," Monroe said drily.

"As if you work nine-to-five," Buck retorted.

"Fair enough. So, what've we got?"

"Did you by any chance see the news today?"

"Sure did. And I'm not gonna lie—I'm a little surprised you two ran your traps like that with so many reporters nearby."

"That's the thing. We didn't. Look at the footage again. Even using zoom lenses, they're not that close. Certainly not close enough to pick us up with that kind of clarity."

"I see. So, we looking at a bug, or…"

"…or someone wearing a wire? Tate, you can see how bad this is, right?"

The other man was quiet for a minute. "All right, I'm gonna need you to come in and chat with me in person as soon as you can swing it. We've gotten a good start, but if Doggett's already infiltrated your JAG team—"

"—or, I don't know, my own command," Buck pointed out.

"Or that," Monroe agreed, "Then this clusterfuck's going to take on a different shape."

"You're telling me. I thought Doggett was just trying to send us a message with this shit inquiry. Now he's going for the personal take-down? What does he think we're planning to do?"

"More importantly, what the fuck does he think you guys *know*?" Tate wondered.

"We've been over it a hundred times. We're missing something. We must be."

"All right, look. We're working on it. I'll shoot you a message with details on when we can meet."

"Roger that."

"Gaines, I know you already know this, but don't…" Monroe paused.

"Trust anyone. Got it, believe me."

"See you soon," the man said and hung up.

Buck dropped his head back. When he squeezed his eyes shut, there was a neon blue snowman with a bucket of ice burned on the back of his eyelids, instead of a smart and sexy brunette professor.

The mole couldn't be anyone in their four-man fire team. Buck knew that in his bones. But someone close to them was trying to help bring them down, and they'd been incredibly short-sighted if they thought he and his men would go without a fight.

Chapter Eight

PEYTON GOT THROUGH the next day without any sightings of the weird man with the camera. There'd been a close call at the grocery store when she was doing her shopping for the week, but when the guy had turned around, she'd realized he was a manager who'd worked there for years.

Still, the incident unsettled her enough that she'd made an unplanned stopped at the liquor store next, where she grabbed a couple of bottles of cabernet to take the edge off the nerves that seemed to rattle her every evening lately, as well as a six-pack of beer in case she had a guest of the tall and brawny variety soon.

Back at home, she'd worked through her impatience for dinner with a light cleaning of the bathroom and kitchen, and forty-five minutes on her brother's fancy treadmill. After that, Peyton made herself grade papers until late afternoon, though it was nearly impossible to focus.

Before she shut down her laptop for the night, she let the cursor hover over the icon for her blogging program, and wondered what enduring hell might still be erupting there.

Peyton turned it off without checking, though. She was already jumpy, afraid of where the stalker guy might show up next. She didn't need a bunch of online vitriol to further poison her mood for her date with Buck tonight.

Buck was…amazing. She still couldn't understand how something so good had dropped into her life in the middle of such turmoil. And as she'd done the day before, Peyton wondered again whether he could really be the gift that he seemed.

How was a guy so handsome and charming still single? There had to be a thousand women out there who could hold his interest, and somehow, she'd been the one he wanted to spend his day with yesterday, and who he wanted to wine and dine tonight.

She groaned in frustration. If she overthought this, along with everything else, she was going to miss out on any joy that might come of it. Peyton had to roll with it—she had to take the bull by the…horn.

She stopped in her tracks, giggling a little. Trust a romance reader to find the innuendo in such a mundane inspirational adage. She needed to pull herself together.

Buck had said he was going to grill for dinner, so she decided to keep her outfit on the simple side. She took a quick shower, spent way too much time picking out her underwear, then threw on a simple shirt and a pair of khaki shorts.

She'd texted Buck earlier to let him know she was going to drive herself to his parents' place, so after one final check to make sure she looked okay, she decided she'd dithered long enough and walked to the door.

The sun was going down when she stepped outside, and Peyton was pinned in place with a sudden rush of memory. Buck's urgent lips. His tongue, hot and sweet, tangling with hers. His hands gripping her hips just tightly enough to get her attention.

She debated for only a second before she darted back upstairs, throwing her toothbrush, deodorant, and a change of underwear into a bag. A quick dive into her nightstand unearthed two condoms that were well past their expiration date.

She threw them in the trash with a huff, checked her watch, and decided she still had time to stop at the drug store to buy more on her way. Buck didn't seem the type to be unprepared for anything—but on the off chance he was not expecting her to be primed for action, Peyton wasn't going to take any chances.

She needed something good in her life right now, and lucky for him, he fit the bill and then some.

* * *

BUCK'S PARENTS LIVED in an upscale community several blocks from the MCC campus. As Peyton parked in the driveway, she glanced at the name on the mailbox.

Gaines. Why did that name seem so familiar? In the face of Buck's charm yesterday, it hadn't jumped out at her, but now…she felt sure she'd heard it somewhere recently. Could she have run into one of his folks around town, perhaps, or at school?

He hadn't mentioned what they did, but surely Buck would have said something if she was likely to have met one of them, right?

Peyton didn't have time to dwell on it. He pulled open the front door open with a smile on his face before she'd even turned off her car.

Good. He'd been watching for her. That had to mean he was looking forward to this as much as she was.

"Hey stranger," she called, grabbing her purse, but leaving her other bag on the passenger seat. "Miss me?"

Buck put that question to rest immediately. As soon as she got close, he pulled her into a hug. He gave her a quick peck, said, "You know it," then kissed her again.

That one lingered a lot longer and sent his hands on a nice tour of her ass.

Soon, though, he pulled her into the house, shut the door, and beckoned for her to follow. "Kitchen's back here," he said over his shoulder. "Can I get you something to drink?"

"Water's fine for now." Peyton trailed Buck down the hall, peeking into large, mostly empty rooms as they passed. Whatever his folks had done for a living, it looked like they'd been successful at it.

He already had plates and utensils stacked on the island, along with an undressed salad and some other things on plates, hidden by neat sheets of foil. There was no table or chairs, and no stools at the island. Peyton faltered, not sure what to do.

Buck held out a hand for her purse, then tucked it in a corner of the counter, away from the food. "Sorry it's not more welcoming," he told her, "Most of their stuff is already at the new place. Do you mind if we eat outside?"

"Not at all."

Fortunately, the patio still held a dining set, along with the grill and a large firepit flanked by two loveseats. Buck already had placemats and napkins lined up on the table, and a cooler full of ice set off to the side.

When Peyton looked in it, she spotted a bottle of white wine, two kinds of spritzers, bottled water, and several brands of soda. She covered her laugh as he held out her chair.

There was prepared, and then there was this.

"Oh, and these are for you," he told her, producing a vase full of sunflowers from behind the grill.

Peyton set them in the middle of the table with a smile. "Thank you. But you didn't have to do all this."

Buck just held up a finger and told her, "Wait here." A minute later, he came back out, set a small platter of dip and cut up vegetables beside her, and parked himself in the chair near the grill.

Peyton stared at the meticulously arranged appetizer, and then at him.

He flushed a little. "I thought you might want something to munch on while I cook the steaks."

She picked up a snow pea, frowned at it, then scowled at Buck. "All right, seriously—are you married, or what?"

"N-no!" he sputtered, looking offended. "Why would you say that?"

"Because these aren't baby carrots you dumped out of a bag, that's why. You've got snow peas here. And three colors of peppers. Did you make this dip yourself?"

"Yes. So what?"

"So, regular guys don't do this kind of thing."

"Sure they do. I do!"

"For a woman you just met yesterday morning? Come on."

Buck gaped at her. "I happen to like you, Peyton Page," he complained. "I made an effort because I like you a lot."

She looked between him and his crudité, weighing his body language against the sheer improbability of his existence. And all at once, the light bulb went off. "*Ohhh*," she said, sitting back and looking him over again. "Oh, I see."

Buck looked skeptical. "Somehow I doubt that very much."

"When did you guys break up?" she asked.

He paled instantly. "What?"

"Who was she, and how recently did she break your heart?"

"How—how did you—"

Peyton just shook her head. "Don't bother fighting it. Just tell me if I'm the rebound or not."

Buck sat back and raked a hand through his hair. "You're not. Not even close. And that," he pointed at her a little unsteadily, "was fucking spooky."

She shook her head. "No, it wasn't. The signs are blindingly obvious. Who was she?"

He let out a shaky laugh. "It's not what you think. She…we weren't even dating. Not really. And she didn't break my heart— she screwed me over. Big time."

"Did she steal from you?" Peyton asked. That had happened to Devon once. At the time, she'd thought it was crazy, but maybe thieving exes were a more pervasive problem than she'd assumed.

"No, nothing like that. More like a…" Buck hesitated, thinking it over. "More like a broken confidence. And it was months ago. I've had plenty of time to get over it, trust me."

Judging by his demeanor, Peyton would venture to say that Buck was not, in fact, over it. Not even close. Then, because she was clearly a masochist, she asked him, "What was her name?"

"Doesn't even matter," he said bitterly. "I guess you could call her a reporter. She started hanging around my squad when we were, uh…deployed a while back. Came on pretty strong, but I didn't think much of it at the time. Figured a little fling between grownups wouldn't hurt anyone."

"But it did?"

"Oh, yes. Fucked up our op six ways to Sunday."

"I'm sorry."

Buck blew out a breath and waved her off, then stood and shook out his shoulders. "You don't have to worry about her. I promise."

"Okay."

"Are you hungry? Want me to start the steaks?"

Peyton dragged the snow pea she was holding through the creamy dip and popped it in her mouth. Damn, even his cooking skills were special. "Sure. That sounds good," she told him.

"How about some wine?"

She spotted the corkscrew on the end of the table. "I'll get it. Can I do anything to help?"

"Nope. Everything's ready to go," Buck smiled. "You just kick back and enjoy the view."

Peyton snorted and brazenly ogled his ass.

"And don't turn me into a frog while my back is turned," he added with a chuckle.

"Don't overcook my ribeye and maybe I won't," she fired back and for some reason, he seemed to find that extra funny.

They made small talk while he cooked. Buck brought out the side dishes he'd put together, and Peyton thought about what he'd shared so far. She was starting to suspect that he was a bit more than a rank-and-file sailor.

There was his hair, for one thing. Even after a couple of weeks of leave, a regular Navy guy wouldn't have let his cut get so overgrown. Buck had repeatedly mentioned his squad and his team, and just now had referred to his messed-up mission as an op.

He also lived in Coronado.

Life-ruining blog posts aside, Peyton thought she'd done enough research about special operators in all branches of the service to know one when she saw one.

"Hey, Buck?" she called to his broad back. "What do you do in the Navy? You never told me."

He stopped poking at the meat and the corn cobs and turned to her. "Uh…"

She waited, letting him fiddle with his tongs for a good long while.

After a while, Buck ducked his head, looked toward the bushes lining the fence at the side of the yard, and scratched at his neck. Once he'd exhausted every stalling tactic in the book, he met her eye again.

"Let's just say," he sighed, "You probably don't need to turn me into a frog—some might say I'm one already."

Peyton blinked at him for a second before his meaning dawned on her. Frog. *Frogman.*

"You're a SEAL."

Buck nodded.

"Are you even allowed to tell me that?"

"Yeah. Just…maybe don't spread it around, I guess?"

"Wow. Okay." Peyton's lungs felt like they had turned to concrete.

This was bad. So much worse than if Buck was a regular, everyday sailor. There was no way on earth she could tell him about her blog woes now. What if he knew the operators involved in that awful ambush?

He would murder her in her sleep and she would never know the difference. *Crap.*

Peyton liked this man. He'd said he liked her. She wanted him to like her all over.

And besides, *Global Lens* had already ruined her life once. Did she have to let it ruin things again?

What was the point of telling Buck, anyway? She hadn't had the nerve to publish anything new since her last article had blown up, and probably wouldn't work up the courage any time soon. If things continued as they had, she might have to shut the whole thing down for good.

Buck would never need to know. They could have these couple of weeks with each other, he could go back to California, and that would be that. *Simple.*

He dropped a steak and an ear of corn onto a plate and set it in front of her. "Did that surprise you?"

"Yes and no. I was beginning to wonder, but…" she shrugged. "I don't know. You guys are sort of like the yeti these days. Everyone knows someone who's seen one."

Buck sputtered out a laugh. "First frogs, and now Bigfoot? Maybe the pinot grigio was a mistake."

He went inside to put his cooking utensils in the sink, then sat across from her with his own plate. "Is it a deal-breaker?" he wondered softly. "What I do?"

"No, of course not," Peyton told him. It should be, she knew, but she couldn't bring herself to cut things off now when it seemed like they had so much potential together.

"Do you like your food?" Buck gestured at her untouched plate. "Do you want something else instead?"

"No, this is great." Peyton took a bite of steak, and another of the potato salad she spooned from a bowl between them. "Really great. Did you make everything?"

Buck nodded, looking pleased.

"And he cooks, too. Not very fair to the other guys, is it?"

"Screw them," he grinned. "If they wanted it bad enough, they'd get out there and earn it."

Peyton smiled. "Oh, you're earning it. And then some."

"Glad to hear that. But, Peyton…listen. You know when I'm done here, I have to head back to base. I just want to say that I hope…I hope we can spend a lot of time together before that happens."

"What about after?" she asked.

"I guess that depends on what you want from me."

"What do you want from me?"

He didn't equivocate. "As much as you're willing to give."

Peyton bit her lip. This guy was a dream. "How much do you have left to do here, anyway?"

"There's a donation truck coming in a few days, and a contractor to take down the wallpaper upstairs. If I can't sell the rest of the furniture to someone, the real estate agent said he can roll it into the listing, so it will convey with the house. My mom and dad will come back to pick up Dad's car, and then…I'm out," he shrugged. "I'll rent a car to get back to base. Probably…in another week or two, at most."

Peyton frowned. "You're going to drive across the country? Why not fly? I thought you guys could just hop on transports when you needed to get somewhere."

"Oh. No…I'm not going straight to California," he told her slowly. "My team's been cooling their heels in Virginia Beach for a bit. We had some…bureaucratic stuff to do. That'll probably last another few weeks. We'll head out west after that's done."

"So, we've got…what? About a month or so, give or take?" she asked. "Some of that with you in Virginia?"

Buck nodded, watching her carefully. "What do you think?"

"I think we can work with that."

Chapter Nine

Buck

THE SUN HAD been down for a while and a lazy post-meal peace had settled over the backyard. Peyton played music on her phone and Buck devoured another frozen fruit bar—they weren't talking much, but it was a nice quiet. Comfortable.

But then, out of nowhere, a sudden burst of light illuminated his parents' patio. Peyton jolted like she'd been shot, her sweating can of spritzer slipping out of her grasp to thunk against the table.

"Oh my god! Was that lightning?" she cried.

Buck rose to his feet slowly and scanned the neighbor's yard to the left. It was hard to see much. They didn't have outdoor lights on in the back.

"I don't think we're expecting weather tonight," he told Peyton. If she hadn't recognized the blast as a camera flash, then he wasn't about to disabuse her. "It was probably a deer tripping someone's security lights."

"We should go inside. I'm sure that was lightning," she said, clumsily gathering up their dinner plates. "You know how it is. Things blow in fast this time of year."

Buck grabbed a few bowls and backed toward the kitchen, trying to keep his body between Peyton and whoever was over there. "True. Let me help you carry this stuff in."

"I was getting eaten alive by mosquitos anyway," she said quickly, though she hadn't mentioned it before, and Buck hadn't noticed her slapping her ankles or itching any bites.

"We can't have that," he smiled, and herded her inside.

He kept the blinds open over the kitchen sink and watched the patio while they cleaned up the kitchen and put the plates in the dishwasher, but no one was bold enough to show themselves in the light.

Maybe they were out there waiting. Maybe long gone.

Either way, Buck felt better with Peyton tucked safely inside the house. The only people likely to be using a flash in his vicinity were asshole reporters, and the very last thing he wanted was for her to get pulled into the whole inquiry shitstorm by accident.

If he had the angles right, they couldn't have gotten a clear shot of her face, though, so it was probably not too late to keep Peyton out of the public eye.

Buck, of course, was a different story—his mug had already been plastered all over creation, so there'd be no harm in him going out to poke around, on the off chance the person had left something behind.

"You know what," he told Peyton. "If we're going to get rain, I'd better put the cover back on the grill."

She nodded and wandered into the nearly empty family room. "Good idea. I'll camp out here if that's okay." She set her phone on the coffee table and dropped onto the couch, but there wasn't much for her to look at. The television was long gone.

"Back in a sec." Buck waited for her to get settled, then casually flicked off the light switch next to the door, slid open the screen, and stepped outside.

It was a still, balmy night. He could hear a frog or two croaking nearby, some cicadas in the grass, and a dog barking a few houses away. Peyton's music was too soft to register, so he kept his steps light.

The dark was pervasive, broken only by a narrow square of illumination slanting from the back neighbor's kitchen window half an acre away.

Buck made his way silently to the fence on the left, followed it a couple of feet to the break in the deer fencing tacked to the rails, and levered himself over. He'd slipped a Maglite into his pocket in the kitchen, and he pulled it out now, panning around the ground until he found the shoe prints.

Size eleven sneakers, give or take, he thought. One adult, slim male, or possibly a tall female. Once the prints left the muddy bed where the neighbors grew tomatoes, they disappeared. Buck kept to the shadows and did a quick circuit of the lawn and house but didn't find anything else.

He didn't want to leave Peyton alone too long, in case that flash had been a diversion to get them separated, so Buck ghosted back to his parents' patio, pulled the cover over the grill, and went inside.

He turned the outdoor lights back on as he slipped off his sneakers by the door and tried not to buckle at the instant stab of pain he felt at the front of his hip. It seemed Buck's strained groin muscle was not on board with his detour into track and field.

Which was unfortunate, given that a really pretty woman was smiling at him from the couch. He'd been recovering so well, too.

"Everything okay?" Peyton asked. "I thought I might have to send out a search party."

"Sorry," Buck said, trying to walk very normally over to her, and failing. "I figured I'd better disconnect the propane tank while I was out there, too. Hard to see what I was doing."

"Yeah, I bet," Peyton said, then glanced at the slider. "I wish my brother's alarm system chimed like that when people go in and out. Ours only beeps when I turn it on."

Buck paused to brace himself on the column at the corner of the family room. "I think most systems have the option," he told her. "I can show you how to turn it on if you want."

"Thanks—that'd be great."

"You live in a pretty nice neighborhood. Don't you feel safe there?"

Peyton shrugged and looked away. "Oh, you know…single girl living alone. Can't be too careful."

Buck took advantage of her distraction to hobble the rest of the way to the couch but naturally, she turned back right in time to see him wince as he sat down.

"What happened?" she asked. "Did you hurt yourself?"

"I pulled something a few days ago. Must've aggravated it crouching next to the grill. It's nothing." Buck took a deep breath and relaxed carefully into the soft cushions, trying to will away the ache through sheer force of will.

It was hard to envision how this date could get any less romantic.

Peyton stared at him, her eyebrows nearly at her hairline. She was too smart to bother refuting his obvious lie, and Buck wasn't about to dig a deeper hole for himself.

The face-off lasted less than a minute, but it felt like ten. That was probably why the chorus of the silly country-rap hit drifting from Peyton's phone landed as clearly as it did. Leaving aside the merits of random white boys rapping about chicks in cut-offs, Buck had to admire the way the lyrics sketched a crystalline image in his mind.

He winked at Peyton, happy for the change in subject. "To be clear, I will leer at you shamelessly if I ever see you in a pair of Daisy Dukes."

A parade of emotions galloped across her features. Eventually, Peyton settled on scorn and stuck with it. "We don't have to worry about that. Booty shorts aren't really my thing, and I think we can all agree that's for the best."

"I have no clue what you mean, and no, I don't agree."

Peyton papered right over his push-back with a haughty, "Believe me, no one needs to see that much of my thighs."

Buck did not want to be included in the *no one* category. Not in the least. He wanted to see so much of her thighs—and more—with nearly paralyzing urgency.

Peyton met his eyes, but only briefly. She concentrated instead on glaring at the blank wall over his shoulder, and her defensiveness stung.

"Maybe I haven't been clear enough," he told her. "I'm not into reed-thin women. If I was, I would've asked out one of them, instead of you."

That got her attention. Peyton's stormy gaze swung back to his instantly, sizing him up in the soft light. "Probably would've taken you five minutes, too," she muttered.

Buck couldn't believe this was happening over a flirty crack about booty shorts. Except this wasn't about shorts at all, he knew. This was about a world that began with pink razors costing more than blue ones and ended with dusty village schools getting blown up for trying to teach girls they could have a different calling than the whims of men.

This was about the kind of misogyny you could see and the kind that you couldn't. Both kinds tainted even the most confident women with self-doubt.

Buck told her, "Peyton, I like you. Exactly as you are. Have I given you any reason to think differently?"

As gently as he could, he pried her arms from around her waist and guided her to her feet. Buck pulled her into a hug and kissed the top of her head, breathing in the warm, feminine scent that filled his nose. She felt just as good against him as he remembered and his residual worry about paparazzi skulking around outside gradually evaporated.

From under his chin, Peyton mumbled, "I'm sorry. I'm not usually this prickly. It's just that you're…like, freakishly fit. I mean, honestly—how about leaving some muscles for the rest of us?"

Buck grinned into the shadows of the echoing room. He'd seen way, way too much of the dark underbelly of the world, but the woman in his arms—the woman of his dreams, he was beginning to suspect—appeared to be feeling aggravated by how attractive she found him.

That *had* to count as some kind of win in the balance of life.

"Peyton. Babe. You can't possibly be worried that you're not going to measure up." Buck supposed that would count as proof positive she wasn't a mind reader. If she were, she'd know there was no reason to doubt him.

On this score, at least.

Peyton turned her head and laid her cheek against his heart. "I didn't think I was. I'm not sure where this is coming from, to be honest."

Buck pulled her tighter against him, and said, "I can promise you that it is not something I am concerned about in the least." She'd undoubtedly notice the glaring evidence of exactly how attractive he found her and her delectable thighs soon enough. However, in case she didn't, he added, "I love how you're soft where I'm not. I want to taste every bit of that softness until you see stars."

Peyton didn't have a ready answer for that. She sighed, though, and the breathy sound shot along his nerves like wildfire.

If Buck could manage enough time with her over the next few weeks, he hoped to convince this woman that he wasn't going to ghost her and he wasn't going to ditch her for the next woman who popped up on his radar.

He had a sneaking suspicion he was a goner already. In it for the long haul. Till death do they part. It was the first time in his life he put any stock whatsoever in the concept of love at first sight.

He took a deep breath and took the plunge. "What do you think? You gonna let me kiss you now?"

"Perhaps," she smiled.

Buck looked into Peyton's face, the seconds ticking past like the beat of his heart. Expectation hung heavy in the air, but it still felt a little off, the energy wrong.

"You're still worried," he said.

Peyton huffed out a frustrated breath. She squared her shoulders, stood up straight, and focused on a point just left of his ear. When she spoke, her voice sounded flat. "I figured tonight…things might get…physical between us." She stopped, as if that explained anything.

Buck touched her cheek, trailing his fingertips across it in a whisper-light caress. "I'm looking forward to it, whenever it happens," he told her. "I want that with you, but not until you're ready."

Peyton licked her lips nervously, so he waited to hear the rest.

Eventually, she came out with, "I know," then stopped, and rolled her eyes. "I know I'm shooting myself in the foot here. But Buck, the way you look has me…"

"Hot and bothered?" he offered.

She didn't deny it, at least. She only blurted out, "Are you sure this isn't some kind of cosmic mistake? What if you only *think* I'm what you want, but you wake up later and realize how disappointed you are?"

The preposterous statement had Buck sputtering, "By *you?*"

Peyton had to have gone off the deep end. She was acting like she was some ancient, haggard crone, haunting the caves of a spooky forest. How could Buck convince her she was everything that pushed his buttons, and more?

"Look, I'm not athletic at all," she tried to explain. "I like to eat, and I hate to exercise. I'm not some California Beach Barbie. I have *scars,*" she said, like that was going to be the deal-breaker.

Buck fought back a laugh, certain that Peyton would take it the wrong way. Her crazy comment had given him an idea, though.

"Scars. *Feh.*" He dismissed them with a careless wave of his hand. "I've got you beat in a scar contest any day." Then he sat down, draped his arm across the back of the couch, and waited to see if she'd take the bait.

Peyton tilted her head. She studied Buck from the top of his head to the toes of his feet, then let her eyes wander north again. A surge of warm desire washed over him before he remembered how many scars he had, and how he'd gotten them. He tried to envision telling Peyton the stories, and the wind went out of his sails like spit off a cliff.

Maybe this was a bad idea.

Of course, that was the moment she decided to roll with it. "Hmph," she snorted, full of her customary confidence once more. "You don't look so tough. And I'll have you know that I've won every scar contest I've ever been in. Easily, I might add."

Buck didn't like the sound of that. "How many of these things have you been a party to? Give or take?"

"Plenty," she asserted, gaining determination by the minute. "It's not like I've had to compete against gunshot wounds or anything, but I can beat a good knee surgery, no sweat." Her shoulders didn't look so tight now, and her posture looked far more relaxed. That was good.

Maybe Buck was on the right track with this contest idea, after all. If it got her bout of nerves out of the way and put a light-hearted spin on it, this evening might still turn sexy. With that in mind, he set his hands on his knees and hauled himself gingerly to his feet.

"I'll go first," he said, then he drew his t-shirt up over his ribs, holding her wide-eyed stare as he stripped it off. *Slowly.* So, she could look her fill.

He couldn't imagine why not, but Peyton clearly had not seen that coming. Buck turned to the side, tucked his wrist behind his head, and showed her his ghastly, game-winning goods.

As he'd expected, she gasped sharply. "Oh my god, Buck— what the hell happened to you?"

He passed his free hand over the bumpy skin and smiled. "Gunshot wound, as it turns out. Plus, some burns. Not so cocky now, are you?"

Peyton reached out without flinching, pulling his hand aside so she could run her own palm across the ruined skin. Buck shivered and added a new want to all the others he'd been accumulating when it came to her.

He didn't only want her legs wrapped around him, and her arms, and her scent, too. Buck wanted to feel Peyton's hot little hands everywhere. He wanted her to touch him with this same sense of possession for the rest of their days.

"Did it hurt?" she murmured.

"Nah," he said. "Like a bee sting."

Her gaze shot up to his and she frowned. "Seriously?"

"A burning piece of metal ripped into me at high velocity," Buck laughed. "It felt exactly like what it was."

"Damn," Peyton muttered, looking down again. "I can't believe it, but I think we might be tied."

He left off his shirt and sat back down. Peyton's eyes searched his torso, traveling over the tattoo on his bicep and the one above his heart before landing back on his face. There were plenty of other dings in his hide for her to discover, but she didn't look like she was going hunting yet.

"Tied?" he complained, hoping to keep her on task. "How did I not just blow you out of the water?"

Instead of answering directly, all she did was look into his eyes and put her hands on the buttons of her shirt.

Buck had no idea what to expect. What could have happened to this woman that would've marked her enough to compete with his side? And how soon was he going to have to hunt someone down and make them pay for it?

Peyton pivoted and presented him with her back. Her head dipped down as she worked at her buttons. He held his breath and waited.

The shirt drifted to the carpet in a wisp of pale blue linen, and his eyes tracked up her legs, hitching on the waistband of her khaki shorts, and the seductive way it curved across the small of her back. Between the twin bows of her hips, the shallow valley of her spine extended upward.

It took Buck a minute to register that Peyton's back was entirely bisected by a long, nasty surgical scar. The stripe stretched from somewhere below her waistband to the nape of her neck, where it tapered into a razor-thin tip.

He followed it with his eyes, and Christ—she hadn't been kidding. It looked like someone had tried to cut the poor woman in half.

Buck stood and let out a low whistle. "That's pretty impressive."

"Told you."

"What happened?" He was close enough to feel the heat coming off Peyton's skin and seeing so much of it exposed at once had him aching to undress her completely.

He touched her shoulder lightly, then drew his fingers down the length of that awful purple line. He hated to imagine what her recovery must've been like.

"Three spinal surgeries," Peyton told him, then flinched when he reached the middle of her back. "Sorry—I have a lot of nerve damage. It feels weird when you do that."

Buck kissed her shoulder instead. "Sorry. Were you in an accident, or what?"

"No, I had scoliosis growing up. First two surgeries failed, but the third has held up okay."

"Yikes. How old were you?"

"Eleven, fifteen, and twenty-two."

"Sheesh." Buck moved his hands around her hips to hold her in place and had to squeeze his eyes closed when he felt the velvet softness of her lower belly.

"You're not grossed out?" Peyton asked. "I know it's pretty hideous. People always comment when I go to the pool or the beach."

Well, at least Buck knew who to kill now. Their murders would have to wait, however, because the way Peyton sucked in a breath when he explored the inch of skin beneath the button of her shorts made his heart go haywire.

He found the side of her neck and the perfect shell of her ear with his lips. "You're not hideous, Peyton. You're gorgeous. So damn pretty I can hardly breathe."

Chapter Ten

Peyton

PEYTON SLIPPED THE button of her shorts free and pushed them down. Buck steadied her as she stepped out of them, then turned her to face him.

He held her by the hips and reared back, looking over her lingerie with an approving grunt. "Probably better I didn't know you were hiding this all night."

"Hiding sounds so nefarious," Peyton told him. "How about saving?"

His fingers traced lightly across the top edge of her bra. "You can save stuff like this for me whenever you want," he chuckled darkly, "But don't be surprised if I conduct regular inspections."

Buck kissed her quickly then, hot and hungry as his tongue stroked hers, and tasting like the popsicles they'd eaten earlier. He jumped when Peyton stroked up his sides, then hummed as she pressed closer.

Chest to chest, he was overwhelming, blazing skin layered over heavy muscle, restrained power and want simmering beneath his gentle touch. Her bout of anxiety before felt like ancient history. Peyton wanted to rub against him like a cat, now.

She reached back to where Buck's hands were softly caressing her ass, and pressed his fingers into her skin so he would grip her tighter.

He smiled against her lips. "It's like that, huh?"

"Oh yes," she told him.

"*Yes* sounds good," he fired back. "Definitely keep saying that."

"Yes, I love the way you kiss me," Peyton smiled. "Yes, I think you should lose those shorts. Yes, I—"

Buck let go of her and shoved down his shorts, revealing a pair of black boxer briefs that did nothing to obscure his impressive erection.

"Oh," Peyton mumbled, eyes widening. "*Oh*."

"Yeah, *oh*," he smiled. "Come here, woman."

He shifted to the couch and pulled Peyton onto his lap. In no time, Buck had his hands full of her backside again, guiding her closer as he kissed the daylights out of her.

She wondered momentarily if she was moving too fast, but realized that concept didn't really apply. Their entire relationship had been barreling along at a faster clip than she usually felt comfortable with. Right here, right now, though? It didn't matter.

Peyton couldn't resist the impulse to grind against all that gorgeous, finely hewn power, so she arched her back and flexed her thighs, and reveled in the deep rumble that emerged from Buck's chest.

He broke away from her mouth and nipped at her shoulder. "Doing okay?"

"Yes," she grinned. "You?"

"10 out of 10, would absolutely recommend," he laughed.

"Excellent." Peyton reached behind her back and popped the clasp on her bra, then slipped it off and dropped it on the floor.

"*Fuck*," he growled.

"Yes, that's the idea."

He dove forward to clamp his lips around one nipple, then the other. "More yeses," he told her, "keep them coming." And then, before Peyton quite knew what was happening, Buck tipped her sideways on the cushions and nudged her thighs apart with his knee.

He hissed in pain immediately. "*Ah*. Shit," he muttered.

"You all right?"

"Just…give me a minute."

Peyton snorted. "I'm sure whatever you pulled is still nothing to worry about. Given that your face just turned the color of old socks."

"Pipe down," Buck grumbled. "Let me breathe through it."

"Oh my god." She held still as long as she could, but there was no holding back her fit of giggles, especially once Buck noticed and started tickling her side, making it worse.

"Stop! Stop," she laughed. "Cease and desist, you big brute!"

"Would a brute make his own vegetable dip? I think not." Buck grabbed her around the waist and moved her further up the sectional, then dipped his head and nipped at the inside of her thigh.

Peyton let out the most undignified squeak she'd ever heard.

"Good god, look at this thigh meat," he grinned evilly. "A man could live for days on these things."

"What!"

"And here you are, trying to keep them all to yourself. Selfish, thy name is Peyton," Buck chuckled, sucking and nipping from her knees to her bikini line like he intended to devour her.

"Buck!" she shrieked, when he hit a particularly sensitive patch of skin, "Please!"

He stopped and raised his head, holding himself over her with one thickly muscled arm. "Yes, darling?"

She took a deep breath, trying to calm down. "Do something."

His eyebrows ratcheted up. "Anything in particular?"

"I'm sure you'll think of something."

He held Peyton's gaze as he stroked up her inner thigh, dragged two fingers across her soaking panties, and pressed them to her clit.

"How's this?" he wondered casually, though his eyes flared when he saw how wet she was.

Peyton's voice came out unsteady and way too breathy. "That'll do."

Buck helped her wriggle out of her panties and reposition herself with no more obvious signs that his injury was bothering him, but she still felt like it was good sportsmanship to ask, "Are you sure you're okay? I don't want you to hurt yourself worse."

"Appreciate you asking, but I could be dragging one leg behind me like a parachute, and I wouldn't quit this," Buck told her. "I'm fine."

"Glad to hear it."

"I'll be even better if I can manage to make you shriek again," he grinned slyly, then lowered his mouth to her core.

Peyton's mouth dropped open when he made contact and she stared at the ceiling in disbelief. "And to think," she gasped a moment later, "I tried to talk you out of this."

Buck was too busy winding her tighter and tighter to bother with words. He was a man on a mission, and before long, Peyton had to brace herself with a foot on the floor and her hands on his shoulders to keep herself anchored to earth.

"Come on," he whispered against her tender flesh, "Let me have it." He did something different and delicious with his tongue, keeping at it until her back bowed and Peyton was panting like she'd run a mile.

Her climax jolted through her body like a thunderclap, sudden and powerful. Buck let up a bit when he felt it, slowing gradually until she collapsed back to the couch with a gasp of disbelief.

"Holy crap. Where did you learn that? Wait—don't tell me. They taught you in BUD/S," she sputtered. "How to neutralize half the world's population in three easy moves."

"Don't be ridiculous," Buck laughed, wiping his mouth on his arm and looking exceedingly pleased with himself. "That's a skill you have to learn on the job."

Peyton snorted and tried to work up the energy to move, but her legs felt like jelly. "I think…you might've killed me."

He levered himself off her, stood, and held out a hand. "Nonsense. The night is still young. I haven't even shown you my bed yet."

She let him drag her to her feet, then swayed against all that deliriously hot skin. "Is that what you want? To show me your bed?"

His grin was even cheekier than usual when he answered, "Among other things. Will you stay tonight?"

"Yes. Let me grab my stuff from the car."

Buck shook his head and reached for his shorts with a hastily covered wince. "I do love a woman who's prepared. Hand me your keys and I'll get it for you."

Peyton was not going to argue with that. She had zero desire to go back outside until the sun was out and camera-brandishing stalkers were easier to spot. So she pulled on Buck's t-shirt and walked over to the kitchen counter, found her car keys in her purse, and tossed them over.

"Passenger seat," she told him. "And no dillydallying. You can check my tire pressure or whatever in the morning."

Buck huffed in offense then lunged at her, catching Peyton easily and bending her backward over one strong arm so he could kiss her into submission again.

When he finally set her upright and waltzed out the front door, she was loopy and grinning like a fool. No, taking their time was something they were not going to do—and that was one hundred percent all right with her.

"IT'S JUST A spasm," Buck groaned several minutes later. "Don't worry."

Peyton took one look at the man splayed out on the mattress in his bedroom and laughed right in his face.

"Buck, would you get a grip? You could barely make it up the stairs. You nearly passed out when you laid down. Just admit you can't do what needs to be done here so we can and move on like adults."

He'd thrown an arm over his face when he'd collapsed, presumably to hide how much pain he was in. Now he balled his hands into fists.

"I'm—"

"You're not fine!" Peyton laughed.

"I'll have you know that I've *done what needed to be done* under far worse conditions than this."

"I have no doubt. You probably didn't enjoy it, though, and that's kind of what we're going for here."

He muttered something under his breath and Peyton shook her head. "I get it, okay? You're very tough. But you're also acting unhinged right now. There's lots of other stuff we can do that won't aggravate whatever you've got going on down there."

"Groin pull," he murmured.

"Like I couldn't guess. Let me help you with these shorts, and I'll kiss it better, all right?"

Buck yanked the arm off his face so fast, he knocked a pillow to the floor. "Don't toy with me."

Peyton bit her lip and grinned. "I knew you'd see reason."

She pulled off the t-shirt and dropped her panties to the carpet. Then she leaned over to work Buck's shorts and briefs down his legs, his eyes glued to her the entire time.

"I'm sorry," he complained. "I wanted this night to be about you."

"Oh, it is. No apology necessary."

"You sure you're okay with doing…that?"

"Buck, please shut up." Peyton licked her lips and was rewarded with his sharp intake of breath.

His hand settled on her back as she bent to slide her lips down his shaft. Peyton explored the tip with her tongue and smiled when his cock got even harder in her hand. Keeping her lips tight, she moved up and down in a steady rhythm, but soon Buck was pulling on her shoulder and telling her, "Stop. Wait."

"Did I hurt you?"

"No. But if I don't get to finish inside of you after the week I've had, I'm liable to shoot something other than my load."

"That will almost certainly affect the house's resale value," she smirked. "Hang on."

Peyton shimmied off the end of the bed, reached for her overnight bag, and found the package of condoms she'd bought on the way over. She scratched at the plastic shrinkwrap with her nails but it seemed to be glued on all sides.

"Rip it," Buck instructed.

"I am."

"Faster," he urged, palming himself with a sexy little frown.

Peyton stopped to watch, and instantly he pulled his hand away to point at the box. "First that. Then this."

"I'm trying."

"Give it to me."

"I'm *trying* to," she cried in frustration.

He barked out a laugh. "The *box*, Peyton."

She tossed it at his head and he snatched it from the air, then smashed the box in his hand like an empty beer can. In short order, Buck had torn off the plastic, extracted a strip of condoms, and ripped one open. Two seconds later, he had himself covered and was smacking her thigh.

"Hop on, beautiful," Buck said. "Let's get you taken care of."

Peyton climbed over him again and sat on his thighs, giving herself a minute to appreciate the terrain of fine man spread out beneath her. Then she ran her palms up his stomach and rested them on his pecs.

"A comfy couch downstairs says you already accomplished that."

His fingers dug into her hips, urging her up and over his straining cock. "I like to be thorough. Sue me."

Peyton guided him into her, sinking down slowly until she'd taken in his entire length. Then she reversed the motion, just as leisurely. Buck let her repeat it a few times before his hands pressed harder, driving her rhythm as he thrust into her urgently.

Buck gasped out a curse and then he was coming, pressing into her the muscles in his torso strained and his face contorted. The sight of it sent Peyton soaring, her tempo faltering as her climax took hold.

Soon though, the adrenaline drained out of her and she collapsed against his chest, boneless and blissed out.

Buck wrapped his arms around her, stroking her hair as they caught their breath.

"You're incredible," he whispered, kissing her temple.

"And you are quite, quite thorough," she told him. "Are you sure you're okay?"

"Yeah, of course. Why?"

"Because at the end there I wasn't sure if your expression signaled ecstasy or agony."

Buck chuckled, the sound rumbling through his chest. "Maybe a little of both. But it was worth it, believe me."

PEYTON DUCKED INTO his bathroom a few minutes later to rinse off and brush her teeth. She put her hair up with a stretched-out elastic she'd found at the bottom of her purse, and put on a fresh pair of panties and the clean t-shirt Buck had offered her.

She expected him to have the light turned out by the time she emerged, maybe even to be asleep already—but Buck was sitting on the bed, watching for her expectantly.

"I guess that storm blew right past us," she said shakily. "I'm not sure it even rained."

She'd agonized about whether to bring it up at all. Peyton didn't want Buck to reconsider whether that camera flash had actually been lightning or not, but she'd also made a big deal about getting inside fast. It felt unnatural to *not* comment on it.

He didn't say a word, though, continuing to stare at her. Her anxiety ratcheted up.

Did he know?

"What?" Peyton laughed, ducking her head and feeling more vulnerable than she had with his face between her thighs. "Do I look that different without makeup?"

She'd been aiming for deflection but wanted to kick herself for her insecure tone. She didn't like to hand people ammunition to use against her, as a rule, but now she'd done it twice in one night.

Buck shook his head, saying softly, "It has been a really long time since a woman has let me see her without makeup on."

Peyton blinked. "Okay?" *Was that a good thing? And how many women were they talking, anyway?*

"You look so…"

"Plain?" she wondered archly.

"No. Maybe…wholesome? I guess that's the word I mean."

"Gee thanks," she muttered drily, flouncing over to the bed and flopping down next to him. "That might sound sexy if we were Amish." *At least the diversion was working.*

"Oh, I don't know," Buck drawled back. "You seem very…accessible."

"Like I haven't been—"

He sprang, pinning her beneath him without any quarter given to his injured muscle. "Look at you. I can kiss you anywhere, and not have to worry about messing anything up. Like here." He planted a sloppy kiss on her cheek. "Or here." Another on her eyelid.

"Buck—"

"This is good. I like this. We should cancel lipstick forever." He punctuated each word with a quick kiss on her mouth.

"You told me you liked my lipstick before," Peyton scowled. "Were you lying?"

He reared back and squinted, thinking it over. "I wasn't lying at the time. But I didn't have all the information I needed to make a sound decision. The situation on the ground has changed."

"The situation on the ground is that it's one in the morning," she fired back. "Don't you have anywhere to be tomorrow?"

"Just here," he smiled, kissing her again. "Cleared my nonexistent schedule the minute I laid eyes on you in that coffee shop."

Peyton rolled her eyes. "I'll believe that when I see it."

"Wait and see," he said, nuzzling against the side of her neck. "Wait and see."

Chapter Eleven

Buck

HE'D MANAGED TO meet Peyton at least once a day for the next week, grabbing coffee here and there, lunch and dinner, and fitting in plenty of canoodling in between with no more visits from unexpected guests. She'd steadfastly refused to hit the sheets with Buck again, however, until he could believably assure her that his groin pull had healed.

He'd about had it with that plan. After they left the coffee shop that morning, he'd spent the rest of the day popping ibuprofen and using the heating pad for fifteen minutes an hour, every hour. Buck's leg felt almost perfect now, and he was determined to redeem himself for his tragically awful performance in the sack last week.

And so, he'd invited Peyton for drinks at a gastropub in the shopping center near his parents' house. If he could convince her was fine while they were here, it would be a nice, short detour before he got her home and horizontal.

So far, however, she'd still been playing it coy.

Buck leaned close to her, his forearm landing on a sticky patch of the bar table.

"Hey, Peyton," he murmured against her ear. Strands of her hair tickled his cheek, but as much as he would've liked to, he resisted burying his hand or his face in the silky mass of it. That wouldn't lead anywhere respectable, and he already knew she was the kind of woman who wouldn't appreciate a five-alarm PDA.

She smirked, probably guessing where he was going. "Yes?"

"How about we get out of here?" he suggested. "You want to come over?"

Peyton leaned back and shot him a dry look. "To your parents' house. Like a couple of horny teenagers?"

"I mean…it's not like they're there. They haven't been in residence for several weeks, as a matter of fact, and they aren't coming back. Ever. So can we really call it 'their' place?"

It'd been days since he'd had his lips on her. Forget about the fact that Buck was working with an extremely limited timetable— which sometimes felt like an enormous train depot clock hovering over his shoulder, tick, tick, *ticking*—it'd been days since he'd licked that soft skin. Days since he'd kissed Peyton's body, days since he'd breathed in that siren scent that seemed to emanate from every inch of her.

He was obsessed and starving and crazy, and he couldn't take it anymore.

"Peyton."

"No way," she scoffed, keeping her eyes on the eager-but-awful cover band across the room. "You are the walking wounded and I cannot stay up half the night again. I have an early class tomorrow."

"Look at me."

"Nope. That way lies temptation." Except then she scooted her chair a tiny bit closer.

Buck draped his arm around her shoulders and noted the way Peyton immediately notched herself against his side, a perfect fit. As if they'd been linked together that way for years.

"You sure?" he asked.

Peyton rested her head on his shoulder. "Positive."

Buck brushed his fingers along the bare skin of her shoulder, torturing himself with the feel of her—but maybe also torturing her a bit if the sound she made was anything to go by. He turned his head and found the rim of her ear, then ran his lips along the curve of it.

"Damn shame," he murmured, clocking the full-body shiver that ran through her.

Peyton snorted, but she didn't pull away.

Oh, yeah. This was going to be the night.

TWENTY MINUTES LATER, his parents' neighbor glared at them through her blinds while Buck struggled to unlock the front door without releasing his grip on Peyton's ass or the lock his mouth had on hers.

Her wicked tongue was going to drive him mad if he didn't get her inside soon, but damn she felt good pressed between him and that impossible fucking door.

The ride over had been an interminable hellscape of hot looks and thwarted desire, the reckless weekend drivers forcing him to ignore Peyton's hand on his thigh in favor of watching the road.

By the time Buck had pulled into the driveway of his folks' sedate colonial, he'd been tempted to pull Peyton onto his lap right there in front of Mrs. Conway *and* her neurotic Yorkie-poo.

He'd gotten Peyton up the front steps, though, but not much farther. Buck broke off the tongue tango to nip at her delectable neck and in response, she tossed her head to the side with a moan. That was when she caught sight of the morality police.

"Oh my god," she gasped, letting out a scandalized chuckle. "Who is that staring at us? Open the door! Hurry!"

"Trying," Buck muttered darkly. At last, he got the key in and the door gave way, allowing them both to stumble inside.

He slammed the door shut behind them, spun Peyton around, and licked deep into her mouth again. She tasted sweet and salty from her margarita, and she was going to be the death of him— but what a fucking way to go.

All of a sudden, the measured beeps of the house alarm flipped into full-on ear-shattering shrieking. *Not again.*

"Fuck!" Buck yelled, setting Peyton aside and lunging for the control panel. The neighbors already thought he was a jackass, just for being less than sixty years old. He could only imagine how testy they'd get if he dragged the cops here for a false alarm at o-dark-thirty.

Buck checked the time on the glowing panel. 12:30. Only half-past midnight. *Christ.* How far had he fallen, that he was worried about *this* being late?

It took a couple of tries to get the code entered properly, what with Peyton's laughing and the screaming alarm slicing through his skull, but silence descended eventually, and Buck could take a breath.

Peyton was doubled over a few feet away gasping and shaking. He went over and laid a hand on her back. "You okay?"

She shot upright and swiped the tears from her face with impatient hands. "That scared the crap out of me." She was still giggling, thankfully. "Is there *ever* a dull moment with you?"

Buck smiled, but the last few months flashed across his brain in a rapid-fire parade of death and destruction, and he had to answer honestly. "No. I'm sorry to say there is not."

Her grin faded, and her eyes dimmed. "Same, dude," she replied. "Same."

Peyton took a couple of steps back, but Buck followed, crowding her against the foyer wall. He cupped her face and gazed into her eyes for a minute, making sure she was still with him before his mouth landed on hers.

She took a deep breath, and Buck swallowed it with his kiss. There was no soft, tender lead-in this time, only desperation.

His head was swimming. He slid a hand into her hair to protect her skull from the wall and used the other to grip her luscious hip. Peyton wound her arms around his waist and worked her hands under his shirt, grazing her nails along the skin of his lower back.

Buck growled at her teasing touch and flexed his hips against hers.

"Your body," she whispered hotly, "God, your body. It's like a machine."

"I promise to wield my weapon in the name of good," he fired back.

She stood on her toes and gave him another fervent kiss, and Buck took that as permission to undo the top few buttons of her jeans and push them past her hips.

It had worked well the first time, so he pressed his thumb on her clit through the damp cotton of her panties, eliciting a sharp shudder that quaked through her with a jolt.

"Buck," Peyton breathed. "Oh my god, I need you to—" She broke off as he pushed the thin material down and pushed two fingers inside her.

"Buck!" she cried again, thrown off track by his invasion.

He shouldn't have been surprised by how slick she was—after that sexcapade of a car ride, he was halfway there himself. But the evidence of how ready Peyton felt still sent a shockwave of lust down his spine.

Buck moved his mouth from her lips to her earlobe, sinking his teeth into the soft flesh. He was having so much goddamn fun. More than he could remember having in ages. Perhaps that was why the stupid joke he'd thought of simply…slipped out of him.

"You going to rhyme, babe? Do it if you want to."

He kept up a slow and deep rhythm with his fingers, sucking on her earlobe in time with his hand. Peyton was already gasping for breath, but some small corner of her brain was still functioning, trying to unravel what he'd meant.

"Rhyme? I don't…what do you…?"

A laugh rumbled through him at her confusion. Buck murmured, "You can do it, beautiful. Sound it out. *Buuuuuck.* Rhymes with—?"

All at once, Peyton grasped his meaning. The breath she'd begun holding as she'd inched closer to orgasm burst out of her in a big, crazy-sounding guffaw. "Oh my god! You're nuts, you know that? How many times have you inflicted that line on some poor woman?"

Buck withdrew his fingers and stuck them in his mouth, sucking the taste of her off his skin. Then he gave her a feral grin, grabbed her around the waist, and tossed her over his shoulder.

Peyton shrieked, struggling to pull up her pants while he carried her off.

He was sorely tempted to take the stairs two at a time but didn't want to tempt fate into a repeat performance. So Buck went carefully, step-by-step, only picking up the pace once he hit the upstairs landing. In his room, he dumped Peyton in the center of his mattress.

Buck followed her a second later, dwarfing her with his larger, heavier frame.

"I am saddened to report that was the first time I've ever used that joke," he laughed. "Though given the reception, I have to think it won't be the last."

"I mean, all this time it's just been sitting there. Unused and unappreciated," she said. "An oversight of that magnitude makes me doubt your critical thinking abilities. You missed the word *suck* entirely."

Her eyes were sparkling, a warm amber as they searched his. "And yet, it truly only came to me now," Buck said, leaning in to drop kiss after kiss on her collarbones. "You clearly inspire me."

He reached down and wrapped Peyton's legs around his hips. With that accomplished, Buck yanked on her t-shirt, attempting to get it off without having to release her.

She watched him as he worked the problem and her mood shifted into something a little more somber. "I've missed you," she admitted, then ducked her head like she hadn't meant to divulge that.

Buck understood. Given the uncertain nature of their relationship, they were supposed to keep their wits about them and not get carried away. Despite all the time they'd spent together this week, they hardly knew each other.

Right?

But it didn't feel like they hardly knew each other. It felt like they'd known each other forever.

"You, too," Buck told her. "And I am so, so, *so*—" He punctuated each word with wet, open-mouthed kisses on her sternum, her ribs, her belly. "—happy that you are here now."

He gave up on removing Peyton's shirt, compensating by shoving his hands under her back so he could undo the clasp of her bra. Peyton had her own agenda, though, somehow managing to get her hand down his shorts so she could cup his junk.

"*Really* happy," he added.

Inside his pocket, his cell started vibrating, making them both jump. Buck gritted his teeth, knowing, *knowing*, who it probably was.

Fuck Bennett. Hell, fuck all of them. Buck had already put his riskiest gamble into play, in whatever shadowy game they were all embroiled in. What more was he supposed to do at midnight on a Friday?

Feeling five kinds of frustrated, he shoved off his shorts and tossed them across the room without checking his phone.

"You don't need to get that?" Peyton wondered.

"Absolutely not."

"Good," she smiled, then wriggled out from under him. A second later, she whipped off her shirt and bra and threw them in the direction of Buck's shorts.

He didn't waste time feeling guilty about ignoring his teammates. They would've done the same in his position, and besides—he deserved this.

Anyone would agree that Buck was sticking his neck out the farthest by contacting Black Watch on the down-low as he had.

And if he got caught, spending a couple of lost weekends with a beautiful professor was going to be the least of his problems.

PEYTON WAS SNUGGLED under the covers and dozing when Buck went downstairs to batten down the hatches for the night. He took a lap around the kitchen and family room, making sure the windows and door were still locked. He turned off the nightlight over the stove and lined up Peyton's shoes near the front door.

It wasn't until he glanced out the big plate glass window in the dining room, that Buck spotted the car parked across the street.

He hadn't noticed that make and model before, though Buck liked to think he'd gotten a bead on the usual comings and goings of the neighbors in the weeks he'd been here.

A man was sitting behind the wheel—not on his phone, not doing much of anything, really. He lit a cigarette and blew the smoke out the open window as if he planned to be there for a while.

Waiting, but for what? He didn't strike Buck as Navy, or any breed of reporter. He was simply…out of place. Buck ran through other options in his head—drugs, sex, theft, police. All of them felt off for one reason or another.

He watched him for a while, but nothing changed in the man's demeanor or position. Eventually, Buck decided to leave it alone—there was no way the dude was getting in here with Hades' own alarm system guarding the place, anyway.

Besides, Buck had a warm woman in his bed to get back to. The fuckery of the outside world could just wait till morning.

WHEN HE LEFT the next morning to drive Peyton home, Buck looked for the car again. It was gone. He couldn't go sniffing around for it without Peyton asking questions, though, so Buck took her through the coffee shop drive-through and headed back to her place.

Once they'd said goodbye and made plans to meet up later, he got back into his dad's car and checked his phone.

One missed call from an unknown number. *Black Watch, no doubt.*

Buck scrolled through his contacts to find the secure number he'd been given and hit send. Tate Monroe answered on the third ring.

"Hey, brother. Just tried to call you."

"Yeah, sorry. I was dropping off a…" Buck hesitated. Monroe didn't need to know anything about Peyton. "…a friend."

"Roger that. I only have a couple things to tell you, and then I need to move boots. I've got a plane to catch."

"Okay. What's up?"

"Listen…Doggett's going to be making the rounds of the morning talk shows in a few days. Technically, it's more promo crap for his campaign, but we've been hearing some chatter that he might be planning to reveal letters that appear to threaten his life. We think he's hoping to tie it back to you guys, bring some public pressure to bear in an effort to wrap up the inquiry sooner rather than later."

"Save a guy's life, man, and the gratitude keeps on coming," Buck grumbled.

"I don't think it's going to go anywhere. My sources tell me that he's already tried to submit the letters to the Congressional committee, but they weren't able to authenticate them."

"Probably because they're fake as shit."

"Yeah. I'm still going to advise you to return to Little Creek as soon as possible. It'll be better if you and the other guys are all together for now."

Buck was grim as the echo of Bennett's words hit his ears. He'd thought he could wring out another week here with Peyton. Now he'd have to say goodbye sooner than he'd planned— possibly even when he saw her tonight.

There was another issue to worry about, however. He asked Monroe, "What about our meeting?"

"I need to push that off for a bit. I'll check in with you once I get back from my trip, and we'll hash out what comes next."

"Got it."

He heard some muffled back and forth on Tate's end, and then the guy came back on the line to say, "One last thing I've been meaning to ask you, and then I've gotta go."

"Shoot."

"Did you happen to save a copy of the original *Global Lens* article anywhere? The links on the blog are dead now. I think whoever runs it took down the post."

"No, I didn't," he admitted. "I only read it once, back when Joely's film came out. I'm afraid I was too furious to digest much."

"Understandable, and no worries. I've got a guy working on it. You head back to base and keep your head down. Once Doggett starts dragging his oily smile around the talk shows, the heat on you boys might get plenty uncomfortable."

"I hear you. Just…let us know what we can do."

"Text the number I gave you if anything strange happens, and don't do anything to make this more complicated if you can help it." Then the man hung up.

Buck glanced at Peyton's house and wondered what the fuck he'd been thinking. What was he doing, screwing around with her like this? She deserved someone nice and uncomplicated in her life, not whatever he was.

Except, it *wasn't* screwing around, was it? If Buck was lowkey courting her, what kind of asshole did that make him? To be contemplating yoking a wife—and maybe even kids, someday— to this mess was the height of arrogance.

He slammed his fist against the steering wheel in frustration, then stabbed at the ignition button with a curse. If he ever found the shitstain blogger who'd helped Joely ruin his life, Buck was going to lights-out that mofo faster than he could blink.

He drove back to his folks' place, fuming the entire way. He hadn't even mentioned his mysterious backyard visitor to Monroe or told the man those photos could find their way into the media at any moment. The ways they could be spun into something sordid felt endless.

Buck pulled into his parents' driveway and nosed into the garage, then stalked across the street to study the ground where that car had been parked last night. As he'd hoped, the cigarette butt was still there, with the brand name printed clear as day on the white label.

The sight of the Arabic letters made the hairs on the back of Buck's neck stand up. The last time he'd seen that logo was at a market in Kabul. They were cheap and plentiful there, but impossible to find here in the U.S.

In all the possibilities he'd considered as he'd watched the man lingering, it had never once occurred to Buck that Kadir's cronies would have the resources or wherewithal to find him here. There was no one else it could be.

Fortunately, his parents were safe at their new condo on the Eastern Shore, and Buck could hold his own if it came down to that—but Peyton had been here three or four times in the last two weeks, and she was a vulnerable innocent in all this. He hated that they potentially had a photo of her with every bone in his body.

The thought sat in the front of his mind all day, too. While Buck bagged the evidence and sent photos and an explanation to the Black Watch number. While he got a receipt from the donation truck driver and sold his parents' patio set to a neighbor two streets over.

Buck thought about it some more when he was getting ready to see Peyton that night, as well. Maybe having to say goodbye was for the best, even if it felt like hell.

Chapter Twelve

Peyton

S INCE SHE WASN'T teaching that day, Peyton hadn't intended to stop by campus—but after Buck dropped her off, she found a terse message from her department head at the top of her email inbox, requesting her presence.

An hour later, she was sitting across from the man, heart in her throat. "I told you about my blog when I interviewed with you," Peyton explained, for what felt like the hundredth time. "And as you requested, I've been careful to keep it anonymous. I have my personal information encrypted and everything."

"Not just a request," Mr. Donnelly pointed out, "The secrecy was a condition of your employment. You signed a binding contract to that effect."

Peyton tried to stay calm. "I understand. And I am still not clear on what the problem is. Yes, the blog itself has been in the news—without my permission, I might add. But my identity has not been linked to the story in any way, nor do I expect it to be." She kept her expression neutral, despite the overreach. *Expect* and *hope* were such different things, after all.

Donnelly's expression was dour, and it said everything about how this was going to go. There would be no negotiation here. Peyton's fate had been decided before she'd ever walked into this office.

"Even so," told her blandly, "given the situation, we've decided not to renew your contract at the end of the semester. You've done a fine job teaching here, but MCC simply cannot afford any more notoriety."

"I'm very sorry to hear that," Peyton said, a gray numbness settling over her.

"We could possibly work something out if you were willing to shut the whole thing down," Donnelly pointed out. "Shutter it, delete it, wipe the records. Then our potential exposure would…"

"No," Peyton said flatly. "I won't do that. Not in this lifetime or the next."

"I see. Well…that settles that, I suppose."

She'd worked so hard to find a position in her field, and now it was being snatched away from her. Up in smoke. Whoever Joely Spitz was, Peyton hoped she stepped barefoot in cat vomit every day for the rest of her stupid life.

Donnelly regarded her with his usual pinched disapproval. She doubted he even knew what a blog was, much less how innocuous most of them were. "Before you go, I have a scheduling change for you," he said. "Mike Harper is down with the flu, so I'll need you to pick up a few of his lectures while he's out."

His casual attitude snapped Peyton out of her fog, a bloom of rage overtaking her despair. The man had just told her she was out of a job for something that might not ever come to pass, and now he wanted to give her extra work before she left?

"I wish I could help," she gritted out, "but I'm unavailable. I'll be using up my accrued vacation and sick days between now and winter break."

"Excuse me?" Donnelly gaped, all semblance of disinterest gone.

Peyton stood up and smoothed down her sweater. Somehow, she managed a civil smile. "Call it a sabbatical. I'll clean out my office on my way out," she said, then stepped to the door. "Just to simplify the process."

"This…this is unnecessary," Donnelly squawked. "You're not thinking clearly."

"That's where you're wrong," she told him, and walked out before she could second guess herself.

PEYTON'S BAD DAY turned even worse that evening. She and Buck had gotten Indian takeout to bring back to her house, but now that they were done eating, Buck was sitting on her couch, looking earnest and explaining that he'd been called back to the base at Little Creek earlier than expected.

"Oh." Peyton's dessert of *gulab jamun* turned to rocks in her stomach. "Oh, that sucks."

"Yes," he agreed, "but I'd love to keep this going if we can. Things have been going so well between us—I don't want to give up before we even get off the ground."

"I…yeah. I think so, too."

Buck searched her face. "So, can we try doing the long-distance thing for a bit? See how that goes?"

Peyton smiled, but she wondered whether he really meant what he said. "I would like that."

He leaned forward and took her hand, kissing her knuckles in an oddly old-fashioned display of affection. "Great. That's great. Just…my schedule might be unpredictable for the next little while. I promise I'll drive back up and see you whenever I can, though."

"As long as you're in Virginia Beach, you mean."

Buck's expression fell a little. "Yeah. After that, we'll have to fly to see each other. But we can text and video call in between visits. It'll be harder, but lots of military couples find a way to make it work."

She thought about that, trying to envision a long-distance relationship with him based on the few short weeks they'd already had together. Surprisingly, it didn't feel as preposterous as she expected. If they both put in the effort, it could work.

On impulse, Peyton told Buck, "Wait here." She ran to the kitchen, scrabbled through her junk drawer, then came back with a key. "Here. Take this with you when you go back to base."

"What is it?"

"It's the spare key. If you get a day off or whatever, don't waste time calling ahead. Just come. Okay? Just…come."

Buck looked so serious, but he nodded, nonetheless. He murmured, "You got it, sweetheart," and sealed it with a kiss.

PEYTON FOUND HERSELF at her desk upstairs a few weeks later, staring at her computer and trying to decide whether to delete her entire blog or just archive more entries.

She'd been at loose ends ever since she'd walked out on the meeting with Donnelly. She hadn't seen Buck once, aside from their standing video call every night, so Peyton had tried to fill her days with mindless chores and half-hearted attempts to exercise and cook for herself—but most of the time she just…drifted.

It was pointless to job hunt before her contract at MCC ran out, and that wouldn't happen for weeks yet. And so, with nothing else to do, Peyton dove into her research on special operators again.

She'd already read everything she could get her hands on for each branch of the military—about the operators' histories and functions, successes and failures—but now it was personal in a way it hadn't been before. With Buck at the forefront of her thoughts, Peyton began to wonder if she'd done the right thing, criticizing the operators the way she had.

Had she truly understood what they did for their countries? Did she have the right to find fault, if she'd never walked in their shoes?

Until Buck, she'd never met a SEAL in person. She'd know only their reputations, how they were called upon to neutralize some of the stickiest conflicts on earth, and were incredibly good at it. *Buck*, she had no doubt, was incredibly good at it. He regularly and willingly risked his life to protect people he didn't even know.

Did Peyton really want to preserve theories derived from secondhand evidence and declassified snippets of information? She recognized now that, given the nature of special ops work, the data she could access only told part of the story.

She'd learned more than most how half a tale could be twisted.

Besides, how could she defend herself to Buck, when the time came to admit who she was?

That time would come, she knew. Even dating long-distance couldn't dent how well they got along. Their relationship already had the potential to be a lasting one.

So why should Peyton keep *Global Lens* live anymore?

Her brother had set it up for her, teaching Peyton the basics of posting and answering comments and adding layers of security and privacy when she'd requested it—but she had no idea if Josh had done enough. After all, neither of them could've predicted how necessary it would become to hide her identity.

Global Lens felt like a time bomb, a catastrophe waiting to explode in the middle of her life. Peyton was no computer genius, however. If she tried to shut things down herself and did it the wrong way—missed some step or failed to delete something crucial—maybe it would make things worse, instead of better.

She had no idea what to do.

As she sat agonizing over it, she heard the unmistakable sound of her front door opening and heavy footfalls in the foyer. Peyton snapped her laptop closed and crept to the doorway of her office, peering into the hallway outside.

Downstairs, Buck called out, "Peyton? Babe, you here?"

She stumbled into the hall and rushed to the banister. "Buck?"

His steps came closer. "Hey, sweetheart. Where are you?"

"I'm up here!" Peyton tried to find Buck's face through the stair rails, but he was only visible from the waist down. But he was in uniform, from the looks of it, something she'd only seen in pictures so far.

She grinned in excitement, wheeling around the newel post and hitting the top step right as Buck stepped on the bottom one.

"Oh my god! It's really you!"

"Sure is," he assured her, face lighting up in pleasure. "As promised."

Peyton started down the stairs, but he immediately leveled a finger at her. "Oh, no you don't. Stay right there," he commanded.

She froze as Buck charged up the stairs. He had a smattering of small abrasions across the left side of his forehead and his cheek.

"What happened to you?" she cried, as he reached her and cupped her face in his hands. "Are you okay?"

"It's nothing," Buck murmured, leaning in. "Training exercise. I'll tell you about it later. God, I missed you." With that, he pressed a kiss to her lips that left her reeling.

"I missed you, too," she whispered.

Buck wrapped his arms around her and kissed her again, deeper this time, intense and hungry. Then he crushed Peyton against him and lifted her, urging her legs around his waist as he carried her up the last few steps to the landing.

"I need to see you. It's been so long."

"I just want you," Peyton admitted breathlessly.

Video calls, even when they turned smexy, could only accomplish so much, after all. She pressed kisses to Buck's neck while he frowned over her shoulder, searching around them.

"We need a wall," he growled. "I am going to fuck you up against the nearest wall if it's the last thing I do."

Peyton moaned against his neck, wholeheartedly approving of that plan.

Buck muttered, turning one way, then another. "I cannot find a fucking wall, woman. Why are there no goddamn walls up here?"

Peyton raised her head and looked around, realizing for the first time that there were more doorways around them than anything else. There were linen closets. A hall bathroom. Two bedrooms and her office, too.

What the hell was going on? The small slivers of wall between all the doors were carefully decorated with framed photos from Josh's travels, leaving nowhere for Buck to safely prop her.

Peyton giggled, stunned by the improbable inconvenience of it. "There're so many doors. Why are there so many doors?"

"You need a new house," he complained, dipping his head to kiss her again. With a huff of irritation, Buck steadied her against him and marched for her bedroom.

"I suspect we'll make do," she answered.

He'd said he would visit, and here he was—straight from somewhere more important, by the looks of it. Peyton's hopes for them quadrupled in her chest.

"I can't believe you came back," she confessed.

Holding her tightly against his chest, Buck levered them through her doorway and only stopped when his legs bumped the side of the mattress.

"Of course, I did," he told her. "I told you I would. I'll always come back to you."

Then he dumped her on the bed and dove on her.

THE REAL REASON for Buck's visit became clear later. His team had finished whatever business they'd had at Little Creek and were preparing to return to their regular station in Coronado, California. He'd come to warn her in person.

"When?" Peyton demanded, trying to control the tremble in her voice.

Buck paled, but his voice was steady and reassuring. "Two weeks. Three at most. I'll spend every second I can with you until then."

"And after?"

"It's going to get harder, obviously. But we talked about this—we can still text and video chat like we've been doing. I'll try to fly through D.C. or Baltimore whenever possible and you can come to see me." He hesitated, then tacked on, "If you wanted. Or—"

Peyton interrupted whatever sad thing he'd been about to say. "Buck, listen. This may sound nuts, but I've been thinking about it a lot. I have an idea to run by you."

He looked so worried, and she couldn't decide whether that worked in her favor, or against it. "Okay," he murmured hesitantly.

She bit her lip, wondering if she was taking things too far. "I'm…I'm not sure what you're going to say."

Buck huffed out a nervous laugh, and when she didn't answer right away, prodded, "Only one way to find out, babe. Lay it on me."

"Okay, so…I know we haven't been an item for very long," Peyton began, easing into it. "But what if—" She broke off to demand, "What?" when Buck grinned.

"Is that what we're calling us? An item?"

"I do not think this is the time to be nitpicky about terminology." Especially because she wasn't sure she had the nerve to broach this topic at all, and the longer it took to get out, the less likely it became that she would.

"Sorry. Sorry, keep going," Buck chuckled.

He'd gone from grim to irritatingly cheerful in about two-point-five seconds. Peyton wanted to smack him.

"*Anyway*, I was thinking that with the semester ending soon, there's not a ton keeping me in Maryland at the moment."

"You're not teaching spring semester?"

"Uh, no."

"What about next fall?"

Peyton swallowed, not liking Buck's suddenly intense stare. "Also, no."

"Why not?"

She'd expected that question and had prepared for it. As she delivered the line she'd rehearsed over and over, Peyton felt pretty good about how casual it sounded. "Nothing dramatic. I've been wanting a change for a while now, and this seemed as good a time as any to make it happen," she shrugged. "So I resigned."

Buck sat up against the pillows, still as a statue and gazing at her blankly. "Sweetheart…what are you saying?"

Peyton took a deep breath and spit it out fast, before she could lose her nerve. "Okay, I don't want you to think I'm some clingy weirdo, but I have family in the L.A. area that I haven't seen in a while. Cousins."

He squinted at her. "And you're…going to visit them?"

"What if I did more than visit? They won't care if I crash with them while I look for my own place. We're close like that."

"Are you…" Buck shook his head like he was trying to clear it, sending a lock of silver hair onto his scraped-up forehead. "I'm sorry—are you saying that you want to move to California? To be with me?"

"Well, it wouldn't, uh…it wouldn't have to be *with* you, per se," Peyton stammered, thrown off by his concise summary. "I'll get my own place and everything, so there's no pressure to level up before we're ready. And like I said, I have relatives nearby, as a safety net if things don't work out. But this way, we'll have more time to see where we're—"

Buck's voice went from cheery to flat in an instant. "Your own place."

"*Ugh*, is it too soon?" Peyton choked down the lump that suddenly seemed to be clogging her airways. "I've been toying with the idea for a few days, but I wasn't sure if you—"

Buck rolled over suddenly, pushing the pillows out of the way and pinning her beneath him. "Stop right there. Did you or did you not just offer to move out to Cali so we can keep dating?"

"Well—"

"Yes or no, Peyton?"

"Yes, that's basically what I—"

The bastard cut her off again, this time by thrusting his devilish tongue in her mouth for a wanton kiss. Just when she began to relax into it, he ripped his mouth away again. Peyton felt like she was spinning, so off-balance she was happy they were having the conversation horizontally.

"If I agree," Buck began, then stopped and redirected. "Wait. Are you sure about this? Have you really thought it through, or is this some kind of reckless impulse because you're afraid we can't last long-distance?"

At least Peyton had a ready answer for that. "Buck, I've thought about nothing *but* this for days. I know we can handle being apart, I just don't *want* to. More than necessary, anyway."

He studied her face and evidently saw whatever he was looking for. "All right. Here's the deal. If this is going to happen, I'm going to need you to make me a promise. A vow, really. Two vows. Maybe three."

Peyton whispered, "What?"

"One, if you move out there, we're not going to disguise it as some trip to visit your cousins. And two, unless you're dead set on it, I don't want you to get your own place." Buck paused, checking to see if she understood.

She nodded.

"I want us to be all in, Peyton. I want to go into this with the expectation that it will be for the long haul. Can you promise that so soon? Because that's how I feel—about you and about us. I know that what I do will take me away from home more than we'd like, and there's always the chance that a mission will go ass-up before I can retire…but you understand that, right? You have to know I'll be one thousand percent yours for as long as I'm living, despite the obstacles."

Peyton gaped at him. "Holy…wow."

"Full disclosure," Buck added, "I share an apartment with two other guys on my team. But I have my own room, and they're good dudes. They won't care if you move in with us until you and I can find our own place."

Peyton could feel her mouth moving, trying to form a reply to this madness that would make some kind of sense. Buck kept babbling, making plans as his hips pressed against hers in emphasis.

Had he really just…

He stopped talking. He placed a couple of careful kisses on her face and sized Peyton up. "Shit. You were already nervous. Did I just blow it by taking this farther than you wanted?"

Peyton tried like hell to catch up to how fast this situation had spun away from her. "How…what?"

"By upping the ante too soon. I know it wasn't very romantic, but I can do better. Let me start over."

She blinked. "No. Stop. You did fine."

"Then what do you think?"

"You said I had to promise you three things. To go all in, do this right and move in with you—that's two. What's the third?"

"Nothing scary. I'll tell you that one later, okay?"

Peyton knew it was madness to take such a huge step after knowing Buck for such a short time. She was half in love with him already, though, and he had a gift for making her feel cherished and safe.

He could keep her safe, as well, and she happened to need that quality in a man these days.

California would be good for her, she thought. There were plenty of places she could work, and no strange men with cameras to lurk around wherever she was.

It could be a fresh start for her—a hard stop between the events of the last year and a new life with Buck. And before

Peyton moved, she could call Josh and ask him how to bury *Global Lens* for good.

Chapter Thirteen

Buck

B UCK HAD BEEN able to steal a paltry thirty-six hours with
Peyton, but all too soon he was on the road back to Little
Creek—psyched about her moving to San Diego, but also feeling
like he was driving a tractor instead of the junker he'd borrowed
from a guy in the barracks.

He wished he was handling his dad's cherry-red muscle car
instead, though I-64 was so congested along this stretch that he
wouldn't have been able to light up all that horsepower anyway.
The sound system would've been better, at least.

He put on his blinker and checked his rearview, wanting to get
over in plenty of time to hit the Norfolk beltway without any
hiccups.

Buck frowned and glanced at the mirror again.

Fuck. The gray sedan was still back there, three vehicles behind
and one lane over. He'd picked it up within minutes of leaving
Peyton's and it'd stuck with him for the whole two hours. The
chances of someone from Peyton's neighborhood having the
same destination as him seemed slim, though.

Off and on, he'd considered taking evasive action, but it hardly
felt worth it. They could only follow him so far. Once he got to
base, they'd be shit out of luck, and he'd be surrounded by a fuck-
ton of armed backup.

Unless the person had a military ID, too, in which case yeah, they could follow him past the gates—and Buck could lure them someplace private to relieve them of that ID and figure out what they wanted.

The car tagged along, pacing him steadily. He watched for details he could use as he got off the main highway and skirted Norfolk. Hair color? Too dark to see. Same with gender or whether the tail was smoking cigarettes.

They'd obscured any make or model insignia and covered their plate with a blurry plastic cover. Buck's heart rate kicked up the closer he got to Little Creek, as he tried to figure out the end game.

Were they only a babysitter, making sure he ended up where he was supposed to? Or did they want to be certain Buck was present when they unleashed hell?

At the gate, he handed over his ID and was waved through with a terse, "Enjoy your night, Lieutenant."

Buck proceeded up the block, then pulled his borrowed ride behind the building up ahead, palming his sidearm and peeking around the corner to watch for the sedan. Eventually, it slid to a stop at the gate and was approached by the duty guard.

Lots of conversation, a smooth gesture by the guard, and a couple of stone-faced MPs strolled over with weapons at the ready.

The car threw it into reverse immediately, squealing its tires and going up on the sidewalk when it turned around and streaked away. The guard trotted back to his station and grabbed the phone, calling in the incident to his duty officer.

Buck suspected they wouldn't see that sedan again, though.

The whole exercise felt like a message, and a test—a pointed *we're here* followed by a soft attempt to see how far they could get and what the response would be. Whatever they'd been trying to learn, they already had what they were after.

He got back in the car and returned to the barracks, finding Bennett and the others sitting around playing poker with a college football game muted on the tv.

Wyatt's head snapped up the second Buck crossed the threshold, looking just as haunted as he had when they'd landed stateside six months ago. He'd said he was getting help now, so at least he wasn't getting worse—but the sooner they could get the man home to Cali, the better.

Joe set down his cards. "Daddy's home," he muttered, "Thank fuck."

Bennett took one look at Buck's face and popped out of his chair, ready. "What happened?"

Buck dropped his ruck and kicked the door shut with a heavy sigh. He'd hoped to have a few more minutes to decide on what to tell them, but Ben was spooky like that. He could tell what people were feeling—sometimes even what they were thinking—with eerie accuracy.

He'd interrogated him about it on more than a few occasions, wondering if the guy was a legit mind reader of some kind, but all Ben had ever said was, *"No ESP, man, just junkies for parents."*

Buck hadn't understood what that meant until he'd looked it up a year or two ago. Sure enough, there were dozens of books explaining why kids of addicts were geniuses at reading minute clues in body language and tone—peak survival-instinct shit that would be impressive if it weren't so fucking depressing.

It didn't change how Buck factored in Ben's skill when they were on an op, in any case. This wasn't an op, though, and it appeared Buck had grown way too fucking complacent while they'd been benched.

"I had a tango on my six the entire drive down here. Didn't bother trying to lose him. Bowser's car has the get-up-and-go of a dump truck and I figured whoever it was would get stopped at the gate, anyway."

Joe scowled. "Were they?"

"Yeah. Took off like their ass was on fire." Buck went over to the beat-up couch and dropped onto it, gripping the back of his neck and staring off into space.

What was he missing? What was he missing...

"You didn't care that they saw where you were going?" Wyatt asked.

"Why should I? If they know me enough to follow me, then they probably know why I'm here."

Unfortunately, that also meant they knew he wasn't with Peyton. The thought was sticking in his brain like a goddamn thorn, but he hadn't figured out what to do about it yet.

Soon, they'd all be out of here, Peyton included. Buck only had to make it a few more weeks before he'd have home-field advantage.

Bennett hadn't moved from his post and still looked like he was ready to throw down. "There's something else," he announced.

"God, isn't that the truth," Buck groaned. "First things first, though. I gotta make a quick call. Hang tight for a few and then I'll get you up to speed."

With that, he pushed to his feet and went into the room he'd been sharing with Ben, then pulled out his phone. He fired off a quick text to Peyton, letting her know he'd arrived in one piece and that he'd call her later.

Then he sent a message to the Black Watch line, requesting a callback. His phone dinged a minute later.

"Gaines," he answered.

"Whatcha got?" Tate asked immediately.

"Apparently a new fan. Picked up a tail almost as soon as I got on the road back to Little Creek. They stuck with me the whole way, then burned rubber once they were turned away at the gate."

"Did you get a plate number?"

"No, they had one of those smoked-out covers. It was too dark to make out the driver, either. But it was a pretty basic gray four-door. I'm going to look at some makes tonight to see if anything looks right."

"Alright, let me know. I'll see if we can pick you up on any video feeds."

"Copy that. Listen, uh…" Buck hesitated, but he had to at least ask—it was physically impossible for him to take care of it himself, at least for the time being. "There's this person up in Maryland. She was with me the night of the stakeout or whatever it was, and now that I'm down here…"

Tate seemed to pick up the subtext instantly. "We got you. Send us her info and we'll look after her."

Buck swallowed, grateful and nervous at once. "Thanks. I appreciate that. But, uh…you can't let her know, okay? She's…she knows what I do in a general sense, but she has no idea about all the rest. The inquiries and shit."

"Say no more," Monroe told him, and Buck recalled a story he'd heard about how the man had married a woman he'd been working for. Maybe Tate got where he was coming from.

"Great. By the way, did you get what I sent you? They're not exactly selling those at 7-Eleven, you know what I mean?"

"I do. We're running DNA now. Maybe we'll get lucky and get a hit."

"If luck is what we're hoping for, I seem to be shit out of it lately."

"Don't sweat it," Monroe told him. "There's a lot of loose threads right now, but we'll tie them all up eventually."

"We have to," Buck answered. "This Kadir guy—he's no joke. If he's fucking with people here in the U.S., we have bigger issues than saving my job or sticking it to a mouthy senator."

Tate went quiet for a minute, then cleared his throat. "All right, look. I have to be frank with you. I've got beef with this fucker, too. I want him neutralized as badly as anyone. You know that. But Black Watch is still getting up to speed with staffing and infrastructure. If al Kadir has expanded such that he has the funding and connections to get his men into the U.S. and hit at a squad of SEALs, then you need to know that I might have to call in bigger fish to help take that fucker out. No way am I going to miss a shot at him again."

"No outsiders," Buck said immediately. "That was the deal. There's no way we can be sure who's clean and who isn't. Whatever we need is going to have to be accomplished by who you have on board now, and me and my guys."

"And you're 100% sure they're solid?"

"Are you fucking kidding me?"

"Gotta ask, dude."

"Yeah, they're all good. And they're all in. So you have the four of us, plus your people. If we need more, I'll reach out to some other people we know in the platoon."

"Roger that. Any official word on how much longer you have to cool your heels there?"

"They're shipping us home next week, so we can sit on our asses and wait for the results of the inquiry and the Board away from D.C. Supposedly, we'll be put back into the rotation after that, but I'm not holding my breath. Doggett's been laying it on thick with the talk show ladies."

"That's the truth," Monroe snorted. "I'd say there wasn't a snowball's chance in hell of him snagging the nomination, but the race seems more like a vaudeville show than an election at this point. The last few jokers they've come up with haven't been much better than old Roy."

"True that. Anyway…I should go bring the guys up to speed. You still want to meet up soon?"

"Yeah, I do. I'm heading out to Wyoming in a few weeks to interview some jarheads working security at one of the resorts out there. Why don't we plan to put our heads together then. I'll set you up with transport so you won't be out of pocket for more than a day or two. Think you can make that work?"

"Dude, making shit work is what I do."

BACK IN THE main room, the guys had largely abandoned their poker game in favor of muttering quietly to each other.

When Buck pulled out a chair and joined them, Wyatt asked, "How did it go?"

"The usual. They're looking into it, and they'll let me know."

"You sure they're the right guys for this?" Joe wondered.

"Yeah. But I'll still feel better once I can meet them face-to-face."

"When's that happening?" Bennett asked.

"Sounds like in a few weeks. I'll have to dip out for a couple of days, but given that we have nothing better to do, it should work."

"We'll be back in Cali by then," Joe pointed out. "Do they know that?"

"Yes. It's not a big deal. But listen, uh…I've got something else I need to ask you guys."

Joe clenched his fists on the table. "We're in. All of us."

"Not that. I know that. Jesus, I already said as much to…to them."

"Then what?"

Buck couldn't believe he was about to do this. "When I was up at my folks' place, I…" He stopped there. How to put the best possible spin on what we wanted?

Wyatt waved his hands in the universal gesture for *out with it*.

"I met someone. Okay? We hit off. A lot. And now…she's going to move out west so we can see where it goes."

Bennett commented neutrally, "This strikes me as a very accelerated timeline."

"Right. I know, but it's hard to explain."

"Okay, so what's the question?" Joe asked, his Boston accent lending characteristic abruptness to his words.

"She has nowhere to live," Wyatt answered.

"Been there, done that," Ben muttered, "Would not recommend."

"Could you…could you just shut up for a minute?" Buck asked, trying to keep them on track. "I told her she could crash with us for a little while. Just until she and I can find our own place."

"What!" Wyatt blurted out. "Why?"

Joe put a hand in the man's face and leaned in to catch Buck's eye. "I'll take over your room. I hate the fuckers I'm shacked up with."

"Slow down," Ben drawled. "We don't know anything about this chick. How do we know she's not a mole? Or a sociopath?"

Joe cocked his head, already problem-solving. "Is she going to help with the rent?"

"What do you care?" Wyatt cried. "You don't even live there!"

"Yet."

"You guys really gonna do me like this?" Buck complained. "You *actually* believe that I would hook up with some random woman, ask her to move in with me, and she's gonna be a witch. Really?"

"There…is a slight precedent in this area," Wyatt said.

"*Really?* Really, asshole? Fuck you."

"I'm just saying."

"Say it again—"

"*Stop.* God, you're a bunch of fucking children," Bennett griped. "I'm sure Buck has done his homework and that his new friend is who she says she is, and won't turn on him once she moves in."

Buck blinked. He hadn't. But he would.

Ben glared at him as if those thoughts had been spoken loud and clear. Buck glared back, daring him to say it out loud.

Bennett smiled thinly and continued, his point made. "Therefore, I am sure we can be grownups about her crashing in his room for a few weeks while they look for their own apartment…or come to their senses and realize they are reckless idiots jumping into a serious relationship without getting to know each other properly beforehand. Whichever comes first."

"Thanks for the support," Buck said drily.

"I have a pertinent question," Wyatt announced. "How hot is this woman?"

"Who the fuck cares?" Buck growled. "She's not available."

Joe shrugged. "I don't know. Maybe he has a point. What if—"

"You. Don't. Live. There!" Bennett yelled.

The guys next door pounded on the wall and cursed them out.

Buck squeezed his eyes shut and pressed his fingers to his lids. "Just…yes or no? If it's no, I need to figure something else out before she shows up on our doorstep, and I have a fuck ton else to do these days, in case none of you noticed."

Bennett sat back lazily. "Fine by me," he said.

"Aye," Joe chimed in with a shady smirk, no doubt redecorating Buck's room already.

Wyatt gaped at them. "No one else thinks this is nuts? None of you?"

"Who cares?" Ben said. "We have her outnumbered. And if she's as bitchy as your last piece of ass, Buck will kick her to the curb long before we have to. Sexy Spitzy notwithstanding, he doesn't exactly gravitate to divas."

Buck sighed. "I promise Peyton is not a bitch. Far from it. She's not going to leave dishes in the sink. She's not going to be loud. And she's not going to stay forever. With you all, anyway."

Three faces turned toward him silently, staring Buck down. No one said a word.

"What?"

"Holy…*shit*," Wyatt breathed.

"*What?*" Buck demanded.

They cut eyes at each other, then turned back to him. For the life of him, Buck couldn't figure out what he'd said to shut them down so effectively. He wished he knew, though, because he'd undoubtedly need to use it again someday.

Bennett readjusted in his chair, dropping his chin on his fist and attempting to keep a straight face. Eventually, he said,

"Peyton, huh?" and eyed Buck like he was the most amusing jackass at the zoo. "Tell us more."

Buck groaned. "Give me a beer. This might take a while."

WHEN HE WAS laying on his bunk later, striving for sleep that wouldn't come, Buck thought again about Peyton, and how much he already cared about her. He trusted her. He trusted his teammates, too, though—and he'd known them a hell of a lot longer.

As much as their doubts about Peyton had rubbed him the wrong way, he had to admit they weren't wrong. He didn't know everything there was to know about her. They simply hadn't had time.

Ben and the others deserved to be reassured with more than vague feelings and hunches. And so, even though it felt paranoid and disloyal, Buck decided to reach out to Monroe again in the morning. If the man was happy to keep tabs on Peyton for safety purposes, he probably wouldn't mind confirming that Buck wasn't wrong about her.

The work of an afternoon, in all likelihood.

Definitely not as difficult as figuring out what Doggett's game was, or who was helping him in Buck's chain of command. No way could a senator, even one as brash as Old Roy, pull all the strings he had without inside help.

As Buck saw it, the Navy had had no reason whatsoever to tarnish their reputations or drive them from the fold. Buck and the others were model SEALs—boy scouts to a man. Not one of them had a single violation or black mark on their records.

The only reason any of them could come up with for their current predicament was that Doggett—and maybe Joely—had done something they were willing to go to great lengths to hide. Something that Buck, Bennett, Wyatt, and Joe were in danger of revealing.

If it was important enough to destroy four exemplary military records, one would think it would be easy enough to pinpoint, however.

It wasn't. They'd gone over the mission a thousand times together, stepping through it from minute to minute, angle by angle, and still, none of them could figure out where they'd tripped the mine.

Buck knew it had to be there—probably hiding in plain sight, too. He only hoped that Monroe and his team at Black Watch would be clear-eyed enough to find it.

Giving up on sleep, he rolled out of his bunk and ghosted out of the room. He tried not to wake Bennett but doubted he'd be so lucky. The man had eyes like a cat in the dark, on top of his emotional Spidey sense. He'd probably provide Buck with an annotated timetable of his wanderings over coffee in the morning.

Great qualities in a sniper. Not so great in a bunkmate.

Buck ghosted around base for a while before landing at the gym. Even at zero dark thirty, there were sailors around, getting in workouts around their graveyard shifts, or exercising away the nightmares that cropped up now and then for most of them.

Buck snagged a treadmill as far as possible from the others, settled into a pace he could maintain for a good long while, and settled into making plans for Peyton's arrival.

Chapter Fourteen

Peyton

AT SOME POINT in the last few hours, Peyton had regressed into a teenage girl. Which was weird, because she'd been sure she was an adult when she decided to pack up her entire life and hie to the west coast in pursuit of a man. She'd managed the necessary degree of maturity for the inevitable discussions with her parents, Josh, and Devon, and even kept her cool on the phone with Buck.

But ever since she'd boarded her flight to San Diego, Peyton had been unable to think about anything but the way Buck was going to greet her once she landed. It was a six-and-a-half-hour flight. The fantasy was getting detailed.

To be honest, she'd been choreographing their reunion for much longer than this flight. Their separation had been unexpectedly hard, and she was looking forward to celebrating the end of it.

Except, once the plane finally touched down in sunny California, Peyton was struck with an unexpected bout of trepidation. She fought through it as she made her way down the concourse, until she could see the open doors to the terminal beyond. Her steps slowed, then stopped.

What was she doing with her life? Was this leap of faith just a massive, reckless mistake?

All this time, Peyton had been envisioning a joyful, emotional reunion with Buck. She was going to find him in the crowd, run to him with a teary grin, and he was going to grab her and hug her tight. Maybe he'd lift her and swing her around when he planted one of his soul-stealing kisses on her, like Peyton was all that mattered—like he'd been waiting for her forever, and couldn't wait to walk into the future holding her hand.

Perhaps she needed more sleep, or less bingeing on romantic tv series. Whatever her issue was, the longer she stood there the more the ball of nerves in her stomach grew.

Peyton doubted she'd cry when she saw him. She was more worried that she'd shut down while she processed her feelings. And Buck, like certain men before him, might interpret that withdrawal as disinterest or cold feet.

Better he knew what he was getting into now, she supposed. Peyton took a few more steps, swept along by the other passengers hurrying toward the baggage claim until, at last, she breached the doorway and found herself awkwardly adrift in the large area.

Bright sun streamed in the windows, and people wandered every which way. She glanced around at the harassed business travelers and flustered families, marking locals returning home and tourists, too—but no Buck.

She was definitely in California, though. Even without a coast in view, there were enough beachy-looking people in evidence to make it clear that one was close. There was also a pervasive, laid-back vibe that was noticeably different from where she'd spent her last several years.

It would be fun, she decided, to be a part of this with Buck.

Since there was still no large, ruggedly handsome man hanging around with Peyton-shaped hearts in his eyes, she checked the signs and found the correct baggage carousel. The other passengers from her flight had already either gathered around it or headed out to the street, and now even their flight crew was beginning to trickle past.

Buck, however, was not there. Had something gone wrong?

It wasn't like him to be late. In the entire time she'd known him he'd never been anything but prompt, arriving ten minutes early to every date they'd ever had.

A tendril of doubt curled through her nervousness, but Peyton walked a little farther, searching the neighboring baggage claims in case they'd somehow gotten their wires crossed.

That's when she spotted the man casually leaning against the wall, a piece of paper dangling from one hand. He was a little taller than Buck, lean and fit, with tousled, sun-streaked hair. His features were so sharply perfect they bordered on pretty.

Peyton couldn't pinpoint what it was that reminded her so much of Buck—maybe he held himself the same way or gave off a similar watchful, capable air? Much like Buck, the man looked like he'd already cataloged every person in this place and had a good idea what they might do next.

When his gaze swept over her, he straightened and smiled, brandishing his sign affably.

It read *PAYTON*—like the football player, instead of the new girlfriend. Peyton scanned behind her to be sure, but they appeared to be the only two people here who were looking for someone.

The guy smiled a bit wider and pushed off the wall, his long strides eating up the distance between them in far too few seconds. "You must be Peyton," he drawled, his soft twang completely at odds with the surfer aesthetic he was throwing off.

"Me?" she stalled, mentally sending out a last, desperate plea for Buck to show up and tell her this was all a big mistake.

Devon had warned her to keep her guard up out here, to not be fooled by snakes with friendship on their faces and hustle in their hearts. At the time, she'd laughed at him. This was San Diego, not a supermax prison.

But perhaps he'd been right to be suspicious. He'd lived in L.A. for a few years after college and was no one's fool.

"Peyton Page, right?" the man asked, cocking his head. When she nodded warily, he barreled on, "Ma'am, I'm Master Chief Bennett Shaw. Lieutenant Gaines asked me to come get you and tell you that he is extremely sorry he can't be here himself."

That was a shade too much like something a kidnapper would say—in her nightmares, anyway. Peyton took a step back and searched the area around them once more. It looked like another plane had landed because a flood of new people was surging around them.

"I don't, uh…Buck didn't say anything about this."

Master Chief Shaw was digging in the pockets of his shorts, but he glanced up then and noticed her undoubtedly panicked expression. He didn't get weird, though. He only explained kindly, "He got the call this morning. Said he'd let you know before he shipped out. He didn't do it?"

Peyton swallowed numbly, utterly bewildered and not sure what to do. "I…no. He did not."

Her phone was in the pocket of her jacket. It hadn't buzzed once since she'd left the house that morning. She felt for the hard plastic of the case, not sure if she wanted to check it or brazen this out.

Whoever this Shaw guy was, he was an expert at reading body language. He kept his posture and his tone relaxed and didn't try to come closer.

He only nodded at Peyton's pocket and asked gently, "Are you sure? Might he have texted you while your phone was off during the flight?"

Peyton gasped in sudden realization. Her phone was still in airplane mode. *Crap.*

She fumbled it free, powered it on, and waited for the airport WIFI to sync. Moments later, notifications started popping up, ding after ding ringing out from her hand. A couple of calls from Devon and her mom.

Three texts, too, all from Buck.

Hey, you. Just got a call—might have to bug out for a few days.
Trying to postpone it—will let you know asap.

A small sound slipped from her throat, and Peyton checked Shaw's reaction. He'd turned away, but not before she caught his sympathetic wince.

Damn it. Peyton thumbed through and read the second text.

No dice. Fuck, I'm so sorry, babe. Shipping out 1300 hrs but back in 3 days. Sending my (our!) roommate Bennett Shaw to get you. He and Wyatt will get you settled until I can get home. I promise you can trust them. I do.

Peyton blew out her breath and quickly scanned the final message, too.

Miss you, Peyton. Can't wait to show you how much. And stop thinking this is an omen of doom LOL. It's not. XO

When she looked back at Master Chief Shaw—Bennett, she corrected herself—he asked her, "Am I cleared for duty?"

"Looks like it," Peyton admitted wryly. "Sorry I doubted you."

"Don't be sorry," he told her, then handed her the card he'd extracted from his wallet while she mourned the death of her reunion fantasies. "Here's my ID. So you know it's me."

Peyton glanced at the card, but it was more for Bennett's benefit than her own. It certainly seemed authentic, with fancy holograms, an official-looking Navy seal, and so on—but she doubted she'd be able to tell a fake from the real thing, anyway.

She handed it back and tried to bury her disappointment. Peyton wished she had time to deal with the change in plan in privacy but telling Bennett she'd rather Uber to the apartment instead of ride with him seemed rude.

"Thanks for picking me up," she told him. "And it's nice to meet you. I appreciate you guys letting me crash at your place." She grabbed the handle of her carry-on and readjusted her purse strap, needing to do something with her hands.

"No worries. We're pretty chill. Stay as long as you want."

Peyton pasted on what she hoped was an optimistic smile. "Okay, great. Now let's…find the rest of my stuff, I guess."

"Let me get that for you." Bennett reached for her rolling bag and grinned easily. "For what it's worth, Buck's told us a lot about you. He's been pretty psyched about you getting here. Thought he might put a hole in the wall when he got that call this morning."

Peyton hurried to keep up with his long, loping strides. "Really?"

"Really," he snorted. With a quick peek at the flight schedule, he beelined for the correct baggage claim.

She smiled to herself, imagining Buck drilling Bennett on her flight details, so he wouldn't screw up her retrieval. "Do you want me to go get one of those metal cart thingies?" she asked.

"Naw, I can handle it. What else you got?"

Bags had already started sliding down the chute, hitting the carousel with muted thumps. Peyton reviewed her baggage in her head and bit her lip. "Well…I think I should get a cart."

Bennett sent an amused look her way, blue eyes sparkling. "That much, huh?"

A wave of pained embarrassment washed over her. She'd had to pack up her life countless times, but this move had swamped her with indecision. Different climate, an incipient job hunt— she'd had no idea what she'd need, or when.

Peyton had agonized over what to box up for the truck, and what to pack in her bags, and in the end, she'd erred on the side of caution, trusting Buck to take it in stride.

"Don't say I didn't warn you," she muttered.

If only Buck had rented an apartment for them before she'd gotten here, instead of insisting that they wait and pick it out together. Then Peyton wouldn't be in this predicament, worrying that his roommates would think she was high-maintenance for arriving on their doorstep with too much stuff.

Bennett startled her out of her thoughts with a heavy arm around her shoulders and a genial squeeze. "Don't worry, ma'am. I have a sister. I know the drill."

Peyton smiled in gratitude. Back in Baltimore, she'd had to pay a $50 surcharge for each of her bags, and had still gotten an earful from the counter attendant for the size of them.

True to his word, though, Bennett didn't even blink as he heaved each of her three oversized duffels off the carousel. Before Peyton could have mercy and procure the necessary cart, he slipped one bag onto his back like a rucksack and lifted another in each hand.

He let her handle her rolling bag and carry-on, and jerked his chin toward the exit with a sunny, "All right, kid. Let's roll."

Then he was off, plowing into the melee of bus shuttles and fumes outside with no obvious effort—like was a Sunday stroll and not a strongman competition.

"Hope you brought something bigger than a hatchback," Peyton panted, trying to catch up with his rapidly retreating back.

"I've been granted temporary usage of your boy's truck," Bennett called over his shoulder. "Believe me, there's room to spare."

IT WAS NO exaggeration. The truck was, in fact, a very big SUV, but Bennett handled it easily. As they left the airport, he followed a road that hugged the coastline, making small talk about her flight and the other guy who lived in the apartment.

"Don't worry about Wyatt," he told her. "He's a good dude. Total mama's boy, though. If you get on his good side, he'll probably try to get you to make him cookies."

Peyton laughed. "Seriously?"

"Yep. He makes pretty decent chili and knows his way around a meatloaf, but he's trash at baking. He's got a sweet tooth, though. Makes things awkward."

"I mean…he can buy stuff at a grocery store," she said. "You just cut open the tube and slice the dough."

"Oh, he does," Bennett agreed amiably. "But he whines the whole time about how his mom does it better."

She squinted at him. "How old is this man again?"

"Too old to be acting like that, that's for damn sure. Don't let him sweet-talk you." He glanced over his shoulder, then eased onto a side street. "We need to marry him off, but so far no one's fit the bill. He's a picky sonofabitch, in addition to being a crybaby."

Peyton grinned, trying to picture them match-making over beers.

Bennett stopped at a light, then turned the truck inland, heading into a pretty, historic-looking area near the water.

She looked around in interest. "Hey, this is cute. Where are we?"

"It's called the Gaslamp Quarter. Lots of shops and bars and stuff. If you look back there you can see the Coronado Bay Bridge, which takes you to base."

"Cool. Is the apartment far from here?"

"Nope. Maybe fifteen minutes, depending on traffic." He stopped at a second light and glanced over. "Hey, you hungry? We can stop somewhere and grab dinner if you want. Can't exactly vouch for what we might have at home. Buck thought you might want to go grocery shopping once you got here."

Peyton smiled, wishing she was doing this with Buck instead of Bennett. Still, the guy made a fair point. She'd barely choked down some pretzels on her flight, and now that her nerves were settling down, she realized she was famished.

"Yeah, actually that would be great," she told him. "What do you feel like?"

Bennett chuckled ruefully. "Nice try, but I'm under strict orders. Ladies' choice or it's my ass on the line."

Peyton rolled her eyes and thought for a minute. "Okay, then how about…sushi? Not too heavy and everyone likes it, right?"

Bennett hesitated. "Yeah, uh…we can do that." He slowed the truck for a turn, then suddenly pointed across the street. "What about that joint? I've never been but I heard it's good."

"Fine by me."

"All right, let me drop you off here, then. Grab a table and give me a few minutes to ditch this beast, and I'll catch up with you."

Peyton watched from the sidewalk as he drove slowly up the block, then pulled out her phone to check her messages. Still no word from Buck.

She fired off a quick text to let him know she'd arrived, but had no idea if he'd even see it. Squaring her shoulders, she marched toward the restaurant and tried to temper her disappointment. This was a minor setback, nothing more.

If she truly intended to date a SEAL, she'd damn well better get used to rolling with the punches.

AFTER SHE'D STUFFED her face and Bennett had driven them home, he'd lugged her bags into the apartment, and introduced Peyton to Wyatt and a third friend named Joe. Together, they'd given her a quick tour of the building and made sure she saved their contact information on her phone.

By the time they finished, she was fighting off jaw-cracking yawns, so they wished her goodnight and Peyton closed herself in Buck's room.

She took a brief shower, changed into pajamas, and climbed into bed in utter exhaustion, expecting to be surrounded by Buck's comforting scent. Instead, all she smelled was the crisp tang of detergent and dryer sheets.

He'd put fresh linens on the bed for her arrival. *Raised right, damn it.*

Peyton got up and prowled the room in annoyance. Aside from her mountain of luggage in the corner, it was irritatingly neat. Eventually, though, she discovered Buck's hamper in the closet and a few things he hadn't washed before leaving.

Peyton sifted through the pile, chose a t-shirt to slip over her pillow, and got back in bed. While she lay there, she roughed out a plan for the next day.

Bennett had given her Buck's keys, so in the morning she could ask the guys where the grocery store was, then begin to learn her way around the neighborhood. Later, she could unpack some clothes and start her home and job search.

Simple.

When she closed her eyes this time, she was out within minutes.

COURTESY OF HER jet lag, Peyton awoke far too early the following morning. She'd been surprised to hear Bennett and Wyatt up and moving around, but by the time she'd showered and dressed, then cracked Buck's door to peek out, they'd already left.

She ventured into the main room, curious to get a better look at it in the daytime. The furnishings were pretty basic, but everything was clean and neat as a pin. It would be fine for now.

Peyton found a note on the counter saying that the guys would be on base all day, but to call if she had questions. They'd also left her half a pot of coffee, still hot and brewed strong enough to fuel a diesel tanker.

There was no milk or cream in the refrigerator, however, and she'd never been able to drink her coffee black. Luckily, she had access to a set of wheels, so she did a quick search on her phone, grabbed Buck's keys, and headed out to find the nearest market with an adjacent café counter.

Once Peyton was fed and caffeinated and had her groceries home and put away, though, she lost any desire to explore more. It would take a few days to acclimate to the new time zone, but at least now she had the apartment to herself and could give in to her exhaustion without bothering anyone.

Grateful for the respite, Peyton crawled back into bed for a long nap, then spent the afternoon unpacking clothes she'd need for the rest of the week and prepping some things for dinner.

While she found her away around the small kitchen, she thought about the rest of her stuff, heading west on a truck at that very moment. Based on what she'd seen so far, she and Buck would probably need to buy more cooking utensils once they moved.

Peyton had used her brother's stuff while she'd lived at his house, and it'd been a great arrangement for both of them. She'd been able to save money toward a down payment on her own place, and Josh had had someone looking after his townhouse while he worked in London.

But it also meant that she hadn't bothered to buy things like cookware herself. Buck clearly hadn't either, and she supposed that made sense if he didn't spend much time at home.

While she waited for him to return, though, she should start a shopping list of stuff to pick out together. Peyton considered what was in her boxes and what she'd left at Josh's, then jotted a few notes on a pad of paper she found next to the phone.

That led her to think about the boxes from her home office, and the binder she'd kept filled with research and hard copies of her blog articles. She'd maintained it as a portfolio of sorts, something she could show to prospective employers as evidence of her skills.

The problem was, it needed to stay packed until she'd had a chance to tell Buck who she was and what had happened to her.

When the truck arrived next week, that binder would go directly into the stall she'd rented at a local storage facility. If things didn't work out between her and Buck, it could stay where it was while Peyton decided what to do next. If they got their own apartment as planned, though…the binder presented a problem.

Fortunately, that was weeks away at this point, and there'd be plenty of time to explain before then. Peyton only wished it didn't feel like she'd kept something important from him.

But Buck would understand, wouldn't he? He wasn't the type to freak out over something that hadn't been her fault. *Mostly*.

True, Peyton had written one reckless article, but she'd done it in relative obscurity. Joely Spitz had been the one to blow the whole thing up, and Peyton still had no clue why she'd been chosen as fodder.

She thought about that as she ate and cleaned up after herself, then went back to Buck's room to read before bed. Her roommates came home soon after, with several other guys in tow.

Their deep voices boomed around the living room in bursts of good-natured bickering, and it soon became clear there was some kind of hotly-contested game being played that night on tv.

So much for reading. Peyton sighed and set her book aside, then stepped outside to plop on one of the folding lawn chairs for a breather from the din. The evening was pretty and milder than what she was used to in Maryland this time of year.

It felt awkward being a stranger, and the only woman in the apartment—and not having Buck there to smooth the way. For lack of something better to do, Peyton texted an update to Devon to reassure him that all was going well, then called up more apartment listings to comb through.

She was engrossed in descriptions of en suite bathrooms when she jumped, startled by a sudden sound that didn't fit the rest of the peaceful evening. Heart beginning to pound, Peyton's head jerked up. A young man was lurking several feet away, half-hidden by some rhododendron bushes.

They locked eyes and he started toward her, eyes glittering in the light from the streetlamp. The guys in the living room let out a deafening roar, booing a call in their game, and Peyton's visitor jerked, looked around wildly, and ran off.

Had he been creeping up on her? Or merely staring? It hardly mattered.

She lurched inside and locked the sliding glass door behind her. She was too embarrassed to go out to the living room and announce what had happened to the roomful of guys, most of them strangers. What was she supposed to say?

Peyton could hardly tell a bunch of worked-up SEALs she was the infamous blogger that patriots all over the country wanted to drag into the light. Or worse, that people had been following her at home, and now, one day after her arrival, were weirding her out here.

She couldn't decide which would be worse—if they didn't believe her, or if they did.

She shut the blinds and cast around the room and bathroom, eventually landing on the plunger under the sink as a suitable implement. Peyton unscrewed the handle and propped it in the track of the sliding door, adding security to the lock.

There was nothing she could do about the door in the living room but figured the crowd of deadly men out there would be protection enough.

Peyton laid awake all night anyway, scared that if she fell asleep, someone would break in and snatch her.

She should have said something to someone. The incident would have sounded unsettling enough without the added context. She wouldn't have had to tell them the whole story.

But the next day, when Peyton was sleepily scrambling herself some eggs and Joe stopped by to retrieve a jacket he'd left behind, she noticed his resemblance to the lurker.

She turned off the stove, made a clumsy excuse, and skidded into Buck's room, locking herself in until he left, then pretending she'd gotten distracted by a call from her parents when Bennett knocked and asked if she was okay.

Peyton was not okay. Far from it, as a matter of fact.

Chapter Fifteen

Buck

THE ONLY THING that had saved Tate Monroe from being strangled to death once Buck came face to face with him in Wyoming was that he turned out to be an incredibly likable motherfucker. Buck doubted Monroe knew how close he'd come to biting the dust, though.

On the precise day that Peyton was due to land in San Diego, the founder of Black Watch Security had summoned Buck to a meeting with zero lead time and even less flexibility. Private plane and luxury resort accommodations aside, it had been safe to say that Buck was ready to commit murder.

Fortunately, the guy had come prepared for their meeting, and then some.

Once Buck had gotten settled, Tate had produced reams of intel about the ambush for him to comb through, as well as a college kid named Noah with a tricked-out laptop and an eager-beaver attitude.

Noah gave off serious "Peter Parker loves Tony Stark" vibes, but he'd quickly demonstrated why he'd been drafted for the job. There didn't seem to be a firewall in existence he couldn't hack through or a detail he couldn't unearth beneath layers of digital security.

Together, the three of them sorted through every official list of attendees at that girls' school ribbon cutting. They'd sifted through airline passenger lists, two censuses that were taken of the village, witness testimonies, and more.

Within hours, Buck had learned more about Joely Spitz and her camera crew than he'd ever discovered from her boastful ramblings—or even from the misbegotten time he'd hit the sheets with her.

He could've done without that part of the conclave but understood why it had to happen. Out of everyone involved, Joely had the shiftiest moral compass and the greatest likelihood of taking a misstep.

He'd gotten a little bogged down, trying to reason out where in the chronology Joely and Old Roy had gotten friendly—or how they'd managed to convince the world that he and his team were like arsonists, setting a bonfire, then putting it out for the glory.

But then, Tate had brought out a detailed hierarchy of the officers overseeing Doggett's original security team, along with a schematic of the brass running the shadow op on the sidelines, hoping to ensnare al Kadir if he emerged during the festivities.

Monroe had led Buck through a chart of the special warfare command, who'd run the extraction and clean-up efforts. There were a few choice candidates in each of the pools who could be playing backstage puppeteer right now.

Tate and Noah had promised to peer under every one of those logs, to see if there was rot to be found.

Finally, there'd been photos from the day of the ambush, and video to scour as well. Buck had hated that part. It wasn't uncommon for his team to enter the chat well after it'd started, but it was jarring to review the lead-in now.

The happy faces of the schoolgirls, holding a ribbon wide so Doggett's polished wife could cut it in half. Their parents gathered around the edges, looking hopeful and nervous all at once.

It was hard to excise the emotion from the equation, reliving the way those innocent people had suffered. Buck and his squad had gotten there far too late to be of much use.

Reviewing everything had been long, tiring work, and Buck still didn't know if his insight had been helpful. He'd been personally involved with only one part of the operation after all—getting the senator and his wife to the extraction point and onto the bird that would carry them to safety.

It didn't seem like the kind of thing a politician would ruin a SEAL's career over, even one who had backtalked him in the heat of the moment. But that was why Buck was here, wasn't it?

Tate had procured all kinds of information on Doggett, to help unearth a motive. He'd gotten financial records dealing with the presidential nomination campaign, tax returns for him and his wife—even bar tabs from the dude's favorite country club.

Doggett's public record had undoubtedly been scrubbed clean in anticipation of his campaign because not one thing seemed to point to a conflict of interest, a personality clash, a side chick, or a hidden addiction.

"Why don't we just bug the guy," Buck had wondered. "With the way that fucker talks, it'll take us about five minutes to figure out what he's up to."

"He's got extra security right now, because of the election," Tate had told him ruefully. "Hard to get past it without giving ourselves away."

Old Roy was dirty, though—Buck *knew* it. They simply had to prove it. Somehow.

The intel on al Kadir hadn't been much better.

"He's still small-time," Noah had explained. "He seems to be focusing mainly on building up manpower and getting funding right now."

"Not a big player in the region," Monroe had added. "Nabarut appears to be personal for him, though. It comes up a fair amount in the little inspirational videos he sends his fighters, but as far as we can tell, he has no family there. Any idea why he's so keen?"

"Not a clue," Buck had sighed in frustration, as he had so many times that day.

He hated how much they still didn't know. His instincts were telling him there was something there, something right in front of them that they simply weren't seeing. But with each passing day, he was getting closer to whatever verdicts the Congressional committee and the Naval board of inquiry were going to deliver.

His days felt numbered in so many ways.

Buck wanted to be anywhere but that high-dollar hotel suite—ghosting out on some op in a forgotten corner of the globe, or even better, home in bed with Peyton's warm luscious curves filling his hands.

Instead, he was holed up with more paperwork than he'd seen since college, with a nerdy kid who was probably ten years his junior and a man who'd come too highly recommended to be making the kind of goofy jokes he did.

When Buck busted Monroe smirking at his phone for the millionth time in two days, the guy finally admitted, "Sorry. It's my wife. She's giving me a hard time for…reasons."

"They're newlyweds," Noah piped up, with the same tone one might use to point out a litter of kittens.

"Hey, congrats, man," Buck told him, not wanting to be a complete jerk. Hell, if he had his way, he'd like to be in Tate's shoes before too long.

Tate attempted a casual shrug and murmured, "Thanks," but immediately redirected them to yet another file full of mind-numbing minutiae. Buck didn't miss the man's smug, secret pleasure, however, and he wondered if he'd be the same one day.

Monroe seemed like a good dude—a smart, savvy guy who loved his work, in addition to his wife. Did he have the chops to get this job done, though?

And did Buck want to work for him long-term?

Monroe ducked out periodically, purportedly to interview a few former spec ops guys working security at the resort. Buck never met the men, never even saw them—but he wondered if meeting Monroe here was functioning as his own consultation.

Buck would've figured the guy would want to see if his potential hires could work together without killing each other, but maybe the man had plans Buck couldn't fathom.

All he knew for sure was that Peyton had been met at the airport yesterday by a too-pretty man who was not Buck. And though Buck had trusted his best buddy with the mission-critical task, it didn't change the fact that Ben could turn on the charm when he wanted to and acted like a goddamn hound half the time.

It wasn't the most auspicious beginning to Buck and Peyton's future, and the shitty cell reception here in the sticks wasn't helping. He would've thought that a swanky joint like this would've invested in a satellite or some shit, but nope—he'd had almost no contact with Peyton since he'd gotten here, and it rubbed Buck all kinds of wrong.

How was she supposed to believe in him, to believe in *them*, if this was the kind of crap she had to deal with? He couldn't decide which would be worse for her—dealing with a tarnished SEAL who'd been vilified by his own community, or with a security group operative acting without a safety net.

When he finally saw her again…he hoped he could find the right words to explain it all.

THE NEXT EVENING, Tate finally got around to the topic that was low on his agenda, but high on Buck's.

"We looked into Peyton Page like you asked," he said. "Everything she told you checks out. Family, employment history…it all squares with what we saw. She's traveled abroad extensively, but never outside the company of her family. Mother, father, and brother all have high-level security clearance. If there was anything shady about her, I have to think it would've come up by now."

"Probably."

"Even that friend Devon you mentioned is clean as a whistle," Monroe commented. "He taught high school history before moving to MCC, volunteers at his church on the weekends, and coaches his nephew's flag football team."

"Peyton's fond of him," Buck replied, then wondered if there'd ever been something more between them. If Bradford was such a great guy, why wasn't she with him, instead?

Maybe she had been. When she was asking him about Joely, maybe he should have been asking her more about Devon.

Tate arched a wry eyebrow at him, as if Buck's thoughts had been broadcast loud and clear. "Even Bradford's super-secret love connection is wholesome," he said. "He's dating a divorced cell biology professor at the college. Brings her mochi every Thursday during her lunch break and babysits her kids when she has to work late. It's like a freaking Hallmark movie up in there."

"Oh, wow…I don't think Peyton knows that," Buck said, placated.

"Doesn't surprise me. MCC has strict dating policies, but the bio professor also has clauses in her custody agreement that probably necessitate keeping things lowkey. Speaking of Ms. Page…"

Buck frowned at him. "What."

"Well…it looks like she's packing stuff up and getting ready to move. Quit her job, too, from what I heard. Thought you'd want to know."

Buck let out a relieved laugh. "Of course I know," he explained. "She's moving in with me. Got there a couple of days ago, as a matter of fact."

"Ah," Tate said, sharing a quick look with Noah, but otherwise not acknowledging that Buck was currently here with him, instead of with Peyton, where he belonged. "That's very…uh…"

"Precipitous?" Buck supplied. "Yeah, maybe. But it's all good. We're solid." Never mind that he'd just had these men do a mini background check on his girlfriend. It'd been a formality, nothing more.

Noah grinned. "When you know, you know!" he announced, like he had one iota of life experience under his belt.

Buck and Tate leveled him with twin looks of exasperation.

The kid flushed a bit behind his glasses. "My…my dad always says that. And I have to say, even when I'm sure he's finally lost it, he usually turns out to be right." He stopped and swallowed, pushing those thick frames up his nose and picking at a UCSD sticker on his laptop. "Anyway."

Tate watched him with a small smile, then turned back to Buck. "I mean…he ain't wrong."

Buck snorted, trying to understand how he'd ended up having this conversation. "We really doing this right now?"

Tate laughed, then yawned and rubbed his eyes. "Nah. I'm beat. I've got an early flight home in the morning, so I'm going to turn in. I get wicked headaches if I don't sleep enough." He pushed to his feet and passed a hand over his face. "Anyway, you two finish up and let me know if you find anything else. I'll be in touch soon."

Monroe rolled his shoulders and stretched his neck like it was sore. He gave them a lazy salute, wandered around the room looking for his room key, and slipped out.

Noah watched him leave with a concerned frown.

After a minute, Buck asked him, "Something wrong?"

The kid sighed. "He had a TBI a couple of years ago. Did you know that?"

"Yeah."

"Well…he doesn't just get headaches when he's tired. He gets brutal migraines when he pushes too hard, and that's kind of his nature. I've heard him use that same excuse at least two other times, and it was always late in the day like this."

Buck looked at the guy with new eyes, surprised that this job wasn't a one-off thing for him. "So what are you saying? You think Monroe was lying?"

"No, I think he's already got the migraine. They have prodrome symptoms, right? And Tate gets them like clockwork. He starts rubbing his eyes and complaining that the light's too bright. Normal noise levels bother him. He gets nauseous, too."

Buck had seen the eye rubbing, but the rest seemed like a stretch. "What makes you think he was nauseous?"

"Well, for one thing, he's been raving about that overpriced craft beer the whole time we've been here, but when you offered him one a little while ago, he looked like a barf emoji."

"Maybe he just didn't feel like drinking."

Noah looked around at the piles of paper they'd been scouring for two days straight, searching for his phone. "If you say so. I'm still going to text him and tell him to take his meds now."

Once he was done, Buck smiled at him fondly. "You're pretty observant, kid. You know that?"

"I do," Noah said. "And for the record, I'm not a kid. I'm 24."

"Okay. Sorry." Buck had eight years on the guy. He was definitely a kid.

Noah shrugged. "It's fine. I get it all the time. Anyway…why don't we start cleaning this crap up. Tate likes it to look like no one was here by the time we leave."

"Don't have to tell me twice," Buck said.

He waited a good ten minutes and took several swigs of one of those fancy beers before he broached the question that had been dancing around in his brain half the night.

"So…you're pretty handy with the computer shit, huh?"

Noah shrugged as he fed papers into the brisk fire they had burning in the hearth. "I enjoy it. I'm doing graduate work now, but I taught myself most of the good stuff."

"The stuff Monroe wants you for?"

He grinned. "Pretty much."

"You have time for one more project in your schedule?" Buck wondered.

The kid looked him over with a funny expression. "Possibly. What's it got to do with all this?" He gestured around at the documents and photos, some of them awaiting their turn in the blaze.

"It's…an ancillary issue," Buck explained. "A bit player, I hope, but one I haven't been able to find on my own."

"Are you going to kill them if I find them for you?"

The urge to laugh was strong, but Buck didn't think the kid would find that funny. "Only figuratively."

Noah blinked and thought for a bit. "Okay. Who is it?"

"I need you to tell me who's behind a political blog called *Global Lens*."

The guy looked surprised. "I'm already on that task, Lieutenant. Whoever that person is, they *really* don't want to be found. Their blog has layers of encryption, all kinds of security—it's like the Fort Knox of blogs. Which strikes me as weird for a little hobby, you know?"

"I do," Buck grumbled. "And that was not what I was hoping to hear."

Noah shook his head, though. "Don't worry. There's a way into their secret cave somewhere. There always is."

"And you think you can find it?"

"I know I can."

Chapter Sixteen

Peyton

ARMED WITH A folding chair and some vague directions from Wyatt, Peyton decided to check out the beach the following morning.

The midweek crowd was light as she dug her toes into the cool sand and watched the fog burn off. In that quiet moment, she was grateful for a few things—mostly for the peaceful break from the last few weeks, but also for the sweatshirt she'd thrown on before she left and the hot coffee she'd stopped for on the way.

Thanks to the chill in the air, she didn't have to expose anyone to her east-coast suburban pallor, or the swimsuit she was now realizing was woefully outdated. At least that problem was easily solvable.

Peyton texted Bennett to confirm she had their mailing address correct, then ordered herself two new bikinis and a couple of bottles of sunscreen. Buck would probably laugh at her version of a southern California starter pack, but she had to start somewhere.

Peyton set her phone aside again, wondering what he was doing now. It was hard not to worry, given his profession. For all she knew, he could be getting his ass shot off while she was sitting here sipping a latte and watching surfers bob in the waves.

The juxtaposition was unsettling, but at least he'd assured her he would be back in a few days. She'd been here for three, so that had to mean he would return soon. Maybe even that day.

With that happy thought in mind, Peyton took off her sweatshirt and snapped a few photos of herself, cropping them somewhat artistically before she propped her phone on the chair and took a silly, tourist-worthy selfie with the ocean behind her. She sent them all to Buck with the evergreen "wish you were here" message and hoped they would speed him on his way.

Smiling to herself, she sat back down and pulled up the job listings again. For the first time in so long, her day felt full of possibility instead of fear, despite that weird incident with Joe.

She could do this. It was going to be great.

THE BLISSFUL CALM lasted for hours, until hunger finally forced her off the sand in search of lunch. Peyton stashed her sweatshirt and chair in the truck and wandered up the block, eventually choosing a tiny taqueria that looked like it was doing brisk business to place her order.

She waited by the graffiti-covered wall for her number to be called and checked to see if Buck had opened her text yet. *Delivered. Unread.*

Maybe he was in a different time zone and wasn't awake yet. Or busy fighting for his life. Or in witness protection somewhere, getting settled in a new life that had no room for her.

She sighed heavily and went to get her order from the counter. She needed to knock it off.

Peyton had her nose in the paper bag, inhaling the divine scent of al pastor wafting up as she walked out the door—so it took her a minute to notice Joe heading into the restaurant with a companion.

They were dressed in casual clothes, and the other guy, at least, looked happy to be there. He was animated and laughing but Joe seemed tense, his stony gaze darting around the sidewalk like he expected to be attacked at any second.

He was too close for Peyton to pretend she hadn't seen him. She gave him a half-hearted wave and received a slight jerk of his chin in response. It wasn't clear if Joe was angry with her specifically or generally unhappy, but in broad daylight it was impossible, once again, to gloss over how much he resembled the man she'd seen in the bushes two nights ago.

His build was the same. The dark wavy hair and the medium skin tone, too. Peyton's heart rate kicked up at the memory. Joe couldn't have followed her here—she hadn't even known she was coming to this place until a few minutes ago.

Unless he'd been watching her all along?

A cold shiver snaked through her. She'd intended to sit and eat on one of the benches facing the water once she got her food. Now, Peyton backed around the corner of the small building, waiting for the two men to emerge to see what they would do.

They didn't act sketchy, though—they only got into their car with their bags of food and fountain drinks, and drove away. Once they were out of sight, Peyton hurried several blocks back to the lot where she'd parked Buck's truck, locked herself inside, and turned on the A/C while she ate.

The food jogged her tired, anxious brain back into proper functioning again. She talked herself down as she chewed. "Okay, relax. You're not in Maryland anymore. No one is looking for you here. No one even knows who you are."

And then, after a few more bites, she told herself, "Joe is not that friendly, but that doesn't mean he hates you. Maybe he's just naturally reserved. And kind of mean."

Buck hadn't explicitly included Joe when he said he trusted his roommates with his life, but Bennett and Wyatt liked the man enough to have him over nearly every day. Surely they wouldn't be friends with someone shady.

There was no reason to assume he knew her secret, either. He would've told everyone by now if he did.

Peyton reasoned with herself while she snarfed down three heavenly street tacos and a big bag of house-made chips, until the food was gone and she felt ready to get out of the truck again and try again.

She locked the truck and strolled down a few more streets, and discovered a big, beautiful library filled with soaring windows and sunlight. Peyton darted in with excitement, making a quick, happy circuit of the first floor, then stopping at the front desk to open an account.

When she left, she had a stack of books under her arm, to keep her occupied at night until Buck came back. Peyton lingered on the sidewalk outside, looking around for her next destination.

Up the way was another interesting restaurant, and across the street sat a boutique that merited closer inspection. She stepped to the curb and glanced to the right, looking for oncoming traffic—and jolted at the sight of two men strolling out of the library, looking around.

One of them was of medium height and build, with dark, wavy hair and light brown skin.

Just like the man in the bushes, and a lot like Joe. Peyton swallowed, trying to decide if the other guy was Joe's companion at the taqueria, but then they turned her way and spotted her.

They hesitated for the briefest moment, then walked toward her with twin scowls.

Peyton pushed past her spasm of fear and darted across the street as the light changed, earning angry honks from the cars in front. She made it across without getting flattened but tripped on the opposite curb—twisting her ankle and banging her knees on the sidewalk, and nearly losing her books in the street.

She forced herself up and into motion despite the burning in her ankle. Peyton bypassed the boutique she'd wanted to explore and bolted down the block, where a big lingerie store's buy-one-get-one sale was attracting a steady stream of lunchtime shoppers.

Peyton peeked quickly over her shoulder and spotted the two men inching up the block on the other side of the street, watching for a break in the traffic so they could cross. She tried to snap a few photos of them then ducked into the store behind three giggling girls in UCSD t-shirts.

Once she was safely inside, Peyton beelined for the nearest sales clerk.

"Hey," she smiled, "Can you point me toward the ladies' room? I can't seem to find it."

The woman gestured toward the clearance section at the back. "Left corner next to the dressing room," she said. "You can't miss it."

Peyton limped past tables of underwear and racks of bras, winding her way through the bargain hunters on their lunch breaks. In the bathroom, she locked herself in the farthest stall, put down the lid, and sat down heavily, debating what to do next.

She couldn't call Bennett or Wyatt, for all the same reasons she hadn't told them about the man in the bushes the other night. It would be pointless to call the police, too. A hunch that people were out to get you was not an actionable offense anywhere in the country.

In the end, all Peyton could think to do was wait. With a frustrated sigh, she cracked open one of the novels she'd just checked out and hoped the throbbing in her ankle would subside by the time it was safe for her to leave.

It was a ridiculous fix to find herself in, but the store was as busy and public a place as anywhere. She'd be okay here until those guys gave up and left her alone—whoever they were.

PEYTON WAITED FOR two hours in that shop bathroom, until she finally noticed the cherry-red heels of the clerk who'd helped her earlier enter the next stall. She tucked her book back into her bag and timed her exit to match the other woman's.

The lady was startled when she recognized her in the mirror over the sinks. "Oh," she said warily. "You're…still here."

"I know. And I'm so sorry. But I've got a big problem," Peyton admitted, then gave the woman a brief run-down of her situation.

Her sympathy was instantaneous. In minutes, the clerk was guiding her out the security door behind the shop, telling her a shortcut back to the lot where the truck was parked, and throwing in a recommendation for a reliable salon nearby.

"Thank you so much," Peyton told her. "I really appreciate this. If I can put in a good word with your manager or something—"

The woman smiled kindly. "I am the manager. And don't mention it. Just come back and buy something next Friday. We're having a sale on shapewear."

PEYTON MADE IT home okay, but five minutes after she got there Joe appeared on their doorstep with spooky precision again. Wyatt beckoned him in, taking the case of beer out of his hand and unloading it into the fridge, while Joe set a stack of pizza boxes on the kitchen bar.

As soon as he clocked Peyton standing near the sink, frozen in place with her iced tea halfway to her lips, he pointed an accusing finger at her.

"Hey, you were at Luisa's," he barked. "Did you like it?" And then, before she could answer, he complained, "It took me three years to find that place, and there you are, waltzing in after two days."

Peyton couldn't decide if Joe meant it as some kind of message or not. There was nothing in his expression to indicate that he'd been following her before, and she hadn't had time to examine the photos on her phone yet.

"It…it was great," she stammered, confused. "I guess I got lucky. It looked popular, so I figured…"

Bennett had shuffled into the room soon after Joe, scratching his neck like he'd just woken up. "Wait, you guys *both* went to Luisa's today? What the hell, man. No one got me anything?"

"I brought three fucking pies," Joe complained, "And more beer. If you wanted tacos, you could've gotten them yourself." He edged around Wyatt to pull a beer from the refrigerator, then tossed the cap in the trash before going into the living room.

The other two followed him to the couch, continuing to bicker over game snacks and which team was predicted to win that night.

Peyton decided to linger, keeping her head down and pulling out ingredients for the meal she'd planned to make that evening since they hadn't offered her any pizza. While she worked, she listened to the guys talk and tried to get a better feel for Joe's personality.

It didn't take long for him to stalk into the kitchen, assess what she was doing, and demand, "You don't like pizza?"

Even after she'd accepted a plate from him, he kept popping in, purportedly to fetch utensils, plates, and napkins but rattling Peyton with the way he was so obviously keeping tabs on her.

Once the game on tv got underway, she rushed through her prep work and cooking as unobtrusively as possible. She'd made the mistake of sharing her lasagne with Wyatt and Bennett the day before, and had been unprepared for how much the two could put away.

They'd demolished it, and there'd been nothing left to save for Buck. So now, Peyton was careful to set aside a portion for herself to eat the next day, and quietly stored the rest in the freezer with the other meals she'd cooked for Buck's return.

Peyton had no idea what he'd endured this week, and she was determined to welcome him home properly. She did not want Buck to have any second thoughts about moving in with her and feeding him seemed like as good a way to convince him as any.

Once she'd cleaned up after herself, Peyton hovered at the side of the living room with a mug of tea and announced, "Hey, thanks for the pizza, but I'm pretty beat. I think I'm going to turn in early."

None of them said much—they were too busy bellowing about a bogus call in the game—but at least Wyatt acknowledged her with a small wave. Peyton returned it and slipped down the hall to lock Buck's bedroom door behind her, still unsure if Joe was someone she had to worry about.

She was disappointed, too. She'd hoped Buck would come back tonight, but it looked like she was going to have to bide her time a bit longer.

PEYTON HADN'T LIED—she *was* exhausted, enough that she'd dozed off easily, despite the noise. She jolted awake sometime later to a loud burst of laughter in the living room, followed by the sound of the front door slamming and heavy footsteps moving around.

The party sounded like it had gained strength, but she had no desire to go out and investigate. It was too cozy here in bed, and she didn't want to change out of her pajamas.

The tea she'd left on the night table had gone cold, though. Peyton debated whether she wanted it enough to go heat it up in the microwave, or whether she should just pour it down the bathroom sink. She didn't want to attract bugs, but she also didn't want to walk through a crowd of strange men to toss it out in the kitchen.

The knob on the door rattled abruptly, as someone tried to force open her door. Peyton jumped and let out a startled gasp, then clapped her hand over her mouth. Her light was off. As far as anyone knew, she was still asleep in here.

Next came a knock, strong and demanding. Peyton wondered irrationally if it was Joe. Somehow it had sounded as brusque as he was, but she didn't answer, hoping he'd go away.

Whoever was out there was not deterred. They called to the people in the living room in a deep, irritated voice, but between the barrier of the door and the cacophony of jeering, Peyton couldn't make out the words.

Maybe someone was looking for the bathroom. Wyatt or Bennett would set them straight.

Heavy boots stomped off, then returned a moment or two later. Peyton pulled the comforter around her shoulders and blinked at the line of light glowing under her door, and the dark shadow in the center of it.

On top of the dresser, her phone dinged suddenly, making her jump again. She scrambled out of bed and snatched it off the bureau, looking to see who'd texted her.

It was Buck, saying simply, Let me in.

Peyton's fingers trembled as she tapped out, Where are you?

Outside the door. Why are you locked in there?

She shook her head in confusion. In where?

My room! Unlock the door, you goofball!

Peyton yelped in relief. Wait, really?

Buck hollered from the hall, punctuating his words with a single thump that might very well have been his head against the door. "Woman, have you lost your mind? Open up!"

Peyton threw off the covers and launched herself toward his voice.

He was home. Finally, he was home.

Chapter Seventeen

Buck

BY THE TIME Black Watch's plane set down in San Diego, Buck was tired and hungry and more than ready to be home. He'd spent the flight from Wyoming getting to know Noah a bit better and had accepted a ride home in the borrowed hatchback the kid had left in long-term parking.

As they exited the airport, it had occurred to Buck that he still didn't know how he was going to explain his radio silence to Peyton. He'd powered down his cell before he left home and hadn't touched the thing since, because he'd wanted to prevent anyone from geotracking him and using it to link him to Monroe.

But the entire time he'd been in Wyoming, enjoying five-star accommodations and outlandishly expensive steak, he'd felt guilty that Peyton was spending her first few days in Cali surrounded by barely housetrained SEALs with far too much time on their hands.

It should've been him there, getting her settled and showing her around. It killed Buck to think that Peyton might already be doubting whether the move was a good idea—doubting whether she was a priority for him at all.

Yes, he'd left on the day Peyton arrived—and yes, he'd gone dark for the duration. That didn't mean he didn't care. He couldn't exactly use the bad cell reception excuse, either. It didn't apply to hotel landlines.

"You alright?" Noah finally asked after Buck had started stewing in earnest.

Buck looked over. "Not really. I need a good reason for why I didn't call Peyton this whole time, but I've got no ideas that aren't bald-faced lies," he said.

Noah pushed his glasses up his nose and peered at the road sign. "Did you tell her where you were going?"

"No, of course not."

"Then I'd leave it be. She has no reason to think you were in a resort instead of a hot zone. She probably won't even ask."

Buck gaped at him, the perfect, simple logic taking him by surprise.

If Noah was correct, the problem he'd been mulling over didn't even exist. Still, it took Buck the entire ride home to get his game face on, to feel confident that he could play his role without giving anything away.

He did not want to deceive Peyton, but she'd be safer if he kept her clear of his messes. So Buck said goodbye to Noah a couple of blocks east of his apartment complex and marched the rest of the way to his place determined to protect her.

But she didn't greet him when he came in, as he'd expected. Instead, Buck walked directly into a football playoff party in his living room, with no sign of his girlfriend anywhere.

He dropped his bag next to the door and looked around. It took a minute for his presence to register, at which point he was greeted with a chorus of groans from several of the men in the room.

"Ah, shit. He's home," bitched Wyatt.

Bennett bellowed, "No! You may *not* come back yet. Turn right around and walk out that door, sir."

And from Joe, a terse but heartfelt grumble, "Mother*fucker*. Already?"

Buck planted his feet and scowled. "Nice to see you too, assholes." He looked down the hall, searching for signs that Peyton had moved in as planned, when someone with a death wish whipped a crushed beer can at his chest.

"The fuck?" he barked, irritated by the chilly reception. Buck had been gearing up for hugs and kisses and instead, he got the damn circus. "Where's Peyton?"

"Dude, you have no idea. She's been like, *cooking* the whole time you were gone," Wyatt said, leaning around some other guys from the squad to deliver his non sequitur. "Why did you come back?"

While that sounded tantalizing—and set off another bout of guilt about his deception—Buck was not the least bit clear on how it applied to the current question.

Besides, he'd only been gone for four days. How much could Peyton have possibly made?

"I live here," he explained unnecessarily.

With each passing second, he grew more impatient to see her. Why were there so many people sitting around? Only two of them lived here, and zero of them were his girlfriend.

"It's not like Peyton was going to let you eat any of it," Joe sneered. "All that home cooking was for Studly over there." He jerked a thumb at Buck. "She was extremely clear about it, and you know it."

Three pairs of sullen eyes shifted to him, along with several sets of amused ones.

Buck blinked. He could not tell Peyton about the filet mignon. *Ever.* She probably assumed he'd been living off MREs this whole time.

Wyatt whined, "Dude, I was wearing her down. She let us have some of that lasagne. With another day or two, I could've gotten her to share the rest with us. I just needed a little more time."

"Bullshit," Joe grumbled. "If Peyton gave you anything, it was only to shut you up."

"What are you talking about? She likes me! We get along great!"

Buck stomped further into the room and grabbed Wyatt's arm. "Hey, where is she? Is Peyton here or not?"

"I haven't seen her for a while," he shrugged. "She might've gone out."

Buck checked his watch. "It's ten o'clock. She doesn't know anyone. Where's she gonna go?"

Another shrug while Wyatt tipped back his beer. "How should I know?"

"Ben?" Buck called, over the rapid-fire play-calling blaring from the tv. "You know where she is?"

Eyes glued to the big screen dominating the wall, Bennett tipped his chin toward Buck's room. "She said she was tired. Went to bed early."

The room erupted into cheers over a touchdown or some shit and Buck sighed heavily. No way could Peyton sleep through this racket. They'd have to move out of here before she killed someone.

Before he left, he asked, "Anything interesting happen while I was gone?"

"We all died of boredom," Bennett snorted. He couldn't say more, not with the other guys from the squad there, but he cut a look at Buck that told him all was well.

Buck strode down the hall and tried his door, and was unsurprised to find it locked. No woman in her right mind would leave things unsecured with this much testosterone swirling around, and the lock seemed as good an indicator as any that Peyton was, in fact, inside.

Buck went to grab his bag, argued with the group some more when he asked them to pipe down, then went back to his door. He pulled his phone out of his jacket, powered it up, and skimmed through the cute messages Peyton had sent him since she'd arrived.

Once he was up to speed, he texted her—which was nearly as exasperating as his conversation with the guys had been. When Buck finally got her to open the door, he dropped his stuff in the corner, shucked his jacket, and reached for her.

"It's you!" she cried.

Joe sauntered down the hall behind him, no doubt heading for the can—but Peyton's eyes snapped to the open doorway at the sight of him, warily watching the guy pass.

That was weird, but it could wait. Buck couldn't.

He kicked the door shut, and told her, "Come here, gorgeous."

When she launched herself off the bed, he pulled her into a bear hug that lasted forever and planted a hungry kiss on her mouth. She was wearing one of his old t-shirts—too big on her and wickedly thin across her breasts—and some cute polka-dotted pajama bottoms. Her warm body felt amazing against his.

"It definitely doesn't suck coming home to find you in my bedroom," he told her.

She hugged him back, almost too tightly. "Oh my god, you're home. I'm so glad you're finally home."

Something in her tone sent a warning prickle down Buck's spine. "What's going on?"

"Nothing. I'm just so happy to see you."

Buck frowned at her, searching Peyton's face for clues. "Babe, this isn't 'happy to see me.' What's up? Did the guys make you uncomfortable?"

They weren't like that, though. What was more, they would've been on their best behavior knowing Peyton was Buck's girl.

She hedged. "Well…"

Buck thought about the way she'd eyed Joe just now and tried not to roar. "Joe? What did Joe do?"

"Wait. Calm down," she said quickly. "I'm not even sure it was him."

"Peyton," Buck fired back, fighting for control, "Tell me what you *think* he did."

She bit her lip, looking conflicted. "Okay, uh…my second night here, there was a man in the bushes, right out there. When he heard the guys in the living room, he took off. But then, earlier today, I was walking around downtown and I thought I saw him again. He was there with a friend and, uh…"

"*What.*"

"I thought they might be following me."

"Did they say anything?"

"No. But Joe's, like, here all the time. And I'm pretty sure he looks just like…"

Buck tried not to lose his shit, but he spun on his heel and found himself yanking Joe off the couch a heartbeat later.

"Can you account for your whereabouts for the last few days?" he demanded.

The entire room fell silent. Out of the corner of his eye, he saw Peyton tiptoe down the hall and peek around the corner, but Buck was focused on the utterly believable confusion wreathing Joe's face.

"I've either been here or on base," Joe said. "And I saw her at lunch today," he went on, nodding toward Peyton. "Bill was there. Ask him."

Buck looked over and Bill nodded, saying, "Drove him to Luisa's, then directly back to base. Tonight, I met him here, after that judo class Lieutenant Snyder does sometimes."

"Why?" Joe asked.

"Because someone who looks like you has been following Petyon."

They stared at each other for the longest moment, then swore in unison. Joe lunged for the slider in the living room, slamming it closed and locking it while Buck barked orders for everyone else to secure the perimeter.

The rapid mobilization unsettled Peyton, understandably, so Buck held her close while everyone rushed around, closing and locking bedroom and bathroom points of entry.

"Buck," she whispered next to his ear. "You're scaring me. What's going on?"

He took a deep breath, unsure how to explain. "Short answer is that we have enemies and whoever was lurking around is definitely not Joe. So, we're just going to make sure that no one out there can get to you before you can give me more details, okay?"

"Are you sure?" she wondered softly.

"I've known Joe a long time," Buck assured her. "He comes off kind of stiff sometimes, but I promise you he's as solid a guy as you'll ever meet."

Her face scrunched up in concern. "He's probably so mad that I accused him," she said. "I need to apologize."

"It's okay. He understands that you don't know him yet. I'm sure he's just worried for you, like everyone else. And at least we have a starting description to work with."

Peyton frowned and looked like she wanted to say more, but after a minute she just shook her head and buried her face in his shoulder. "This is not happening," she murmured.

"Welcome to California," Buck snorted, kissing the top of her head and rubbing her back. "And my life. At least you'll never be bored."

Inside, though, he was equal parts shaken and seething. He'd been hoping that whoever had been watching them that one night in Maryland had stayed on the east coast. The idea that they'd relocated out here, along with Buck and his squad—and Peyton, an innocent in all this—was enough to make his head explode.

Senator Doggett and al Kadir, or whoever was playing this cat and mouse game, might think they had the upper hand, but they were wrong. Buck and his squad, along with Tate Monroe and the team at Black Watch, did not intend to lay down quietly.

Soon it would be time to make that clear.

TWO HOURS LATER, the apartment had emptied of guests, and Buck and Peyton were finally able to sit on his bed and catch up properly. Asking her how her flight went seemed ridiculous at this point, though, and launching directly into an interrogation of her movements over the last four days didn't feel like fair play either.

While Buck debated how to ease into things, it became clear that Peyton already had her own questions locked and loaded. They were barely settled before she wondered, "Why didn't you let me know you were on your way? Probably would've saved us all a lot of angst."

He couldn't account for the way the simple inquiry caught him off guard, and he couldn't help the nonsense that spilled out of his mouth. "I…I knew you'd want to know. I *wanted* you to know," he said. "But I sat there with my phone in my hand, and I just…" Buck shrugged. He had no idea how to say, *I didn't want to lie and I can't tell you the truth.*

"You didn't want to jinx it," Peyton commented.

"Pretty much," he agreed, relieved by the lack of judgment in her tone.

"You do know how much I like you, right?" she asked.

"I have some idea, yes."

"Then you ought to know that one phone call isn't going to break us," Peyton smiled softly. "You don't need to be superstitious—at least, not about me."

"I'll have you know that my hunches have saved my neck more than a few times."

"I don't doubt it, but this is different. Next time, just…let me know, okay? Don't make me worry longer than I have to."

In all his dithering, Buck hadn't considered her perspective in quite that way, and it knocked him back a step. "You got it," he told her.

Then he relaxed against the pillows and pulled Peyton into his lap, cradling her against his chest like he truly could shield her from everything evil in the world.

"Tell me what you've been up to," Buck said, brushing his lips against her hair and filling his lungs with her sweet scent. "Other than the creepy dude, did you make out all right this week?"

"Yeah, it's been fine. Bennett picked me up from the airport and we stopped for sushi on the way home. It was a nice place. We sat outside on this cute patio with fairy lights in the trees. You and I should go back sometime."

Buck chuckled, picturing Ben trying to be polite while he poked suspiciously at his food.

"What? Was that too date-y?"

"I'll say. Ben hates sushi."

"Are you kidding?" Peyton cried. "He never said a word!"

"Probably because I threatened grave bodily harm if he didn't take you where you wanted. Happy to see he can follow orders."

"Buck," she scolded, "Don't you think that was a bit much?"

"No?" he laughed.

"You should apologize," Peyton complained. "That one is not on me."

He shook his head, knowing Bennett would've done the same. "Don't worry about it. Tell me what else happened."

"Nothing much. I went grocery shopping, slept a ton, and looked through apartment and job listings. This morning I hung out at the beach and people-watched for a while."

"I saw that. Thanks for the photos, pretty girl."

"You're very welcome," she winked, then gestured to a stack of plastic-covered hardbacks on the bedside table. "I found a cool library, too. I want to go back soon."

Buck snagged a thick book on European post-war economics off the top, then peered at the one beneath it. A couple of ripped models were scowling on the cover, slightly sinister-looking in their low-rise leather pants.

"*Princes of Darkness?*" he inquired wryly. "Plural?"

She snatched the economics book from him, flushing an impressive red as she placed it carefully over the shirtless wonders again. "Never you mind. It's for a project I'm working on."

"Project," Buck repeated, laughing and nipping at her neck.

Peyton smirked. "Yes. I'm helping dismantle the patriarchy."

He snorted, but their back-and-forth was ridiculously entertaining. "Pro tip—that job might require more than one cute professor with a library book."

"Oh, don't worry," Peyton waved airily. "There's a ton of us. You guys are doomed."

"Awesome. I'll tell the other—" Buck broke off when his stomach growled too loudly to ignore. "Sorry. I'm famished. What time is it, anyway?"

She yawned and looked at her phone. "12:30."

"That late? Damn. I meant to eat when I got home."

"That's my fault," Peyton groaned, cheeks blooming pink again. "I can't believe you guys launched into full lockdown mode like that."

"Better we overreact and keep you safe than sit back and let something preventable happen."

She accepted the explanation without noticeable qualms, then pushed off his lap. "There're eggs in the fridge. You want me to scramble you some?"

"No, babe—you get some sleep," Buck told her. "I'll grab something quick and be right back."

She rolled her eyes. "You're hungry. Let me feed you." With that, Peyton marched out of his room, as determined in her pajamas as some men were in uniform.

Buck trailed after her with a smile, the promise of a midnight breakfast too tempting to resist. If they worked together, they could hit the sack even sooner.

Peyton had to be exhausted after worrying someone was following her the last few days. Buck was, too. He couldn't wait to crash in his own bed tonight, with a full stomach and his arms wrapped around his woman. And if some fucker decided to pay her another visit, he'd have to go through Buck to do it.

Come morning, should Buck and Peyton still be tangled up in each other...well, he knew how to navigate that, as well. He hadn't had a chance to welcome Peyton to Cali properly yet, after all. Time to do it right.

They snuck out to the condo's kitchen, Peyton stumbling a bit through the dark living room, where Joe was murmuring in his sleep on the couch.

She turned on the nightlight over the stove, then found the eggs in the fridge. Buck got the frying pan out of the cabinet, added a pat of butter to it, and set it on the stove just as she winced and caught the edge of the counter.

When she hobbled over to get a bowl, his brain finally caught up to what his subconscious had clocked five minutes ago. "Hey. When did you hurt yourself?"

"What?" Peyton looked startled—and cagey.

"You're limping," he pointed out. "Why?"

"Oh. That," she hedged. "Uh…I twisted my ankle earlier. It's nothing."

She shuffled to a drawer, pulling out a whisk and a spatula, but the pool of illumination cast by the nightlight was enough for Buck to see her lopsided gait and her grim expression.

"Babe. What happened?"

"I told you," she murmured. "I turned my ankle this morning. I'm sure it'll be better tomorrow." With jerky movements, she started cracking eggs into the bowl.

It didn't take a rocket scientist to figure out that her explanation was only part of the truth if any. "What aren't you telling me?" Buck prodded when she didn't elaborate.

He stared at the back of her head until she turned around. Peyton took one look at his face, huffed out a weak laugh, and tossed the whisk in the sink.

"I just…hit the curb weird when I ran across the street," she said, eyes skating away. "I tripped. That's all."

Buck walked over, turned off the stove, and moved the pan to a cold burner. He turned Peyton toward him, and as gently as possible told her, "Okay. Now the rest."

"It's so stupid," she muttered, a hint of fear creeping into her eyes.

He frowned, trying to piece the puzzle together. "I bet it's not."

She chewed on her lip, then blurted in a rush, "The guy from the patio…Buck, he was staring at me with the creepiest look on his face. So when I thought I saw him again today, it totally freaked me out. I thought he was Joe, and *that* freaked me out. So, I ran."

"That's good. Always trust your gut. Don't get caught alone."

Peyton blinked, like the affirmation was unexpected. But then she continued, "Anyway, I crossed right as the light changed, and I tripped on the opposite curb. But there was too much traffic for the guys to follow me right away, so I don't think they saw where I went. I hid out for a long time, just in case, though."

"And you don't know if they followed?" Buck asked.

She shook her head, pensively lining up the spatula with the chrome edge of the range. "No. When I left, the manager let me go out the back. I don't think the men were around, but I'm doubting myself about a lot of it now."

Buck scanned Peyton's posture and the tiny quiver of her chin. *Something* was going on—that much was clear. "Where did you hide?"

"A lingerie store's bathroom."

Buck tried to hold back the laugh that bubbled out of him but didn't quite manage it. "Seriously?"

"Yep," she admitted sheepishly. "I know better than to lead some weirdo right to my house, and the store was busy. Great sale on bras."

Buck rubbed his hand across his mouth, but it didn't erase the confusing mix of mirth and doubt he was feeling. "Babe, I'm so sorry I wasn't with you. It sounds like you were really scared."

Peyton nodded mutely, turning the heat back on under the frying pan and adding the eggs and some shredded cheese. While she pushed things around with the spatula, Buck wrapped his arms around her waist and rested his chin lightly on her head. "I need to ask you a question."

"Shoot."

"Anything like this ever happen to you before?"

There was the briefest pause, then Peyton said, "No. Never." She didn't sound terribly convincing, but she still tacked on, "I'm sure I was just jumpy after that dude showed up outside the other night."

"Understandable," Buck agreed. He kept his tone as soothing as possible, but the flash of amusement he'd felt at her going to ground amidst the lace and satin panties had evaporated nearly as quickly as it'd appeared.

He gritted his teeth, feeling fury take its place. A pair of strangers following her downtown, coming on the heels of someone lurking outside the apartment, was too much of a coincidence—particularly after that incident back in Maryland.

When he thought he could fake calm again, Buck let her go, shoved a few slices of rye into the toaster, and leaned against the counter. "Tell me again what the guys looked like."

Peyton sighed and hung her head. "Like…Joe, I guess. Average build. Dark wavy hair. Sort of tan. One guy was a little taller and looked older." She turned off the burner with a decisive snap, moved the frying pan off the heat, and wheeled to reach for a couple of plates in the cabinet beside her.

The extra weight on her foot made her gasp, though she tried like hell to hide it.

Buck sighed and shook his head. "Stay there," he ordered, then trotted back to his bathroom for the first aid kit.

He couldn't decide who was fucking with him and, by extension, his girl—so he was going to have to work out his frustrations by wrapping Peyton's ankle and feeding her breakfast in the middle of the goddamn night.

Tomorrow morning, though? The gloves were coming off.

Chapter Eighteen

Peyton

PEYTON WOKE TO another hazy California morning, wide rays of light slanting through the blinds and across Buck's bed. She was too warm and not a little exasperated. The sheer *sunniness* of it seemed egregious, given how far into the night they'd been…not sleeping.

Turning away from the worst of the glare, however, made it clear she had bigger problems. Not only was Buck's side of the bed empty, but the rest of the room was so utterly still that he had to be gone.

Peyton blinked away her disappointment. He'd just gotten home. She'd hoped to have a lazy morning or two with him before he had to leave again.

Maybe he was just running an errand, or on the other side of the apartment, brewing her coffee.

Peyton's eyes landed on her phone, set precisely in the center of his pillow. She snatched it up and scanned the screen, where a text from Buck was waiting for her.

Morning, Gorgeous.

She rolled to her back and smiled, a nicer kind of warmth filling her chest. She swiped on the message and saw that he'd sent it more than an hour earlier—Buck had gotten even less sleep than she had.

Wincing in sympathy, she typed, Empty bed. So lonely. :(

Buck's response pinged almost immediately, like he'd been waiting for her. Temporary situation. In my mind, I'm still wrapped around you like a cheap suit.

Peyton grinned at the image that elicited, then tapped the icon to flip the camera around. She snapped a quick selfie and sent it to him, and as she'd hoped, little reply dots started blinking a second later.

It's me. Pick up.

A scant second later, her phone started ringing, his number flashing across her screen.

"Hey."

Buck didn't waste time with preliminaries. "Even when I'm not there in body, I'll always be there in spirit. Sorry I had to leave, babe."

"It's okay," Peyton told him, a little loopy from his sweet reassurance. "What happened? Where'd you go?"

"Took a little run. You looked so comfortable—I didn't have the heart to wake you."

"I appreciate that. I needed the sleep."

"I figured."

Peyton could hear cars in the background, and possibly the ocean. She pictured Buck standing on the beach, shirtless and sweaty, and wished she'd been awake to go with him. There was no way she could've kept up, but at least she could've ogled him from a bench or something.

"Hey," he said suddenly, I just had an idea. What's your favorite donut flavor?"

"Boston cream," she said. "No question. Why?"

"Wait and see," he laughed. "I'll be home in a bit."

Peyton flopped to her back, grinning from ear to ear. Hopefully, she had enough time to haul herself out of bed, shower, and down some much-needed coffee before Buck arrived with his treats.

They hadn't discussed their plans for the day yet, but she was more than ready to tackle some sightseeing with him. Maybe Buck would go back to the library with her, or drive around to investigate neighborhoods they could move to. They could walk around one of the local colleges, so she had a better idea of where to apply for jobs.

There were undoubtedly places he wanted to take her, too, destinations she didn't even know about yet.

It wasn't until she was standing under the hot spray of the shower that Peyton's guilt caught up with her enthusiasm. Somewhere out there, her boyfriend was probably buying her favorite donut.

Within the walls of this apartment, there were another two or three men who had gone out of their way to make her feel safe last night, and who would undoubtedly rush to her aid again if the lurker ever reappeared.

Peyton hoped the people who'd followed her gave up trying to get close because Buck and his friends would make their lives a holy hell if they caught them. Because of her.

She cringed, her shame from last night coming back tenfold. Peyton had to say something to Buck, at a minimum—and soon. He deserved to know who he was living with, and what he'd be up against if the people Peyton had angered with her reckless words ever found her.

Bennett and Wyatt and Joe deserved the same. Their lives could easily be turned upside down, the same way hers had.

She shut off the water, wrapped a towel around herself, and went to sit on the bed. With a glance at the time, Peyton grabbed her laptop off the nightstand and booted it up.

Seconds later, she was staring at her blog's homepage and biting her lip with indecision. She should shut the whole thing down. Just deep-six the entire site and walk away. There'd be snippets out there in the ether that she couldn't do anything about, but at least the originals would be toast.

All that work, down the drain.

It felt so confusing to skim her entries now, knowing the kind of people Buck and his friends were. There had to be hundreds more just like them in the world, leaving their loved ones behind to fight hidden battles for the common good.

Of course, there were bad apples. Every profession had them, because humans were, by nature, flawed. But Peyton had painted *all* special operators with the same critical brush, and she had a sick feeling in the pit of her stomach now, realizing how wrong she had been.

The front door squeaked open on the other side of the apartment, and she jumped up guiltily.

Buck was home.

Peyton slammed her computer shut and shoved it under the econ book from the library, then darted into the bathroom to throw on her clothes. She was combing out her wet hair when Buck sauntered in, flushed and sweating from his run.

"Best Boston cream you've ever eaten is in the kitchen," he grinned, leaning in the doorway. "Along with a latte, since I finished the last of the coffee before I took off earlier."

"Aww, thanks."

He pulled a bouquet of peonies from behind his back and said, "These are for you, too, pretty girl. I'm sorry I wasn't here to greet you with them last week."

Peyton nearly choked on the lump of guilt trying to climb up her throat. "Thank you. They're beautiful."

"Give me five to clean up?" he asked, leaning in to peck her cheek, but trying not to get her sweaty.

"Of course. I'll need more than that to assess whether those donuts are up to my standards, anyway," she told him.

"Fair enough. After you've filed your report, I thought we could get out and see the town. What do you say?"

"Can't wait," she smiled back, but inside…inside, Peyton wanted to cry.

She was the very worst person in the world for lying to him. She didn't deserve Buck in the least, and she wondered how disappointed he'd be when she finally told him the truth.

PEYTON'S GUILT ATE at her for most of the day. So that night, while Buck was in the shower, she flipped open her computer and set up a hasty post to her blog. It would take time and an expert to erase the whole thing from the face of the earth but for now, she could simply tell people the blog was on hiatus.

Peyton checked to make sure the viral article was still inaccessible to anyone but her, then quickly archived several more posts for good measure. She'd closed the editing portal and was getting ready to sign out when Buck suddenly flopped down beside her.

"Look at you, all smart and sexy," he grinned. Then his eyes fell on her screen, where the homepage of her blog was still prominently centered.

Peyton gulped. "Uh…"

"*Global Lens?*" he spat. "I'm surprised you'd give that piece of shit the time of day."

She blinked at his venom. In the entire time she'd known him, Buck hadn't gotten so angry about anything. It seemed to come out of left field.

"You…you know this…this blog?" she stammered.

"Wish I didn't. The internet is full of crackpots like that, though. Running their mouths and acting tough behind their little keyboards, but half the fuckers wouldn't know their ass from a hole in the wall."

Peyton stared at her screen for a long moment. He knew her blog. Buck *knew her blog*. And he despised it.

"Why…why do you hate this one so much?" She clicked the keys to shut down her computer and tried to keep him from seeing the way her hands were shaking.

"Long story," Buck seethed, "But suffice it to say, that little shit nearly tanked my career." He glanced at her and paused, seeming to come back to his usual demeanor with a deep breath and a shake of his head. "Sorry, babe. That got away from me. I've got some history with that site, and seeing it took me a little by surprise."

Peyton set her laptop aside and gripped her hands tightly together in her lap, fighting to keep calm. *Global Lens* had always felt a bit like screaming into the void. She'd worked hard on her articles, and but for one inexplicable exception, no one had ever given her the time of day.

The notion that her words had any impact whatsoever on real people, trying to do their jobs in a messy, chaotic world, had never once occurred to her. The idea that one of those real people would end up being a man she cared an awful lot about was fantasy in the extreme.

And yet, here Peyton was. It had been hard enough to envision telling Buck who she was when *Global Lens* meant nothing to him. Trying to picture it now, with the knowledge that he had a personal grudge against it, was near impossible.

"Why were you reading it, anyway?" Buck wondered.

"It's my field," Peyton responded numbly. "I follow a lot of stuff like that. I think it's important to look at all sides of the issues."

"No doubt. But someone needs to put a bullet in that fucker. They're playing with fire and people are getting hurt because of it."

She sat there, panicked and chagrined by Buck's ire. They'd had such a nice day—the best of days, in fact. Now, she couldn't make herself sit next to him a second longer.

"I'm going to brush my teeth," she said, jumping up. "Be right back." *After she'd pulled herself together, anyway.*

Safe in the bathroom, Peyton stared at her reflection and tried to figure out a way through this mess. Her thoughts were whirling, but as she washed her face and flossed, they settled into something resembling sense.

She had to find out what Buck's issue with her blog was. If she knew why he'd reacted the way he had, maybe it would show her a way to explain her side of things.

It was a long shot, but it was all she had.

Peyton dropped her toothbrush in the glass on the sink, smiling sadly at the way it immediately dropped to the side to rest next to Buck's. Even her toothbrush wanted to be close to him.

After another minute or two, she straightened her shoulders and opened the door. The bedroom was dark.

Buck could fall asleep at the drop of a hat, so Peyton slipped into bed as quietly as she could, in case he'd nodded off waiting for her.

She was so focused on not waking him, she failed to notice that Buck was still propped up on some pillows against the wall—exactly where she'd left him.

An instinctual jolt of fright had her sucking in a huge lungful of air, but the backend scream never came because Buck's hand dropped over her mouth and pressed firmly against her lips.

Peyton's eyes went wide, and her fear tightened around her. She twisted around to push at Buck's chest, trying to gain purchase with her legs, but he rolled over her, neatly pinning her in place with his heavier frame.

A thousand thoughts crashed together like bumper cars in her brain. He'd found out about her blog. He was having a waking nightmare or an episode of PTSD. He'd made her fall for him so he could lure her out here and kill her.

Or maybe Peyton was wrong, and it wasn't really Buck holding her down. It could be his evil twin that no one liked to talk about. The man from the patio, or even the one who'd shown up in the lecture hall at MCC, with the unnerving stare.

Buck let more of his weight drop onto her, flattening Peyton beneath him and nearly pushing the air from her lungs. He put his mouth against her ear, his breath hot as he murmured, "Don't move," so quietly she was surprised she heard it at all over the cacophony in her brain.

She tried to tell him it was okay, that it was just her and not an intruder or an enemy. Buck shook his head and pressed his hand a little harder against her mouth.

"Shh," he breathed against her ear, before pressing a—was that a *kiss?*—against her cheekbone.

Now Peyton was confused, on top of scared. Was this some kind of sex ambush? Was it a role-play, was he a sadist, did he…?

Buck's body against hers, his lips on her ear…it should've been hot. But this was terrifying.

At last, he spoke again. "Someone's outside," he whispered. "When I say go, get on the floor next to the bed and stay there. Okay? Stay there and don't make a sound."

Peyton's eyes rolled toward the window. Was there a darker shadow moving among the bushes and trees? She wasn't sure. But the sliding glass door was wide open, and if someone *was* out there, all they had to do was waltz right in.

She nodded quickly. Maybe Buck had stepped outside and seen something while she'd been in the bathroom.

"Now," Buck hissed, shoving her toward the far wall and launching himself at the patio in one efficient explosion of movement.

Peyton slid to the floor and crawled as close as she could to the bedframe, but it sat too low to the ground for her to fit underneath. She didn't hear much out of the ordinary outside—a breeze rustling the leaves on the palm trees. A car passing on the street, music thumping.

The door to the bedroom creaked open, and she shrank down. The comforter was already hanging half off the bed above her, so she reached up and tugged it over her, hoping the mass would obscure her shape in the dark.

The light in the hall went out, and Bennett stuck his head in the opening. "Peyton," he whispered. "You good?"

"Yes."

"Stay put for a couple more minutes, okay? I'll be out here in case they circle back."

"What's going on?" she asked him softly.

If he'd heard her, Bennett didn't answer. She couldn't hear him at all, only the sound of a commercial playing on the tv in the living room.

It felt like an eternity before Buck finally stepped back through the door, sliding the screen and the door closed and locking them behind him.

He closed the blinds, then snapped on the bedside lamp. "Babe," he called. "You still here?"

Peyton pushed off the comforter and sat up, heart hammering in her chest. "Buck, what's going on?"

With the light on, it was clear that he'd thrown on a pair of sweat shorts at some point after she'd gone into the bathroom. Other than those, it seemed he'd been running around out there without a shirt or shoes—not that he appeared to care.

Buck darted for her, breathing hard. "Sorry," he said, falling to his knees next to her. "I'm so sorry. Did I scare you?"

All Peyton could do was nod. "What's happening?"

He exhaled, reaching out to tuck her hair behind her ear. "I stepped out for a minute to cool off. Dude was creeping around out there again. So I came in and laid down, then texted Joe and Wyatt to meet me out back. Ben was supposed to watch you in case anyone tried to double back."

"He did."

"Did you see anyone?"

Peyton gestured to the bedding mounded around her. "No. But I didn't have the best view."

For the first time, Buck's face relaxed into a smile. "Nice ghillie suit, by the way."

She couldn't return the amusement. This had gotten too far out of hand. "Did you catch the guy?"

"No. He took off like a jackrabbit and disappeared. He must've had a car waiting."

Buck and his roommates thought there was someone after them, but Peyton knew better. She couldn't let this go on any longer, no matter what the consequences turned out to be. She had to say something.

"Listen, Buck—I have to tell you something."

There was a knock on the door, and this time it was Joe who stuck his head in. "Hey, Buck? Can I talk to you for a sec?"

Buck sighed and stood, looking sympathetically at Peyton. "Give me a minute?"

"Yeah. Go." She stood up and started to set the bed to rights. Was there any way to convince the guys that the person who kept showing up was after her, not them—without telling them why?

She didn't think so.

And if she had to tell them about the blog, then she was going to have to face Buck's wrath when he found out that the real enemy wasn't lurking out there in the oleander bushes—she'd been right here in his bed the whole time.

Chapter Nineteen

Buck

B UCK STEPPED INTO the living room to find Bennett, Wyatt, and Joe standing in a loose knot, staring down at a clear baggie in Wyatt's hands. They broke apart and fanned out when he murmured, "Hey."

Bennett looked past him down the hall. "Peyton doin' okay in there?"

"Seems to be," Buck said. "I was confirming when Bruiser busted in with his summons to the party."

Joe shrugged. "It seemed important."

Buck scowled at him. "Define *it.*"

Wyatt extended the bag he was holding while Joe explained, "Peyton's new buddy left a note on one of the chairs. I found it on my way back in."

Buck took the thing by the edges and looked it over. At first glance, it seemed like nothing more than a sheet of notebook paper sealed in a sandwich bag, with a few lines of handwriting scrawled across the center. The cramped penmanship screamed male, but that didn't necessarily mean anything. People altered things like that all the time.

The note read, "*We have a common interest. Let us arrange a meeting somewhere private and safe, so we can join forces against our shared enemy.*"

Buck looked up and laughed. "It's a joke. This is a joke, right?"

Wyatt frowned. "I don't think so."

"I admit it's a little goofy, but we still ought to have someone look at the handwriting and dust for prints. Just to make sure," Joe said.

"Joe's right," Wyatt chimed in. "Those people you know can do stuff like that, right?"

Buck scanned the note again, searching for signs that this was a legitimate offer instead of a prank—or worse, a trap of some kind. "I don't like this," he grumbled.

Whoever's operatives had been toying with him in Maryland had made the jump to the west coast, and that irritated the fuck out of him. It indicated a familiarity with his movements that a random stranger should not have.

"Seems like a breakthrough to me," Bennett commented. "I'd rather the little shit deal with us directly instead of spooking Peyton every other day."

"Good point," Buck agreed. "But he didn't leave instructions. How do we reach out?"

They tossed around a few half-assed plans before Wyatt interjected, "Hang on—I've got an idea. A buddy of mine's wife is a real estate agent. You remember, Buck? The one I said I could hook you and Peyton up with?"

"Yeah."

"Well…when she has a listing and the sellers have already moved out, she keeps a keypad lock on the door in between showings. Other agents can enter the code, and the little lockbox opens with the door key."

Joe nodded, "I've seen those."

"I bet I could get her to let us use one of her listings," Wyatt went on thoughtfully. "We could leave one of her sales postcards on the chair out back. If anybody sees it, they'll assume it's junk mail we left sitting around."

"But our guy would know where to go. If we gave him a day and time, could your friend's wife block it off, so no one else shows up unexpectedly?" Bennett asked.

"I'm sure she could. She schedules the buyer agents all the time."

Buck eyed Wyatt critically. "Should I ask why she'd be willing to do that for you?"

Wyatt licked his lips and looked shifty. "She might…still be holding a little torch for me. Every once in a while, I get drunk texts from her."

Joe tossed up his hands and waved Wyatt off, booing in disgust. "Dude, she's fucking married. To your supposed friend, I might add."

"It's not like that. We only had a short thing a few years ago, before she got hitched. Besides, give me *some* credit. She and my buddy are happy. I wouldn't get in the middle of that."

"Yeah, they sound real happy," Ben muttered.

"I mean…it could work," Buck mused, pondering the details. "I like that the place would be locked up before we meet, so no one's getting in to plant bugs."

"Unless he arranges a showing or goes to an open house before us. That's what I would do," Bennett said thoughtfully. "Tricky to hide it in an empty place, but it could be done."

"He could also wear a fucking wire to the meeting," Joe complained. "You gonna strip search the guy?"

Buck shrugged. "Maybe. Let's see if he shows, first." To Wyatt, he added, "Tell her to pick a place that has no one going in or out before us. You think she'll do it without knowing the details?"

Wyatt nodded, a little sheepishly. "I do. Yes."

"Who're we talking about, anyway?" Joe demanded. "Maybe we need to vote on whether she can be trusted."

Wyatt turned a narrow gaze on him, eyes glinting dangerously. "You don't believe me?"

Buck sighed. "Don't start. Wyatt, you can give me—and only me—more details in the morning. In the meantime, I will share this development with other interested parties, but only *after* I make sure Peyton is okay."

Wyatt's forehead scrunched as he searched Buck's face. "Peyton knows about the inquiries, right? She's in the loop?"

"Uh, that's a negative. Still working on that part."

"Excuse me?" Wyatt yelped.

"Your ears work fine."

"What do you mean, *that's a negative*?" Bennett pressed. "You let the woman upend her life for you and you haven't given her a sit-rep yet? That's not like you."

Buck cracked his neck. "We haven't been together very long yet. I was trying to make sure we were solid before I started telling tales, you know?"

Joe sneered, "With all due respect, that's complete bullshit, Lieutenant. You had plenty of time to decide you wanted to play house with her. You expect us to believe you were so busy hitting it, there was not a single spare second to inform Peyton your life is FUBAR?"

Buck pinched the bridge of his nose, feeling a headache forming behind his eyes. "I know what I'm doing, *Chief.* Okay? Now can we please wrap this up?"

The three men he trusted most in the world stared back at him, but they might as well have been a hundred grandmothers judging by the weight of combined disapproval they were radiating.

"Suit yourself," Joe said eventually. "But don't come crying to me when Peyton goes running for the hills."

Wyatt smirked evilly. "Peyton, on the other hand, is welcome to come crying to me whenever the hell she wants. You better believe I'll be accepting that call."

Buck took two steps and put a finger in the man's face. "Not if you're at the bottom of the ocean, you won't."

Bennett grabbed his shoulder and yanked him back. "Down boy. Go back to your girl and take care of your shit. When she goes to sleep you can call…whoever. We'll all check back in tomorrow. Okay? *Great.*" He shoved Buck toward the hall and Wyatt toward the couch.

Joe rolled his eyes, stalked to the kitchen and grabbed his keys off the bar, then gave them a lazy salute. "I'm out," he said and marched out the front door grumbling to himself.

Buck took a couple of steps, then turned. "What about—"

Bennett groaned. "Please go. Nothing else is getting accomplished tonight, I swear. And the longer you sit out here arguing with us, the more worried Peyton is going to get in there."

Buck scratched his jaw and gave up. "Yeah. Catch you tomorrow," he said, then went to his room.

THE TELEVISION WAS on a twenty-four-hour news channel when he stepped in, the anchor looking grim as he announced, *"The congressional inquiry into a rogue SEAL team operating in the Middle East has stretched into its…"*

Buck moved in front of the screen in one big stride and hit the power button on the side of the set a split second later.

Heart hammering, he looked at Peyton. She was propped in bed hugging her knees, curled as tightly into herself as she could possibly manage. Her gaze looked haunted.

"You were watching that," he said. "Sorry."

"I wasn't paying attention. I only put it on for company."

He sat on the edge of the bed and squeezed her leg. "How're you doing?"

"Buck, we really have to talk," she told him, tearing up. "I need to—"

"Babe, I know," he interrupted, before she could tell him she'd made a terrible mistake and was leaving him. "And I am so, so sorry I scared you before. Tonight was…an unusual situation. I never have work 'follow me home,' so to speak. But someone needed to get us a message, and they wanted to backchannel it. That's all it was, I promise."

Peyton's brows came down and she started to speak, but then she clamped her mouth shut and tilted her head. She was blinking fast, something she always seemed to do when she was trying to figure things out.

"You said they needed to get *you guys* a message."

"Yep. It's not ideal that they know where we live, but that's probably why you kept seeing someone around. They were looking for me."

She looked confused. "How did they know I'd—"

"Not sure. But you can bet your cute ass I will be asking that question first."

Peyton stared at him for a long moment. "They must have seen us together in Maryland. That's the only way."

Buck had hoped she wouldn't make that connection, but he should've known better. She was way too smart for her own good, even if he adored her for it. "You could be right."

She swallowed and took a few slow breaths. "Did…did any of you guys see who it was?"

"No. The person left their note and slipped away again. That's it."

"So, now you're going to meet whoever it was and…and ask about me?"

"Among other things," Buck smiled, sliding his arm behind her back and nudging her closer.

Peyton turned and burrowed into him immediately. She asked, "When?"

"I can't tell you that. I'm sorry. You need to stay as removed from this as possible."

She nodded into his chest and held him tighter.

"You sure you're okay?"

"I'm fine," she murmured. "I think I'm crashing now that the adrenaline has worn off."

"We did a lot today, too," Buck agreed. "But I still have to run out for a couple of minutes, okay? I need to give someone the run-down on what happened tonight. You'll be safe, though. Ben and Wyatt are staying here, and they'll make sure nothing happens to you."

She looked up at him, worried all over again. "Will you be gone long?"

"Half an hour, tops," he told her. "Try to get some rest, and I'll be back before you know it."

He got up and helped Peyton under the covers, then triple-checked the locks on the window and door. Buck turned off the bedside lamp and clicked on the one in the closet so she wouldn't get scared.

"Be safe," she whispered as he headed for the door.

Buck went back over and kissed her lightly. "You got it, sweetheart."

He checked in with Bennett and Wyatt on his way out, then got in his truck and drove to an empty beachside lot that still had its entry barriers up. He sent the usual message to the secure Black Watch line, and tapped his fingers on the wheel, waiting for the callback.

The ocean was an inky smear against the horizon, the regular surge and retreat of it setting up a steady backdrop to the silence in the cab of his truck. Buck couldn't stop thinking about that look in Peyton's eyes, or the way he'd trampled all over her words to keep her from voicing what would have been utterly reasonable doubts about their fledgling relationship.

Was he really going to be the asshole who held onto her, even if it meant she'd be in danger? *Possibly.*

He groaned, dropping his head into his hands and gripping his skull to keep it from exploding. He had no idea what the fuck he was doing, and he hated it.

His cell went off in the cupholder. Buck stared at the screen for a beat or two, then grabbed it and connected the call.

"Hey, man."

"Do I even want to know?" Tate wondered.

Buck massaged his aching head, realizing for the first time that Monroe was undoubtedly in a different time zone, and therefore even less inclined to talk than he was.

"Somehow I figured you'd have people fielding your calls for you," he said. "Especially in the off hours."

"How do you know I don't?" Monroe snorted, then went on, "Maybe you're getting the VIP treatment."

"That would be a first," Buck muttered.

"Noted. Now how about telling me why you're calling."

He launched into a weary recitation of the night's events, then gave Tate the details of the plan going forward.

Monroe was quiet for a bit. "All right," he said eventually. "Go ahead and see what you get. Do you still have Noah's contact info?"

"Yeah."

"Good. Hit him up and arrange a meeting as soon as you can, but definitely before you do the other one. I want him to look over the note and see if he can pull anything from it. He'll have a few party favors you can bring along as well."

Buck sat back. He'd assumed the kid was involved strictly for his computer skills. It was startling to realize Noah had other skills, too.

"Okay."

"Anything else?"

"Only…" Buck gripped his phone, not wanting to overstep. "I need to know if we're any closer to figuring out whether we're looking at one of al Kadir's guys, or Doggett's, or what. I'm worried about Peyton. How did they know to connect the two of us, or where to find me in Maryland *or* California?"

The silence on the other end of the line stretched longer this time. When Monroe finally decided to speak, however, he wasn't exactly forthcoming. "So…I don't want to get too far out ahead of this, in case it turns out to be a dead-end, but we may be zeroing in on a couple of names. If Noah is correct, we're looking at a third option."

"What the fuck does that mean?"

"I should know more in a couple of days," Tate hedged. "No use calling out the posse until then."

Buck wanted to roar with frustration. "There has to be something we can do in the meantime. Every day the inquiry drags on is more time for Old Roy to drag us in the press. And we're going to have to testify before the Special Warfare board any day now, too."

"I get it. Meet up with whoever is behind that note. I have a feeling it's going to clear some shit up. And don't sweat the backup. Take your boys in with you and I'll put some folks outside to make sure the conversation stays friendly."

"Who is driving this inquiry train?" Buck asked, the urgency to fix this clawing under his skin like a rash.

"Got a few leads on that issue, too. Stay the course, brother. We're not going to leave you hanging in the wind. I promise."

"God, I hope you mean that," he told Monroe.

"I do."

After they hung up, Buck sat there for a few more minutes, staring out at the beach and debating what to do about Peyton. It didn't feel right keeping her in the dark, but maybe the big reveal could wait a little bit longer.

It would be a far easier tale to tell if he could make it past tense. Tacking on an 'all's well that ends well' finale would be the bow on top. And then, he and Peyton could ride off into the sunset with his conscience clear and her safety assured.

Buck nodded to himself and started his truck. It was a plan, and for now it would have to do.

Chapter Twenty

Peyton

W HEN BUCK CAME to bed an hour later, Peyton was still
stewing, getting nowhere with her rioting thoughts but
unable to stop herself. He lay beside her on the mattress and
curled carefully against her back, probably hoping she was asleep.

"I'm so glad you're here," he whispered into her hair. "And
I'm going to keep you safe. I promise."

Peyton rolled to face him. "You didn't actually think I'd leave,
did you?"

He kissed her forehead gently. "After the way things have been
going, I wouldn't blame you."

"Buck," she sighed, "I know what you do for a living. I
expected you to do stuff you couldn't tell me about."

She felt his quick laugh more than heard it. "Somewhere else,
though. Not where we live. And not your first week here."

Peyton stroked his side, the solid weight of him anchoring her
in the dark, reassuring her despite her confusion and questions.
She shrugged. "Shit happens. Doesn't help to fight it."

"Ain't that the truth." Buck touched the side of her face, then
lifted a piece of hair from her shoulder and gently wrapped it
around his finger.

She asked, "What's wrong?"

He dropped her hair and shifted closer. "I'm worried that you'll want to throw in the towel before we have a chance to make a go of this. The last week or two has been a lot, but it won't always be like this."

"No, you'll only have to leave at the drop of a hat, not be able to tell me where you're going or what you're doing, and…probably miss plenty of special occasions, too," she retorted.

Buck pulled back a few inches. "Uh—"

Peyton smiled and closed the distance between them. "I'm teasing. Like I said, I knew what I was getting into," she told him, "So you can stop worrying. We'll figure it out."

He gathered her close, enveloping her in his strength and warmth and settling her mind. "Thank you for the leap of faith."

"Ditto."

IN THE DAYS that followed Buck seemed eager to take Peyton to every one of his favorite spots around town, almost certainly trying to undo whatever damage he'd incurred with his absence the week before.

Fortunately, he also squeezed in time to help Peyton rent a storage unit because her stuff arrived on the moving truck soon after, along with her car. Buck helped supervise the unloading but grew busier as the week progressed, leaving the apartment at odd times, sometimes for hours at a stretch.

Bennett and Wyatt were the same. They came and went at a moment's notice, and were careful not to discuss specifics in front of her.

Peyton didn't want to pry—for all she knew, this was their normal routine—but she couldn't help wondering if all the strange activity stemmed from the meeting with whoever had left that note.

It was hard to wrap her mind around the notion that her "shadows" had been after Buck all along. Hadn't she been noticing them before she'd ever met him? The math didn't add up, but she couldn't deny that ever since the night of the note, she hadn't noticed anyone else following her.

Though maybe that was because she lived with a phalanx of trained killers now? Surely they would act as a deterrent if Buck's assumptions proved incorrect.

Instead of worrying about what-ifs, Peyton ought to have been taking advantage of the situation. She could have buckled down on her job search or explored on her own while Buck was out being mysterious. After all, she couldn't wait forever to figure out where she was going to work, or where they should live when they moved out.

She'd hoped Buck would be more involved on the moving front, but he didn't seem to feel a lot of urgency to get going. Peyton, on the other hand, was motivated. She wasn't used to crowded living arrangements and even though Wyatt and Bennett were freakishly neat, they took up a lot of space and teased and bickered with each other constantly.

They were relentlessly nosy, too. Even though Peyton and Buck had tried to be discreet, they'd been subjected to snide comments over coffee about their bedroom activities, and it had only gotten worse now that Joe was crashing on their couch more often.

But today—today, Peyton was blissfully on her own. She'd slept in, waiting until Buck and the others left before going to the kitchen to brew fresh coffee and eat a piece of toast.

With no real plan in place, she put on sneakers when she was done and wandered across the courtyard to the apartment complex's gym. As she pedaled on the stationary bike, Peyton's thoughts circled as well, eventually landing back on the issue of who'd been following her.

It was difficult to believe that all the time she'd thought people were after her, they'd really been trying to get to Buck. How could that be true when she had her own reason for weirdos to be harassing her? Not to mention the fact that she'd noticed having a shadow weeks before she'd met Buck.

Goosebumps erupted across her arms and Peyton pedaled faster, determined to quash the eerie feeling along with her doubts. Buck knew what he was doing. He wouldn't tell her she was safe if she wasn't, even without understanding her connection to *Global Lens*.

She was happy she hadn't jumped the gun and shut down her whole blog, though. If Buck was right and her recent woes were all about him, then Peyton could still go back and unarchive articles after this whole thing was over.

Maybe she really would ride out her crazy notoriety and recover from Joely Spitz's interference in her life. She might even get the chance to turn *Global Lens* into the respected voice she'd always hoped it would become.

The A/C kicked on suddenly, and the vent overhead turned the sweat on her back to ice. Peyton stabbed a few buttons to end the cycling program, got off the bike, and drifted over to the weight machines in the corner.

Hope felt like a tricky thing, but as she settled into a set of lat pulldowns Peyton allowed herself to indulge in a tiny bit of it. Perhaps her luck had finally turned and her life was going to start making sense again.

How else could she explain meeting a man like Buck amidst the chaos? It had to be an improbability of lightning strike proportions.

And later, once everything blew over, perhaps she'd find a way to laugh about her bizarre brush with infamy. She could join a recovery group for former internet sensations, and make friends with other hapless souls brought low by virality.

Peyton caught her expression in the mirror on the wall and snorted. That was so not going to happen.

Over her shoulder, she saw a couple of guys come strutting in, arguing about football and slyly peeking at her when they thought she wasn't looking. It wasn't hard to tell they were the type to offer unsolicited exercise advice, so she grabbed her keys and water bottle and ducked out without finishing her workout.

Surprisingly, she still had the apartment to herself. With a happy sigh, she left her keys on the counter and tossed together a rice bowl with last night's leftovers, then carried it to Buck's room and set it on the bureau to cool while she took a quick shower.

Afterward, she sat on the bed in her towel and turned on the tv, flipping through channels while she ate her lunch. It was nice to be completely alone. She'd gotten used to it in Maryland, and liked the feeling of just existing, free from judgment or expectations.

When Peyton recognized who the news channel was interviewing, however, she nearly choked on her bite of steak. None other than Joely Spitz sat across from that reporter—her long, highlighted curls spilling in a mane over her shoulder, her utility pants and hiking boots more suited to the places she filmed her documentaries than to the elegant seating area of the set.

The camera zoomed in on Joely's expressive face as she talked, and Peyton peered at it with interest. Before today, she'd only seen still photos of her, searched out online once she'd figured out who was responsible for dropping the bomb in the middle of her life. It was fascinating to see the woman in 3D now, to hear her husky voice and see the way she worked the camera.

Joely was a pro, that much was clear. She understood how to angle her head, when to chuckle through a response and when to look somber. She fielded every question as easily as if she'd had a year to study her responses.

Maybe she had. It certainly sounded as if she had a preexisting report with her interviewer, a handsome middle-aged woman in pearls and a lavender twinset. There was a wink-wink quality to their back and forth, a cozy sense that the women were, if not actual friends, at least in on the same joke.

Peyton forced herself to pay attention to their actual words, instead of the theater of their performance. They seemed to be discussing the way manufacturing companies could transform the towns they were based in, and focusing on one entity in particular.

"Have you documented much pushback from the surrounding community?" the interviewer asked. *"Any 'Not in My Backyard' sentiment interfering with Landry Cox's expansion?"*

"We haven't. But remember, this part of West Virginia is not at all like the cities and suburbs that line the coasts. The people here are, for the most part, very comfortable with guns. And Landry Cox employs more than half the adult residents of Hyersville, many of whom have grown up hunting and target shooting as a way of life. So guns are not the enemy—they're a familiar part of day-to-day life, and not demonized for the mistakes of reckless humans."

"Even the newer assault models that Landry Cox has begun to churn out?"

Joely smiled, smug and superior in her armchair. *"Even those."*

There was a split second where something flickered under the surface of the interviewer's expression, but she was too suave to let it rise to the surface. She simply turned to the camera and told her audience, *"We had the opportunity to speak with Dan Cox, the director of administration at Landry Cox. He had this to say about the people of Hyersville."*

Peyton watched as the face of a skeevy man filled the screen, spewing nonsense about how close he'd grown to the Hyersville residents, and how much he admired their "pioneer spirits."

"My deep respect for these folks made the decision easy," he said. *"Once I got to know them, no way was I going to put them out of work by hiring from somewhere else. Not when we could invest in training these good people to run the new equipment and assembly lines themselves. It's just good business."*

Peyton grunted in disgust. She'd bet her life savings that Dan Cox spent more time schmoozing in country clubs than in the company of his workers, but he made it sound like he was getting named godfather for their babies right and left.

The camera cut back to the interviewer, who made vague references to contradicting opinions, then quickly pivoted to a topic she found a bit juicier.

"Joely…we've heard from a few sources that Dan Cox has befriended more than the people of Hyersville. Is it true that during filming you and he also became close? Maybe…more than close?" Her large blue eyes crinkled at the corners as she delivered the softball that Joely tried to look coy about, but was absolutely waiting for.

"I think that falls outside the scope of this interview," Joely said, but her smirk communicated everything that her words did not.

Peyton swallowed hard when the woman pushed her hair over her shoulder, casually flashing the gargantuan rock on her finger in the process. Viewers on the moon could've seen that stone, and that was definitely Joely's intention.

Peyton set aside her food so she wouldn't be tempted to throw it at the screen. She'd been living on a razor's edge for months, fretting constantly that her real identity was about to be exposed. She'd spent countless sleepless nights wondering when she would be fired before it had come to pass for real.

Peyton had been terrified by threatening calls and emails, by strangers showing up at her work and her home, trying to take her picture. And this…this…*caricature* had been out in the world living her best life, getting engaged to the subject of one of her documentaries.

Joely Spitz probably didn't feel one speck of remorse for her careless distortion of Peyton's ideas. She probably didn't remember Peyton's involvement at all.

Well, Peyton remembered. For the rest of her days, she was going to feel a burning in her soul when she heard the name Joely Spitz, especially if she never got the chance to confront the woman to her face—to demand to know why she'd picked Peyton, of all people, to destroy so cavalierly.

Next to her on the bed, Peyton's phone chimed with an incoming text.

She scrambled for the remote in the folds of the comforter and shut off the tv. With the click of a button, Joely's plastic smirk winked clear out of existence, but not before Peyton noticed the little badge in the corner of the screen, announcing *"Live from Los Angeles."*

Joely was here? Out in California like her? The realization added to her shock. First D.C, and now L.A. If she were feeling more paranoid this afternoon, she'd wonder why the woman seemed to keep showing up wherever she was.

That way lay only madness, though. It was a coincidence. Nothing more.

The screen of her cell showed a message from Buck. He'd sent Peyton a link to yet another real estate listing from Wyatt's friend Geena, asking, What do you think about something like this? We can't see this specific one, but Geena said there are others available in the same development.

Peyton clicked on the link and toggled through the attached photos. It's cute! Let's go look.

Buck replied with a thumbs-up emoji. She's also got a couple of freestanding cottages that look nice. You want me to make a viewing appointment?

Peyton liked the sound of that. Privacy, no upstairs or downstairs neighbors, and maybe even a yard. She told him, Yes please! then set her phone aside.

Part of her wanted to ask when he was coming home, but she could probably use the next few hours to get her head straight after watching her nemesis joke her way through afternoon television like she wasn't a horrible person.

Somehow, someway, Joely Spitz would get her due. What's more, Buck's out-of-the-blue text reassured Peyton that he was thinking about her even while he was busy with whatever he and the other guys were up to.

She'd made the right choice, moving out here. She knew she had. Now she just needed to stay the course.

Chapter Twenty-One

Buck

WELL, WELL, WELL, the text from Tate Monroe read, If it isn't your old friend, Ms. Spitz. There was a hyperlink included, so with a quick glance at Bennett, Buck clicked on it.

The live broadcast was already airing, and Buck couldn't tell how much he'd missed so far, but Tate wasn't wrong—the woman sitting in the interview chair was definitely Joely, smiling and looking a bit like the cat that ate the cream.

It must have been the end of her segment, because within seconds the camera cut from that cozy sitting room to a utilitarian broadcast desk.

The journalist who'd been across from Joely looked decidedly more serious as she explained, "*Despite their happy news, neither Joely Spitz nor Dan Cox has made an appearance on Roy Doggett's campaign trail. Most candidates would be thrilled to parade such an attractive couple in front of voters, but theirs is, of course, no ordinary family dynamic.*"

Buck's buddy cut eyes at him over the truck's center console. "What the fuck?"

He shrugged and frowned down at his phone, trying to make sense of what they were seeing.

"*Viewers may recall that Ms. Spitz was briefly linked to Senator Roy Doggett last year, in the aftermath of the rogue SEAL incident currently being investigated by the senator's Congressional committee. At the time,*

Doggett's wife, Lena Cox Doggett, was notably chilly when asked about that connection, and has since made no statements to the press about her son's engagement to Ms. Spitz. However, sources close to the family report that the relationship between mother and son, already strained when Dan moved the family company from its longtime home in Louisiana to Hyersville, has now been made even more fraught by Dan's betrothal."

"Holy shit," Buck mumbled. "There is so much going on here, I don't even know where to start."

"How about with the news that Sexy Spitzy was banging Roy at the same time as you?" Bennett said.

"I refuse to go there."

"While this might sound more like an afternoon soap opera than a political campaign," the newscaster went on, *"there is more at stake than romantic machinations, for more people than Doggett's constituents in Texas. As we reported earlier in this broadcast, Dan Cox is in the process of repositioning and expanding the scope of Landry Cox to take advantage of rapidly expanding global demand for automatic weapons. And while that might appeal to right-wing factions within his stepfather's party, it will undoubtedly be a trickier sell to the broader electorate."*

"Ya think?" Bennett drawled.

"Keeping Dan and Joely on the sidelines allows Landry Cox to continue benefiting from lucrative government contract deals through Roy Doggett's placement on the Armed Services committee without widespread scrutiny. In turn, sources tell us that Lena Cox Doggett will be more amenable to certain personal concessions if her family's legacy is assured—and might even be willing to lend her support to outreach aimed at the far-right evangelical groups her husband has not yet been able to sway."

"Let me guess," Buck commented drily, "the church folk don't like philanderers."

Bennett retorted, "Not ones who get caught, anyway."

"As the granddaughter of Cyrus Cox, Lena would be uniquely positioned to fill that role. Evangelicals across the South still admire her grandfather for his fiery preaching style and bestselling books on everything from..."

Buck tapped the screen of his phone and let it drop into the cup holder. "I can't listen anymore. This is complete insanity."

"You are correct," Bennett agreed, sinking back into the passenger seat. He blinked at the windshield for a couple of minutes, then asked, "I don't suppose you noticed they were broadcasting from L.A.?"

Buck closed his eyes and reconstructed the layout of the tv screen in his head. Ben was right—there had been a little flag in the corner that read, *Live from L.A.*

His blood pressure ticked up a few notches. "What in the hell is that woman doing here? Shouldn't she be in a rainforest profiling deforestation? Or filming floating barges of garbage out in the middle of the ocean? Or something in outer space—space would be a great place for her."

In front of them, Wyatt and Joe walked out of the ground-floor condo they'd all just scouted, reset the lockbox on the door, and strolled over. Wyatt stopped beside Buck's window and gestured for him to roll it down.

"Why are you still here?" he asked.

"Had to take a quick call," Buck told him. "We all squared away here?"

"Yup. I'll let Geena know we're done, but we gotta tell her soon if we're gonna use it. She said she can't delay the listing for much longer."

"Can it wait till morning?" Buck asked. "We were going to go check out that warehouse next."

"I'm sure that'll be fine. We're heading to Skippers now. Stop by when you're done, if you want—we can take a vote tonight."

The two men walked across the lot and got into Wyatt's car, then pulled away a moment later. Buck took one more look around, studying the modern, Mediterranean-looking buildings, the tidy landscaping, and the well-maintained cars parked in the resident spots.

It looked like a nice little development. Quiet and safe.

"Gimme a second," he told Bennett, then grabbed his phone and sent a quick text to Peyton. No way on earth would Buck take her to see the condo they'd just profiled, but it couldn't hurt to look at what else was for rent in the development—for comparison's sake, if nothing else.

Besides, apartment hunting here with his girlfriend would lend Buck plausible deniability, should anyone he knew spot him loitering around. That couldn't be a bad thing, right? It was crossing streams, but the efficiency of it was hard to argue.

"All set?" Bennett asked, clapping his hands together like he was fed up waiting.

"Yep." Buck shook off his uneasiness and rolled out.

THEY DIDN'T SPEND long at the warehouse across town. What had looked good on paper had way too many blind corners in person and no earthly way for the four of them to cover themselves adequately. There was also far too much foot traffic outside the building to keep their meeting on the down-low.

That left Wyatt's condo as their best option.

Skippers was on the way home, so Buck and Bennett headed over to let the others know. Though it was a foregone conclusion, the four of them took a vote over a dollar pitcher of beer anyway, speaking in vague generalities that the music roaring over the speakers drowned out.

Buck knew it was the right decision, despite the overlap with his and Peyton's house hunt. Now they just needed to put a plan of action in place and follow through with it.

He was too antsy to sit still, though. Thoughts of the meeting coupled with the unwelcome memory of Joely's face earlier—and the even less welcome insight into her current activities—and buzzed under his skin like bees.

He made it through two watered-down beers then pushed out of his seat, more than ready to leave the noise behind and head home to his girl.

"Testimony is at one tomorrow," he reminded the others. "Don't stay here all night. We need to get there bright and early. Okay? Don't give them a single thing to ding us on."

Buck endured a predictable number of eye rolls and catcalls for the nagging, mostly deserved. His guys wouldn't let him down, though. They never did. He knew that, but going through the mother hen routine made him feel like he had an iota of control over tomorrow's outcome.

It enabled him to leave with a clear conscience, knowing Bennett, Wyatt, and Joe would continue to have his back whether he was sitting with them or not. If they were reading his relationship situation the way he thought they were, they'd have Peyton's back, too.

If it ever came to that.

As he got in his truck and drove home, Buck hoped like hell it wouldn't.

AS BUCK LET himself in and silenced the alarm, he checked his watch again—it was only eight. Peyton wasn't going to be expecting him back so soon, and definitely wouldn't expect him to show up alone.

It was utterly quiet in the apartment, but there was no way she would be asleep this early. Good thing, too, because they almost never had the place to themselves like this.

Buck left the mail on the counter and thought about surprising her. It was an enticing idea, but it could get tricky. If he overdid it, she'd get scared, and no one wanted that after the last couple of weeks she'd had.

If he played his cards right, the soft entry could be just as fun, though. So instead of barreling into the bedroom and jumping on Peyton like a puppy, Buck hung out in the kitchen for a few minutes to her ease into the realization that they were here alone.

He made a normal amount of noise as he surveyed the contents of the pantry and the fridge, looking for a snack to bring her.

She'd clearly been busy today. There was a hell of a lot more interesting food in the place than there'd been before, and it all looked good. It was a perk he hadn't anticipated when they'd planned her move out here, but he wasn't going to give it up easily now that he had it.

Buck snagged a pitcher of water from the fridge, poured himself a glass, and studied the array of groceries, trying to decipher what Peyton was planning on making for dinner this week.

He shouldn't get too comfortable with the home-cooked meals, though. He needed to take her out a few times, too, or whip up something himself so she wasn't doing all the work.

Buck made a mental note to ask Peyton what she felt like as he put his glass in the dishwasher, then paused and shook his head. The adrenaline that had powered him through the last few hours was wearing off, leaving a grinding level of exhaustion in its wake.

Dinner decisions could wait. Right now, all he wanted to do was get cleaned up, love on his woman, and grab some Zs. He had just one thing to do before that could happen.

It took less than five minutes to send the message to the secure Black Watch line, then arrange a meet-up with Noah to hash out the preliminaries of the condo rendezvous.

With that accomplished, Buck headed down the short hall toward the bedrooms, hoping his steps sounded familiar and safe instead of threatening. The closer he got, the more his anticipation rose.

What was Peyton wearing? Was she sitting in bed reading some five-pound book, dwarfed by a t-shirt she'd pilfered from his dresser? When she put up her hair and took out her contacts at night, it slayed him every time.

Buck paused with his hand on the knob, picturing the smile that sometimes lit up her face when she let down her guard. That smile…it had become his reason for living.

He pushed the door wide, ready for it. His room was pitch dark, though, the only pinpoints of light coming from the smoke alarm and digital clock on the nightstand.

Buck stepped in to let his eyes adjust, searching for the shape of Peyton's body under the covers, and for the sound of her breathing. She was there—out cold, it seemed, huddled on her side with the covers pulled up to her ears and the fan twirling overhead.

Damn. She hadn't texted him to let him know she wasn't feeling well.

He crept to the bathroom and shut the door as quietly as he could, shucking his clothes and stepping into a blissfully scalding shower that drained the last remaining gas from his tank.

Buck felt a little guilty for standing there as long as he did. There was no way Peyton could've slept through the clanking pipes, the dropped bar of soap, or the groan he hadn't quite been able to suppress when the water hit his shoulders.

When he emerged, however, Peyton hadn't budged an inch. Buck left the bathroom light on and tiptoed over to get a closer look at her. That's when he spotted it—a neon pink earplug like the ones he used at the shooting range.

If she'd used one of his, he probably could've set off an IED next to the bed and she wouldn't have noticed. It would've seemed funny if a chill hadn't skated down his spine as the implications became clear.

Peyton had slept through a large man entering the apartment, disabling the alarm, and walking around right next to her. Buck got that their roommates acted like a bunch of cavemen, but after all the close calls she'd had recently, Peyton making herself vulnerable like this was not his favorite.

Much like his dinner plans or hopes for a goodnight kiss or twelve, that conversation would have to wait, though. Buck grabbed a pair of pajama bottoms from his bureau, pulled them on, and slid under the covers as carefully as he could.

On the nightstand, his phone vibrated. He glanced at the screen, then grabbed it and hightailed it back into the bathroom.

"What's up?" he murmured, once the door clicked shut.

"Quick heads-up about your testimony tomorrow," Tate Monroe barked. "There was a last-minute change to the board roster. Zero out of two people on this call will be surprised to hear that the new guy is a golfing buddy of your pal Doggett's."

"Motherfucker," Buck hissed. "This never fucking ends."

"We're going to end it. But you and your boys better tread real carefully in what you say tomorrow. Don't give the brass any more rope to hang you with than they already have."

"And how exactly are we supposed to do that? If we tell the truth, we're slandering a United States senator. And if we leave stuff out, then we look like we're lying by omission."

"I get it. Just…see where they lead you and watch for the potholes. I'll be in touch."

Tate hung up and Buck stared at his screensaver. He'd forgotten to ask which one of the medal monkeys was the problem child. He sent another text to the Black Watch line but gave up waiting after only a minute or two.

Buck climbed back into bed, rolling to his side and stretching along Peyton's back, a wall of protection between her and the outside world. He listened to her breathing for a few heartbeats, reassuring himself that it was regular and even. Normal. Healthy.

Buck relaxed and let himself drift then, the soft orange-blossom scent of her shampoo surrounding him. He pressed a kiss to the top of Peyton's head and tucked her closer, and smiled when she sighed in her sleep and snuggled into him.

Before long, Buck was out cold, too.

Chapter Twenty-Two

Peyton

WHEN PEYTON WOKE the next morning, Buck's side of the bed was empty and already cold. He was usually an early riser, but this was particularly bad—it was barely light out, and the running shoes near the closet indicated that he'd already been on a run.

Peyton caught the sound of the shower turning on, so she slipped out of bed and padded to the bathroom door. It swung open when she knocked, and she stepped in.

Buck had his forearms braced on the tiled wall, the hot spray pounding against the crown of his head. Muscles bunched across his shoulders and down his arms and his broad back tapered to a lean waist. His body was almost dream-like surrounded by the mist.

Peyton's eyes followed the water sluicing down his spine, over his ass, and down his thighs. Would she ever get used to this sight? *Doubtful.* She hoped she'd get enough time with him to find out, though.

A lump rose in her throat at the thought. "Sorry I fell asleep so early last night," she told him. "I was really tired, but I can't possibly have jet lag anymore."

She had, however, stomped out of the apartment after seeing Joely's interview, spent two hours combing through three different specialty markets, then hauled everything back to the kitchen so she could rage cook recipes she'd looked up on the net.

Buck stood straight and slicked his hair back. "You don't have to apologize," he said gently. "I get it. It's been a weird few weeks."

Peyton got a clearer look at his face when he cracked the shower door. He looked tired, and she wondered how early, exactly, he'd gotten up. "Are you okay?" she asked.

"Yeah, I'm fine. Tossed and turned last night. Figured I may as well get up and get rolling. Sorry if I woke you."

"You didn't."

Peyton peeked again at all the brawn on display and couldn't help but notice the way his cock twitched when her gaze wandered down. She snapped her eyes back up to his face, but she was already busted.

Buck arched a brow at her. "Don't just stand there," he smirked. "Lose the pj's and get in here."

Peyton scrambled to comply. "Don't have to tell me twice."

He opened the door wider and moved aside for her, then closed them into the warm confines of the glass enclosure. Buck pulled her into his arms and pivoted so she'd be under the water, then ran his fingers back through her hair, keeping it out of her face.

His kiss was soft and slow. Lingering in a way that added to the sense that this was a fantasy, instead of real life. The crisp scent of his body wash rose all around them.

Peyton ran her hands over Buck's slick skin, over his hard chest, and down those big biceps.

He pulled back and smiled softly. "Good morning," he murmured.

"Bet I can make it better than good." Peyton bit her lip and sat on the small seat in the back corner, and moved Buck to face her.

His eyes flared and his cock jumped again, growing harder by the second. She pressed her fingers into his thighs and drew him closer. Buck didn't say anything, so she looked up and asked, "Is this okay?"

"Very okay. But you don't have to—"

Peyton shook her head. "Yes, I do." Then she leaned forward and took the head of him into her mouth.

Buck's inhale was sudden and sharp over the steady rush of the water. He set one heavy hand on her shoulder and reached overhead with the other, redirecting the spray so she wouldn't get water in her eyes.

Peyton worked her mouth down his length, cradling his cock on her tongue and taking him deep, then tightening her lips on the retreat. Buck swayed toward her on a groan, grabbing the top of the shower frame to steady himself while she repeated the motion.

She spent a second or two teasing his tip, but it was too fun to see someone so strong and capable fall apart like this. So, Peyton circled his base with her fingers, sliding them up and down in time with her mouth and listening to Buck's breath sawing in and out of his lungs.

When it seemed like he was getting close, she cupped his balls in her other hand, fondling them and pulling gently in the way that always set him off.

Sure enough, Buck let out a dark and urgent, "*Fuck,*" and went tense all over. He tried to pull away but Peyton followed him, gratified when he sunk both hands into her hair and came in a hot rush on her tongue.

He held still for a moment, then pulled back and leaned against the wall, his hair plastered to his skull like molten silver and all that tanned skin tempting her to give things another go.

Buck stared down at Peyton with a dazed expression. "Jesus," he rumbled. "How are you so fucking perfect." Then he reached for her hands and pulled her to her feet.

"You're one to talk," she told him, going up on her toes to kiss him.

Buck wrapped his arms around her and stroked his broad palms down her back, landing on her ass and squeezing her tight against him.

"I'd like to take care of you right here," he said, "but thanks to you, my legs feel like overcooked linguine. So, you and I are going out to that bed right now, and you are you to spread your legs for me like a very good girl, aren't you, Peyton."

The command in his voice sent a jagged thrill through her. "Yes. Yes, I am."

He yanked the towels off the rack as they stepped out of the shower, slinging one around his hips and enveloping Peyton in another. And then Buck towed her directly to his bed and pushed her back.

She sank to the edge and watched him kneel between her feet. If she hadn't already been achingly aroused from going down on him, the sultry promise on his face would've done the job all on its own.

"I want to make you come so hard you see stars," he growled. "So if you want that too, I suggest you lay back and undo your towel."

Peyton blinked at him, stunned speechless by how much she loved the edge in his words.

Buck sat back on his heels. "Peyton?"

She took a breath. *Right.* Once she laid back, his strong hands were there immediately, smoothing the damp towel flat, urging her legs over his shoulders, and gripping her ass tight.

His mouth was a molten shock when it hit her core, moving over her with wicked intent. Peyton was already well on her way when Buck curled two fingers inside her, stroking them in and out as his devilish tongue wreaked havoc.

Her legs started to tremble. Peyton turned her head and tried to muffle her desperate whimper in the comforter.

"*Now*," Buck demanded, his lips hot against her skin, "Come now."

Peyton squeezed her eyes shut and just like that, she did, shattering into a thousand brilliant shards like a mirror exploding into space.

Buck eased her back to earth, setting her feet on the floor, and stroking her calves as he dropped soft kisses on her thighs.

When she could put words together again, she laughed shakily. "What the hell did you just do to me?"

Buck got to his feet and grinned. "What can I say? You're very inspiring."

"Holy shit."

"Payback's a bitch, babe," he chuckled, then stretched out on the bed beside her.

Peyton scooted up so they were face to face. "I could get used to this," she told him quietly. It was painful to admit, like saying it out loud might make it disappear.

Buck's eyes were warm, though. "And to think—my friends used to tease me for having high standards. I didn't even know how good it could be."

Peyton nestled into his chest. "*Aww.*"

He draped a heavy arm across her waist. "What do you have going on today?"

"I might look around a campus or two. A few have open positions that I'm looking at. If I can get in and introduce myself to the department heads, they'll be able to put a face with my resume when I submit it."

"Such a pretty face," Buck murmured, then kissed her on the nose.

Peyton kept babbling so she wouldn't melt into a puddle right then and there. "Oh, and later I thought I'd try to see a couple of those freestanding houses Geena suggested. Unless you'd rather I wait for you?"

"No, it's fine. I've got some long meetings today on base. You go ahead."

"Well, how long will they be? Maybe we could go together later this evening."

"I gotta be honest," Buck said, "Sometimes they drag on for a while. But if you see something you love, just text me, okay? We'll probably get a break or two, and I can try to reply then."

If she saw something she loved. A wave of awareness shimmered through her, wrapping around Peyton's heart and turning it golden. She had a feeling she was looking at something she loved right now.

It was way too early to tell Buck that, though. Instead, she said brightly, "Sounds good. I'll see you when you get home, and we'll see what's what."

He dropped his hand to her ass and gave it a squeeze. "I already know what's what, babe. And when I get home, we are going to finish what we started here."

With that, he pushed up and hopped to his feet. "Now I've got to get dressed, though. Let me grab a couple of things and then the bathroom's all yours."

WHEN PEYTON CAME out a little while later, she felt like she was glowing from the inside out. That feeling only intensified when she got a look at Buck, standing in front of the mirror and brushing a nonexistent piece of lint off his dress whites.

"Oh, lord. Would you look at yourself?" she gaped. He'd shown her photos but seeing it in the flesh was a whole new level of five-alarm hotness.

"You're one to talk," he drawled, hooking a finger in the top of her towel and tugging her closer.

Peyton touched a finger to his trident pin and sighed. "Do not move. I need a picture of this magnificence right now."

Buck rolled his eyes. "Come on."

"Do not take this moment from me, Buck. I have so little."

"What are you talking about?" he complained, as she played paparazzi and took a barrage of snapshots one after the other. "You literally have me. In the flesh. Whenever you want me. How does a picture even come close?"

"Sometimes you leave me and go to meetings," Peyton huffed. "Obviously. What's the one today about, anyway?"

Buck frowned and looked away. "Nothing special. Just a routine debriefing with the brass. It's going to be a waste of time, but there's no getting around it."

"Such is life."

"For sure. Anyway, if you're enjoying this so much, you probably ought to throw on shorts and come out to the kitchen. You'll get four frogs for the price of one."

Peyton blinked. "You're all going?"

"Whole team. Gotta look respectable," he told her.

"Give me two minutes," she sputtered quickly. "I'll be right there."

THE SECOND PEYTON walked through the door of the lemon-yellow cottage, she knew it was the one. It was old and small, but it was awash in sunlight, had cute palm trees in the front, and a little backyard surrounded by a brand-new privacy fence.

There were tall succulents by the mailbox, and two large blooming lilac bushes flanking the front steps. The outside looked quaint, with fresh paint and bright white trim, and the inside felt cozy, not cramped.

Peyton wanted it so much, it was like an ache under her ribs.

Buck, she was sure, would love it too. He had to—it was perfect. It wasn't far from the beach or base and was situated on a quiet side road with easy access to a shopping center.

She tried to listen patiently while Geena talked about the utilities and the school system. She looked in each of the bedrooms, checked out the garage, and nodded along while the real estate agent pointed out the appliances in the kitchen.

When the woman finally broke off her spiel, Peyton said without hesitation, "I want it. Where do I sign?"

"Oh. Okay. I also wanted to say that the owners might be willing to extend an option to buy in a year or two, if all goes well."

"Even better."

"Great. Well, as you can imagine, this place is going to go fast. So, I recommend having Buck arrange to see it today, if possible. That way you all can—"

"No need. I can follow you back to the office and sign the lease right now. I'll text Buck and let him know, and I'm sure he will swing by and sign his part as soon as he can."

"Alrighty," the woman chirped, "That certainly makes it easy. You want to look around for another minute before I lock up?"

Peyton nodded, then went through the place one more time, taking photos for Buck. Once she'd covered the highlights, she texted him, Isn't it so cute? I'm going to do it! Privacy here we come!

Excitement thrummed through her, imaging the two of them settling in together. The house was too small to make sense for more than the two of them, and she didn't know if they'd even reach the point where that would become a factor. It was far down the road, in any case.

For now, this place was perfect.

Peyton followed Geena outside and dutifully took down the address of the woman's office. On the way there, Buck called her.

"Hey!" she cried. "Are you all done or on a break?"

"Quick break," he told her. "But I saw your texts. The place looks great. I say go for it."

"Really? It's cute and it's clean. Geena said it looks well-maintained, but it is pretty small. And old. Appliances are new-ish, though." She stopped and took a breath. "I really love it, Buck. It has soul. It feels…like us."

Buck laughed at her enthusiasm. "I trust you. Send me the address and I'll do a drive-by when I get out of here later. Tell Geena I'll swing by her office to sign the lease after that, or in the morning if she's gone by then."

Peyton did a happy dance in her seat and almost missed her turn. "Oh my god! This is so exciting!"

He chuckled again and told her, "I can't wait to see it."

She could hear a fair amount of activity in the background—trucks, maybe, and deep voices barking orders. "Are you still on base?" she asked, trying to picture him pacing outside in his white uniform.

His voice was muffled for a minute, as he spoke to someone. Then he told her, "Yes."

"Would I be able I visit there someday? I'd love to see where you work. Or…well, you know what I mean."

Buck paused, and she began to wonder if she'd overstepped. But then he told her, "Of course. Once I get this mess wrapped up we'll do all that stuff. I have to go now, though, okay? I'll see you later. I'll text when I'm on my way."

"Can't wait."

"Me either, Peyton. Good things are happening. All good."

BY THE TIME Buck came through the door that evening, he was bearing a copy of the signed lease along with a sweating bottle of champagne and a big bouquet of roses for her.

Their roommates had beat him home by an hour, uniforms still as perfect as they'd been that morning but with grim expressions on their faces.

Wyatt watched as Peyton accepted the gifts, then groaned when Buck bent her over his arm for a breath-stealing kiss. "Oh, fuck this," he muttered. "I am not sticking around for part two of this movie today."

With that, he shoved his feet in a pair of sneakers next to the couch, grabbed his keys off the bar, and saluted them on his way out the door.

"Oops," Peyton told Buck, her face turning hot.

Buck was looking at Bennett, though, sprawled on the couch and eyeing them with a frown.

"What? I have to leave, too?"

"Couldn't hurt," Buck retorted.

"Been a long day, bro," Bennett said. "How about I put on these headphones, and we call it good?"

Buck looked at Peyton, his eyebrows raised in inquiry. She shrugged, "Don't ask me. I don't know what you've got planned."

"That is a blatant lie. Let's put these flowers in some water, so we can go to our room and discuss it in detail."

"Jesus lord, you two sound like parents on tv," Bennett grumbled, before snapping a large gaming headset over his ears and propping his feet on the coffee table with two heavy thumps.

Buck looked back to her, smug and expectant. "Well?" he said.

Peyton stepped into the kitchen, found a pitcher under the sink, and dropped the flowers into it, plastic and all. She ran a few inches of water into the bottom, set it on the counter, and turned back.

"Lead the way, Lieutenant," she smiled, shooing him down the hall.

LATER, AS THEY lay side by side whispering plans in the dark, Peyton admitted something that had started to worry her soon after she'd left Geena's office that afternoon.

"Buck, I'm so excited about this. Don't get me wrong. But…what if I can't find a job soon? I have some savings, but I need to be working to afford that rent."

He stroked his hand down her arm. "Please don't worry. I've got plenty saved up, too. I can take care of you as long as it takes.

Besides, I don't want you to settle for the first job that comes along. You should hold out for something you'll really love. I'll worry about the rest until then."

"I appreciate that. But what if it doesn't happen?" She didn't dare voice her bigger worry—that the hiring staff out here might already be able to connect her to *Global Lens*, somehow.

"I have faith in you," Buck said, strong and sure. "Someone out there will see your worth in no time. And until then, I got your six."

Peyton could not form any of the words she wanted to say. So, she kissed him instead and hoped that would do.

Chapter Twenty-Three

I THINK IT'S Flannery," Bennett said, resting his chin on his hand and staring out the side window of Buck's SUV.

"Who is?" Buck's mind was on the backup Tate Monroe had said he would have in place for the meeting today, and wondering whether they would move into place before or after he and the others got there.

It was categorically *not* on whatever stream-of-consciousness thought process Bennett was currently dragging out.

"The dog-faced boy," Ben answered, "Who else?"

Buck glanced at him and snorted. In the last twenty-four hours, *Doggett's boy*, their original nickname for the BOI member Black Watch had warned them about, had deteriorated into *Dog-faced Boy*.

In the case of Lieutenant Commander Flannery, the circus-style sobriquet was particularly apt. The man looked and acted like a damn bulldog.

"Why Flannery?" Buck wondered, though they'd been parsing this topic since yesterday.

"You saw that fucker. Between the fake tan and the lip gloss, he was right up Doggett's alley."

"Come on. He wasn't wearing lip gloss."

"You willing to put money on that? Cause ten bucks says I can get in that dude's bathroom in five minutes flat to find out."

Ben wasn't wrong, but Buck wasn't going to admit it. Instead, he commented, "Joe still thinks it's Zielinski."

"Nah. It's not him. He's a hardass, for sure, and he looks like he's been eating gravel for breakfast for forty years, but he's not a dick. He'd have no use for a guy like Old Roy."

Buck tapped on the steering wheel as he stopped at a light. "What about Wyatt? What's he think?" After he'd left the apartment last night, Buck hadn't had another chance to talk to him about their testimony. He'd been too occupied with celebrating with Peyton.

"Wyatt's with me," Bennett replied. "Flannery. No contest. Think about it. He had a total hard-on for all that shit they asked us about Spitzy."

Buck dry-heaved a couple of times, mainly for effect, then hit the gas when the light changed.

"Tell me I'm wrong."

Buck shook his head. "I'm sticking with my guess. It's Azevedo."

"How?" Bennett complained, as irritated now as he'd been when Buck first brought up the commander. "The asshole wasn't even there. That's not interference, that's disinterest."

"Think about it, though. Every other guy there was either desperate to make an example of us or trying to get us off the hook before their dinners hit the table at home. Why would Azevedo work so hard to get himself on that board if he was only going to blow it off on the day we came in to testify?"

"Maybe he was sick."

"He wasn't sick."

"And you know this, how?"

Buck snagged his phone out of the cupholder, unlocked it with his thumb, and showed Ben the photo he'd screen-shotted from the morning paper's society page.

Azevedo had attended some country club party the day before and had posed between a younger man with strikingly similar looks and a tall, glamorous woman in a gold sequined dress and platform heels.

Bennett squawked, "Is that his *family*?"

"The kid's his nephew Ozzie," Buck explained. "He's apparently heading to BUD/S in a few months. The woman is Adriana Márcia. She's some pop superstar in Brazil."

"Okay, so what is this picture supposed to prove?"

"That party was held at the Anchor House Yacht Club yesterday from noon to six."

"Gotta be honest, bruh—I would've ditched ya'll for that set of legs, too."

"I believe you. But more pertinent to the matter at hand is that there was a Doggett on the guest list as well."

"Roy? Or Lena?"

"Neither. Roy's brother, Leon, was there, and he had Joely with him."

"Jesus. How'd you find that out?"

"You remember that chick I went on a few dates with a couple of years ago? Bree? With the pink hair?"

Bennett sighed. "Who could forget Bree?"

"Certainly not you, since you banged her two weeks after I did. She tends bar at the yacht club now, and was happy to make small talk given the right incentive."

"Does she know you're shacking up with Peyton?" he scowled.

"No. But she does think you were mentioning her last weekend." With that, Buck made the final right into the condo complex where they were planning to meet their mysterious pen pal, and a few turns after that parked his truck in the busy community pool lot.

He checked his watch for the hundredth time. "We're a little early. I'll start over there and begin setting up."

Bennett hung his shades on his t-shirt and pulled a ballcap from his bag, pulling it low over his eyes. "There's Joe and Wyatt," he pointed. "I'll give it a few minutes, then loop around the back."

Buck nodded and let the other two pass, looking like nothing more than a pair of buddies out for a run. After they rounded the corner, he watched the sidewalk for another minute or two, but everything looked as excruciatingly normal as it had every other time they'd been here.

If Black Watch's people were here, they were hidden well.

"Just out of curiosity," Buck asked before he got out of the truck, "if you thought it was Flannery yesterday, why'd you give him so much crap when he fucked up the timeline?"

Bennett turned suddenly in his seat and glared. "Because fuck him, that's why. This whole shitshow is getting on my last nerve. We did the right thing in Nabarut. You know we did. We should be deployed right now, doing our jobs, not sitting around scratching our asses and meeting up with little punks who think they're tough for scaring an unsuspecting woman."

Buck looked him over and nodded. "Fair enough. I'll see you in a bit." With that, he got out and strolled up the block, heading for who knew what.

THE TWO MEN who walked up to the condo a little while later looked for all the world like they were popping in to visit friends, not waltzing into a den of wolves. They chatted casually on the sidewalk, knocked on the door, then smiled and bowed when the thing swung open—as if there weren't four guns pointed at their heads and four mean fuckers holding them.

They kept up the routine as Bennett pulled them inside, relieved one of his messenger bag, and patted them down. He led them to the chairs they'd placed in the center of the living room.

Once they were seated, Joe caught Buck's eye, asking the question they'd left for a game-time decision. *Restrain them, or not?*

Buck shook his head. So far, their visitors were taking great pains to be inoffensive—full of gracious gratitude, and keeping their hands where everyone could see them. They could stay the way they were for now.

There might have been a little nervous energy under all the tea party manners, but Buck wasn't picking up any hinky vibes from them. The messenger bag was similarly inane, containing nothing more than a large manila envelope and the usual detritus of energy bars and lip balm.

He lifted his chin at Joe and Wyatt, giving them the go-ahead to fade back to their posts near the front and back exits.

Bennett would keep an eye on the bedrooms, in case anyone managed to slip past the Black Watch team that was supposedly outside and enter through a window. And Buck had to talk to these two.

He stood in front of them, weapon down beside his leg. The pair mirrored each other in looks and posture, both with medium brown skin, black hair and dark eyes, and a marked familial resemblance. They seemed as relaxed as they could be under the circumstances, with their hands resting on their thighs and sporting identically neutral expressions.

Buck cleared his throat and said, "You two weren't exactly furtive."

The older one shrugged. "What do we have to hide? I'm a man taking his nephew apartment hunting. Nothing wrong with that."

"You guys can relax," the other chimed in. "We're not going to blow you up or anything. We just want to talk."

Buck slid his eyes to Bennett, who sniffed quietly in recognition. The accent was unmistakable—to the people in this room, anyway. The last time they'd heard it was in northwestern Qahat, the site of the ambush that had tanked their careers, and home base to the warlord Asif Abd-al-Kadir and his growing militia.

Joe shifted on his feet near the back slider, looking wary.

Their visitors were surrounded by an antsy squad of SEALS, but neither was acting the way Buck would've predicted. They simply sat and blinked at him, waiting for Buck to take the lead. It was weird, and it was unnerving.

Buck gestured for Ben and Joe to lower their weapons.

"How about we relax once you've explained why the hell you've been following us all over town?" he said.

The one on the left spoke up again. "All over town? Hardly." He was younger than he'd first appeared. Buck had pegged him as mid- to late-twenties, but he was probably no more than nineteen.

"Dude," Bennett said, "Sarcasm is not a good look for you right now."

The older man held up his hands like he wanted to calm everyone down. "Rohaan, start at the beginning," he instructed.

The kid opened his mouth, thought for a minute, and nodded. "I am Rohaan. This is my uncle, Mohsin. Our family has lived near Nabarut for hundreds of years."

The confirmation set Buck back a step. These guys could easily be Kadir's people. He'd thought the warlord didn't have the funds to send operatives all the way to the States to track down American service members and exact his revenge—but hate had a long reach, and Buck had learned not to underestimate what it could do.

"Okay," he answered. "Now why are we here?"

The one called Mohsin put a hand on his chest and bowed slightly, the picture of amenability. "We have been searching for you gentlemen for months. Thank you for agreeing to speak with us."

"If you needed to talk to us so badly, why bother with all the skulking around? Why not approach us directly?"

The kid laughed. "I didn't want to get shot before I could take my midterms."

His uncle shot him a quelling look. "I am responsible for Rohaan's safety now. I needed to reassure myself that you could be trusted before we tried to reach out."

"Besides, there's a lot of Qahatis around here," the kid added. "And even more Navy people. If we marched up to you on some street corner, anyone could've seen us."

Mohsin nodded, worry clouding his features. "There is…danger in what we have to tell you. For us, and for you."

Bennett's steady gaze shifted from the pair to Buck. Buck could hear the radio chatter from the day of the ambush like it was here in the room with them right now, and not six months and a world away.

"We're ready to go in. We've been ready to go in. Let us evac the village before it gets caught in a crossfire."

"Negative, Lieutenant. We have a U.S. senator on the ground in Nabarut. Repeat, U.S. senator and entourage at Nabarut. Echo Company will hold off opposition until the senator has cleared the area."

"Clear him out now," Buck had demanded. *"Do you not see what's about to happen?"*

"Echo has opposition cornered, Lieutenant. Stand by. Repeat, stand by."

Kadir hadn't been cornered. Not at all. Within minutes of the exchange, his forces had come streaming through the Boshad pass—reaching it through some tunnel none of the U.S. forces had known about—and Nabarut had quickly been overrun by two days of ugly fighting.

Buck swallowed and refocused on the men seated in front of him. "Who sent you?" he asked.

Mohsin put his hands together like a supplicant. "No one sent us. We are on our own, as you and your men are. We believe, however, that we can help each other."

Did Buck dare accept the gentleness this man exuded? Or the kid's whole regular teenager schtick?

"Buddy, I'm gonna need a hell of a lot more information before we get to that point. How about you start filling in some details here."

"We know you're the SEALs that tried to halt what happened in Nabarut," Rohaan said, "and we know Senator Doggett is trying to get rid of you for it. We've seen the news. But I was there, Mr…uh…sir."

Bennett zeroed in on the kid's face with that laser-sighted stare of his. "You were in Nabarut during the ambush? Why?"

Rohaan deflated abruptly, his bravado evaporating as he sagged in his chair and looked heartbroken. "Nabarut is my home. And Mohsin's too. What happened that day…"

Mohsin cleared his throat and took up the tale. "I left Nabarut fifteen years ago. I haven't been back since, but when my sister called, wanting to send Rohaan to me, how could I refuse? After the ambush, Kadir's thugs were combing the area, trying to conscript as many of the young men and boys as they could. We couldn't risk him getting caught up."

"Understandable."

"It's worse than you think," Rohaan said. "I translated when they came to take pictures of the school. I helped arrange the party for the opening. I even got to drive Mr. Roy Doggett and his wife around for a tour. We were so proud the Americans picked me. *I* was so proud." His voice cracked on the last words, and he looked away, blinking rapidly to clear the tears spiking his lashes.

Mohsin explained, "Rohaan's girlfriend was to attend the school when it opened."

Rohaan grew more agitated, making Joe and Bennett tense. "No one knew about us. We had plans, though. We were going to get married, but she insisted I wait. So, I saved my money, and I was going to ask her family for her hand when she graduated. I promised her I would wait, but if I hadn't…maybe she wouldn't be gone."

His uncle continued, "He was lucky. They used the money he'd saved to sneak him out, to send him here where he'd be safe."

Buck scrubbed a hand across his mouth as he watched the kid's performance unfold. If these two were lying, they were really fucking excellent actors. The best he'd ever seen.

However, if what they said was true, Rohaan was probably even luckier than he knew.

"I am sorry for your loss," he said, "But I'm sure you can appreciate that we don't have a lot of time here. Can either of you fill me in on why you think we can help you?"

Wyatt's voice crackled in Buck's tiny earpiece, one of an array of items Noah had given them before the meeting. He said softly, "Team B marked. In position twelve o'clock."

Black Watch's operatives were outside. Buck relaxed slightly with the confirmation.

In front of him, Mohsin clasped his hands in his lap and looked around the room. "Lieutenant Gaines, we have information that will help you put the inquiries to rest once and for all. In the right hands, it could end Doggett's presidential campaign—and maybe even his career."

As unexpected gifts went, this one was too much to hope for. Buck tried not to let his shock show. "And in return?"

"You help us find out what happened to the girls of Nabarut. Their loved ones deserve closure. Rohaan deserves closure."

Chapter Twenty-Four

Peyton

I LEFT BEFORE he got back from lunch," Peyton told Devon. "His secretary looked at me like I'd sprouted horns."

She veered around a man stocking cans, then made her way into the main aisle of the market.

"Which job was this for, again?"

"The Intro to I.R. class at San Diego State."

"Peyton," Devon sighed, "You could teach that class with your hands tied behind your back. Why didn't you stay?"

"I just…I got nervous, I guess. It was stupid of me. Buck and I signed the lease on our new place last night, and I picked up the keys this morning. I need a job, Dev—I'm going to have to split bills with this man soon."

"Did you at least leave your name?"

"I did. But I still haven't gotten Donnelly's recommendation letter yet. I feel like I'm jumping the gun applying for stuff without it." Peyton swung into the next aisle and stared blankly at the bags of snacks. "That dickwad is really going to make me call and beg for it, isn't he?"

Devon was silent for a long beat, enough for Peyton to snap to attention and demand, "*What.*"

He let out a pained exhale. "Yeah…I would not do that if I were you."

She looked around, then inched toward the rows of tortilla chips and lowered her voice. "Explain."

"Because Donnelly's been dragging you to anyone who will listen. He's been doing it ever since you left. What the hell happened between you two?"

"Nothing happened," she lied. "He just didn't have the budget to renew my contract."

"That must be why he's trying to refill your position so hard."

"Oh."

"Yeah, *oh*," Devon snarked. "Listen. There's something else."

Peyton didn't like the way her friend's voice had lowered ominously. She took one last look around, decided that Buck's neighbor was wrong about this market being better than the one near them, and strode for the front door.

"Hang on," she said. "Let me get to my car." Once she'd reached it and locked herself in, she told Devon, "Okay, I'm good. What's going on?"

"Donnelly had some guy call him the other day. I was supposed to meet with him right after, so I was sitting there chilling with Verna while they argued over speakerphone."

"Okay."

"I wouldn't have thought much of it," Devon explained, "Except the first thing I heard was the other dude telling Donnelly to stop bullshitting him—that he'd said Ms. Page would shut the whole blog down and she hadn't."

Peyton felt her blood run cold. "What?"

"My guy wanted to know if you intended to play ball or not. Peyton, what's that all about?"

"I…wait. What did Donnelly say?"

Devon told her, "He freaked. Told the guy that you left. Donnelly said he tried to talk to you but you up and quit, and then pulled up stakes and took off for California. He said, and I quote, 'Whatever you think I can do, I can't anymore. It's out of my hands.'"

Peyton choked back the bile trying to climb up her throat, but she couldn't seem to force words from her mouth.

"Girl, what's up with that? You had a blog and didn't tell me?"

"I did. But I don't know why anyone would care about it," she lied again. "Do you know who Donnelly was talking to?"

"I asked Verna, because the way they were talking had me worried. She said it was some high school friend of his. Tim something. Uh…I think…Stein? Tim Stein. Ring any bells?"

"No. But I'll look him up after we hang up. Did they say anything else, Dev?"

"Donnelly was waxing poetic about ethics or some shit, and this Tim character asked him, 'The same ethics that took my money six months ago?'" Devon replied. "Look, I'm all for people roasting Donnelly, but that was mafia-sounding shit right there. Should I be concerned?"

Peyton had to say something to reassure her friend, but her thoughts were so convoluted, she couldn't come up with anything remotely convincing. "Don't worry," she managed. "I am completely fine. Whatever wingnut Donnelly is friends with can't touch me out here in California, and even if he tried, I am sure Buck would take exception."

Devon hesitated for a second or two, then asked, "And your dude's treating you well? All systems still go?"

"It's all good. I promise," Peyton said, then started her car. "Thanks for letting me know."

As they said their goodbyes and hung up, she wasn't really paying attention to where she was going. She was only desperate to get out of there—to go home, where she could hopefully figure out what to do about this newest fly in the ointment.

After a few unfamiliar turns, however, it became clear that she'd exited the shopping center a completely different way than she'd gone in. Peyton drove for a couple of blocks, looking for a good place to pull over and reset her car's navigation system.

When she noticed the sign for the community pool, she figured that was as good a place as any to get turned back around.

The problem was, once she'd parked, her hands were shaking too much to make headway on the nav directions.

Her brain felt like it had turned to cotton candy. Peyton rolled down her windows and turned off her car, then fished her phone out of the console so she could google Tim Stein.

An assortment of accountants and veterinarians popped up, along with a high school wrestler from a few towns over and a crime novelist. But then, high on the second page of results, came the business profile of Timothy Stein, public relations manager for Senator Roy Doggett's presidential campaign.

And she knew, she *knew*, she had the right guy. Peyton scanned his bio and tried not to hyperventilate. Senator Doggett. Joely Spitz. This Stein person *had* to be the connection—the reason Peyton's little blog had gone from innocuous to viral as the flu.

She had no idea what to do with the information, though. If Donnelly wasn't going to write her a recommendation, then her job search was going to go absolutely nowhere.

And if Stein was as unhappy about her keeping *Global Lens* active as Devon had made it sound, then there was a good chance that Buck was wrong.

At least some of the people that had followed her hadn't been looking for him.

Shit. There was no getting around it. Peyton had to tell Buck the full story as soon as possible. He'd been nothing but wonderful since she'd gotten out here. He deserved to know who he was dealing with, especially if money became an issue or Peyton ended up in real danger.

Like she'd conjured it with her whirling thoughts, the SUV facing her across the lot came into focus. A black SUV. *Buck's* SUV.

She frowned and got out of her car, walking toward the truck and looking for the little details that would tell her if it was the same make and model, but not his. Buck was supposed to be in a meeting on base today, not hanging out at some neighborhood pool.

But the small dent near the gas cap was right where it always was. So were the faded Navy sticker and the parking permit for base. Even his license plate number was familiar—Peyton would never have been able to call it up from memory, but faced with that combination of numbers and letters now, she knew it was correct.

This was Buck's truck. Where was he?

She stood there with her hands on her hips and looked around. For some reason, her eyes kept landing on the sign at the entrance to the pool, until eventually, it occurred to her that the name of the community was one she'd heard before.

Peyton went back to her car and got out her phone. She scrolled through Geena's emails, finding the one with the open condo in this development a split second before she remembered Buck's text, pointing out a different unit for sale.

Peyton decided to drive by that one first. She took a deep breath and sent the address to her phone's mapping app, then restarted her car.

It took three minutes to get there. She parked a few rows back from the front of the building, then peered around at the other cars. Sure enough, Wyatt's car sat off to her left, stashed next to some overgrown shrubs in the shade of a big eucalyptus tree.

If some tiny part of her brain had worried that she was about to bust her boyfriend cheating on her, the sight of that car dispensed with it.

This still felt weird.

Peyton lifted her phone again, scrolled through her contacts, and called Geena. The agent answered in two rings. "Hey, Miss Peyton! Can't stay away, huh?"

"Pretty much," she answered. "Listen, I ended up near that condo in the Las Palmas development this afternoon. Totally by accident, but is there any chance you can tell me the lockbox code? I'd love to pop in and take a peek at it real quick. Just to compare, since Buck hasn't seen the inside of the cottage yet."

"Do you mean the one on Buena Verde Court? Or San Pedro?"

"San Pedro."

On the sidewalk in front of the ground floor unit, an attractive couple in running clothes stopped to chat with a man walking a large German shepherd. The scene was excruciatingly normal, but for Peyton's pounding heart.

"Oh, rats," Geena said. "Someone's viewing that one right now. They should be done by three, though. Maybe you could get in after that?"

As Peyton watched the door of the condo, waiting for Wyatt or Buck to emerge, a white Mercedes pulled into the lot and rolled past her. Geena was behind the wheel with her phone pressed to her ear.

The agent didn't look up and didn't see Peyton. She simply parked on the other side of the lot and sat in her car, waiting like Peyton.

Peyton asked, "Is it Buck or Wyatt? Viewing the condo right now?"

Geena laughed. "Why would they do that? You just picked up your keys!"

"You sure?"

"I mean…I didn't make the appointment. It's possible, I guess."

Peyton watched the other woman frown through her windshield, twirling a piece of hair nervously around her finger. "So, I can go in after three, you said?"

"Yup. Go run some errands, and by the time you're done, it'll probably be ready. We just need to have someone from our team go in after the last appointment to straighten up, but I can tell them you're on your way, if you want."

Someone from our team. Not "me."

Peyton looked from Geena to that condo, from the condo to Wyatt's car, and back again. Then she made a decision.

"Sounds good. Will you text me the lockbox code, so I have it for later?"

Once the numbers came through, Peyton grabbed her purse and got out of her car. She wouldn't have a lot of time before Geena spotted her, so she marched across the lot and headed straight for the condo's front door.

The people on the sidewalk did a double-take as she approached.

The woman stepped neatly into her path with a big smile. Peyton veered around her, murmured, "Sorry," and kept going.

"Wait," the lady said, reaching for her arm. "You can't go in there. Someone's looking at it."

Peyton shrugged her off. "It's okay. I know them."

Now the man with the dog stepped up, looking far less friendly. "You heard her. She said you can't go in."

Peyton continued backing toward the door, keeping her eye on the dog. "I don't know who you are, but my agent said it was okay." She glanced behind her and saw something shift in the front window.

The woman's companion noticed it, too. He moved closer, the other two hanging back a step on either side. "We represent the landlord and the people viewing the place. If you wouldn't mind waiting in your car until the appointment is over, we'll be sure to let you know once it's your turn."

If these three were real estate agents, Peyton was a faerie princess. "I literally just watched you walk up this sidewalk from opposite directions. You're lying. So I'm going in there and you can't stop me."

She spun and reached for the lockbox hanging from the handle, then tried to enter the code as fast as her trembling fingers allowed. The man was faster, though. He knocked her hand away from the keypad and pushed between her and the door.

"Hey! Hands off," Peyton complained.

"Ma'am!" he shouted in her face. "We asked you politely to step away. If you do not leave immediately, we will call the police and report you for trespassing." Over his shoulder, the other man put his fingers to his ear like he was listening to an earpiece.

"Who are you talking to?" Peyton called. "Someone in the condo?"

That pissed off the woman. She put her phone to her ear immediately, squawking nonsense about trespassers and disorderly conduct while shooting death glares at Peyton. The German shepherd sat near her feet, alert and watching Peyton's every move.

Across the lot, Geena was watching the fracas with wide eyes, talking a mile a minute into her phone, but not coming closer.

Peyton had one move left. She lifted her chin, reached behind her, and pounded on the door with her fist. "Wyatt!" she yelled. "I need your help!"

The group on the sidewalk froze in unison.

Behind her, the door swung open.

Chapter Twenty-Five

Buck

A S YOU MIGHT recall, we kind of have our hands full at the moment," Buck said, fighting not to let his confusion and frustration show. "What makes you think we can do anything?"

Rohaan brimmed with the confidence of youth. "Easy. You are American SEALs. You have resources that no one else does."

"That's debatable," Bennett muttered.

Buck glared at him. "Why don't you tell us what you know, and we'll decide if it's actionable, or not."

"Roy Doggett was in a relationship with Joely Spitz. Might still be," the kid announced.

From his position near the sliding glass door, Joe snorted. "Nothing we haven't heard on the news, bucko."

"Not a romantic relationship," Mohsin corrected. "A mercenary one. Doggett promised to get Ms. Spitz her own show on the Explore network in exchange for her help."

Joe scowled. "God, that guy's a dick. How's a senator supposed to pull that off?"

"The yacht club pictures," Bennett said, his mind making the same lightning-fast connections it always did. "Joely was there with Leon Doggett, remember?"

Buck nodded. "Yup."

Rohaan nodded too. "Yes, you see. His brother, Mr. Leon in Hollywood, is how he does it."

"Show us the proof," Buck instructed, "Right now."

"We didn't *bring* it," Rohaan sneered, affronted. "We had to decide whether we could trust you first."

"Fun fact," Joe retorted, "It doesn't exist until we get a look at it."

Buck cut eyes at him while he weighed what they'd learned so far, trying to decide how it impacted their current situation. "Guys like Doggett promise people stuff all the time," he told the kid. "No one will blink an eye at him smoothing the way for an attractive woman."

Mohsin shrugged. "That's correct. But they will blink an eye at what Senator Doggett needs Ms. Spitz's help with."

Buck's gut tensed with foreboding. "Which is?"

The men seated in the center of the room paused and looked at each other, but they'd apparently worked out everything they were willing to share ahead of time. It took only a quick nod from his uncle for Rohaan to explain, "The ribbon cutting at the school was a diversion. Mr. Doggett was really there to make a deal with al-Kadir, and he needed Ms. Spitz to make sure no one discovered that."

The pieces slotted into place with a sickening sense of logic. Wyatt made a disgusted sound from his post in the foyer but didn't say more. Buck glanced at Bennett and Joe and saw the truth written across their expressions, as well.

There was only one deal Roy Doggett could have been making in the tiny mountain village of Nabarut, but Buck had to ask anyway. "What kind of deal?"

"The kind with guns."

Guns. Landry Cox automatic weapons, no doubt, sold for what had to be a pretty penny to an unhinged zealot who'd been wreaking havoc all over northwestern Qahat.

The subsequent takedown of Buck and his squad had never made a lick of sense before now. Doggett would have to be a grade-A narcissist to pull this inquiry crap over a few sharp words in a helo, but if he thought they'd seen something damning on the day of the ambush?

The inquiries and the smear campaign were probably the least the guy would try.

Fuck. This was bad.

"You say you didn't bring proof, but you brought something." Buck hoisted Mohsin's messenger bag and showed them the inside. "What's in the envelope?"

"Photos," Mohsin explained, "Gathered from the mothers who survived the fighting. For the girls whose families were killed, we used stills from Joely's camera crew. Take them out, Lieutenant. See who we are risking our lives for."

Buck slipped the pile of pictures from the envelope and shuffled through the first several images. Bennett looked over his shoulder and let out a low whistle. He wasn't wrong—they might have been looking at headshots for a modeling agency, one looker after the next.

Rohaan knew very well what they were seeing. He raised his chin and said proudly, "Nabarut is famous for the beauty of our women. Men come from all over Qahat, hoping to marry them, and the girls are allowed to choose as they wish."

"Obviously, Kadir finds this unseemly," Mohsin added. "He can't tolerate the thought of women having that kind of autonomy. To him, educating them on top of that gives them far too much power."

Insisting that they look at the faces of the girls was clearly a heavy-handed ploy for sympathy. Buck knew that, but he couldn't seem to tear his eyes away from all the fresh, hopeful expressions. The promise of the future in the line-up of clear, direct gazes.

He'd bet good money there were more than a few keen minds behind those pretty eyes.

A thick silence descended on the room, punctuated only by the two sharp barks they heard outside.

A beat after that, the powder keg erupted.

Someone pounded on the front door and instead of holding the line, Wyatt opened the damn thing and scuffled with whoever was trying to push their way inside.

There was a bit of back-and-forth and then he shouted, "*Shit. Incoming!*"

Rohaan and Mohsin exploded into motion, lurching first for the messenger bag on the floor and then bursting toward the back door, where Joe had planted his feet and raised his weapon.

They came at him too fast for him to get off a shot, but Joe grappled with the men instead, getting a forearm across Mohsin's neck to hold him off and sending Rohaan to the carpet with a swift kick to the knees.

The hand-to-hand was over before it began. Neither of them was a skilled fighter, and they were more focused on flight than self-defense.

Buck sent Ben to back up Wyatt with a quick jerk of his chin, then collared Mohsin from behind and manhandled him back into his chair.

With that taken care of, Joe wrested Rohaan to his feet and deposited him beside his uncle, growling, "Where the fuck did you think you were going? We're not done here."

Mohsin looked aghast. "You don't understand. Our family— what's left of it—is still in Nabarut. They will be slaughtered if anyone sees us with you."

"No one's telling on you, okay?" Joe fired back. "Cool your jets."

Buck expected Rohaan to have something snarky to say in return, but instead, the kid was staring at the foyer with a knowing expression.

Buck spun and nearly choked at who he saw there.

Peyton? Flanked by Wyatt and Ben, and looking shaken and alarmingly pale.

"I'm sorry," she whispered. "I saw your cars. I didn't know what you—"

Naturally, Rohaan decided to run his mouth. "Hello, Miss Peyton Page. You're late. I was beginning to think you wouldn't come at all."

Buck swung back and stared at the kid in confusion. How did he know Peyton?

Joe kicked his chair. "Hey. You don't talk to her."

Peyton locked eyes with Rohaan, though, asking, "You…why would you say that?" Her voice was barely audible, but it still echoed around the room like an RPG blast.

Buck really didn't want to know Rohaan's answer. "Leave her out of this," he told the kid. And then, with a sense of panic he couldn't quite explain, he added, "Wyatt, get her out of here."

Rohaan's avid gaze swung back to Buck. "We don't need to talk to her, anyway. She's done what we'd hoped she would."

Buck looked at Joe, and then at Ben. *Yup*—they'd heard that too.

"Explain."

"We thought she might be able to tell us where to find you," Rohaan shrugged. "But Miss Page made it easy. She led us to you before we ever had to ask."

There was a lot to unpack in that statement. Buck took a breath, weighing where to begin. It sure as hell sounded as if these two jokers had been following Peyton long before they'd asked for a meeting with Buck and the others.

Exactly as she'd thought.

"Rohaan is right in a sense," Mohsin commented calmly. "We *don't* necessarily need to talk to Ms. Page anymore. But I thought she'd be curious about what we had to say, given her role in all this."

The air in Buck's lungs seemed to lock up all at once. "Peyton is my girlfriend. She has no role."

Everyone ignored him, because the kid was looking at his uncle in admiration, saying, "You told me it would work, and it did."

"Nothing *worked*," Buck corrected. "You were stalking an innocent woman. That does not help your case."

Mohsin held up his hands, trying to placate him. "We weren't trying to stalk. But we had to make sure we had the correct person before we approached her. We couldn't risk the wrong people finding out what we were doing."

Bennett asked, "How long has this been going on?"

"Since August," Rohaan answered readily. "Once I had access to a decent computer, it was simple to find her."

Buck glanced back to see Peyton frozen in place, not saying a word and looking like she might toss her cookies at any moment.

August, he realized with dawning dread, was before he'd met her. Well before.

"Where'd you get access to a 'decent computer'?" Joe wondered.

"UCSD," Rohaan explained proudly. "Mohsin helped me apply once I made it here. In four years, I'll get a computer science degree and a job, and they'll let me stay here permanently."

If he was lucky. Buck wasn't about to get into the vagaries of immigration, however. That would only drag this shitshow further off the tracks.

He caught the kid's eye and demanded, "So you went to Maryland, and what—just trailed Peyton around everywhere she went?"

"I didn't go. I had classes to attend. Mohsin went."

Buck blasted the man with a fiery glare, now that he'd been confirmed as a suitable target for his welling fury. "You were the asshole taking pictures."

"I'm a photojournalist," Mohsin shrugged. "For the WPA. Taking pictures is how I process things. Besides, then we had something to compare to the information Rohaan had dug up about her."

Bennett stepped closer, subtly nudging Buck aside. "Explain why you thought Peyton would know how to find us. Why does she matter?"

Rather than answer directly, Mohsin turned to study Peyton. "You must be invested in the outcome of this meeting, too. Why aren't you saying anything? Your life's been ruined as much as any of ours."

Buck gritted his teeth. None of this was making sense. He growled, "When I said leave her out of this—" at the same time Ben insisted, "Answer the question. Why were you following her?"

Peyton didn't utter a word, but Buck felt the hitch in her breath like a blade to his ribcage.

He didn't turn around. He couldn't. He just asked, "Babe? What's he talking about?"

Rohaan laughed in disbelief. "Come on. You can't be serious. Peyton Page. The *Global Lens* blogger. Why are you pretending you don't know who she is? She came to you for help, just like we did!"

"Peyton?" Buck pressed.

"Didn't she?" Rohaan pleaded, eyes getting round.

Beside him, his uncle was frowning, looking from face to face with dawning comprehension. "No. Rohaan…I don't think that's what happened."

"Of course, they know," Rohaan argued. "How could they not?"

Mohsin stared at Peyton, trying to figure her out. His nephew wasn't nearly so circumspect. He cried, "What, I'm supposed to believe they just hooked up by accident?"

Buck swallowed back the bile climbing up his throat. He did not believe in coincidences, and stumbling across the very blogger he'd been searching for seemed exceptionally far past the realm of lucky accidents.

Peyton's continued silence spoke volumes though, didn't it?

Joe had been quiet, brooding near the back door, until he murmured, "What the fuck is going on?"

Buck held steady and forced himself not to react. These clowns were bluffing. This was only a clumsy divide-and-conquer ploy, designed to set them against each other.

Rohaan looked exasperated, however. "When all of you came back here and got into so much trouble with the authorities, we thought you might be willing to help us. But it wasn't until you took in Miss Page that we knew for sure."

"Please shut up!" Buck bellowed. Inside his head, his thoughts were spinning out.

Maryland. The political science teaching job. The dots that didn't quite add up when Peyton left that job so readily, to move out here with a guy she'd just met.

Was she standing behind him, making connections like he was? Had she understood what Rohaan meant about the crap Buck was embroiled in?

Funny how all this time he'd assumed the asshole behind *Global Lens* was a man, though. Buck ought to have guessed it would take a woman to destroy him so handily.

Rohaan continued to ramble from his chair, as if he didn't feel the tectonic shift happening in the room. "Mohsin suspected that if we found the blogger first, they'd know how to reach the SEALs Doggett wanted to silence." The kid stared at Peyton, beseeching her to agree. "And it was true. Bloggers are like part of the press here, right? So, did you come to San Diego to report on the trial? Are you staying with them so they can protect you?"

Joe let out his breath in a long, pained, "*Ah, fuck.*" His blue-collar Boston accent was front and center when he tacked on, "Here we go."

Buck looked around, wanting to get a read on what the others thought of this. Wyatt's eyebrows were sky-high, and his mouth was hanging open. Bennett's face was impassive, but his knuckles were white where he gripped his weapon.

And Peyton. Pretty, brilliant, once-in-a-lifetime Peyton.

Buck recognized the instant she put it all together, the second she realized that her new boyfriend and his roommates were the subjects of the drawn-out Congressional inquiry she'd seen in the news—in addition to a lower key, no less serious, board of inquiry in the OSW.

Buck knew because she let out a disbelieving little gasp and swayed like she might faint. The sight unlocked something in his chest, and he pivoted, finally, to face her.

He stared at the same face he'd looked at first thing that morning, back when he'd thought he'd never loved a set of human features more.

Buck had been blind, as it turned out. The dark truth was there, written all over Peyton's expression. *Guilt. Horror. Shame.*

She'd lain in his bed how many times, letting him fall in love with her? *Making* him fall in love with her? And she'd never said a word about who she really was.

Buck was such a fool.

He wanted to roar at the betrayal, at the injustice of first Joely, and now Peyton, manipulating him to further their own agendas. But he had two informants bearing witness to this charade, and a team of operatives outside waiting to wrap up this soirée.

Buck supposed Rohaan could be blowing smoke, stirring shit up to throw them all off balance—but he didn't think that was the case. As soon as the kid's words had landed, he'd known them for what they were.

The god-awful truth.

He had to get this show back on the road before he lost his mind.

"Get Peyton out of here," he told the room. When no one moved, he stabbed a finger at Wyatt. "Get her out of here. Take her home and keep her there until you hear from me. You got me? She does not leave your sight until I say so."

"Roger that," Wyatt said.

Then, Buck heard Peyton's voice, small and scared. "Buck?"

He could barely make himself look at her, afraid of what he'd see—and yup, her gray pallor did not fill him with confidence at all. "Go with Wyatt. I'll come home as soon as we're done here."

"But—"

"Later," he promised her. Or was it a threat? "We will figure out the rest of it later."

"Please don't hurt them," she said on her way out, "It's not their fault."

If that wasn't the most damning statement of all, Buck didn't know what was—and Peyton didn't get to ask for promises from him anymore. "I'll be back as soon as I can," he said.

Wyatt looked grim as he took her arm and led her away. Peyton stumbled on the throw rug in the foyer, and it made Buck want to punch a hole in the wall. Maybe ten holes.

Bennett and Joe watched him, warily waiting for orders. Buck bent to gather the scattered photos from the floor and told them, "The rest of you sit tight for a minute. I've got to make a quick call."

With that, he made his way blindly down the hall, finding the largest bedroom at the end and closing himself inside. Buck sent a text to the secure Black Watch line and sat on the fussy bench against the wall.

While he waited for Tate to call him back, he worked on his breathing, and on not wreaking holy havoc on the entire fucking building.

Chapter Twenty-Six

B ACK AT THE apartment, Wyatt had insisted Peyton stay in the living room with him, so she'd sat in uneasy silence on the couch, enduring his curious stare for long, torturous minutes before he finally spoke up.

"Peyton, listen," he said. "I don't want you to worry about what those assholes said. Okay? I know it doesn't make sense, but we're going to take care of it. We'll figure out what their game is and—"

She couldn't let him finish. "Wyatt, what doesn't make sense to you?"

"Why they'd accuse you of being the *Global Lens* blogger," he said. "You showed up at that condo completely by accident, right? So why would they—"

Oh god. She really couldn't do this now. "Wyatt." Peyton shook her head, trying to order her stampeding thoughts. "They weren't lying. Those guys *do* know me. They found me in Maryland, and they've been following me for months. Exactly like they said."

He sank back on the couch and stared at her in shock. "So, you're really…"

She nodded sharply.

"Seriously?" he bleated. "That wasn't subterfuge, or a—"

"Wyatt. I'm telling you, it's me. I'm the blogger."

"But why—" He stopped and pressed his fingers against his eyes, then stared at her again. "The reason I ask is that... *Jesus*, do you have any idea how much Buck hates *Global Lens*? Like... truly loathes it? He's been looking for them—for *you*—for months."

"I am aware. He's made that clear on a number of occasions." Peyton couldn't make herself say Buck's name. If she did, there'd be no way to keep herself from crying.

Wyatt sat across from her, blinking like she'd started speaking in tongues. "Is that why you didn't tell him who you are? You've been here for weeks. And you never said a word. To any of us."

Peyton stood up. "I can't do this with you."

There was no way they'd let her sleep in this apartment tonight. They'd probably never let her cross the threshold again. She had to gather as much of her stuff as she could, and go. *Now.*

She already knew what Buck would have to say to her once he arrived, but it'd dawned on her rather abruptly that there were three other men who lived in this place, too—and they would all want a reckoning.

She skirted the end table and headed for the hall.

Wyatt shot off the loveseat. "Whoa. Where are you going?"

"To pack my bags," Peyton announced. "You can come with me or not, but I think we both know your roomie is going to kick me to the curb the second he gets back. I'd like to have my toothbrush when he does."

Wyatt didn't have a ready answer to that. He simply followed her into Buck's bedroom and waited near the sliding glass door while she tossed things into bags.

After a while, he said, "Peyton, I have to ask."

She stopped and stared impatiently at him.

"We're the only special operators you've ever met, aren't we?"

She turned back to the dresser to hide the flush that heated her face. "I figured that part was obvious."

"Even so... how could you do that to us? To any of us?"

"Wyatt," she sighed, closing her eyes and resting her forehead against the bureau. "I wrote that post long before I met you guys. It had nothing to do with you."

From the doorway, Buck grunted in disgust. "That's where you're wrong, babe."

Wyatt lifted his chin. "What happened? Did you let them go?"

Buck shrugged. "We…" He glanced at Peyton, then continued, "Their story appears to be legit. If they have what they claim, they know where to find us."

Peyton let out the breath she was holding. It sounded as if he hadn't punished those men after she'd left. She wasn't thrilled that they'd outed her like that, but they hadn't known her true situation. They shouldn't have to pay for her transgressions.

Wyatt indicated Peyton with a casual tilt of his head. "She says it's really her, by the way. They weren't fucking with us."

Buck's eyes landed on her again. They were nearly black with fury. "Your recklessness, as it turns out, had everything to do with us. You know how long I've waited to say that? To tell you that, thanks to you, four men are probably out of a job? We've been vilified for months, Peyton, just for doing that goddamn job. A job most people are too squeamish to do, I might add."

Peyton tried not to flinch at the disdain dripping from his words. She couldn't bear to look at Buck or Wyatt, so she stared at the comforter instead, waiting for him to get it all out.

Mercifully, Wyatt left, murmuring something to Buck as he edged past. Peyton could hear Bennett and Joe knocking around out in the kitchen, but they fell silent when Wyatt joined them.

She grabbed a shopping bag off the bed and went into the bathroom.

"What are you doing?" Buck demanded.

"I'm leaving," Peyton explained, though it probably should have been obvious.

"The hell you are," Buck retorted. "It's getting dark out."

"I'm not a child, Buck. And I'm pretty sure neither of us wants me here."

She hadn't thought it possible, but Buck grew even more pissed. "Even so, you're not going out to wander an unfamiliar city at night." He reached for her bag full of toiletries. "Would you please knock that off?"

Peyton yanked the bag back and held it against her chest, staring Buck down until he stepped aside and let her leave the bathroom. "I imagine we've navigated an equal number of strange cities at night," she told him, scanning what she'd gathered so far and deciding it would hold her for a few days, at least.

"I'll be fine," she added, then zipped up her large duffle bag.

With a start, Peyton remembered her shoes in the closet, so she ducked around the bristling man in the center of the room and grabbed her sneakers and a few pairs of sandals off the floor.

Buck was spitting mad. He looked like a drill sergeant in a movie—feet spread, hands on his hips…all he needed was the hat and a mouth full of vitriol to complete the scene.

He did not look like her boyfriend—former boyfriend?—anymore.

"And what are you gonna do if someone comes for you? Insult them with your fancy theories?" he snapped.

Peyton smiled tightly at him. "I do not intend to put myself in harm's way to begin with. But should trouble find me, I know plenty of self-defense. My family took care of that, at least."

Buck turned red from his collar to that remarkable silver hair of his. "You're not using your head. Stop throwing shit in bags and listen to me."

Peyton shook her head and hefted the straps of her big duffle onto her shoulder. She picked up the shopping bag full of bathroom items, then looked around for her purse, eventually spotting it on the chair near the door.

If she had to go around in circles for much longer, she was going to break down in front of this man—who was suddenly the last person on earth she could bear to be vulnerable in front of.

"My head is working fine," she said, "Perhaps for the first time in recent memory. And you know what else works? My car, my phone, and my credit card. I. Will. Be. Fine."

She marched toward the bedroom door and to Buck's credit, he shifted to the side and let her pass instead of using his size and formidable skill set to stop her.

He still followed her to the living room, though, where three sets of wary eyes latched onto them and tracked their every move.

Peyton's bag slipped off her shoulder, so she stopped to readjust the unwieldy bulk of it.

Buck stationed himself beside the front door. "Damn it, woman. Would you give me that?"

"Please get out of my way."

"Not until you tell me where you're going."

"Don't you worry about that," she retorted. "I'm not your problem anymore."

Bennett stepped closer, looking between them cautiously. "Peyton. We can't just…let you leave. Not if you're involved with whatever someone's been trying to pull on us."

All at once, she realized that she represented more than a girlfriend who'd lied about her inconvenient hobby to them. She was as good as a suspect.

For someone who claimed her brain was in fine working order, Peyton sure was dense.

She swallowed and forced herself to meet Bennett's eyes. "You know I would never do anything to hurt you. Not intentionally. Please tell me you know that."

"We don't know squat," Joe piped up from the kitchen, but not unkindly.

"Before this afternoon, I'd never spoken a single word to those men. All I've done is write one blog post, then spend the next several months hiding from the people trying to find me."

Bennett looked at Buck over her head. A minute later, he was searching her face again, asking, "Where are you going?" once more.

Peyton squeezed her eyes shut for a second, then squared her shoulders. "I'm going to my storage unit to get a few things, and then to the new rental. I'll stay there until I can find something else. And guys…I'm sorry I didn't say anything. Really."

Wyatt tossed a set of keys at Buck, who snatched them out of the air without paying much attention to the action.

Then Buck opened the front door and gestured Peyton through. "Lead the way," he told her.

"I do not need a chaperone," she muttered, as she maneuvered through the opening.

"Too bad. You're getting one anyway."

"I'm driving," Peyton said, marching to her car and dumping her bags in the back seat.

"Go right ahead," Buck told her. "I'm going to follow you there."

BUCK STAYED A respectful distance behind her, but his truck was a constant presence in Peyton's rear-view mirror for the entire drive to the storage facility. *God forbid he let her get away*, she thought. *She might have time to pull out her laptop and blog about him.*

He didn't say much when she parked and entered the code to get into the building. He just loomed grumpily while she got a cart and pushed it to the bank of freight elevators.

The ride only lasted two floors, but it felt interminable. Peyton barrelled out of the car with relief. Her unit was at the far end of the wide hall, but as she looked around the empty, cavernous space, she had to admit she was a teeny bit glad she wasn't there alone.

It looked like something out of a crime movie.

Possibly because the man beside her wanted to commit a crime against Peyton with every fiber of his being.

She tried to ignore Buck's scowl and think through what she needed. A lamp or two, probably. The box with her coffee maker, plates, and utensils. Her sleeping bag.

She used her keys to open the padlock and blinked into the dusky interior.

Crap. Peyton was never going to find anything in this light.

Behind her, Buck clicked on the Maglite he usually kept in his glovebox and shined it around. She forced herself to step forward and peer at the labels she'd stuck on the first few boxes.

Books. More books. Comforting, but not helpful.

Buck cleared his throat, and she braced for what he would say.

"I'm sorry, but I just don't get it," he grumbled. "I don't."

Peyton shrugged like his flat tone hadn't sliced her heart in two. "Now you sound like Wyatt."

"Wyatt's a smart guy and I've been told worse."

"You don't say." She shoved aside the book boxes and searched for anything that looked like it might contain kitchenware. She had a tried-and-true system when it came to packing and moving. Number or letter the boxes, and keep a list of what was inside.

Except, she'd left her master list stuck in a library book on Buck's night table. Without it, Peyton had no idea what was where, and her entire soul was screaming to be alone, so she could mourn their dead relationship with all the agony it was due.

"Why aren't you trying to defend yourself?" Buck complained. "Or trying to explain?"

Peyton straightened and looked him in the eye. "What is there to say? I did it. You despise me for it. Pretty cut and dry if you ask me."

She cut the tape of the box next to her with a key, and wanted to groan at what was inside. *How appropriate.*

"So, you did write that post. You are the person behind *Global Lens.* You're not going to deny it?"

In answer, she reached into the box of office paraphernalia, withdrew her blog binder, and held it up for him. Like she was reading a story to a child, Peyton opened the cover and showed him page after page.

"Here they are, Buck. Every one of my published posts." She flipped to a second section. "The notes for stuff I was working on next." And the last section. "Receipts for my computer backup service, my hosting company, and my domain name. Is there anything else you'd like to see?"

Buck looked gutted, seeing the proof waved in his face like this. But what else could Peyton do? Facts were facts, and he didn't seem terribly interested in more than a handful of them.

"I think I'm good," he murmured.

Peyton returned the binder to its designated box and cast around for something that might help her survive this night. Her sleeping bag was nowhere to be found, and neither was her kitchen stuff. It was time to leave.

"I give up," she sighed. "I'm never going to find what I need without my list."

Buck didn't appear to hear her. He was staring off into space, muttering to himself.

"Did you hear me?" she asked. "I'm just going to lock up and go."

He refocused on her and the empty cart. "You're not bringing anything?"

"Were you not paying attention? I can't find where anything is. I'll come back and deal with it tomorrow."

Buck rolled his eyes and flicked off the flashlight, looking exasperated in addition to angry. "And what? You're gonna just sleep on the floor?"

"If I have to."

He clenched his jaw and looked away, then barged past her to grab the strip of packing tape the movers had used to seal her mattress in plastic. "Grab the other end," he instructed. "We can throw it in the back of my truck and bring it to the house now."

"Now? I hardly think—"

"Peyton," he growled, "Move the damn cart out of the way and get the other end of the bed. For crying out loud."

She had to be hallucinating. Peyton did as he instructed, though, then stared daggers at the back of his head the whole way down in the freight elevator. Instead of acknowledging her, Buck watched the floor numbers.

Outside in the parking lot, he took a minute to fold down his back seats, then heaved the heavy mattress into the back of his truck like a supervillain tossing a car.

He turned to her and snapped, "I can't understand how I missed so many signs with you. Was lying to me all a big game, or what?"

"First of all, if it was a lie at all, it was one of omission. And buddy, I missed some huge red flags myself."

"That's a real choice, coming from you."

"Is it?" Peyton cried. "You've got a lot of goddamn nerve. All *I* did was write a stupid article that the wrong person got ahold of, took out of context, and distorted so much I barely recognized it as my own. Then she left me swinging in the wind. I was terrified for my safety on a daily basis, but I still fell for you."

Peyton shoved her hair back with frustration. "But you…you and your boys are the ones who sat on your asses while an innocent village got slaughtered. If we're going to talk about lies here, you've got a lot more to answer for than me—and I won't let you make me out to be the only bad guy."

Buck stared at her in shock. "Of course," he sputtered. "Of course, you'd believe that. Why am I not surprised?"

"If I hadn't had strange men stalking me, I might've taken a second to wonder why a normal man would hate someone he'd never met so much. Stupid me, right? But here we are."

They faced off for a long minute, all out of accusations on both sides, it seemed.

Finally, Buck jerked his chin at Peyton's car. "Get in. I'll follow you to the house and put this in the bedroom, then leave you to it."

She blinked back the hot wash of tears trying to spill over and turned her back, stomping away from the best—and worst— thing that ever happened to her.

Chapter Twenty-Seven

Buck

AFTER THEY'D MOVED Peyton's mattress into the bedroom, Buck had retreated to his truck—but he still couldn't seem to make himself leave.

They were supposed to be spending their first night in that house together. Instead, he was out here, parked in the driveway next to Peyton's practical sedan and trying to picture what conditions would be like for her inside.

She'd stopped at a convenience store on the way from the storage facility, and when she'd dumped her bags on the kitchen counter, Buck had spotted bottles of iced coffee, cereal and a pint of milk, and plastic utensils she'd probably snagged from the deli counter.

Peyton would be set for breakfast, at least.

The ceiling fans had lights on them, so she wouldn't have to sit around in the dark, but Buck doubted that she'd remembered to grab towels, or bedding to use with the mattress on the floor.

Peyton also hadn't memorized the code for the alarm yet, so he'd had to change it to her birthday before he'd left, to make sure she'd use it.

He shouldn't care about any of this, Buck thought, watching her shadow move behind the old-fashioned window shades. It seemed that he did, though.

He couldn't fathom why he was so annoyed that Peyton had insisted on roughing it, instead of spending one more night under a roof with him. After the way she'd deceived them all, he would've thought he'd be happy to be rid of her.

As he sat there fuming, he supposed he should've seen this coming. Snippets from the past several weeks drifted through his mind, tainted by hindsight—Peyton's odd skittishness when Mohsin had snapped that photo of them on Buck's parents' patio. Her seeming reluctance to talk about her hobbies when they'd first met. How meticulous she always was about powering down her laptop when she wasn't using it.

In all the time that he'd been hoping to delay her finding out about the inquiries, Buck had been unwittingly aided by the fact that Peyton was busy keeping her own damn secrets.

Could she have figured out who he was before today? He didn't think so. But if she hadn't accidentally stumbled into the meeting this afternoon, he had to wonder how long she would have kept lying to his face and kissing him like he was her entire world.

But maybe…Peyton's arrival at the condo hadn't been an accident at all. Maybe she was still working with Joely. With Doggett. Maybe she was a mole, sent into their midst to gather intel no one else could.

Buck raked his hands over his face and groaned, remembering Peyton's horrified expression in the condo all over again. If that had been fake, it'd been some top-notch method acting.

At the sound of an approaching vehicle, he turned his head and scanned the street. A car rolled slowly along the road, then turned into a driveway several doors down. After a minute, a tall Black kid got out, retrieved a backpack and a set of football pads from the backseat, and let himself into his house. In the window at the back, an older woman was setting plates on a table.

Buck nodded to himself. This was a good, family neighborhood, he thought, sitting back. A quiet one. Peyton would be safe here without him.

Again, not that he should care—not after the accusations she'd thrown at him at the storage facility, in lieu of explaining herself.

Why did it sting so much that Peyton believed everything the press had printed about him and the rest of the team? She'd proved with that fucking blog that she wasn't able to delve beneath the surface of what mainstream media circulated about special operators. Naturally, Peyton would swallow that whole "stood by and did nothing" nonsense, too.

Buck might've been able to forgive it if she hadn't spent the last several weeks sharing a bed with him, and an apartment with Bennett, and Wyatt, and Joe. For her to parrot Doggett's character assassination to Buck's face tonight seemed like an especially cruel insult.

He remembered again the way they'd ground their teeth, while command put them off again and again. The sounds of that lone Army unit crumbling under Kadir's onslaught, and the utter confusion when Kadir's forces somehow found a way through the Boshad Pass and into the little village of Nabarut.

When OSW had finally allowed the SEALs in, the mess on the ground was already out of control. Buck's team had drawn the short straw, assigned to evac the senator and his wife while others waded in to hold off Kadir and rescue whoever was still standing in the village.

Doggett had still been spewing crap about "allowing allies to handle their own business" as they'd bundled him into the bird extracting him from the hot zone. Later, though, when Old Roy initiated his inquiry into the SEAL response, he forgot to mention any of that.

And ever since then, he'd been alleging that interbranch squabbling had caused the catastrophic delays and subsequent, preventable tragedy. The senator alleged that Buck and his brothers hadn't wanted to cut their R&R short, squandering precious minutes while they lobbied for a splashier mission.

It was all bullshit, of course. Doggett's PR people hadn't wanted to deep-six their photo op, and when it went south they used every connection at their disposal to pin their stupidity on the SEALs who'd saved their sorry hides.

Peyton hadn't witnessed any of that, but Buck still could not understand how, as smart as she was, she didn't smell the rat in the whole fiasco.

It felt personal. Unconscionable.

Like she didn't have his six and never would.

It bugged Buck to no end that no one had uncovered Peyton's connection to *Global Lens* before now, when it had apparently presented no challenge whatsoever for a first-year computer science major to figure out.

The kid had been in the U.S. for less than a year. By his own admission, he hadn't had a decent computer before a few months ago. Noah should have cracked the code in minutes.

Buck needed to call Tate again, to update him on what was happening, but he couldn't quite make himself do that yet, either. The Black Watch team that had been outside the condo earlier had undoubtedly given Monroe a rough outline of the afternoon's events. Buck would only be filling in details.

He sighed heavily, not wanting to think about it. What had he missed, when his life was imploding for the second goddamn time? What *else* could Buck be missing now?

BUCK WAITED IN his truck for an hour, maybe more, before Peyton finally shut off the lights and presumably turned in for the night. After that, he put his seat back and waited some more. And some more.

For what? She knew he was out here, and it wasn't like she was going to suddenly decide to invite him in. Buck didn't *want* her to invite him in. He didn't want to be here at all.

He dozed off at some point, though, because he when woke up the first streaks of dawn were coloring the horizon, and he had a stiff neck and a headache burgeoning behind his eyes.

Peyton was watching him from the front window.

In that moment, Buck hated everything about his life.

Without acknowledging that he saw her, he started his truck and put it in gear, then drove home on autopilot. He'd missed dinner the night before, so he grabbed a protein shake from the fridge and hot-footed it down the hall before any of the others could wake up and question where he'd been.

Joe, he noted, was asleep on their couch again. Bruiser had been looking forward to ditching his current roommates and sliding into the empty berth here. He was going to be pissed that Buck wasn't leaving after all.

He didn't have the energy to worry about it now. The dude could bunk in the living room or find someplace else. Or Buck could find someplace else. It didn't matter.

In his room, he chugged the shake and headed for the bathroom. His clothes smelled stale after the night spent in the truck, so he peeled them off and tossed them in the hamper on his way. He didn't want to look around too carefully, in case he spotted something of Peyton's that she'd left behind.

Buck stood under the hot spray for a while, hoping to slough off the fog he was shrouded in, but it didn't help much. He shaved quickly and pulled on a fresh pair of shorts, then propped himself in bed and stared at his phone.

Peyton hadn't called or texted. Of course, she hadn't. Right now, she likely despised him as much as he hated her.

The thought was depressing as hell.

Buck thumbed through his contacts with a bitter snort and sent the usual coded message to the secure Black Watch line. He couldn't put off the inevitable any longer.

Tate called back in seconds. "Hey, brother," the man said. "Ten bucks says I know why you're calling."

"I assume you heard what happened yesterday?"

"Some of it. For crying out loud, you boys ever take a day off?"

"Apologies, your majesty. Next time, I'll schedule the betrayal with you ahead of time."

Monroe was quiet for a minute or two. "Is that what you think happened? Peyton sold you out somehow?"

How the hell was Buck supposed to answer that? "I mean…she sure didn't tell anyone she was the blogger behind *Global Lens*. That was pretty pertinent intel, wouldn't you say?"

"I would. Kind of like you being the subject of two separate inquiries was pertinent."

Buck gritted his teeth and looked away, but his eyes landed right on the stack of Peyton's saucy library books on the nightstand. "You gonna armchair quarterback my love life now?"

"Not at all. I'm just pointing out that there might be equal amounts of obfuscation to go around here."

"Duly noted. Alas, the point of my call was to make sure you knew who Peyton was. Since someone has already told you that, I'll simply add that she moved out last night and call it a day."

"Okay. Where'd she go?"

"Just to the house we rented. Do I need to be concerned about having her out of our sight? Is this woman a flight risk, or what?"

Monroe chuckled. "You're the one banging her. You tell me."

"Wish I could, bro, but it turns out I don't know her from a houseplant."

The head of Black Watch blew out a long breath, but he didn't seem terribly concerned. In fact, Buck thought he sounded almost…amused.

"Am I missing the joke here?" Buck asked.

"No. There's no joke," Tate told him, despite letting out another low laugh. "And I don't think you need to worry about Peyton. Noah's been digging all night and he hasn't found a single link to Joely Spitz or Roy Doggett. I think your girl was collateral damage, not a primary player."

Buck wasn't so sure about that, but he wasn't going to debate it until he had a chance to get back into that storage unit and take a closer look at Peyton's fancy binder—along with whatever else she had stashed in there.

With that in mind, he slid free the list she'd stuck in a book to save her place and scanned what she'd noted was in each of her boxes.

"Did you guys find anything else on Rohaan or his uncle?" he asked absently.

"Nothing so far. Their stories check out. We'll keep an eye on them and wait to see what kind of proof they bring you. As eager as the kid is, I don't expect we'll be waiting long."

"How about Doggett? Where are we on him?"

"He and the missus are in D.C. right now. The Armed Services Committee is voting on a few things this week, and they're scheduled to attend a few fundraisers."

"Has he released a statement about Dan and Joely yet?"

"Not so far. It's a little odd, but he's never been one to broadcast his connection to Dan. I've got someone keeping tabs on it."

"Okay," Buck said, setting Peyton's meticulous list aside. "Then what do we do about Peyton?"

"For the time being? We leave her be."

Buck didn't know whether that sounded good or abysmal. "That's it? Just leave her alone?"

"She's not the problem here, Champ. We'll make sure she's safe but you need to stay focused on the big picture, all right?"

"My focus is fine, Monroe."

"If you say so."

Buck took a deep breath and fought to stay calm. "Anyway, next steps are to evaluate whatever proof those guys produce and let Peyton roam free. But what about the inquiry? Or the BOI?"

"Keep your heads down and ride them out," Tate instructed. "I'm hearing from a few different sources that they'll be wrapping up soon, and sentiments are leaning heavily in your favor. Whoever's running this show won't appreciate that. They're going to want to push back and that's when they will show us their cards."

"Whoever besides Peyton, you mean."

"Correct. As I said, I think she's a bit player at most."

"We'll see about that."

"Look," Tate sighed. "I know this tree hurts, but I need you to step back and see the whole forest. We have bigger targets to aim at, okay?"

"Yeah. Okay," Buck said. "So…we wait, I guess. You should know, I do not enjoy that."

"Who does," Monroe fired back. "Who does?"

THE PROTEIN SHAKE wasn't cutting it, so after he and Tate hung up, Buck risked another trip to the kitchen. Joe was sitting up on the couch, yawning and cracking his back.

"Did you kill her?" the man asked.

Buck took in his rumpled Bruins t-shirt and plaid boxers and sighed. "Of course, I didn't. Why would you even ask me that?"

"Probably because you've spent the last few months vowing to murder the *Global Lens* blogger with your bare hands," Ben said from behind him.

Damn that dude was quiet. Or Buck was losing it.

"It was figurative speech," he said. "Asshole."

Wyatt ambled up the hall and shouldered past Bennett, beelining for the coffee pot. "Said the stone-cold killer."

Buck tossed up his hands. "It's hardly as if any of you fuckwads wanted to buy the person wine and chocolates!"

"That was before we saw the set of legs that went with the keyboard," Joe pointed out.

He glared at him. "Watch it, fucker."

"He's got the right idea, though," Wyatt called, as he spooned coffee grounds into a filter. "Knowing Peyton changes things."

Buck scowled harder. "Makes things worse, you mean."

"I wouldn't say that," Bennett shrugged. "More complicated, maybe."

"It's actually very simple," he told them. "Monroe told us to leave Peyton alone, and that's what we are going to do. Once she vacates that house, she will not be our problem anymore."

There was a heavy pause as the other three men went still. "What do you mean, *vacates*? Where's she supposed to go?" Joe objected.

Buck shrugged. "What do I care? She has cousins in L.A., or she can move back to Maryland if she wants. All I know is that I've got first, last, and security tied up in that cozy little house she's bunking in and I'm not going to just let her have it."

They all shot looks at each other, but it was Bennett who finally spoke up. "Dude…Peyton hasn't found a job yet. You guys got that place with you as the primary wage earner. If you make her move out, she's not going to be able to get anything else."

Buck stuffed his hands in his pockets. "I guess she should've thought of that sooner."

His best friend on this dumpster fire of a planet faced him head-on and ducked a couple of inches to look him square in the eye. "I realize that you're hurt, bro, but this ain't you. You are not the guy that kicks a woman out on her ass over money you don't need."

"Who says I don't need it?" Buck retorted. "You might remember the special friend we currently have on retainer. Plus, if this inquiry doesn't go our way, I could end up just as unemployed as Madam Blogger."

Wyatt strolled out of the kitchen in his pajama bottoms like some kind of shirtless barista, handing steaming mugs of coffee to each of them before going back for his own. "We're all chipping in on the 'special friend' business," he pointed out when he returned. "You can afford to give Peyton a couple of months to get her feet under her."

"And who knows?" Ben added. "Maybe by then, you two will be back together."

Buck blinked at him, trying to make sense of those words. "You can't possibly be serious."

Joe stood and shuffled closer. "Why not? All this time we've been thinking of Peyton as this shadowy villain—but what if she's been jobbed like the rest of us?"

Buck looked around at the three faces he trusted most in the world and couldn't understand how they'd taken such a collective leave of their senses. "I'm dreaming. This is a bad dream. Has to be."

He set his mug on the bar and walked toward his room. If he was sleeping, he ought to be doing it in bed, not standing in a huddle with these jokers.

Back in the kitchen, Wyatt was cracking open the freezer and calling out, "Yo, if you two are really done-zo, can I eat the meals Peyton stashed in the freezer for you?"

Buck gripped his doorframe and rolled his shoulders. "Be my guest," he said, then slammed his door behind him.

Nightmare. Had to be.

Chapter Twenty-Eight

Peyton

A M I SPEAKING to Peyton Page?" the woman on the other end of the line asked.

There was a familiar cadence to her voice, and Peyton tried to place where she'd heard it last. Could this be one of the people she'd spoken to about jobs in the last few weeks?

No, that didn't seem right.

Peyton had spent most of the night supine on a bare mattress, however, running through the day before over and over in her head instead of sleeping. And then, after Buck drove away without a backward glance early this morning, she'd parked herself at the kitchen table and spent the next two hours ruminating some more.

This time with coffee.

Current conditions weren't terribly ripe for feats of cognitive brilliance, but Peyton was still nearly certain that her caller was a documentary darling who inspired very, very stabby feelings in at least five people.

"May I ask who's calling?" she inquired, just to be sure.

"Absolutely. My name is Joely Spitz. You've probably seen me on tv."

Peyton stuck her finger in her mouth and pretend-gagged at the sheer audacity, though no one else was in the kitchen to witness it.

Joely brazened out her silence. "I did a special on school shooters last year, with families from tragedies all over the country. Also, one on indigenous communities in Alaska, and how they're being impacted by climate change."

"Good for you," Peyton muttered, glaring down at the kitschy linoleum under her feet.

"Have you seen them?" Joely prodded.

If Buck could hear this woman, he'd be ripping the phone from Peyton's hand and tearing into her with a vengeance.

Peyton pushed that thought away with irritation. No one was riding in to save her from this but herself.

"Ms. Spitz, I have never seen either of those programs. And yet, I still seem to know who you are. I wonder why that is?"

A knowing laugh rang over the line. "Great. Let's dispense with the small talk, then. I have some good news for you."

Peyton would bet her entire retirement account that no news exiting this person's mouth was ever going to be good. "How did you get my number?" she wondered.

Another husky chuckle. "You're not so hard to find, sweetie. Moving to Cali changed nothing."

Peyton didn't need to fake-retch at that assessment. Joely's cheerful words, and the implicit threat beneath them, made her feel sick for real.

She forced words from her lips. "What do you want from me?"

Joely hesitated a beat, barely noticeable but definitely there. "I've got a proposal for you," she announced. "Win-win for both of us. You want to hear it?"

"Not in the least," Peyton said.

"Tough. Here's how this is going to go. You are going to work for me on my next project as my director of research. You can geek out with all your foreign affairs crap, earning a hell of a lot more bank than you ever did teaching acne-faced losers at that stupid community college. Travel costs are rolled into the production. If you do well, the path for advancement is guaranteed."

Shit.

Shit, shit, shit. Peyton's brain stumbled ahead, tripping over every red flag jammed into the ground along the way. For someone she'd never met, Joely Spitz knew an awful lot about her. And what she was offering sounded more like a gilded cage than a career boon.

"And in return?" she whispered.

"Shut down that ridiculous blog of yours for good. Delete everything. Wipe the drive, salt the earth," Joely instructed. "I have no idea why you haven't done it already, but it's time to bury that little headache of yours once and for all, wouldn't you agree?"

Peyton's heart was hammering, and she felt like a refrigerator was sitting on her lungs. "No. I would not agree," she said, louder this time. "Why do you care, anyway? I'm no one to you. You took what you wanted, changed it to fit your agenda, and left me to pick up the pieces."

"Come on, Peyton. Read the room. It's over."

"Not for me, it isn't."

"Look. You had a little hobby, showed off for a while, proving how smart you are, and it was a total flop. Now I'm offering you a gig where you can actually make a difference. Anyone with half a brain cell could see you're trading up."

Did Joely often get what she wanted by insulting her marks? And for that matter, what was even happening here?

Peyton sat back as her brain finally caught up to her panic response. "Why are you trying to buy me off?"

The other woman paused again, longer this time. "Is that what you think this is? Don't be ridiculous. I just felt bad for how everything shook out and thought I'd extend an olive branch."

"Then why make me kill the blog?"

"Because it was a *disaster*, Peyton. You think I want something that pathetic associated with my brand anymore, even indirectly?"

Peyton traced the whorls and medallions on the floor with her eyes, listening to the nervous energy simmering under Joely's words. "You're lying."

Joely let out an offended huff of laughter. "You're a joke, you know that? I thought I'd do something nice, make amends, or whatever. Meanwhile, you're out here thinking this is Watergate or something. Grow up."

Peyton took a deep breath, frantically trying to slot the pieces of this bizarre conversation into their proper places. "*Global Lens* is still a problem for you. Why?"

"All right, I can see you're going to be pigheaded about this, so let me be perfectly clear. You *will* shut down that piece of shit blog of yours. You will destroy any trace of it. Erase it from the face of this earth. Do you understand?" Joely asked. "Because if you do not, all that careful separation you've kept from *Global Lens*, all that precious anonymity, is history. Forget about what's on the dark web—I am going to broadcast your name and whereabouts far and wide, Peyton Page. Every single crackpot that you pissed off with your pedantic bullshit six months ago is going to know exactly where to find you and I will not spend one second worrying about what happens next."

Peyton tried not to let Joely hear the fear icing her veins. "You're threatening me."

"You're damn straight I am. Why don't you chew on that for a bit? I'll be in touch soon and you can give me your answer then."

"Wait," she said, unable to resist asking the thing that had bedeviled her for nearly half a year now. "I have one more question."

"What's that."

"Why…why me? There must be a million political blogs out there. Why did you pick mine?"

Joely snorted and offered up the first thing that sounded true in this whole conversation. "I didn't. The PR team for the production did."

Peyton held her breath. Did she dare? "Oh, right. That was Tim Stein, wasn't it?" *Guess she did dare.*

There was a long pause. "Couldn't tell you."

"Got it. Well...I'd say thanks for calling, but...yeah. Anyway."

"Talk soon," Joely said and hung up.

Peyton set her phone face down in front of her and stared blindly at the case.

Holy fuck. What just happened? If Buck were here, he'd be having a complete meltdown. She was ready to break down herself.

And then she thought...Buck. And Joely. All at once, she remembered him talking about his ex, back when he'd asked her to his parents' place for dinner. "*Doesn't even matter,*" he'd said, and then, "*I guess you could call her a reporter.*" He'd told her that reporter had screwed up their mission.

What were the odds that Buck's ex and Peyton's nemesis were the same individual? At the moment, they seemed quite high. And if that were the case...why hadn't Joely said a word about the man she and Peyton apparently had in common?

Even after a ten-minute call, she could tell Joely wasn't the sort of woman to forgo that kind of chum in the water. That meant she knew Peyton and Buck had already split—or that she didn't know they'd gotten together, to begin with.

It felt important, but she wasn't sure what to do with the information.

Sometime overnight Bennett had texted her, however, telling her that he, Wyatt, and Joe would still be looking out for her. The show of support had made her teary at the time, but Peyton called up the message again now, reading it over and reassuring herself this was a good idea before she tapped out a reply.

Hey, you have a minute to talk privately?

His response popped up quickly. Sure. Give me 5.

When he called, she asked him, "Do you guys have my phone tapped?"

"Peyton, no," Bennett protested. "No, of course not."

"Not like you'd tell me if you did."

"Girl, what the hell are you getting at? What's going on?"

She explained what had happened in a rush. "If that college kid could crack my blog security so easily, and now Joely—how long before everyone else does, too?" she wondered. "Joely threatened to expose me if I didn't agree to work for her. I'm scared."

"Don't worry. We're keeping an eye on you, okay? No one's gonna fuck with you, but if you see anything weird, you have to promise me you'll call the cops right away. All right? Call 911 first, *then* one of us."

"I will. I promise."

"Good. Now, what are you doing the next few days? We thought we could take shifts helping you move some of your stuff out of storage."

"That's nice of you guys, but maybe I should leave most of it there," Peyton said. "Buck is probably going to want me out of here before long."

Bennett scoffed. "Nah, you're good. Stay as long as you need to. He doesn't care."

Peyton pulled the phone from her ear and frowned at the screen. *Huh?*

"You sure about that?"

"Sure, I'm sure," Bennett chuckled. "We'll get your boy in hand. Don't you worry about a thing."

LATER, AS SHE drove down increasingly familiar roads on her way to meet Ben at the storage facility, Peyton thought again about Buck. All the time she'd been worried about hiding her identity, it'd never once occurred to her that he might be doing the same.

He'd never let on that his unit was under investigation or told her the real reason he despised the blogger behind *Global Lens* so much.

What bothered Peyton now was how he'd made their first meeting seem like a coincidence instead of a calculated plan. Buck could've lied about that nice colonial being his parents' house, and about what he was doing in Maryland—but how could he have known she was going to be at that coffee shop that day? Even Peyton hadn't known.

If he'd known who she was all along, though…why had he looked so utterly shellshocked at that condo yesterday afternoon?

In any case, Peyton didn't believe what Bennett had said. Buck definitely cared if she stayed in the cottage. And if Bennett and the others told him she'd been in contact with Joely Spitz, what was to say he wouldn't beat his ex to the punch and out Peyton to the world?

He'd been vowing vengeance on *Global Lens* for months, after all. That would be the perfect revenge.

Was there anywhere Peyton could go to be safe? Her cousins in L.A. were far too close for comfort, and her parents would not be remotely interested in taking her in if it meant their reputations would be put at risk.

Maybe Peyton could fly to London and hunker down with her brother for a while. No one would care who she was across the pond, and Josh would help her find work if she asked. But the thought of hanging out with him, pretending everything was fine when it patently wasn't, made her droop with exhaustion.

Peyton could run, but who knew how long Joely would wait before she called again, demanding a final answer? Before she made good on her threats? In a couple of days, or a week, or a month, Peyton could be public enemy number one, for real this time.

And then—then normalcy would be a thing she never experienced again.

Chapter Twenty-Nine

Buck

A S MONROE HAD predicted, they didn't have to wait long for Rohaan's message setting up the evidence handoff. Only a few days after the first meeting, the kid once again managed to slip a note onto their patio chair with none of them the wiser.

With that kind of stealth at his disposal, Rohaan wouldn't need to worry if the whole computer science degree didn't pan out. Tate was bound to offer the guy a job with Black Watch at this rate.

Who knew, though—maybe Monroe already had. He could be handing out jobs like Mardi Gras beads, with Buck's own offer an inconsequential blip among the rest.

Regardless, as he pulled up to the swanky seafood joint where Rohaan supposedly bussed tables, Buck was grateful to have something to do besides sulking about Peyton. She'd consumed his thoughts every minute since she'd left, and he hadn't done himself any favors with his drive-bys at the cottage, checking to see if she was home.

Buck hated the way she'd managed to insinuate herself into his life so smoothly, and that he still couldn't figure out what Peyton's angle had been. And, though he'd go to his grave before he admitted it to anyone else, he despised the fact that he missed her.

Turned out she'd taken more than her toothpaste with her when she bolted—it seemed Buck had lost several brain cells to the woman, as well.

He cursed and threw his truck in park, scanning the restaurant lot for anything off before he got out. He only saw the usual lineup of vanity vehicles, however, row after row of sleek and shiny, burnished by the setting sun.

A small marina sat off to the side, sailboat masts bobbing next to the low roof of the restaurant, their furled sails clanking in the chilly breeze.

This would've been a great place to bring Peyton on a date, had they managed many of those before the crap hit the fan.

Another curse and Buck got out of his SUV, pulling his baseball hat lower on his forehead as he marched toward the entrance. The doorway was all chrome and glass and flanked with potted palms, and would've made him rethink his casual clothes if he'd been planning to stay for longer than five minutes.

As it was, he'd stand out from the patrons—but he'd fit right in with the delivery drivers and dishwashers, and hopefully remain completely beneath the notice of whoever might be dining here this evening.

Inside, Buck bypassed the hostess stand and went to the takeout station off to the side. Rohaan hovered behind it in a navy-blue polo shirt, joking around with a coworker and looking for all the world like the average college student he most definitely was not.

He caught Buck's eye but gave no sign that they knew each other.

"Welcome to Sea Chase," the kid intoned. "Here to pick up?"

"Yup. Should be all paid for." Monroe had taken care of that, using some Black Watch card no one could trace.

"What's the name for the order?"

"Johnson." It was a common name, but none of them had a single relative with it, should anyone decide to go looking.

Rohaan nodded at his little computer screen, tapping a few times with perfect professional neutrality. "Okay, looks like it's ready. Let me go grab it from the kitchen, and then I can close out the transaction."

The kid stepped away, allowing a waiter with a laden tray to sweep by before ducking into the kitchen through the swinging doors.

His coworker stayed behind, shifting in her sneakers behind the podium and smiling shyly when Buck looked at her. She had just opened her mouth to say something when a large party came pouring through the side door from the dock, swirling into the space between them on a cloud of briny air and expensive cologne.

The group made its way into the bar area adjacent to the dining room, taking up residence on stools and at high-top tables as they looked around at the other drinkers, baldly assessing who merited their notice and who could be ignored.

Buck watched them from under his brim, recognizing a couple of socialites that occasionally made the papers, as well as an injury attorney who ran constant ads on tv.

And then his heart stopped, a mass of familiar blonde curls presenting itself toward the edge of the crowd like a punch to his solar plexus.

What the *fuck* was Joely Spitz doing here, now of all times?

She was leaning over a smarmy old man sitting in the shadows at the back of the group, smiling as if she didn't care that he was ogling her cleavage. From Buck's angle, he looked tanned and Botoxed, and was sporting a goddamn seersucker blazer as if he'd just popped in from back-to-back boat christenings.

Buck drifted further into the corner near the kitchen and hoped like hell the hostess stand would obscure him. Then he peeked through the porthole window of the swinging door closest to him, spotting Rohaan in the kitchen, winding his way through the prep tables with a large brown bag in his hands.

Buck tapped his ear and murmured under his breath, "Kid, time for you to get gone. Tell your manager you're sick or something. Leave through the back. Send the bag out with someone else."

Rohaan stopped in his tracks, barely hesitating before he collared a young woman to hand off the food. Seconds later, he was wading deeper into the kitchen, lost behind the line cooks and sous chefs as he hopefully found a back exit.

His proxy came out and set Buck's order behind the takeout podium, then returned to the kitchen. Rohaan's coworker beckoned Buck over and transferred the bag to him with a sentence so softspoken it was inscrutable. Buck kept his back to the bar and turned to the door, hoping to make his escape without Joely spotting him.

No such luck. Buck didn't even have time to alert the others before her fingers slid around his biceps and held him firmly in place.

"Hey, Beau Gaines," she purred. "I thought I recognized those nice, broad shoulders."

Of all the things to wash up on his shore right now, Joely Spitz was akin to a week-dead fish. Rotten through and through. Buck's chest erupted in a cascade of furious fireworks.

He could not—would not—harm this woman, but damn he wanted to. He wanted to drag it out and make it hurt, too.

Joely fluttered up at him, laying on the sex kitten schtick. "Miss me?"

Buck's jaw was tensed hard, but he managed to push out a few words. "Can't say that I have," he muttered, "And I expect you know why."

Joely scoffed at him, chirping tipsily, "Are you still mad about the show? Come on. No hard feelings. You know I have nothing to do with how they turn out."

"You told me you were there to profile the girls' school, Joely."

"I was!" she protested, her long, manicured nails digging into his skin. "The producers changed everything during editing. It wasn't my fault."

"Not your fault? It was your documentary. You expect me to believe that you had no say whatsoever in how it came out?"

Joely gave him a worldly Cheshire cat grin. "I've got to pay the bills, big guy. Just like everybody else. Now, tell me. Are you in town long? When can we hang out?"

Buck cringed at how the oily come-on slithered across his nerves.

"Hang out," he said. "You're serious."

"Yeah, I'm serious. It was good between us. Surely you remember that much."

They'd had a handful of hot-and-heavies, no more. Danger banging. Nothing close to what he'd shared with Peyton these last few months, not that it was any of Joely's business.

"I remember hearing you got engaged," Buck pointed out.

She rolled her eyes and snorted. "I'll worry about that ink once it's dry," she laughed.

Oh, yeah. She and the mister were definitely going the distance if Joely was out here propositioning former flames within weeks of his ring landing on her finger. Buck shuddered to think what Dan was getting up to.

He tipped his head toward the bar and said, "All right. Then how about focusing on the horse that brung ya?"

Joely peeked over her shoulder a shade too quickly. "Who, Leon? Give me some credit. He's my producer, not my sugar daddy."

Buck checked the guy out once more and as he zeroed in on him, Joely's brazen advances faded into background noise. For all intents and purposes, Leon looked like any other rich man, enjoying an evening out with his privileged, oblivious friends.

But Buck had instincts honed from years on the Teams, and he'd bet his left nut that guy was a bad dude. The worst, in fact.

Leon sat, still and watchful, as his pals joked around him. He emanated coldness behind his canned smile. The fine hairs on Buck's neck prickled with the recognition of evil.

He didn't want to stare too long and draw the man's notice, however, so he refocused on Joely and paid more attention to her vamp act. When he'd known her before, she'd been one-hundred-percent cool girl, worldly and chill, out for a good time.

Now, there was a jittery edge skating under the surface. Buck had assumed it was because she'd rolled him and his team under the bus with her fucking documentary, but now…now he wondered.

"You work with that character a lot?" he asked.

Joely angled her body between him and Leon and frowned. "Sometimes. Why?"

"Was the hatchet job his idea?"

Joely pressed her lips together and looked away. *Direct hit.*

Buck said again, "You told me you were there for the girls' school, Joely."

"I was. At first," she admitted. "But it turned out that a bunch of cocky-ass men with guns had more entertainment value."

Her total lack of shame pissed him off something fierce. "Is that what Leon told you?"

Joely perused his body like they were at a steakhouse and not a seafood joint. "Figured that one out for myself," she muttered.

"I appreciate the reminder."

For the life of him, Buck couldn't figure out why he was bothering to spar with this woman. She was old news, his "fish of the day" was rapidly getting cold, and he needed to get on his way.

"You know what, Beau? Forget it," Joely spat. "You're clearly hung up on stuff that had nothing to do with me. I thought we had a good time together, but you weren't this surly when I met you the first time."

The sound of his given name startled him out of his bitter spiral. For months he'd felt so betrayed by this woman, but she'd never even known him well enough to start using his regular nickname.

And now, having had a taste of what a real relationship could be like with Peyton, Buck realized what a big nothing his tryst with this woman had actually been. Joely's infractions felt like a flash in the pan compared to the forest fire of emotional destruction Peyton had lit in his heart.

"I am absolutely hung up on the way your fucking documentary exploded multiple landmines in my life," Buck told her. "And thanks a bunch for that. Now, why don't you march yourself back over to your buddies and find yourself a new mark. Ruin someone else's life. I don't care."

He turned and walked away, Leon Doggett's icy gaze drilling holes in his back—but Joely surprised him by chuckling and following him out. Her demeanor changed the instant they got outside, her smile falling away as she grabbed his arm again.

"Listen, I didn't take you for an idiot, but I'm beginning to wonder if you've had a few screws come loose since last I saw you."

"Excuse me?"

Buck pulled free of her hand and clocked the two goons lounging near the corner of the building a split second before Wyatt murmured in his ear, *"Deuces, 2 o'clock."*

He really hoped Rohaan had followed his instructions and gotten the hell out of Dodge.

"Someone's been nosing around where they don't belong, Lieutenant Gaines," Joely hissed, just as the men straightened from their leans and began to head over. "And I bet you know who it is."

He kept an eye on the incoming bogies and stepped back from her. "I think you're letting your conspiracy shows get the best of you, hon. Might be time for a vacation."

The pair of meatheads were uniquely Hollywood types, heavy on the muscle and easy on the eyes. Joely noticed them approaching with a scowl of irritation.

"You have no idea what kind of hornet's nest you're poking," she told him. "Call off your people, whoever they are, and let this drop. You are not going to win this fight."

The thugs rolled to a stop next to her. Buck shifted the bag of food to his hip and held up a placating hand, though he was so pissed off he dearly would've loved to punch at least one of them.

"What fight? There's no fight. I'm taking my food, and I'm leaving. That's it."

"Don't be thick, Beau," she called as he reached his truck. "I'm trying to help you."

"Catch you later," he smiled thinly and got behind the wheel.

Buck's earpiece was silent as he set the takeout order on his passenger seat, so he looked down at his gearshift and murmured under his breath, "Tell me you heard all that."

Joely and her guard dogs stayed put, watching as Buck pulled out and rolled toward the exit.

The reply came a split second later.

"Roger that, Romeo. Head back home and we'll cover your six."

Chapter Thirty

Peyton

PEYTON SAT ON a folding chair on her back stoop, watching Mr. and Mrs. Fujikawa putter companionably around their back yard next door, weeding vegetable beds and pruning fruit trees. They'd brought her six avocados the night before. She'd eaten one on the spot, but five were still in a bowl on her kitchen counter, waiting for her to turn them into guacamole.

Peyton didn't want to feel forlorn, watching her sweet neighbors tend their garden together, but she did—and the reason, quite clearly, was Buck. Or rather, the lack of Buck.

Did this constitute as sulking? *Probably.*

She didn't care.

After Joely Spitz's crazy call the other day, she hadn't been able to stop thinking about Buck and, for that matter, the rest of the guys.

Peyton had thought about Bennett cheerfully eating sushi he didn't like, Wyatt begging for kitchen scraps, and Joe rushing to protect her moments after she'd basically accused him of being a stalker.

She'd thought about Buck, finding out she'd lied to him for their entire relationship then moving a mattress here so she wouldn't have to sleep on the floor. She thought about him sleeping in his truck in the driveway the first night she'd stayed in the cottage, watching over her even while he licked wounds that she'd inflicted.

Peyton groaned and dropped her head in her hands. They were good men, and she'd hurt them. She'd undoubtedly hurt others like them, as well.

In retrospect, she could see where she'd been careless with her words, trying to be clever and stand out from the crowd. Instead, she'd managed to open the door for people like Joely Spitz and Senator Doggett to use her for their own ends.

Now that she'd served her purpose, they thought they could bury the evidence of what they'd done. They thought they could bury her.

Unfortunately for them, sometime during all her brooding, it had occurred to Peyton that they could only keep her in check if she allowed it. If she played along.

What if she *didn't* toe the line, though? What if she took the anvil they were holding over her head and seized it for herself?

Peyton looked over at Mr. Fujikawa, meeting his eyes when he straightened and waved at her. She smiled and waved back, then got to her feet and went inside to get her laptop.

Regret was only useful if it spurred you to do better going forward, and she thought she might have figured out a way to do that. She'd been too tangled up in her own panic and pride to think of it before, but these last days alone had given her clarity.

It was time to use her voice—and well past time to take back the power that'd been stolen from her.

* * *

PEYTON STOOD AT the front window, watching for Bennett's pickup truck to turn onto her street. She'd invited all of them over for dinner as thanks for their help the last couple of weeks, but she knew he'd get there first.

He always did. Out of all of them, he'd taken her welfare to heart the most.

The guys had been quick to offer their big vehicles and strong backs so Peyton could move her stuff out of storage. She'd put them off at first, but after receiving word that two of her job possibilities had been filled by other people, she'd eventually agreed.

With no paycheck coming in, she needed to keep her spending down, and the monthly rental fee at the storage facility was a bill she could do without.

Whenever they'd had time, Bennett, Joe, and Wyatt had stopped by to pick up her key and carted her possessions to the cottage. Before Peyton knew it, they'd brought her most of her clothes, an assortment of end tables and lamps, and her meager collection of kitchen utensils.

They'd even procured her a second-hand sofa, from a family they knew that was relocating.

Once the necessities were in place, the guys brought the rest over haphazardly. She unpacked some boxes and stacked others in the guest room untouched.

It hardly mattered, anyway—she would have to move it all right back into storage if she couldn't find work soon.

Peyton would deal with that when and if it came to pass, though. For now, she still had options.

Her chief priority tonight was to stop hovering at the window and stop trying to imagine how Buck felt about being excluded.

He should be here. He and Peyton should be cooking this meal together tonight. They weren't, though, and at some point, she was going to have to get used to the fact that it was mostly her fault.

At the end of the street, a black sedan rounded the corner and cruised slowly up the road. It wasn't Bennett or any of the others. Not even close.

Peyton knew their cars well now, and she'd grown used to nondescript minivans and older four-doors of her neighbors, but this car—this car demanded attention. With its dark tinted windows and flashy chrome hubcaps, it belonged somewhere far different than a modest suburban sidestreet.

It was inching up the block now, like the driver was looking for an address, or was lost.

Peyton ran through possibilities in her head. She supposed it could be a real estate appraiser, pulling comps for someone getting ready to sell. A person taking video for a mapping app, perhaps. Or a location scout for a film.

It definitely wasn't a criminal scoping out her street, hunting for a pariah blogger. It *wasn't*.

Peyton shifted out of sight as the car rolled by, spooked by how fast her heart was beating. She really wished Bennett and the others would get there soon.

AFTER THE GUYS helped her clear the table, they stood awkwardly around the kitchen while Peyton spooned the leftovers into take-home containers for them.

Bennett leaned against the counter watched her for a minute, then exchanged a quick look with the others. "Peyton…do you mind if I ask you something?"

She looked up from a bowl of rice. He was trying to look casual, but his tone had been anything but.

"Shoot."

Ben took a deep breath. "You're a smart woman. Okay? So, I'm sure you had your reasons. But I can not for the life of me figure out what you had to gain from writing that blog the way you did."

Peyton set down her serving spoon and stared at it for a moment, before forcing herself to meet each set of eyes aimed at her. "Nothing, as it turns out. And for what it's worth, I *am* sorry. I hate that I was responsible, even indirectly, for what you guys and…and…"

Her voice cracked. She shut up before she embarrassed herself.

"Buck," Wyatt supplied.

Peyton nodded and took another few seconds to compose herself before agreeing, "And Buck. What you've all gone through—I never meant for any of it to happen." She chuckled bitterly. "You have to understand. Six months ago, no one even read my stupid blog. No one. It was easy to forget that it was public and I wasn't thinking in terms of real people—it was only macro scale ideas to me. I could've been dissecting a chess game from fifty years ago, or a tv show. It was just…concepts. That's it."

Joe looked away, his dark features stormy.

Peyton went on, "The thing is, I do know you guys now. I know where I went wrong and what I can do to make things better."

Bennett frowned and started to speak, but she held up a hand to stave him off. "I need you to know that what was printed in the papers and broadcast on tv was not an accurate recounting of what I said. I *was* off-base in some respects, but the media twisted my words far past that point. They took stuff out of context and mischaracterized my intentions."

Peyton swallowed down the familiar wave of frustration that had haunted her for months and continued, "That reporter, Joely Spitz? I will never understand why she and her PR people chose to use me the way they did."

She rubbed her stinging eyes. "Once the horse was out of the barn, though, I was really scared by the way people reacted. I had no prayer of setting the record straight, while staying anonymous."

Wyatt folded his thick arms across his chest, looking uncomfortable. "By the time Buck found your site, half your stuff was archived. I've never seen him so furious."

"Yeah, the sudden onslaught of traffic crashed the site for a bit," Peyton explained. "When I finally got it up and running again, it seemed safer to limit access until things died down."

Wyatt studied her. "So…what *did* you say in that post? I never read the original."

Peyton shrugged. Telling them couldn't make things much worse. "Basically, that special operators are not the supermen people make them out to be. You're human, and therefore fallible."

She looked around at their faces, wanting them to understand. "You've been glorified since 9/11, but the truth is, bad apples exist in every barrel. One or two can compromise a mission. More than that, and entire theaters of operation could end up destabilized. Add to that the closed-door nature of what you do, and it becomes a breeding ground for hubris and corruption. Consequently, your track record doesn't always merit the carte blanche you receive."

Joe turned back to squint at her in confusion. "What?"

Peyton smiled weakly. "I listed a few examples of commanders pushing ahead with doomed missions and outlined the ripple-effect of damages when things inevitably went south."

Wyatt's eyebrows were nearly at his hairline as he shared a look with Joe. "Peyton, that is…very different from what we heard."

"Tell me about it," she muttered. "I imagine what they've said about you has been similarly distorted."

"I mean…you weren't really wrong, though," Joe said.

Bennett nodded slowly. "Forgive me for saying this, but it wasn't exactly ground-breaking, either. Why bother writing it?"

Peyton had wondered the same thing and hadn't liked what she'd come up with. "I guess…I needed to sound smart? Maybe? As they say, I didn't know what I didn't know. I just wanted to prove I knew *something*. Doesn't make a lot of sense in retrospect."

Wyatt asked, "Were you, like, trying to impress someone in particular, or…?"

She shrugged again, shaking her head. "Prospective employers, perhaps. I thought *Global Lens* would help establish my credentials as a current affairs expert. That way, when I was ready to level up to a new position, I'd look like I was bringing something unique to the table."

"That's a laugh," Joe scoffed. "Half of those dudes in academia wouldn't know a blog if it bit them in the ass."

The bile tried climbing her throat again. "You're probably right," Peyton admitted.

Wyatt was rubbing a hand across the stubble on his jaw, weighing her explanation. "I think…there's more to it," he said eventually. "Isn't there?"

Peyton brushed past him and sat at the kitchen table with a sigh. "I don't know, Wyatt. It probably had something to do with my mom and dad. They never said anything to my face, but I know they were disappointed when I was passed over for the foreign service. I wanted to show them I could still make a difference, just…in my own way."

Joe said, "Who the hell outed you, though. You were good enough at staying anonymous that we couldn't find you. So how did Spitzy discover who you were?"

Peyton had wondered that very thing. "I think it must've been my old boss at MCC," she told him. "Outside of my immediate family, no one else knew. But I disclosed the connection when I applied for that job, and a couple of weeks ago my friend Devon overheard Doggett's PR guy arguing with the dean. It sounded as if he offered me up for money. Probably told them I wouldn't put up a fight, too."

"Well, that's shitty."

"Agreed."

"Peyton." Bennett's blue eyes drilled into her, intense and hyperfocused. She could almost see the gears turning behind them. "Listen, we all know Joely Spitz better than we'd like to, and we've gotten an unfortunate crash course on Doggett, as well. We know what they're capable of, and it's easy to believe that what you're saying is true. But I think you *really* need to tell Buck all this."

Peyton dropped her head to the table with a thunk. "That's going to be a problem since Buck never wants to talk to me again. And for the record, he also withheld who he truly was. I'm not the only one to blame." *Even if it felt that way most of the time.*

"He was burned by Joely, too," Ben said gently. "When Buck thought you were in cahoots with her, it reopened a wound that had barely scabbed over."

"And what am I supposed to do with that?" she retorted, straightening up. "I'm not going to chase him down, Bennett. He supposedly cared so much about me, but he wasn't terribly interested in giving me the benefit of the doubt or asking me what the truth was when it came down to it."

"If I may," Joe said, coming over to lean his hands on the table, "you never gave him the chance, Peyton. You bolted. It made you look guilty as sin."

"Was I supposed to wait around in the hopes that he'd have a sudden change of heart?" she fired back. "You know full well how Buck felt about the *Global Lens* blogger. If anything, finding out it was me just made him hate me worse!"

Her voice cracked again, and Peyton blinked back the sudden wash of tears filling her eyes.

Damn it. She didn't want to do this in front of them.

"Buck helped us load up your stuff at the storage place," Bennett said suddenly. "Did you know that? He drives by here every day on his way back from base, too."

"He wants to make sure I haven't taken off," Peyton grumbled.

"He wants to make sure you're safe," Bennett corrected, in his soft Texas drawl. "You're the best thing that's happened to him in a long time. Trust me when I say, he'll come around. What will you do when he does?"

"You really think I'll get a chance to figure that out?" She hated how small and hopeful the words sounded exiting her mouth, but the fact that these three had stood by her, even after learning who she was, made her think she could trust them with the one question she hadn't dared to ask herself.

Wyatt piped right up. "Buck will find a way back to you because he knows, deep down, that you're worth it," he said, patting her back. "Current meltdown notwithstanding, he's no dummy."

He didn't seem like he was tossing out a line—he sounded sincere. Peyton still checked the other's faces for confirmation.

Bennett nodded, and Joe—dark, brooding Joe, tracing nervous patterns on his leg with fingers that never seemed to still—murmured, "He's right. Just give him time."

Could Peyton believe them?

As she said her goodbyes and saw them out, she looked up and down the street in case, Buck was out there somewhere, watching out for her like they'd said.

She didn't see his SUV, however, only that same flashy black sedan from earlier. It was parked a little way up the street, faint tendrils of steam curling from its exhaust as it idled at the curb.

Why was it still here?

Peyton frowned. The sedan had some kind of shield obscuring its license plate.

As the guys got in their cars and pulled away, she shut the front door quickly, then went around the cottage, double-checking that all the doors and windows were locked tight.

Peyton set the house alarm for the night, and told herself not to worry. Someone on the street had a visitor, that was all. A very normal, very non-threatening visitor.

She could still do what she'd planned.

Chapter Thirty-One

Buck

THE VOICE CAME from Buck's left, as excited as it was unwelcome. "Oh my god," the woman cried, "You're that guy from tv! The SEAL, right?"

Buck cringed internally, wondering if he'd ever get past this notoriety. Externally, he only pulled down the brim of his hat and gripped the case of beer a little tighter, grunted something noncommittal as he shuffled forward in line.

Maybe he'd bore her with his lack of response, or she'd decide she was wrong and take off.

Alas, this was southern California—and tripping over people who fed off celebrity sightings was a daily occurrence, even in the grocery store.

Buck *wasn't* a celebrity, though. He was a deadly weapon in the shape of a man, and he hadn't been used for his intended purpose in way too long. Coupled with the fact that he was still smarting over Peyton, it meant his mental state was basically at basement level.

It was a wonder he didn't have a cartoon storm cloud hovering over his head, warning the woman away.

The line inched forward, slowed down by a motley collection of teenagers, people on their phones, and older folks trying to make sense of the self-checkout stations.

Beside him, Bennett rocked on his heels and gestured with his basket full of steak and spinach, flexing his forearms in the chick's direction. Lest there be any mistake, he also unleashed one of his wide, cocky grins.

Distract and deflect—one of Ben's specialties. Buck wanted to hug the guy and his fucking empath tendencies.

"How about me?" Bennett asked the woman. "Recognize me?"

Buck peeked at her, long enough to see her tilt her head while she puzzled it out. Soon enough, her eyes went wide.

"You know what? I think I do! You're the blonde one, right?"

"Might be," Ben shrugged with a smirk.

"You guys look so hot in your uniforms! You could be models."

Buck moved forward a few more inches and glanced around. The volume of their conversation was a bit too loud to stay under the radar for long. Heads had already started to swivel in their direction, including the elderly man buying carrots with his wife in front of them.

The guy was wearing a pristine, stiff-sided ball cap that proclaimed him a Vietnam vet from the USS Tattnall, and had a scowl to match. *Shit.*

Buck had intended this beer run to be a targeted strike. In and out. But in less than five minutes, he'd already attracted an oblivious fangirl and an incoming lecture from Gramps there. And while he appreciated Ben trying to help, his buddy was simply too big and blond to not make things worse.

"B, shut it," he hissed. "Let's just get out of here before this turns into a circus."

A mom at the head of the line finished buying her laundry detergent and diapers and pulled her double-wide stroller to the side, so she could whisper with her friend and pretend it wasn't about them.

Bennett drawled, "It's all good. Right, sweetheart? We're just shooting the breeze. Don't mean a thing."

"Fine," Buck grumbled. "Since you have things under control, you can take care of this. I'll be out in the truck." He shoved the case of beer at him and stomped past Grandpa before the man could load up a *back in my day* speech.

Ten minutes later, Ben pulled open the passenger door and dropped the beer and the food behind his seat. "What the hell, man? Now you're throwing temper tantrums in stores?"

"What's that supposed to mean?"

"It means you just stomped away like a petulant child. When I was attempting to render aid, I might add."

Buck scowled. "You weren't helping. You were drawing more attention to us, not less."

"I was drawing more attention to me, thereby turning you invisible. That's how you like it best, right? Nothing to see here, folks, just a grumpy-ass bastard."

"We're operators, fucktard. We *all* like to disappear."

"Not near pretty women, we don't."

"You can have the women," Buck said, slamming his truck into gear and gunning for the exit. "I'm done with them."

Ben busted out laughing. "You keep telling yourself that, you giant dick. You won't be over Peyton when the world comes to an end."

Buck gripped the wheel so hard he wondered if he might actually snap the thing in two. "Don't…don't say her name."

"Who, *Peyton*? The one who shall not be named? The one who got away? The girl who doesn't deserve this crap from the man who was supposedly in love with her?"

Buck yanked the wheel and pulled into another shopping center, veered into a free spot, and turned to stare at his supposed friend. "What exactly are you implying?"

"That a man who goes all-in on a whirlwind sexfest, uproots the woman and moves her clear across the country, then dumps her ass without making sure he has all the facts—*might* not have been as in love as he liked to claim."

Buck stared at him in shock.

"Tell me I'm wrong," Bennett said.

"You're wrong."

"Prove it."

"That I loved her? Or that she's a liar? Because I might have had an easier time proving what a viper she is if you assholes had let me into her storage unit."

"Dude, for the last time. You were not going to go through your ex-girlfriend's boxes because she is not the enemy. You were on lifting and hauling duty, and that is all."

"Just…where does she keep the key?"

Bennett shook his head. "Give it a rest. The key is no more. We cleared out the last of her stuff last night, before we went over there for dinner."

Buck was still pissy about that dinner.

On the one hand, the maelstrom in his chest had grown quieter, knowing his brothers were making sure Peyton got squared away and settled. But on the other…who in the actual fuck did they think they were? Apparently, loyalty meant nothing in the face of those chicken enchiladas she'd made them.

True, Buck wasn't positive that's what they were. Joe had busted him this morning before he could get a decent bite. He was hoping there'd still be some left so he could try again later.

Next to him, Bennett was massaging his temples. "Could we perhaps get moving, bro? I dropped fifty bucks on that meat and I'd like to get it in the fridge before it spoils."

Buck rolled his shoulders and stretched his neck from side to side, trying to shake off the way the careless dismissal of his agony stung.

He had to face facts, however. While Bennett had hooked up with his fair share of women in the time he'd known him, to Buck's knowledge the man had never fallen in love with any of them. That meant Ben had no clue what Buck was going through, and therefore no idea how he could get past it.

They'd had each other's back for a long time, but not now. As much as it sucked, Buck was going to have to walk this road alone.

BACK HOME, BUCK left Ben at the apartment and walked across the courtyard to the gym. He ignored the kid doing a circuit on the weight machines, turned on the tv mounted to the wall, and climbed on one of the treadmills.

By the time Ben rolled in a while later, a beer in his hand and a pitying look on his face, the teenager was long gone and Buck's t-shirt was drenched.

Bennett looked him over, peered at the treadmill screen, and sighed. "You really gonna make me do this?" he asked.

Buck picked up his pace, despite the screaming in his thighs.

Bennett reached out and pulled the emergency stop string. He yanked Buck to the side before he could bite it, then supported him when he wobbled a bit on *terra firma*.

His legs felt like jelly and his vision cut in and out. Buck sat his ass down and put his head between his knees.

"Why the fuck did you do that?" he gasped.

"Because otherwise, you were going to run yourself into the ground. For the love of god, dude—what's it going to take for you to admit that you miss her?"

"I do not miss that…that woman. She betrayed me. I am rightly furious with myself for not seeing the signs sooner."

Bennett took a long swig from his beer bottle. "Man, we've been over this. You did not see signs, because there were not any signs to see. Peyton is a good person, who got caught up in a complete clusterfuck, just like you. And you aren't furious, you numbskull—you're heartbroken. So is she, I might add."

"I do not care one whit what Peyton is feeling." Buck pushed to his feet, wove his way toward the door, then grabbed onto the jambs for support. "I do not give a flying fuck, Ben."

His buddy looked at him like he was the sorriest stray he'd ever seen. "Oh, you poor dumb soul."

Then Ben came over and shouldered under Buck's arm, helping him stay upright. He pushed his beer into Buck's free hand. "Drink that. Or not. But let's get you home before you keel over."

* * *

ROHAAN HAD BURIED a flash drive in the takeout bag, but they'd passed it on to Noah first so he could work his magic authenticating it and making copies. It hadn't taken the guy long. Buck and his team were directed to one of Black Watch's satellite locations a few days later to review the footage.

The warehouse was nondescript, one gray block in a scruffy row of them on the outskirts of town. They scoped the exits and pulled their vehicles into the bay, then followed Noah into a smaller war room carved out at the back of the building.

He had quite a set-up back there. Buck and the others clustered around his bank of computer screens while Black Watch's young genius got everything cued up.

Before he started, Noah swiveled in his ergonomic chair to look at them. "Okay, so full disclosure before I run through this. While we were looking into Rohaan and his uncle, I realized that he and I are basically in the same program at UCSD. You don't need to worry, though. I'm in the last year of my masters, and Rohaan is only a freshman. We haven't crossed paths yet, but it's possible I could end up as his teaching assistant or something going forward."

Buck looked at Bennett, who shrugged. "UCSD is a big place," he commented.

"It is," Noah agreed. "And Rohaan has no idea who I am or what I do in my spare time. If he and I do end up meeting, he'll have no reason to think I'm anything other than another student."

"Monroe knows? And signed off on it?" Wyatt asked.

"Yes. We wanted to be completely transparent, though. Let you guys know, in case you had an issue with it."

Joe rubbed his hand along his jaw, considering the young man seated in front of them. "Couldn't hurt to have another set of eyes on the guy. Make sure he's not doing anything hinky."

Noah smiled quickly, like he appreciated the acquiescence. "Our thoughts exactly. I'll tell you what—I took a peek at his records and the kid's smart. Like, *really* smart. Given the right tools, he could end up a real asset to this job. Maybe to others, too."

Buck held up a hand. "Let's not get ahead of ourselves. Show us what he brought, first."

Noah spun back around to face his screens. "Right. So, the first file is a document that lays out the timeline. What Rohaan did for Doggett's people, and when. He claims they had no clue he understood English as well as he does, and the audio supports that."

They crowded closer to scan the document he pulled up on the left screen. Joe asked, "Where'd a kid in the hills of Nabarut learn to speak English so well?"

"I wondered that, too. It seems there's been a steady stream of Americans passing through there ever since the Army moved into the area, and some of them spent months teaching at his school. Add in whatever Rohaan found on the internet and his uncle being fluent, and he probably ended up getting a pretty decent foundation in English. Moving here and speaking it all the time would've helped him polish it up, I expect."

"Makes sense. So, what else we got?" Wyatt wondered.

"Audio files," Noah said, "And a few photos. Rohaan notes on his timeline where he recorded his passengers, and that he started doing it because he thought it would help him practice vernacular English. Didn't take long for him to realize they were acting oddly, focusing on the wrong things and whatnot. You can't blame him. I had to clean it up a bit but check this out."

Doggett's brash Texas drawl belted out, *"Look, no one is disputing that Kadir wants in on Landry's M16s, but he doesn't think he needs what Dan wants him to take. The guy's an imbecile, though. He can't see the possibilities."*

Another man cut in, *"Maybe we need to give him a reason to stock up, then."*

"You've seen this place, Tim. It's the middle of nowhere. Fuck all happens, and they like it that way."

"Fuck all but a girls' school opening, you mean. Kadir can't be too keen on that."

"You're assuming he knows. He's not going to pay attention to a shithole like Nabarut when he's got an entire Army unit breathing down his neck."

"Again, maybe we need to give him a reason."

Noah paused the recording. Wyatt and Bennett stared at each other, then turned to Buck with identical stunned expressions.

"Holy shit," Joe breathed, "The kid wasn't playing. This alone is some damning shit."

"There's more," Noah told them.

"And you can verify this stuff?" Buck asked. "It's not doctored or anything?"

"Timestamps line up. Chronologies match Doggett's public schedule. No splicing or any other tampering that I can find," Noah said.

Bennett frowned, staring at the audio graph cutting across the large center display. *"Tim.* Doggett was talking to a *Tim.* Why do I know that name?"

"We checked the guest lists for the school opening," Noah replied. "We think it's Timothy Stein, his PR guy. Should be easy enough to confirm."

Buck waved at the screen. "You said there's more?"

Monroe's computer prodigy nodded. "I suspect you'll all recognize this next guest."

"Darlin', what you need to do is think next level," Doggett said. *"I'm talkin' Ken Burns projects. Blockbuster movies. That kind of stuff. Our connections can make that happen for you like that."*

"You mean Leon." Joely's voice. No question.

"Of course. But you gotta pay to play, sweetheart. You do for us, and we do for you. Easy as pie and win-win for all."

There was a long pause, then Joely asked, *"Who is this person, anyway? What's their deal?"*

"Tim found her. Friend of a friend, apparently. She won't make a fuss."

"But Roy…all our footage is of me interviewing the girls and their families. How are we supposed to…"

Doggett cut in with characteristic impatience, "*You're the star, kid. Do what you gotta do and make it happen. It's not like you're ever going to see these people again. And what are they gonna do? Call CNN from their mud huts?*"

Noah stopped the recording again, giving them a minute to digest what they'd heard. No one spoke. It was the evidence they'd all hoped to find, but…

"It seems too good to be true," Joe rumbled.

Noah nodded. "I know. But we're gathering everything we can to support it. All together, it just might be enough to get you guys off the hook. Create some reasonable doubt, at least."

Buck looked off into the depths of the warehouse, staring blindly at the random containers draped in tarps. "Maybe. I was hoping for something to show that Doggett's team was the one holding us at bay, though. Something to prove he wouldn't let us in until all hell broke loose."

The corner of Noah's mouth ticked up in the whisper of a smile. He tapped his keyboard, and a chaotic argument filled the room. Doggett shouting that his photo op was going to be ruined. Navy brass trying to convince him the Army unit was too far away to assist. Old Roy pulling rank, saying he refused to be upstaged by some "posse of arrogant cowboys."

Bennett looked at Wyatt and murmured, "*Yeehaw.*"

Noah looked awfully proud of himself, and rightfully so. Buck could've hugged him. Rohaan, too. The poor kid had been out there hoping to learn some slang and get the girl, and instead got mixed up in the middle of a global incident. That he meticulously documented.

Buck let out a long, slow breath. It was hard to conceive that this whole Hail Mary they were pulling might actually work.

"What have you found on Leon?" he asked.

"Glad you asked," Noah said, indicating the third screen in front of him. "The deeper I dig, the worse he gets. He's had at least two harassment charges that've been buried with NDAs and big payouts. His second wife filed a few domestic violence reports but ended up dropping all of them. He still dumped her a few years later, though."

"Delightful," Joe muttered drily.

"Not delightful," Wyatt countered. "Man, I want to nail these fuckers to the wall."

Noah looked from one to the other, earnestness radiating from him. "And we're going to do it," he announced calmly. "With this, we can do it."

Chapter Thirty-Two

PEYTON READ THROUGH yet another rejection email, snapped her laptop shut, and sighed heavily. There was nothing left for her to do. She had to make some concessions before she drowned.

With that depressing thought in mind, she opened the computer again and clicked out of email. A few more taps on the keyboard, and she'd submitted her application to substitute teach for the San Diego school district. Maybe one of the high schools needed a temporary social studies teacher. At least it would bring in some money.

Peyton left the table and went to stand at the back door, staring into the yard and wondering how far Joely's reach would extend once she was refused. Would anyone in the country hire her if Joely made good on her threats?

Peyton suspected she would. Somehow, she would end up paying another hefty price before this was over.

As she stood there, a young man reached over her back fence and nimbly hoisted himself over the top. He approached the house slowly, giving her plenty of time to note his dark hair, light brown skin, and careful expression.

She blinked in surprise. It was the guy from the condo, the one Buck and the others had been interrogating. What was he doing here?

The kid stopped and waved when he noticed her watching him. For reasons Peyton barely understood, she stepped outside and waved back.

"*Ahlan wa sahlan.*" he said. "I assume you know that there are two men sitting in a car out front, watching your house?"

Peyton had been sitting at her kitchen table for the better part of two hours, combing job listing sites and mulling over her shrinking list of work possibilities. She had not, in fact, known she was being staked out.

"What kind of car?"

"Black. Tinted windows and flashy wheels."

"Stay here," she told him. "I'll be right back."

Sure enough, the strange black sedan was back, parked across the street with the windows down, and at least two burly men lounging silently inside. Peyton debated pretending she hadn't seen them, but that wouldn't work. She didn't want them to see the kid out back, regardless of why he'd come.

These two had to go.

She opened her front door, met the driver's eye, and raised her phone like she was taking his picture. He didn't seem phased at first, but then the Fujikawas' daughter and her kids spilled out of the house next door, laughing as they headed for the minivan in her neighbors' driveway.

Only then did Peyton's new fans face forward, raise their windows, and pull smoothly away. She waited for a minute, making sure they were really gone before she returned to the back.

Her visitor was still standing where she'd left him. "I don't suppose those guys were with you?" she inquired.

"Sorry, no," he said. "I've never seen them before."

She bit her lip and looked away. "Dang it."

He smiled a little. "I'd make a joke about you being a popular lady, but I think maybe you would rather not be."

"True," Peyton agreed.

He took a cautious step forward. "My name is Rohaan. Do you remember me?"

"I do. How'd you find me here?"

He shrugged. "You would not believe what a person can uncover with a little time and a good computer," he pointed out. "Public records, for example, include lease agreements. It was much harder to find you in Maryland."

"Rohaan, don't take this the wrong way, but you probably need to stop stalking me. Use your techie skills for good, not evil."

"You think I'm here to do evil?" he laughed. "I'm not. I only wanted to apologize for scaring you before. You were much more observant than we expected. We didn't consider how things would seem from your perspective."

"You really should have."

"Perhaps you're right. My ideas about Americans are not always accurate…though, to be fair, your ideas about Arabs are even stranger. Our peoples do not understand each other very well, do they?"

"Rohaan, listen—I appreciate your apology, but you probably shouldn't be here. As you've already noticed, I've got bad people watching me. If you're in a big enough pickle that you need Buck's help, I doubt you want to draw their notice, too."

"Yes, well…that's why I chose the back door instead of the front."

Peyton sighed. "Fair enough."

Rohaan looked her over and after a moment or two, his brow furrowed in concern. "Are you okay, Ms. Page? You seem…upset."

She leaned against the door jamb and shook her head. "It's nothing. Just a job hunt going absolutely nowhere. You'd think more people would be hiring political science professors these days—but you'd be wrong."

From his vantage several feet away, he studied her again. After an uncomfortably long silence, Rohaan straightened his Star Wars hoodie and announced, "Maybe you're approaching things from the wrong direction."

"What do you mean?"

"Instead of trying to sell schools on a professor they've seen a hundred times before, what if you marketed yourself differently? Think about it. In the last six months, you've been through something few people have. My uncle Mohsin—the man you saw with me at the meeting—says we should celebrate what makes us unique, instead of trying to hide it to fit in. That's an American idea, no?"

Peyton blinked at the kid in front of her, startled by his unexpected burst of insight.

Her expression must have flustered him. "I'm sorry if I overstepped," he rushed to say. "I know it's none of my business, but I'd feel bad if…"

"No, no—it's okay. And I can't believe I'm saying this, but…you might be right."

The kid grinned at her happily. "That's good."

She gazed blindly over his shoulder, thinking it through. "If I leveraged this whole mess…"

It could help turn her plan into a reality, in ways she hadn't considered before. Peyton looked back at Rohaan.

"I could put together my own class. Pitch it to the big schools. Something about…how social media and virality can actually impact politics, instead of only the reverse. Would that be interesting? Would kids want that?"

"I would definitely take that class," he nodded solemnly.

"Okay. Okay, yeah—I think that could work."

"I am very happy to be of service."

"Rohaan, thank you for stopping by. Seriously," she told him. "But please don't keep popping up out of nowhere like this."

"I won't," he laughed, coming a little closer. "Maybe I should leave you my number, though. In case I can help more."

Peyton rolled her eyes in amusement. "You just worry about working hard in school. I'll be okay, I promise."

"It would make me feel a lot better about before," he wheedled, his big brown eyes as lethal as a puppy's.

She ducked inside and grabbed her cell off the table with a huff—caving faster than a tissue in a rainstorm. "Okay fine. What is it?"

Rohaan rattled off his digits, then turned to go back the way he'd come. "Would you like me to give a message to Lieutenant Gaines?" he called over his shoulder. "I hope to be hearing from him very soon."

Peyton laughed, charmed by his childlike eagerness. "Thank you, but no."

Except then, a thought occurred to her. "Rohaan…can I ask you something? About Lieutenant Gaines?"

"Yeah, sure."

"Were you, by any chance…there? When Buck and the others went into Nabarut?"

The kid's guileless eyes clouded over. "I was. Yes."

"Did they really do what they've been accused of? Are they as awful as people say?"

Rohaan began shaking his head before she'd even finished speaking. "No, Ms. Page. Lieutenant Gaines and his men saved people that day. They arrived in the middle of hell, and they did the best they could to protect the innocent."

She sagged against the doorframe, something hard inside of her giving way to relief. "That's…good to hear."

He nodded at her. "There are many men in the world with guns, who wield power but not honor. Your friends are not among them."

"*Shukran*," she told him, remembering a word she'd learned once, visiting her parents in Dubai. "Thank you for coming to see me."

He put his right hand over his heart and bowed slightly, then turned to go, saying, "Call me if you need anything. I'm good at fixing broken laptops. Setting up home networks. Whatever."

Peyton watched his slender frame amble away and thought about him being the target of people like Joely and Tim Stein. She tried to picture him standing up to those two thugs who'd been loitering in front of her house, or to a slick politician like Roy Doggett.

Rohaan could do it, she suspected. He'd survived the ambush in Nabarut, navigated a touchy meeting with four wary SEALs, and god only knew what else.

He was still a kid, however, despite weathering a horrible situation, not of his making. He deserved normalcy as much as Peyton did, and she hoped he'd find it here with his uncle.

He—and she—also deserved justice, though.

"Rohaan, wait," she called out.

He turned back, looking curious.

"If I had an article that I wanted to broadcast as far and wide as possible—I'm talking every major media outlet I could reach—would you know how to do that? Could you help me make it go really, really viral?"

Rohaan's grin was immediate, and not a little mischievous. "Absolutely, I can."

Chapter Thirty-Three

Buck

DEEP IN THE Black Watch war room, Buck closed his eyes and thought back to the extraction in Nabarut, chaotic memories swirling behind his eyes.

He'd been trying to hustle Doggett and his wife toward the waiting bird, but they'd been arguing—first, with a man he hadn't recognized, and then with each other.

Old Roy had been chewing his wife out, trying to make her move boots, but Lena hadn't wanted to leave the other man behind.

Who was he? And what had happened to him?

His eyes popped open and he looked at Joe. "Those photos Rohaan and Mohsin brought. Where are they?"

Joe turned to Noah. "Here, they're right here," the guy said, rifling through the folders strewn around his worktable. He landed on the one he wanted and passed it over.

Buck carried it to another table, flipped it open, and spread out the images one by one. The surface was halfway covered before he landed on the image he wanted.

"This guy," he asked the room. "Who's this guy?"

Noah and the guys crowded around, but no one had a ready answer. "Looks kind of familiar," Wyatt mumbled.

"Give me a copy of the guest list."

Wyatt handed it over and Buck scanned the names. There'd been few males of the right age or ethnicity traveling with the Doggetts that day and Joely's crew had been the only other outsiders present.

Buck lifted the photo of the man and showed it to the group. "I need a name for this person."

Noah took the picture and turned back to his screens. "Let me do an image search. That should turn something up."

Two seconds later, he blew out a stunned breath and sat back in his chair. "Well, shit."

"You get a hit?" Buck wondered.

"Sure did."

"Care to share it with the class?" Joe asked wryly.

Noah looked from face to face, but his gaze settled on Buck's and stayed there. "It's Dan Cox. Lena's son."

Buck searched the guest list one more time, but he already knew that name wasn't on it. "Why the hell…" He stopped, shook his head, and refocused. "Is he in any more of the pictures?"

Joe and Wyatt hurriedly laid out the rest, pulling three more with Cox in the background. "Got him."

Buck studied the shots, frowning. "Who took these shots? Rohaan?"

"Some of them," Noah replied. "Others are from the Doggett's publicity photos. I captured stills from Joely's camera footage, too."

"And Dan Cox is not on any list of visitors that day? He didn't sub in at the last minute for someone who was sick or act as a plus-one for his mom or something?"

Noah tapped rapidly on his keyboard, shifting from screen to screen. "No, nothing. He's not here anywhere."

Bennett took the photos from Buck and looked through them, too. "So, they slipped a gun manufacturer into a volatile region, and *oops*, a battle broke out. Am I reading this right?"

Buck locked eyes with Noah. "Call your boss. This is proof that Dan Cox is dealing arms to al-Kadir. I'd bet my life on it."

"Yeah, but how did our friendly neighborhood warlord fund it? And do Mommy and Daddy Doggett know?" Joe wondered.

"Guess we're going to have to find that out, aren't we?"

* * *

THE GUYS HAD been on the patio for a while, whispering about who knew what, before Buck's curiosity got the best of him. Their hushed voices were indiscernible as they filtered in through his bedroom window, so he wandered out to the living room to see what the furtiveness was about.

He expected to give them shit for not inviting him to hang out, but it took two-point-five seconds to realize they were discussing a woman, and not just any woman. *The* woman.

Joe had apparently grabbed lunch with her the other day. Ben, it seemed, had just gotten back from having dinner with her.

Buck inched closer to the sliding door, hungry for scraps of information and hating himself for his inability to stop caring.

"She seems to be doing okay. I didn't get rock-bottom vibes from her or anything," Bennett announced. "What about you?"

"Nah," Joe agreed. "But you know how Peyton is. She wouldn't share that with us. She'd put a brave face on it and keep on trucking."

Wyatt chuckled. "If that's her brave face, it sure looks good on her. *Damn*. What's our boy thinking, anyway?"

Buck edged right up next to the screen, his blood pressure skyrocketing.

"You got that right," Joe fired back. "Some dickhead is going to snatch her up before long."

"I dunno—Buck pisses me off good enough, that dickhead might be me."

"Not if I get there first, fucker."

Buck ripped open the door and stepped through the opening, his gut feeling ten shades of sketchy as he stood there fuming.

"Who you talking about?" he demanded.

Bennett was the one who answered, cold-eyed and even colder-hearted. "Peyton," he announced, sizing Buck up like he was the asshole here.

The dread in his belly flipped into rage, and he grabbed the Judas closest to him like he could shake the betrayal right out of Bennett's skull. "Living up to your rep, Easy B?"

His buddy wasn't too keen on having the old nickname thrown in his face. Bennett narrowed his eyes and jutted out his chin, yanking free of Buck's grip to shake out his fists. "Is that what you think? Fucker. You didn't make it too hard for any of us, that's for damn sure."

Doherty was up and out of his chair instantly, sliding between them to get up in Buck's grill. "Stand down. All we're doing is looking out for her while you get your act together."

"Is that right?" Buck growled. "That's what you were doing? I never figured you for the sloppy seconds type."

Joe's right hook came out of nowhere, landing like an anvil and stunning Buck into an ungainly backward shuffle that landed him flat on his ass against the grimy glass door.

Buck pressed his hands under his eyes, trying to figure out whether his nose was broken under all the blood rushing to his face. "Seriously? What the fuck."

Bennett did an angry little pace around the patio, then lunged over. "You believe the audacity of this fucker?" he asked, then leaned down and hissed, "I've about had it with you. Peyton is one of the good ones, you piece of shit. You made her love you and you left her swinging in the wind right when she needs you the most."

"She's a liar," Buck explained, for about the millionth time. "Just like Joely. Maybe worse." It didn't feel as real as when he'd first started saying it, though.

Buck rested his forearms on his knees and looked around. If he got up, one of them would probably try knocking him down again. Then he'd have to kill them, and murder and heartbreak didn't strike him as the healthiest cocktail for a Tuesday evening.

There was no "maybe" about what Peyton had done to him, he knew that for sure. At least Joely hadn't pretended to love him.

"Peyton ain't nothing like Joely Spitz, and you know it," Bennett growled, sliding into a thicker Texas drawl that signaled just how angry he was.

"Do I?" Buck wondered. "Hey, not for nothing, but just because you can bag any chick you want, doesn't mean you should. Some things are supposed to be sacred."

Joe groaned and shook his head. "This? This is how you treat your friends, dickhead? Jesus. Remind me not to ever fall in love."

"If you wanted that girl all to yourself," Bennett spat, "You might've tried hanging on to her. Worked your shit out like a grownup instead of running like a little bitch at the first sign of trouble."

Buck got to his feet, throbbing face be damned. "I have never run from a fight in my goddamned life."

"First time for everything," Joe muttered.

Buck couldn't believe his ears. "*What?* What are you talking about?"

Bennett scrubbed a hand through his hair. "You know, I always thought you were sharp. Can you possibly be this dumb?"

Buck shook his head. "What…is going on right now?" he asked again.

"If you could've heard the way you talked about reporters and bloggers, you would understand a little better, dumbass. If I were Peyton, I wouldn't have told you who I was, either."

Buck blinked at his best friend, his brother, in disbelief. "Are you siding with her? She's not innocent, Bennett. Our careers could be over because of her."

"Hold on. Let's be clear, here," Joe interjected. "Peyton did not intend for her blog to blow up like it did, and she's not responsible for the way her words were twisted. That's on Doggett and Joely. Peyton is guilty of nothing more than being a small-time academic working with a partial set of facts. She's collateral damage, same as us."

Wyatt snorted. "So, she didn't tell you right away. So what? You gonna try to act like you had no secrets from her? Your whole adult life is a secret."

Buck spun and went inside, taking a few steps toward his room—planning to lock himself inside before he abruptly decided he needed to get out of there. Another pivot and he made for the front door, grabbing his keys and cell off the counter on his way.

"Do not go out and get wasted," Bennett ordered as Buck stepped outside. "After the things you said to me, I refuse to wipe the snot off your face when you come home crying."

Buck paused a moment, gritting his teeth and wondering whether he had time to kill the bastard. But no—that could wait. He knew where the shithead slept, after all.

Joe marched into the living room and beelined for him. "Where the hell do you think you're going?"

"Out."

The others came in, as well.

"You two were really going to let him leave and not tell him?" Joe wondered. "Come on, assholes. Bickering is just going to make it easier for them to take us down."

Buck turned and narrowed his gaze on Doherty. "Tell me what?"

The rest of his team stared back at him, and all at once the testosterone simmering in the air drained away.

"Peyton called Joe the other day," Bennett explained grimly. "She's been seeing some people hanging around that don't belong there. She's scared, dude."

He looked from face to face. "What? Why didn't you tell me?"

"You told us you didn't want to talk about her," Wyatt sneered. "Remember?"

"This is different," Buck protested.

"Relax," Joe said, holding up his hands. "That's what we were talking about when you were trying to be all stealthy. We're taking care of it. We've been hanging out with Peyton as much as we can. Whoever's watching her is going to see that and back off."

Buck pushed back into the apartment and slammed the door. "Not bloody likely. Who is it? Who's watching her?"

"We don't know," Bennett admitted. "Not yet, anyway. They're being careful."

"Well, I'm not about to wait around for them to make a mistake. We have to do something."

"Oh, now he cares," Wyatt drawled, but it lacked the ire from before.

Bennett looked him up and down, like he was trying to gauge Buck's seriousness. "Assuming you can summon the stability to not fuck this up, what do you have in mind?"

Chapter Thirty-Four

Peyton

TO MY READERS:

I'd like to introduce myself. I am Peyton Page, the blogger behind *Global Lens*. You may have noticed that it has been several months since my last post, and while I don't normally share personal details in this space, I think it's time you know why.

PEYTON READ THROUGH the rest of the draft, tweaking words here and there until there was nothing else to adjust. Then she sat back and stared at her screen, nodding to herself.

She'd done her part. The post was perfect. She was satisfied with her message and determined to see this gambit through.

The only thing left was to make it live at the appointed time.

By outing herself and giving testimony to what the last several months had been like for her, Peyton would own her part of the events that had taken down Buck and the rest of the guys. She would neutralize Joely Spitz's threats and those of anyone else who thought to extort her, and take back her voice.

Since there were no more finishing touches to be made, she shut her laptop and looked around her cozy kitchen, wondering how to keep herself busy until noon.

With eerily precise timing, her cell began buzzing, each vibration sending it skittering closer to where her hand rested on the table. Peyton eyed the unfamiliar number on the screen, but she knew in her bones who was calling.

She couldn't say she was surprised, exactly. She only wished she'd had more time to get her head around how this conversation was going to fit into the larger picture.

For what, though? Her plan was as good as it was going to get and postponing the inevitable was not going to make this part of it any easier. Peyton simply had to get it over with.

She picked up her phone and connected the call. "Hello?"

"Peyton, darling," Joely chided, "Time's up. Why is your dumbass vanity blog still live? I thought I'd made myself clear."

Peyton lifted her chin. *Game on.* "Oh, you did. And I made my choice."

"Excellent. In that case, I'll send someone by with a couple of routine contracts for you to sign, and we'll be up and running before you know it. Just take that damn website down before my person shows, and we'll be good to go."

"You've misunderstood," Peyton said calmly. "I won't be working for you in any capacity, and I won't be shutting down *Global Lens*. If that offends you, so be it."

There was a beat of silence before Joely laughed, harsh and disbelieving. "*Offend* doesn't even begin to cover it," she said. "You know, I didn't take you for stupid, but you obviously don't understand what you're up against."

Peyton smirked, feeling lighter and surer by the second. "I know exactly what I'm doing," she told the other woman. "And no matter how much you threaten me, I'm not going to change my mind."

Joely fumed for a few seconds, then hissed, "Everyone on this planet is going to know your name. Do you hear me? *Everyone.*

And they're all going to know exactly where to find you. Every single gun-toting yahoo from New York to L.A. is going to come for you and I will not spend one second crying over your ashes."

Peyton tried not to let Joely's words sink claws into her resolve. She'd made her plan. She was sticking to it. It was the only way to get out from under the cloud that'd shrouded her life for months now. If, by extension, it somehow helped Buck and the others, that would simply be an added bonus.

Besides, supposing people did try to find her…what were they going to do? Yell at her? Picket her house with homemade signs?

Peyton would get the police involved long before things got truly dangerous, and make sure to press charges against anyone who tried to get physical.

"You have your answer," Peyton told Joely. "It's *no*. Now stop calling and leave me alone."

"Gladly," Joely Spitz said. "And, hey—enjoy hell, you stupid bitch. You deserve what you've got coming." Then she hung up.

Peyton blinked at her phone. *What an evil, evil shrew.* She couldn't imagine what Buck or that senator's son had seen in the woman, but it hardly mattered now. She had other fish to fry.

She checked her watch, curious how much time the exchange had eaten up.

It was ten minutes shy of noon. Time to tango.

Peyton opened her laptop again, aimed the cursor at the large "Publish" button to the right of her blog post, and clicked on it. With that accomplished, she got up, poured herself one last cup of coffee, and settled on the couch.

With the remote in one hand and her mug in the other, she counted down the minutes. *Eight. Five. Two.*

At twelve o'clock, she turned on her television and began flipping through channels, searching for hints that Rohaan had done what he'd promised.

It didn't take long for the *Breaking News* banners to pop up at the bottom of the screen. Talking heads picked up the story one after another, and soon every single new anchor was delivering some version of her story.

There was no doubt the kid had knocked it out of the park. Before long, every sentient being on the planet was going to know Peyton's name.

A text pinged from her brother, in London. And another from her dad, in Dubai, though it was after midnight there.

How long before Peyton's landline started ringing off the hook? Before reporters pulled up on her lawn in their boxy white vans, hoping for a glimpse of her? A soundbite? A bigger scoop?

Would it be overstepping to warn the police that her house was about to become a neighborhood nuisance? She ought to at least tell the Fujikawas, so they could go stay with their daughter before things got bad.

The speed with which her story was going viral was stunning, and not a little terrifying. But it also felt exhilarating to taste vindication so thoroughly. Every broadcast was leaning heavily in her favor.

Peyton shuttled between channels, absorbing the outrage on her behalf, and the increasing calls for a response from Joely Spitz and her producers.

There would be consequences for this ploy, she knew—but at least now she could face them in the light of day. No more cowering in the shadows. Not for her. Not anymore.

AFTER A WHILE, Peyton's fascination with the cycling news-to-social media engine ebbed, so she shut off the tv and went to fetch her laptop. The morning's events had given her a lot more material to add to her seminar proposal.

Hell, the dichotomy between accidental buzz and engineered hype alone would keep her and her future students busy for weeks. Once she talked to Rohaan, to discuss the machinery he'd used to execute her instant virality, she'd have more than enough to flesh out a syllabus. By next week, Peyton might even be ready to start shopping her class around to see if any of the big schools would bite.

If no one wanted to hire her, she'd simply pack up and take her show on the proverbial road. She could become a public speaker. Or write a book.

The important part was that she'd be free.

Peyton clicked out of her working document and onto her browser, searching for stories similar to hers, that she could use to support her talking points. It proved to be an unexpectedly rich topic, case studies piling up by the bucketload until a queasy feeling in her gut reminded her that she'd consumed nothing more than three strong cups of coffee and a toaster waffle all day.

Peyton set aside her computer and went to make herself lunch. As she stood at the counter fixing a tuna sandwich, her mind was still on all the other people, the ones out there like her.

How many had stood in kitchens just like this one, waiting for the other shoe to drop? How many patsies and fall guys, whistleblowers and pawns—all waiting in uneasy limbo, wondering if their next day might be their last?

Thanks to Rohaan's incredible handiwork, Peyton hoped Joely and her henchmen wouldn't be able to dispense with her so easily now. Forget about catastrophic injuries, with all eyes on Peyton, even a few too many minor accidents would look suspicious to the authorities and the press.

She hoped so, anyway. It was a gamble, but at least this way, if she went down, she wouldn't bring anyone else with her.

Her family would be safe. Buck, too.

Peyton carried her sandwich to the front window and looked out at the still-quiet street while she chewed. No one but a regular dogwalker was anywhere to be seen.

When everything stayed normal, she wandered back to the kitchen to rinse her plate. Peyton was reaching for the spigot when a thunderous pounding on the front door nearly scared her out of her skin.

Her plate clattered into the basin, splashing water onto her arms and shirt. She brushed at it absently as she sidled up to the front window again, trying to peer out without being seen.

The four hulking men on her doorstep saw her immediately, though, calling out, "Peyton! Open up!"

She threw open the door. "Hey, guys. What's—"

Buck shook his head, grim and stone-faced at the head of the pack. "Jesus, woman—what the hell did you do?"

Chapter Thirty-Five

Buck

PEYTON BLINKED AT them, attempting to look innocent and failing wildly. "I fixed my life," she announced. "Okay? That's it. That's all."

Buck shook his head at her. Based on what they'd seen on tv, she'd done a hell of a lot more than that. "You didn't fix your life," he corrected, "you made it way more complicated. You have no idea what Joely and Doggett are mixed up in. None."

She tilted her head. "Doggett? So, you saw that show too?"

Bennett came up and nudged Buck aside. "Peyton. Honey, this is serious. They're not going to take kindly to you telling them to fuck off. Do you get that?"

Peyton scowled at him. "That's so interesting. As it happens, I didn't take too kindly to them ruining my life."

Buck heard Joe snort behind him, and then Wyatt muttered, "Same, girl."

Buck shoved in front of Ben again, telling her, "Peyton, like it or not, you need our help, and you need it now. Okay? No fucking around."

At last, she looked him in the eye. *Really* looked. And after a minute of searching his expression, she finally relented. "Alright," she sighed, shoulders sagging in resignation. "You may as well come in. Lord knows you're going to do it anyway."

After they'd crowded into the front room, she planted her hands on her hips and her feet on the rug, staring them down. Buck drank in the sight of her, surreptitiously cataloging every minute change in her appearance since he'd seen her last.

Her preppy little shorts showed off the tan she'd gotten on her legs—a tan that appeared to extend everywhere else, too.

He shook his head. "Joely and her minions are not going to like that you defied them. They're going to retaliate, and soon."

Peyton didn't disagree. "So I'll call the cops," she shrugged. "I'll let them know that I might be the target of some unsavory people."

"Then what?" Wyatt asked, from the armchair in the corner. "Are you going to ask them to station a round-the-clock guard?"

"Good luck with that," Joe muttered.

Bennett was gentler with her. "Peyton, without any proof that you're in danger, they won't be able to do much. What we need is preventative action here, not remediation."

Buck watched as her bravado began to slip, doubt and uncertainty clouding her pretty features and making his chest ache with the need to fix it.

"So…what's the plan, then?" she asked, looking from Bennett, to Wyatt, to Joe.

She didn't look at him, though, and while Buck hated it, he supposed it was fair. He turned to the others and said, "We need to intercept them. They're going to come here, so let's make sure they meet with resistance when they do."

Bennett laughed, shaking his head like Buck was off his rocker. "*You* are not doing jack shit. *You* are too close to this issue to keep your head. Therefore, *we*," he gestured to himself and the others, "will do what needs to be done, while you keep your distance."

Buck stared at him, affronted. Once he regained the power of speech, "Bullshit," was the best he could come up with.

"As I understand it, Doggett and the others still don't know you two are an item," Ben pointed out, looking to Peyton for confirmation. When she nodded, he went on, "For everyone's sake, we are going to keep it that way as long as possible."

* * *

"HOW MUCH LONGER do we have to wait out here?" Wyatt asked over the comm. "I think there's a hornet's nest in these bushes."

Joe's voice cut in, even more exasperated than usual. "Get a grip. We're going to wait for the guys Peyton saw to show up. Then we can call it a day."

Equally irritated, Wyatt fired back, "Can we talk about how she knows who belongs here and who doesn't? She's lived here…what? A few weeks?"

Buck dropped his forehead onto his arms. *Every mission. Impatient as fuck.* "Peyton is observant," he muttered into the comm clipped near his shoulder. "If she says she's sure, then she's sure."

"I also don't like that those dudes rubbed her the wrong way on the same day Rohaan paid her a visit," Bennett pointed out. "It's weird. So, let's just hang out for a bit longer and see if they show."

Naturally, Wyatt had an answer for that, too. "And how long is *a bit*? We talked about every fucking detail but that last night."

Buck was tired, hot, and anxious about approximately nine thousand things. He truly couldn't take Wyatt's bullshit one second longer. He shifted his torso, trying to get comfortable on the hot shingles, and growled, "Listen, asshole. We stay here as long as it takes. Got it?"

Wyatt didn't get it. "Not for nothing, but if our *friends* cleared that kid, why are we even worried about him?"

"Rohaan's not the problem," Joe snipped. "The fuckers Peyton saw out front are. A million bucks says they're Doggett's muscle."

"Oh, you mean the fuckers *Rohaan* pointed out?" Wyatt demanded. Relentless, but not wrong. "How do we know they weren't together? Huh? Just because he said so doesn't make it true. What if he set the whole thing up to scare her?"

Buck groaned. Maybe he'd been overreacting when he'd concocted this plan. Surely the four of them had better things to do than stake out his ex-girlfriend's house, waiting for mysterious individuals who might not even show.

Perhaps Joely had accepted Peyton's rejection and subsequent "fuck you," and moved on with their miserable lives.

Right. And he was the king of England.

Peyton was as sharp as a tactical blade and unlike some people, she was not prone to overreaction. If she'd had a bad feeling about those characters in the car and her conversations with Joely, then there was undoubtedly a good reason for it.

Once Buck got past the sting of her calling Joe about it, instead of him, that was the detail he kept fixating on.

He knocked his head against his arms again. Who was he kidding? He wasn't *over* the sting of Peyton asking for help from anyone but him. He wasn't over any of it. It was part of the reason everyone had demanded he keep some distance on this op—because he was too emotional to be effective at close range.

The other part, of course, was that Sexy Spitzy and the rest of Doggett's toadies still didn't seem to realize that he and Peyton had been an item. The longer they could keep it that way, the safer Peyton would stay.

None of that meant Buck couldn't help ensure Peyton was protected, however. And the others, despite all their bickering, had finally agreed.

Bennett's voice filtered over the comm, steady and reasonable as always, "Listen, we're here and we're gonna do this thing. All ya'll stop crying."

There were a few blessed moments of quiet before Wyatt was back, asking, "Why couldn't we just tell Peyton we were going to be out here? Shouldn't she know?"

"Will you shut the fuck up?" Joe complained.

"Amen," Buck muttered, scanning the street below. "The less she knows, the better."

While he watched, a squirrel jumped onto the corner of the gutter and dug around in the dry leaves. When it noticed him splayed out on the roof, inches away, it let out an aggrieved squeak and took off down the tree.

Buck trained his eyes on the shrubs across the street, where Wyatt was holed up. He couldn't see the hornet nest from up here, but he should probably try to get rid of it this weekend, so Peyton wouldn't get stung accidentally.

"I just don't want her to be scared if she sees one of us," Wyatt said.

"She's not going to see us," Bennett assured him. "We've done this shit a thousand times."

"Don't remind me," Joe grumbled.

Buck slid forward a bit more, straining to see over the edge of the neighbor's garage roof. Shingles dug into his belly, and a small branch was wedged under his knee…but his position was going to have to do for now.

He had clear sightlines up and down the street and of Peyton's front door, but he was relatively hidden by a peak of the neighbor's roof on one side and the leaves of a big sycamore tree on the other. And if Buck needed to get to ground level quickly, it was a short drop down.

Ten feet. Maybe twelve.

Bennett murmured, "How's it look up there, Mr. Owens?"

Buck rolled his eyes. "Clear."

Joe paused, then barked, "Not from my end. Incoming vehicle. Red hatchback heading eastbound, rolling slow."

Buck trained his scope up the street. "Stand down," he said after a second. "That's the neighbor kid." He glanced quickly at his watch. "Probably coming home from football practice."

"Peyton said it was a black car, anyway," Wyatt reminded Joe, "with dark tinting."

"Yeah, but only a dumbass would keep the same wheels after she marked them. They'll be changing things up," Joe muttered back.

"You keep the same wheels when you want to send a message," Wyatt pointed out. "They *want* Peyton to see them—especially after what she pulled with Joely. They want her to know they're watching her."

"Shut up right now," Buck told them.

"Oh, like I'm not—"

"*Shut. Up*," he hissed, squinting into the scope. "Second vehicle turning the corner. Pretty sure it's our hostiles."

Sure enough, the dark car drifted past Peyton's house, turned around in a driveway up the block, then slotted itself into an empty spot on the street, right under Buck's nose—right where he couldn't see them well.

"Give me a visual," he demanded. "Who's got eyes on these fuckers?"

Below him, the car doors swing wide, ejecting two muscleheads in perfect synchrony. Buck craned forward, trying to get a better look without sliding onto their heads.

"Ah, shit," Joe hissed into the comm a moment later.

The men did a quick scan of the street before jogging across, then headed straight for Peyton's front walk.

"Where the *fuck* do they think they're going?" Wyatt grumbled, rustling in his hide next to the side fence.

As the goons passed the gate, Peyton opened her door and ratcheted Buck's anxiety level into the stratosphere.

"No, Peyton," Bennett muttered. "No, no, no—what are you doing?"

Buck tried to calm his breathing. His heart was hammering at Mach 5 in his chest, and spots were starting to dance across his vision. He'd promised the guys he'd stay out of the way no matter what went down on the ground. He'd *sworn* it.

Even though he was the closest thing to a sniper they had right now, no one in their right mind would fire shots in a residential neighborhood like this. Besides, he reminded himself, Doggett's camp didn't know Buck was in love with Peyton. For her sake, they had to keep it that way.

All at once, a wave of bile tried to surge up his throat. *Love.* He was still in love with her.

Of course, he was. *God damn it.*

Peyton stood on her doorstep, proud as a queen and glaring daggers at the men. "Stop right there," she told them. "Don't you dare come closer. I've already called 911 and told them you're trespassing. They'll be here any minute."

The fucker on the right chuckled darkly. "I think you're bluffing, Miss Page."

The other one added, "This won't take more than a minute anyway."

Buck knew that tone like he knew his own name, and it never heralded anything good. He shimmied to the edge of the roof and barked, "*Now*," into his comm.

Bennett, Joe, and Wyatt burst from their hides and zeroed in on the pair.

Bennett yelled, "Peyton, get inside and lock the door."

The man on the left was fast, though, faster than he had any right to be with the kind of bulk he was hauling around. He shot forward on those tree-trunk legs, reached for Peyton, and sent her stumbling backward into the house.

Wyatt and Joe took his partner to the ground behind him, scrambling to pin the man in place while Bennett shot toward the front door before it could close.

Inside the house, Peyton let out an outraged shriek, and that was what did him in. Buck went over the edge, dropping twelve feet to hit the packed turf of the neighbor's side yard with a bone-shuddering impact. He rolled to his feet a heartbeat later, ignoring a twinge in his ankle as he barrelled across the street, gunning for the dude trying to put hands on his woman.

"She's not a part of this," he growled, once he made contact. "This is between us and Doggett."

Bennett didn't miss a step as he rolled his eyes and grouched, "Seriously?"

The goon shrugged out of Buck's grasp and turned to square up. "Hands off, squid."

"She stays out of it," Buck reiterated.

Bennett shoved Peyton behind him and glanced at the door. Joe and Wyatt were having their own convo with the knuckle-dragger outside, but they seemed to have him well in hand.

Buck's new buddy, however, was rolling his shoulders and putting up his dukes, like he was looking forward to a fun little bout. "I'd love to exclude her," he said, "but this chick is in way over her head. Cute as fuck, though, right? I might as well enjoy the work, know what I'm saying?"

Buck looked to the sky for deliverance as the guy feinted left, then sucker-punched the bastard before he could make it an inch in Peyton's direction.

For all the guy's machismo, he turned out to be a two-trick pony—not much of a challenge, despite having a good twenty-five pounds on him. The problem was, once Buck got in a few good shots he couldn't seem to stop connecting his fist with all that meat.

Eventually, Bennett set Peyton aside and waded in, tossing Buck an exasperated, "All right, guy. That's enough out of you," as he pulled them apart. Ben dragged the man out the door and jerked his chin at Wyatt and Joe as he passed, indicating the black sedan at the curb as his destination.

Buck locked eyes with Peyton. "Did you really call 911?" he asked.

She shook her head. "Bluffing," she admitted. "Damn it. I thought I was a better faker than that."

Buck rolled his eyes and went outside. The guys were shoving the backup thug into the backseat of the vehicle, while Bennett got up in the bigger guy's face. "You tell your boss this—Peyton Page is off-limits," he said. "You hear me? No one touches her again. Not one hair on her head."

The dude's eye was already swelling up, and both his upper lip and his nose were oozing blood. "Fuck off," he sneered.

Bennett locked a hand around that thick throat and squeezed. "I think you meant, *yes, sir*," he growled. "Now drive your shiny shitmobile outta here before we change our minds about letting you go. And like he said, don't come back."

Buck strolled up the front walk and waited on the sidewalk until the guy looked over at him. "I will end you," he said. "Like that."

He snapped his fingers, then had to swallow back the crazed wave of laughter that tried to bubble out of him. He sounded like a Bond villain. Probably looked like one too.

The goon growled in frustration, ad flexed enough that Bennett felt obliged to give his head a solid knock against the door frame. After a drawn-out moment of indecision, the man gave them the barest of nods.

Bennett let go of his neck and stepped back, and didn't react at all when the dude grumbled, "Fucking frogs," as he got behind the wheel and started the engine.

Once the car pulled away, Joe turned and smiled at Mrs. Fujikawa, hovering nervously near her front door. "No need to worry," he told her. "Everyone is safe now."

"Is Peyton okay?" she called. "I heard her scream."

Peyton rushed out to wave at her. "I'm fine," she called. "Sorry about that."

Mrs. Fujikawa's eyes strayed to Buck, then landed on each of the others before she looked back at her neighbor with a worried frown.

"They'll make sure no one else bothers us," Peyton assured her. "I promise. I called the cops, too. I'm sure they'll be here soon."

Buck had to hand it to her—Peyton sounded perfectly convincing, though she probably wanted to throw him out with the same degree of prejudice that Bennett had exercised on that thug. Mrs. Fujikawa nodded in response, gave her a meaningful "call me" sort of look, then disappeared inside her tidy stucco house.

Bennett marched up the front walk a second later, Joe and Wyatt steps behind. He gripped the back of Buck's neck and propelled him inside, leaving Peyton to shut the door.

"Nice work, dipshit," he said, once they were all closed in. "Cat's outta the bag, now. You just broadcast loud and clear how important Peyton is to you."

"No, I—"

"Peyton, honey, may we use your bedroom for a moment?" Bennett inquired. "We need a moment to speak privately to our boy here."

"Sure, go—"

Bennett yanked Buck toward the back of the house. "Awesome, thanks," he called, then shut the four of them inside.

"Thanks to Loverboy and his uncontrollable territoriality, Peyton cannot be left alone any longer," Bennett scowled. "Someone's going to have to stay with her 24/7. Who's it gonna be?"

"Me," Buck said. "Obviously me."

Joe arched an eyebrow at him. "Dude, really?"

"Try me. Just...try me," he shot back.

Wyatt threw up his hands and looked at Ben in disbelief. "They hate each other."

"That remains to be seen," Bennett drawled, staring at Buck. "But he's not staying here alone. I'll camp out, too, and keep them from killing each other before they can make up."

Chapter Thirty-Six

Peyton

W HEN PEYTON HAD learned that Buck and Bennett would be staying with her, she'd known it might get awkward. She just hadn't anticipated *how* awkward.

They regularly traded off shifts, one watching the front and one the back—which had only seemed reasonable until Peyton realized that it placed Buck squarely in her personal space for roughly half of each day.

Nights weren't much better, since they insisted that she sleep with her door open, and true privacy had become nonexistent.

Her phone had been blowing up with interview requests for days, rattling everyone, and she had no idea how long it would continue. Peyton was exhausted. She was a wreck.

She sighed to herself and wiped down the kitchen counter for the third time that morning. She was grateful for Buck and Bennett's help. She really was.

She only wished that her protective detail could've come in the form of total strangers instead of her ex and his bestie, who'd been worrying over her welfare like a couple of neurotic spinsters.

While Buck hovered nearby, Peyton glanced into the living room, trying to think of a way to forestall the stilted small talk he seemed determined to inflict on her this morning.

Bennett wasn't going to be any help, though. He'd pulled his favorite armchair up to the front windows and was watching intently for bad guys.

She supposed she could try drowning out the awkward conversation with vacuuming again, but the last time she'd tried it Buck had insisted on doing it for her—leaving Peyton to sulk on the couch, trying not to stare at his muscles.

What else was left? Punk rock on the radio? Car racing on tv?

Buck took advantage of her distraction, sidling closer and catching her eye. "I like the curtains," he told her, tilting his head toward Bennett's position. "Did you bring them from Maryland?"

"No, I found them on sale last week. The guys hanging around outside were weirding me out. I didn't want them to be able to look inside so easily."

Buck flinched and looked away. "Peyton, I'm so sorry. We shouldn't have left you here alone, but I just…didn't think you would have to deal with shit like this." He glanced back warily. "I thought I was going to lose it when I saw those assholes coming for you."

Peyton could take Buck being snippy, or even all-business, but she could not stand being in such close quarters with him if he kept acting so *nice*. It felt like salt rubbed into the wound of her loss.

She turned away, searching her little kitchen for deliverance from her memories. "Life happens. We just have to deal with it as it comes." It didn't sound terribly convincing, but it was all she had.

"Peyton," Buck pleaded, "this wasn't how I meant for any of this to go. We should be buying curtains and stuff together. Not doing…whatever this is."

"Believe me, I know." She darted for the fridge, wondering if she could start making dinner this early. Something complicated would fit the bill, with lots of chopping and a million steps.

Buck followed her, though, leaning his hip against the counter and crossing his arms across his chest. Peyton gazed at the milk so she wouldn't be tempted to measure the way his t-shirt pulled taut across those broad shoulders.

Those shoulders were not for her. Not anymore.

Buck said, "I shouldn't have dragged you into my mess. If I'd told you who I was from the start, maybe…" He trailed off, mumbling something under his breath and gripping the back of his neck with both hands in frustration.

When he didn't go on, Peyton risked a peek at him, but he only muttered, "Anyway," as he studied the floor.

She sighed. "Buck, listen…I know. Who we really were wasn't supposed to matter. I also thought it was okay to hold off telling you who I was because whatever was happening between us was supposed to be temporary. Fun while it lasted, and then over forever."

Buck looked up sharply. "It was never that."

"No, it wasn't. And we were both fools not to see it from the beginning."

"Ah, hell," he said, shaking his head and looking agonized. "What are we—"

Her phone buzzed to life on the counter, another unlisted number flashing across the screen. Peyton stepped back and let the fridge swing closed, and held up her hands to forestall whatever Buck intended to say.

She was excruciatingly aware that Bennett had to be listening from the other room. "Just…just tell me when you think those guys will come back. Will they show up with friends next time, or what?"

Buck shot her an arch look, but he didn't fight the change in topic. He only paced stiffly away, scanning out the back door as he answered, "They won't come back right away. My guess is they'll take a little time to regroup, try to figure out what it means that we were here with you."

Peyton winced at the reminder, embarrassed that the guys hadn't trusted her enough to tell her what they were planning.

Was it so surprising, though, given the way she'd managed to screw up her life?

"Maybe they'll think I reached out to you guys in solidarity," she said hopefully, "like some kind of *Burned by Joely* club."

His eyes crinkled in amusement, and for an instant he looked so much like he'd been before that it sent a pang echoing through Peyton's chest.

"That is not a great club," Buck smirked.

"The worst."

"I think that's the best-case scenario, in any case," he shrugged. "They were probably incensed by the stupid stunt you and Rohaan pulled." He paused, then clarified, "Incredibly brave, but stupid. Next time I see that kid I'm going to strangle him with my bare hands."

"Buck, he was just trying to help."

He blew out a long breath. "I know. But I'm worried. We have no idea how deep these people's connections go—or what they can find out once they decide to look."

Peyton already had an uncomfortable inkling of Joely's reach. "A lot," she told him.

Buck didn't bother to correct her. "Probably," he agreed. "I'm sorry."

"Not your fault."

Buck glanced quickly into the front room as she had, then set his hands carefully on the chair closest to him. "Peyton," he murmured softly, "I…don't know how to move forward. I don't know where we go from here."

The angst in his voice caught her attention, morphing her urge to flee into something else. She peered at his downturned face, looking for…who knew what.

"What do you want to happen?" she wondered softly.

He looked up, his glittering blue eyes a startling contrast to his silvery hair. "I want for everything else to go away so we can figure ourselves out. I know that's not gonna happen, but…a guy can dream, I guess."

Peyton swallowed, a tentative glimmer of hope flickering to life like a firefly in her soul. "Well…to me, *first steps first* means wrapping up those two inquiries, right?"

Buck straightened up and looked sheepish. "Didn't anyone tell you? Congress punted yesterday. The committee closed out their inquiry with no resolution. Said they were 'deferring to an active Navy investigation of the matter.'"

Peyton blinked. "Really? But that's good, right?"

Buck shrugged. "I'm not sure. We're more inclined to get a fair shake from fellow Naval officers, but…the board of inquiry has some people on it that we aren't sure of. All it'll take is one bad vote and we're screwed."

Peyton's phone was vibrating again, so she grabbed it and flipped it over. "Maybe I could tag along when it's time. Lend my support to you guys, or whatever."

Buck shook his head, looking so remorseful she felt tears threaten.

"That's not allowed. I'm sorry, babe."

Peyton shot another glance at Bennett and attempted to look nonchalant. "No worries. I just thought…"

Buck stepped quickly to her, taking her arms in his hands and ducking his head to meet her eyes. "Hey. It's okay. We've been working with a, uh, a company—to help unravel this whole shitshow. They're going to send people to look out for you while the guys and I are tied up with the board. You'll be safe. I promise."

"That's not what I'm worried about," she whispered, looking up at him. "I want to be able to help you like you've helped me. I mean, look at you—even mad at me, you keep doing nice stuff, and I—"

She couldn't get through the rest. The words locked right up in her throat, and the tears she'd been fighting began to spill over.

Buck tracked them down her cheeks with a troubled expression. "Peyton. Sweetheart," he murmured. "I'm so sorry I didn't listen to you. I never gave you a chance, and that was not fair." He pulled her into his arms and stroked her hair while she cried. "I should never have freaked out on you like that."

"I'm sorry I didn't tell you about the blog sooner," she managed eventually. "I didn't think we would ever get far enough that you'd have to know. By the time I realized how deep I was, I just…couldn't stand the thought of losing you so soon. I hated that you were going to despise me."

Buck chuckled ruefully, the sound rumbling under her cheek. "God, would you look at us? Everything we tried to prevent happened anyway. And we still ended up alone."

"Buck, I'm miserable," Peyton admitted.

"Me too."

He tucked her head under his chin and held her tight. Before Peyton could say anything else, though, Bennett ambled up to them, looking very smug.

"Y'all got your shit worked out now?" he asked wryly. "Cause I'm starving. I need a snack and it's Loverboy's turn at bat."

"Ben, for Christ's sake," Buck muttered, pulling away. "Another couple minutes wouldn't have killed you."

Bennett shrugged, then picked up Peyton's phone when it began buzzing yet again. He peered at the screen and handed it to her. "It's UCSD. You want to take this one?"

Peyton snatched it from him and connected the call. "Hello?"

"Hello. This is Dr. Hank Wu, from the University of California at San Diego. May I speak to Peyton Page, please?"

Peyton met Buck's curious eyes and put the call on speaker. "This is she."

"Professor Page, I realize you must be a very busy woman right now, but I'm hoping you might be willing to spare me an hour of your time this week," Dr. Wu said. "UCSD is in the process of forming a new School of Global Studies, and we'd love to talk to you about how your proposal might fit into our vision."

Peyton's mouth dropped open, but she couldn't seem to form words. Bennett waved his hands at her, urging her to hurry up, so she cleared her throat and murmured, "I think I can swing that."

"Excellent. When's good for you?"

She shook her head, looking between Ben and Buck for guidance.

Buck mouthed, "Board meets tomorrow at two."

"How's tomorrow at two sound?"

"Perfect," Dr. Wu agreed. "My secretary will forward the details to your email this afternoon. We are very much looking forward to meeting you, Professor Page."

"Thank you. You, too," she said and disconnected the call.

"Well, there you go," Buck grinned. "The flower growing from the ashes."

WHEN PEYTON WENT to bed that night, Buck checked her room first, the same way he and Bennett had done it every night since they'd moved in. This time he lingered, though, trailing his fingers along the end of the bed as he finished his circuit of the room, then waiting in the doorway as Peyton went in to reclaim her space.

Out in the living room, Bennett was quietly watching a football game on tv and setting up the pull-out couch. Buck was taking the first shift, and Peyton had learned quickly that Bennett would be out like a light, catching a few hours of sleep before it was his turn to stand watch.

As she gathered her pajamas to go change in the bathroom, Buck watched her thoughtfully.

"Being here like this had been hard," he whispered. "Playing house together, but not *together*, you know?"

"I know, Buck. It's not going to last forever." *And didn't that suck*, she thought.

"For a while there, forever sounded pretty good," he countered.

Peyton faced him, clutching her PJs and adrift in her own home. "Not anymore, I take it?"

Buck took a deep breath, then stepped back into the room and swung the door most of the way closed behind him. "Depends. Is there any hope that you'll eventually forgive me for the way I treated you?"

She dropped her clothes on the bed and started toward him, noting the way his thumbs started tracing circles on his fingertips, barely noticeable at his sides. He was nervous.

Peyton missed him. God, she missed him. He'd been trying to edge across the abyss separating them for days, and maybe all she needed to do was set aside her hurt and pride and toss him a line.

"Buck, I don't blame you for losing your cool," she said. "You were completely blindsided, and it's hard to think straight when everything is blowing up around you."

He chuckled. "It's literally my job to stay calm when things are exploding."

"Hearts are different," she retorted, "And you know it."

Buck smiled and moved forward, dispensing with a little more of the space separating them. "True," he murmured.

"What about you, though?" Peyton asked. "You still hate me?"

Another step, more distance gone. "Do you have any idea how hard it is to hate you?" he scoffed. "I tried, believe me. I couldn't do it."

"I don't know—you were pretty convincing for a while there."

Buck looked her over, shaking his head. "I needed a target, and it blinded me to the facts. I should have seen from the start that you were getting jobbed the same way we were."

"It's done now," Peyton whispered. "We have no more secrets now. We can choose what comes next for us."

Buck reached forward and took her hands in his, tugging her against him. "I'm not gonna lie. The next thing I want is to kiss you."

Peyton's breath caught in her throat. Standing so close to him, surrounded by his familiar scent, had thrown her entire nervous system into overdrive. "Why don't you?"

"Because I was stupid, and I lost that right. Now I have to wait for you."

She focused on his chin, not daring to believe it could really be so easy. "I don't have that right, either. Not anymore."

"Let's assume you do," Buck grinned, touching her cheek gently.

When she lifted her eyes to his, his gaze sparked with a dangerous mix of hope and heat.

"Fine," Peyton huffed, covering her almost frantic need to beg with a bravado she didn't feel. "Kiss me."

Buck snorted and arched an eyebrow.

She rolled her eyes. *Should have known.* "Please, kiss me."

His lips crashed against hers. Buck crushed Peyton against his chest, his urgency igniting every iota of love and desire she'd been trying to suppress for weeks now.

Peyton moaned under the onslaught of his lips, needing it to go on and on. Needing more.

Buck's pleasure rumbled through his chest, his tongue stroking deeper as he backed her toward the bed.

From the living room, Bennett bellowed, "Would you two fucking get a room!"

Buck yanked back, shocked out of the spell they'd been under.

"Bennett, we *have* a room," Peyton yelled.

Buck laughed and gave her a little peck on the forehead, obviously meant to quell her ire. "I should go," he whispered.

"Damn it," she fumed. "Why is he such a pain in the ass?"

"Good night," Buck said, backing toward the door. "Get some sleep. I'll see you in the morning."

Peyton was most definitely *not* going to sleep—not when she was sexually frustrated and had the murder of a 6'3 Texan to plan.

"Good night, Buck," she scowled, and tried not to melt when he winked on his way out.

Chapter Thirty-Seven

Buck

BUCK HAD TO HAND it to him. Bennett's performance was flawless—all sparkling blue eyes and easy grins on top of his pristine white dress uniform. However, when he stepped away from the young woman at the desk down the hall, it fell away like desert dust.

By the time he'd trotted back to Buck and the others, clustered in the hall outside the room where the board of inquiry was preparing to hand down their fate, Bennett was as grim as the rest of them.

"She said Flannery has been out all week. A stomach bug, apparently. He didn't even participate in the final deliberations."

"So, did they bring in someone new or blaze on without him?" Joe wondered.

Buck frowned. "Good question."

Flannery was Doggett's lackey, the board member they'd been least sure of, so him bowing out of the proceedings was, on the face of things, a good sign that Monroe had managed to lobby the correct contacts through backdoor channels.

An unknown entity stepping in after him was a complication they hadn't anticipated, though.

"She said no," Bennett murmured. "That's all she would tell me."

"What a fucking cluster," Wyatt groaned. "I can't believe Buck was able to look Peyton in the face this morning and tell her this was only a formality."

"Give me a break. She was already nervous about her interview. I didn't want her to worry about us, too," Buck said.

"Right," Joe fired back, "because fudging the truth has gone so well for you, so far."

There was no time to defend himself. A lance corporal Marine stuck his head out of the door and said, "Gentlemen. They're ready for you."

He moved aside to allow an angry-looking ensign and his lawyer to exit and Buck and the others to file in.

Lieutenant Commanders Zielinski and McMurtry were there, along with the stand-in, whose placard proclaimed him "LTCDR William Colson." Commander Azevedo was still seated in the center of the group, staring down from the same wide wood dais they'd testified in front of weeks ago.

They stood at attention while Azevedo recited a perfunctory summary of the Nabarut investigation, then wasted no time whatsoever in cutting to the chase.

"After extensive review, this board of inquiry has found that none of the four parties committed misconduct before or during the incident in question."

Buck allowed himself the smallest exhale, wondering if it was possible that the stars had aligned, and their long nightmare was finally coming to a close.

Unfortunately, Azevedo wasn't quite done. "Public scrutiny subsequent to the conflict has reached a truly unprecedented level, however, and has compromised this team's ability to perform their functions as required. Because of that, the board cannot recommend retention for any of the parties in this case."

Did he feel Bennett flinch beside him? Or had Buck himself twitched in dismay?

"Therefore, in the case of Lieutenant Junior Grade Beau Gaines, the board recommends discharge at the convenience of the government, with an honorable characterization of service and all of the attendant rights and privileges concomitant with that designation."

Buck didn't move another muscle, didn't so much as blink—but he could feel the tenor of the room change subtly. Someone up there on the dais was not happy with this decision. Possibly more than one someone.

So how had the vote gone so wrong?

Azevedo went on, "In the case of Master Chief Petty Officer Bennett Shaw, the board also recommends honorable discharge."

Buck's mind went blank as shock washed through him. All along, he'd wondered if the Navy might make an example of him—if he might end up taking the fall so the rest of the guys could continue on with their lives with some semblance of normalcy. On one level, he'd almost made his peace with it.

But to discharge Ben, too, was a far harsher punishment than he'd ever envisioned.

Azevedo kept going. "In the case of Senior Chief Petty Officer Wyatt Oaks, the board recommends honorable discharge. And finally, in the case of Chief Petty Officer Joseph Doherty, the board also recommends honorable discharge. As stated previously, the remainder of Foxtrot platoon is exempt from this ruling and will continue to serve in its existing capacity."

Azevedo set down his paper, his broad, leathery face impassive as a bronze monument. Buck was dying to scan the lineup of brass more closely, to see what he could pick up in terms of expression or body language. He didn't dare release the death grip his stare had on the vague middle distance, though.

He refused to give those fuckers the satisfaction.

Each of his brothers had to be reeling as much as he was, but not one of them moved, either. Their assigned counsel sprang forward, and to her credit, Lieutenant Nuñez took a long, centering breath before she smoothed down her uniform and announced, "Thank you, sirs. My office will be filing an—"

Azevedo held up a meaty hand to silence her. "Given the unusual nature of this investigation, Command will not hear further appeals."

Lieutenant Nuñez was visibly shocked. She didn't seem to know what to say next, or even whether she ought to sit or stand or run for the hills. Buck could empathize. He felt like he'd stepped into an alternate reality, where everything looked correct, but was vaguely, inextricably wrong.

Lieutenant Commander Colson leaned forward and spoke into his mic. "Thank you for your service, gentlemen. Your commanding officer will provide you with further instructions. Dismissed."

The lance corporal who'd been manning the door appeared at Buck's elbow to hustle them back down the aisle and into the hall, where their counsel sputtered something about *lack of precedent* and *circumventing established procedure* before she stomped off in a fury, promising to call soon.

The four of them were alone, blinking dumbly at each other—like a row of bowling pins instead of a team of highly decorated SEALs.

"What…what the fuck just happened?" Wyatt asked.

"That's it? Snap of the finger and we're out?" Joe complained.

Bennett stretched his neck from side to side, clearly trying to rein in his temper. "Something went wrong. I thought Monroe was supposed to hook us up."

Wyatt shook his head. "Maybe the hookup part was not getting our asses court-martialed."

Buck watched them try to make sense of things and his thoughts splintered, weighing variables, testing theories, trying to spot the catch. When the doors burst open at the end of the long hall, though, he grabbed the two sleeves closest to him and hustled his team in the opposite direction.

"Lieutenant Gaines!" someone shouted from behind them. "Can you comment on the—"

"No comment," Buck hollered, not looking back.

The four of them rounded the corner and took off, slipping down corridors and cutting through empty offices as they wound through the maze of the building, and finally reached the garage where Buck had stashed his vehicle earlier.

Ben took shotgun as always, and Wyatt and Joe piled into the back. Buck wished a thousand things as they pulled into the glaring sun and got a look at the crowd of reporters and news trucks gathered on the front steps of the building.

He wished he could redo those days in Nabarut, and that he and his brothers had pulled a different mission.

Buck wished he could've taken all the heat, and that his three best friends in the world hadn't been pulled under because he couldn't stop himself from mouthing off to some fucktard senator in the heat of battle.

He wished like hell he'd never laid eyes on Joely Spitz.

Most of all, though…most of all Buck wished he knew what he was going to tell Peyton when he got home.

IT WAS EVEN worse than he expected it to be.

When they pulled up to the cottage's garage, Peyton was all smiles and nearly levitating from happiness. Her car was already parked inside, but she threw open the kitchen door and danced around as they filed in, then threw her arms around Buck with a squeal.

"I got it! I got the job!" she exclaimed.

He swung her around and dropped a kiss on her cheek while the other guys looked at each other, no doubt wondering whether they ought to give them some privacy or stay to back up Buck when the inevitable landmine exploded in the middle of the conversation.

"Babe, that's great," he said, forcing himself to smile back at her. "They're lucky to have you."

"I didn't even get through my whole presentation before they offered it to me," Peyton went on. "The pay is okay. I can probably negotiate for something a little better. But I'm going to be on track for tenure, so that's awesome."

"Awesome," he echoed. Over her shoulder, Bennett met Buck's eyes and winced.

Peyton glanced around at the others, her incandescent joy dimming slightly. "Did you see my babysitters outside? It was that couple from the condo. The ones with the dog, remember?"

Buck nodded. They'd saluted him and driven off just as he and the others had arrived.

Peyton frowned, growing more uncertain. "Are you okay? What's going on?"

Joe and Wyatt mumbled to each other and sidled into the living room with pained looks.

Bennett was more direct. He asked him, "You want us to take off, or…?"

Buck shook his head. "Just…could you give us a minute?"

Ben nodded and headed into the living room too, starting a conversation with Joe and Wyatt that was undoubtedly intended to function as background noise.

Buck tipped his head toward Peyton's bedroom and pulled her after him.

Once they were shut inside, he sighed as he looked at her worried face. "Peyton. I've got some not great stuff to tell you."

She stared back at him. "That wasn't a routine meeting, was it?"

"No. It wasn't."

"The board of inquiry findings?"

He nodded.

"I can tell by your faces that it wasn't good," she said.

Buck shook his head. Peyton was making this easy on him. At this rate, he wouldn't need to say anything at all.

"I don't understand," she frowned. "I thought it was good when Congress deferred to the BOI."

"Well…we did, too," he agreed. "But they discharged us. All of us. It's honorable, but still."

"But you said those people you hired were going to pull some strings for you. You said they were going to help, right?" Her voice was going uncharacteristically shrill as she got more worked up. "How the heck are *discharges* helpful?"

Buck shrugged. "Maybe the board had something worse planned. I don't know. It just happened, though, so there's a lot we have to figure out."

Peyton's face went white. "Oh, my god. You're right. I'm so sorry, Buck." She spun away, rubbed her hands over her face, and turned back to him. "And here I was, hopping around like a doofus when you got home. You guys must be so upset."

Buck walked over and gently touched her cheeks. "Peyton, what happened to us does not invalidate what happened to you. I am thrilled for you, babe. I really am. You *should* be happy because you deserve this more than anyone."

"Thank you," she whispered.

"As for me and the guys, this is a setback, for sure, but I don't think any of us believes it's the end. We have to work out what this means, though, and what we should do next."

"Of course," Peyton said quickly, slipping her arms around his waist. "I get that."

Buck dropped his forehead against hers. He couldn't resist the feel of her. "Once we have a plan to move forward, maybe you and I can figure out what comes next for us, too. Would that be okay with you?"

Peyton snuggled closer, and the sweetness of holding her in his arms again, and of the warmth and comfort she was trying to extend to him, unfroze some of the ice trying to form around his soul.

"I want that," she whispered.

"Even if I end up unemployed at the end of this?"

Peyton shrugged. "Well, it's kind of your turn."

Buck smiled. He didn't deserve her. "Would it be okay if we commandeered your living room for a bit, while we make some calls and stuff?"

Peyton leaned up and kissed him lightly. "Commandeer away. I'll go make you guys something to eat and try to make myself scarce."

"You don't have to do that. We can just order something and have it delivered."

"That's one more stranger coming to the house," she pointed out. "Let me do this. I don't mind."

Buck sighed, not having the energy to insist. "Okay. And thanks. I'm sure the guys will appreciate it."

"Can I do anything else to help?"

He shook his head and stepped back. "No. But Peyton…" There were too many things he wanted to say to her, too many questions and promises and pleas for any one thing to come out of his mouth easily. "I don't know what to…"

"It's okay," she assured him softly. "You might not be able to see it right now, but somehow it's all going to be okay."

Buck watched her leave and hoped she was right.

After she was gone, he looked around her room once more. Would he ever find himself living here with her? He was out of a job, now. No, more than that—he was out of a career, a life's calling, a community in which he'd played an integral part.

Maybe Peyton wouldn't want someone so anchorless now that her life was back on the upswing. He'd find out soon enough, he supposed.

For now, he had other bombs to defuse.

HIS PHONE STARTED buzzing before he'd even managed to rejoin the others.

"Gaines," Buck answered.

"Dude, tell me I got bad intel," Tate Monroe barked. "Tell me those fuckers did not just discharge you."

"Word travels fast," Buck said.

"Colson replaced Flannery, right? He sat in on the deliberations?"

"As far as we know."

Monroe fell silent. Then he let out a filthy string of cusses, and Buck could so relate.

He wandered into the living room and sat on the sofa next to Bennett, then set his phone on the coffee table and put it on speaker.

Eventually, Tate gritted out, "I hope I don't need to explain to you that that was not how this morning was supposed to go. I had it on excellent authority that you guys would be in sympathetic hands."

Buck sagged back against the cushions, indescribably exhausted. "That was certainly our hope."

Wyatt and Joe murmured to each other from their armchairs, disgruntled and pissy until Peyton tiptoed up and handed them each a steaming mug of coffee.

She might have been Florence Nightingale with the way they lit up.

She pointed at Bennett, but he waved her off with a soft, "I'm good, darlin'. Thanks, though."

Monroe asked, "Is everyone there?"

"Yes," Buck confirmed.

"Okay, good." There was a sudden rush of background noise, a flurry of activity that Buck couldn't quite place.

Not a busy street…an office maybe? A newsroom?

Tate went quiet long enough for Buck to wonder, "You still there?"

"Yeah, sorry. Just fuming." The connection stabilized, as if the other man had arrived somewhere calmer. "You guys know what this means, I assume?"

Buck looked around at the steady gazes of the others. They were all on the same page, no doubt about it. He said, "Doggett got to the others."

"I have no fucking idea how, but he must have," Monroe agreed. "This goes up the ladder farther than we thought, boys. I don't like the look of it."

"No shit," Joe grumbled.

"Just out of curiosity, were any of those guys in D.C. when you testified before the committee?"

Buck thought back. "McMurtry was. Why?"

Before Monroe could answer, Joe interjected, "Azevedo, too."

Buck shook his head. He didn't remember that. "You sure?"

Doherty nodded, then asked Tate, "Why does it matter?"

"Just spitballing, but that might explain our hot mic issue."

Buck and Joe stared at each other. If Doggett had moles within the chain of command…

Bennett had been listening thoughtfully, but he suddenly leaned forward to say, "Maybe that's not it. Maybe the board got new intel when the inquiry moved from discovery to deliberation. Something that tipped the balance against us."

Buck tilted his head and eyed his friend. "Okay. If Rohaan found us, who found the brass?"

Monroe agreed, "Something to consider, for sure. But if that's what happened this time, we need to remember that the same thing could also work to your advantage during your appeal. If you catch my drift."

"No go," Wyatt told him bitterly. "They said no appeals."

Monroe paused. "That's a breach of protocol."

"Our lawyer agrees. She was spitting mad about it, in fact."

Buck caught sight of Peyton bustling around the kitchen and thought about how she'd just leveraged an information leak herself, using it to shore up her position. His mind leaped ahead, searching for ways to make that tactic work for them.

"Not for nothing, but we're sitting on a cache of interesting information right now," he mused. "Maybe we need to play show-and-tell with some of it."

Monroe paused. "We could. It might prevent us from tracking down all of the players if sources get antsy, though."

"It might also get these fuckers to show their hands," Bennett said.

"True. We'll have to be smart about who we share with," Tate muttered. He held a rapid, muffled conversation with someone on his end, then asked, "So, what do you guys want to do?"

Buck looked around, waiting until he got a nod from each of the others. "We are sitting here speculating that these assholes have infiltrated the chain of command of the United States Navy," he said. "That's a level-up from trying to deep-six a few frogmen. I say we cut that vine off right the fuck now, while we still can."

Chapter Thirty-Eight

Peyton

BENNETT LEANED AGAINST the doorframe, filling the narrow opening between the living room and kitchen with his tall, lanky body.

"Hey man, I'm going to head out for a run, then grab lunch and go home for a bit. I've got to do some laundry, and I need to call my sister and give her an update on what's going on."

Peyton was curious. She'd never heard Bennett mention a sister before. Buck seemed unsurprised, though, because he only set down his spatula and said casually, "Give her my best."

"Roger that. You need me to pick up anything while I'm there?"

Buck glanced at Peyton, then shook his head. "That's okay. I'll swing by after you get back. I could stand to run a load of clothes, too."

Ben tipped his chin at her and let himself out, and Buck resumed bustling around her little kitchen, making breakfast.

Peyton had been working at the table for the last hour, breaking down her seminar concept into distinct lessons and researching more case studies, but now she closed her laptop and set it aside.

"Didn't Bennett go for a long run this morning?" she asked. "He's going to hurt himself doing it all the time like this."

Buck smiled at her. "He'll be fine. Trust me, he could use the stress relief." He turned off the stove and slid some food onto a pair of plates. "Besides, I think he's trying to find ways to leave us alone now that he knows we're not going to kill each other."

With that, he walked over and set a plate of blueberry pancakes and bacon in front of her, announcing grandly, "Compliments of the house."

Peyton laughed. "It's my house!"

Buck didn't laugh, though—he grabbed her mug and darted back into the kitchen, keeping his back to her as he refilled it. As if he was hurt.

Peyton bit her lip and looked down at her food. Maybe that'd been the wrong joke, all things considered. "Thanks for breakfast," she told him, hoping to soften the blow. "It smells great."

Buck returned with her coffee and sat across from her, his face composed and his tone all business. "I think we should talk about your schedule for the next few weeks," he said. "The guys and I are mostly clear, but we do have a couple of meetings with our lawyer and our CO. If there are any conflicts, Black Watch—that company I told you about—can send someone over. I want to make sure you'll be covered, though."

Peyton smiled softly at him. Between guarding the house and doing his level best to pick up cooking duties and other chores, Buck had been tying himself into knots trying to mend fences and keep her safe.

She appreciated the effort, but she obviously hadn't made it clear that he'd more than made up for his sins. It was past time to make sure Buck knew she still loved him. She suspected she always would.

"I don't have a ton going on yet," she told him. "Some orientation and training at school later this month, but that's about it. We'll be okay."

So far, the stuntman thugs had not returned, and the angry hordes Joely Spitz had threatened her with had fortunately not materialized. For one thing, the news cycle had moved on, but the university had also graciously taken over Peyton's P.R. once they'd hired her officially.

In the last week, they'd had her sit for a friendly interview with the local news station's morning program and facilitated a longer print piece with the *D.C. Post*—and both had done wonders to help rehabilitate her image.

Were there individuals out there who still thought she was the devil's handmaiden? Probably. Peyton intended to stay vigilant, just in case.

She was more worried about retaliation from Joely herself—the woman was far more connected than Peyton had realized, and she wasn't going to take defeat lightly.

She looked across the table, where Buck was gazing pensively into his mug.

Peyton reached out and covered his hand with hers. "You know you can do laundry here, right?"

"That's okay. It's bad enough we took over your living room. No need to make things worse and get in your way everywhere else, too."

"I'll admit Bennett is often in the way," Peyton conceded. "Nice guy, but he's a massive third wheel. You, I don't mind. You belong here."

It was the truth, too. She and Buck had fit together from the very beginning, but now that secrets weren't clouding the air between them, they'd begun building real emotional intimacy.

It confirmed what she'd suspected all along. If they put in the work, they could really go the distance.

Buck stared at her, trying to process her pronouncement.

Peyton set down her fork and laughed at his blank expression. "Come on, who are we kidding here? It's getting ridiculous, Buck. We are obviously back together, so just…acknowledge it and move in already."

His mouth dropped open. "Peyton, don't play around with me. Are you serious right now?"

Okay, maybe it hadn't been obvious to him, Peyton corrected. The truth was, they'd had a few close calls, but with Bennett underfoot 24-7 they hadn't exactly found time to kiss and make up officially yet.

That part had mostly happened in her mind.

She said, "Yes, I'm serious. Assuming you want that, anyway."

Buck surged out of his chair and stood over her, hands out and gazing expectantly into her face until Peyton reached out and set her palms on his. When she did, he pulled her up and out of her chair.

"Damn straight that's what I want," he told her, then dipped his head and kissed her slowly. Reverently.

He dragged his hands from her shoulder blades to her ass, then used his grip to yank her hips against his.

"Hey, there," she gasped.

Buck's eyes glinted dangerously. "Hey yourself," he murmured, then kissed her again.

He reached down and hooked his hands under her thighs, lifting Peyton so she could wrap her arms around his neck and her legs around his waist, then maneuvered them through the door and headed for her bedroom.

"Where we going, Buck?" she smirked.

"To make up the right way," he fired back, diving in for another heart-stopping kiss.

A minute or two later, Peyton pulled away to catch her breath. "Wait, what if Bennett comes back? Shouldn't we go somewhere else, or…?"

"You heard the man," Buck smiled. "He won't be back for hours. I suspect we can accomplish what we need to in half that time."

She grinned back, knowing it was true. "Why does this remind me of sneaking around your parents' house?"

"Hush, you. We are grown adults doing perfectly allowed grownup things. No sneaking required."

With that, Buck tipped her onto the bed, whipped off his t-shirt and gym shorts, and climbed over her, nuzzling into the side of her neck with a groan of relief. "God, Peyton. You have no idea how much I've missed this."

"I have some idea."

"Aww, really?" he teased. "Did you miss me too, babe?"

There was no use denying it. Peyton told him, "Oh, yes," and tugged him closer, his skin hot and tempting under her hands.

Buck trailed a line of kisses across her jaw, then leaned back to pull off her t-shirt so he could tickle the skin along her waistband with soft licks of his tongue.

She squirmed under the onslaught, clutching his skull and urging him to press harder.

Buck chuckled and resisted her, the stubborn man. He took her hands off his head and held them down beside her hips, using his mouth to work the button on her shorts free instead.

After teasing her belly some more, he broke off with a gasp. "Hang on. Peyton, I have to say something."

"What's wrong?"

"I want you to know that whatever happens with this new gig of yours—or with everything else—I'm so, so proud of how brave you've been. Through all of this, no matter how people try to intimidate you, you keep finding ways to live life on your terms," he said. "Out of all the things I love about you, I think that might be the thing I love best."

Peyton took a shaky breath and felt her eyes mist up. "Buck, that's…that's really sweet."

He shrugged sheepishly. "It's true."

When he tried to kiss her again, she held him off. "Wait. I love you, too, you know. It's not fair what's happening to you, but I promise I'm going to do everything in my power to help you get justice."

"I appreciate that, but…it's always been about more than me. You know that, right?"

"I do. And I know you won't quit until the good guys win."

Buck swallowed thickly. "I can't. Not wired that way. I'm sorry."

"Don't be sorry. Just be yourself. That's who I love, anyway."

"No idea how I got so lucky." He looked away for a minute, then back at her. "Okay, this took a turn. Now I don't know how to get back to sexy time without looking like a total Neanderthal."

Peyton grinned. "Allow me to assist you, then. You were about to remove my clothes and use that magic tongue of yours to make me see stars."

"Oh, is that all?"

"No pressure. I mean…I have been living a sad, celibate life for weeks due to your rage issues, but I'm sure I can survive a little longer if I have to."

Buck narrowed his eyes and scowled at her. "That's a thrown gauntlet if ever I've seen one."

"Then you should probably pick it up and do your worst," she retorted.

He worked her shorts and underwear down her legs with fierce determination, then rolled them until he was flat on his back and Peyton was straddling his hips.

"You're gonna need to park it up here for this next part," he instructed, his blue eyes bright. He palmed her ass and urged her toward his mouth.

Peyton braced herself on the wall while Buck went to town, working her body with his lips and tongue until her legs were trembling and she was moaning with need. She arched her back, tilting her hips to find the perfect angle and pressure, while Buck held her firmly and doubled down on bringing her over the edge.

Her orgasm hit like a tidal wave, washing through her with sudden force and locking her in position as it sizzled through her body.

Buck eased her down to earth with long, gentle strokes of his hands. When Peyton could move again, she braced herself on his thick shoulders and shifted back. Buck's cock was hot against her thigh, and he jumped at the contact.

He moved quickly, propping himself against the pillows and finding a condom in the nightstand before hastily removing her bra, wrapping his hands around her waist, and positioning her where he wanted her.

"Good girl," Buck growled as he slid deep. "Now I want you to burn for me."

His hands were everywhere, mapping her terrain with fevered touches as he pushed into her, again and again.

Peyton gasped with every deep thrust, clinging to him and keening as she raced toward another shattering completion.

"Love you, love you," he murmured repeatedly, surrounding her with his strength and heat as they moved together.

She clung to his neck, the achingly familiar scent of his soap surrounding her, the overwhelming force of their desire and love knitting them together into one unbroken entity.

"Now, baby," Buck gasped near her ear. "I can't wait. Please, I have to—"

His desperate pleas unlocked something inside of her, hurling Peyton from the precipice she'd been teetering on and sending her straight into shuddering bliss.

Buck followed a breath later, pressing into her and holding her tight as he groaned into her hair. They stayed like that, clinging to each other as their hearts settled into a hypnotic, soothing synchrony.

Eventually, Buck cradled her head in his hands and met her eyes. "I missed you," he said softly.

"Same," Peyton murmured. "Let's not fight like that again, okay?"

He smiled gently. "More action, less reaction," he pronounced. "We can do that."

She nodded, knowing it was true. "We can."

LATER, AS THEY lay there with the fan moving the warm midday air slowly around them, Buck turned to trail light fingers up and down her arm.

"Hey," he murmured. "Have you thought about what you might want to do going forward? Like…in the next couple of years?"

"Well, hopefully I'll still be teaching my new class," Peyton mused, confused by his sober expression. "What do you—"

Buck flopped on his back, tucked his hands behind his head and watched the shadows on the ceiling, flickering hypnotically every time a breeze gusted through the palm tree outside the window. "What about five years out? What do you think you'll be getting up to then?"

Peyton blinked at him. Buck didn't usually daydream. He was a planner. A situation-on-the-ground kind of guy. This was a strange mood for him.

She said, "I guess I—"

He cut her off. "I've been thinking about it."

"You have?"

His head lolled toward her. "What you'll be doing, I mean. I can picture it perfectly."

After the hot-and-heavy passion that had exploded to life between them not too long ago, Peyton wasn't sure where Buck was going with this. Was it innuendo, or something else?

"You…you can?" she stammered.

"Sure. Clear as day. You'll have sarcastic coffee mugs in the sink. Books piled everywhere. Birthday cakes and holiday decorations. Flowers on anniversaries and date nights, and bubble baths on bad days…" He trailed off, waiting for her to catch up. "You're probably going to watch me mow the lawn with some sexy librarian glasses."

"Sounds nice," Peyton said, swallowing hard. "Are you—are we—"

Buck's eyes were warm, but also amused. "Do you remember when we first went out, and you told me what kind of woman I wanted?"

"I do not remember that," she admitted in surprise. "Was I tipsy? Because that's a pretty bold opening gambit for me."

"You might have been. That's not the point."

"What is?" she wondered. Then, as she took in his mischievous expression and sparkling eyes, Peyton figured out how to play along.

She sat up and smirked at him. "Hang on—I seem to recall something, now. You had a list of preferred traits, didn't you? *Medium height. Not too skinny.* Brunette, too, I believe?" Somehow, she managed to deliver the list with a matter-of-fact tone. "Just one long collection of physical attributes, as I remember it."

"No, I…god, no." Buck sat up, too, and shoved playfully at her arm. "Come on. Play nice."

Peyton laughed at his frustration. "I will if you *make your point,* Mr. Mysterio."

"My point is that I see us together! For fuck's sake, Peyton!"

She grinned and gave him a quick peck. Buck shook his head and smoothed back a tendril of her hair.

"Listen," he sighed, more serious now. "I'm not sure where I'm going to land if our attempt to appeal gets shot down. Most of the likely places will want me to travel for work. You'd be safer if we moved to a secure building, with a guard and keyed entry. Then I wouldn't worry about you so much when I'm gone."

"I love it here, but I see your point. We can negotiate that."

"Good. Next item." He paused and searched her face. "I'll admit I'm kind of traditional and would enjoy seeing a name change in your future, but I realize that part's up to you. I'm more concerned with getting some shiny jewelry on your finger at some point. Soon-ish, if you agree. How do you feel about that?"

"Did you have a particular finger in mind?" she inquired, heart starting to thump faster.

Buck took her left hand and traced her ring finger thoughtfully. "This one would do nicely. So, what do you think? Can a dude make a reservation on this? Maybe arrange a preorder or a *save-the-finger* or something?"

Peyton flushed and pressed a hand to her chest, trying to will the galloping organ behind her ribs to settle the heck down. This wasn't a proposal—not yet. It was the promise of one.

"I believe that can be arranged," she replied shakily. "What kind of lead time are we talking?"

Buck sat back, looking smug. "You know, I think I'd like to keep it open. Stay nimble," he said slyly. "I'd hate to rob all the romance from the moment. Plus, it leaves me room to seize an earlier opportunity if one presents itself."

Peyton looked back at him, and knew he wasn't trying to hedge his bets so much as give her a chance to start making plans of her own. Thoughtful to the very end.

"You aren't going to last six months, are you?" she laughed, hoping she was right.

Buck laughed right back, devastatingly sexy and full of determination. "Probably not. When it comes to you, I am both very motivated and very impatient to make you mine for good. Best be ready, babe."

Chapter Thirty-Nine

Buck

IT'D ONLY TAKEN a handful of trips to ferry his possessions to Peyton's the following day, and even less time to dispense with their chaperone. Once the move was done, Bennett had declared that he wasn't needed anymore and with no prompting whatsoever, had returned to the apartment for good.

So, when evening rolled around and Buck parked himself next to Peyton on the couch, he was well aware they had the house to themselves. They could watch a movie, cuddle up close, and follow wherever the mood might lead—without fear of interruption.

Awash in the possibilities and relishing the sheer normalcy of it all, Buck draped his arm around his woman and cheerfully clicked on the tv. He gave Peyton's shoulder a squeeze, imagining hundreds of nights together, just like this one.

An oddly romantic commercial for prescription medicine flickered across the screen, then segued directly into the evening news. Peyton snickered at the clunky transition, but it was the tagline running along the bottom of the frame that caught Buck's attention.

Breaking News: New Arrests in Qahat Investigation.

The anchor looked solemnly into the camera as he recited, *"News 4 can now confirm that disgraced filmmaker Joely Spitz has been arrested and charged with a number of counts stemming from her actions around last year's international incident in Nabarut, Qahat. She's accused of taking bribes to defame special operators who intervened in the conflict, as well as substantially altering the copyrighted work of a low-profile political blogger to support her false assertions. Ms. Spitz originally claimed she was in Nabarut to document the opening of a groundbreaking school for girls, but the film she eventually produced became a scathing condemnation of the service members widely credited with saving her life—as well as those of United States senator Roy Doggett and his family—when fighting broke out."*

"Low profile seems like an unnecessary dig," Peyton commented dryly.

"What do they know," Buck scoffed. "You'll show them."

"Ms. Spitz's subsequent project has been billed as a profile of her fiancé Dan Cox, head of West Virginia arms manufacturer Landry Cox, as well as Senator Doggett's stepson. In light of the current allegations, that has now been shelved."

"Tough break," Peyton drawled.

"She had it coming," Buck shrugged, but he couldn't help being impressed by the effectiveness of Black Watch's controlled leak.

Once they'd made the decision to go ahead with it, Monroe had warned them that the story would hit the media soon—but Buck hadn't expected more than talk to stem from it.

Actual arrests were a thing he hadn't seen coming.

"Spitz is only the latest individual in Senator Doggett's inner circle to experience a messy fall from grace. Former Doggett publicist Timothy Stein was also among the group of bad actors uncovered in recent probes of the incident, though sources in the Texas senator's camp insist that Stein and Doggett parted ways weeks before authorities searched the publicist's home and business, and well before Doggett's political party snubbed him by nominating the former governor of Maryland as their presidential candidate."

Buck's phone dinged with an incoming text. He grabbed it off the table, scanned the message, and tapped out a quick reply. Peyton eyed him curiously.

"It's Bennett," he explained. "Just making sure we're watching."

"What do you think this means for your case?" she wondered. "With you guys vindicated like this, won't they have to let an appeal go forward?"

Buck shook his head. "Not necessarily. The board didn't leave a lot of wiggle room with their decision. They might decide it's easier to just stick with their original verdict."

Peyton blew out an unhappy breath, disgruntled on his behalf. Buck, however, felt mostly contentment—his conscience lighter now that justice was being served, and he didn't have to lie to her anymore.

He lifted Peyton's hand and kissed it, smiling when she swiveled right back to the tv to marvel, "Whoever did this for you really refined Rohaan's playbook. It's a circus, but I like how they kept the focus off you guys and trained it on Joely and Stein, instead."

"Agreed," Buck laughed. "It's kind of terrifying, watching it unfold like this. Makes you wonder how many times it's been done before, with no one the wiser."

"Annnnd…that's why I have a job now," she said wryly. "At this rate, I'll have to scrap my story and use you guys as a case study, instead."

Buck dragged her onto his lap and told her, "Hold up there, Professor. Let's wait till there's no hope for an appeal before you splash my business across campus." Then he blew a loud raspberry on her neck to make her giggle.

On the screen, the view of the news desk broke to old footage from the ambush, drawing Peyton's eye and making her brow furrow in dismay. She wriggled off Buck and stood up with a sigh.

"Those poor people. Caught between a rock and a hard place and all they probably wanted to do was live their lives in peace."

"Literally caught," Buck agreed. "That terrain is incredibly treacherous even without a warlord lurking in their backyard. People can't get out easily, even when they want to."

Peyton's eyes were glued to the desolation flashing across the screen. "Do you think Rohaan's family is okay? They got him out, but what happened to the rest of them?"

Once it'd become clear that the kid was not a threat, Buck had inquired about that very thing—so he had a decent answer for her.

"Rohaan told us he left them with his uncle's people in the capital. They promised they'd stay there until things settled down back home, but now that he's settled he wants them to come here instead. If they like it, he's going to try getting them to emigrate permanently."

Peyton brightened up at that. "Maybe I could help," she said hopefully. "My mom is career foreign service. I bet she knows someone who could pull some strings."

Her earnestness warmed Buck's jaded heart, as it always did. "I'm sure Rohaan would appreciate it," he smiled. "And between your help and the goodwill he's earned from the Black Watch folks, he should be able to make it happen one way or another."

"Good. He's a nice kid," she murmured.

Buck thought back to that empty condo, and Rohaan's insistence that they look at the photos of the missing girls. Every one of them.

Was Rohaan nice? Sure. But he was also a young man who'd lived through the unimaginable and had come out on the other side bound and determined to see his mission through to the end.

Every man on Buck's team could respect that. What was more, if he and the others played their next few cards right, they'd be able to ensure the kid got a chance to do what he'd come here for.

Buck grabbed the remote off the table and switched to their streaming service before he could dwell too much on what came next. "How about we lighten things up?" he asked Peyton. "You want to watch a movie with dinner? There's that superhero one that just came out."

"Sure, we can—"

His phone started buzzing again, this time with an incoming call. Buck eyed it warily. "What're the chances that's my mom and dad, freaking out about the news?"

Peyton peered at the screen, then back at him. "Unlisted number."

Only one person that could be. "Shoot. I need to take this. Sorry, babe."

"It's okay. I'll put a pizza in the oven and make a salad. Just let me know when you're done."

When she was out of earshot, Buck connected the call. "Gaines."

"Hey brother," Tate Monroe said. "I assume you boys caught the evening news?"

"We did. Little more dramatic than I expected, but I'm not about to look a gift horse in the mouth."

"Yeah well, chips fall where they're going to fall," he said flatly. "We've got other shit to worry about than Spitzy's rap sheet. Any developments on the appeal front?"

"Nothing yet," Buck told him. "Lieutenant Nuñez said she'd get back to us sometime this week."

"Roger. Let's try to meet the week after next, then. I'll be in town, and we should hammer out next steps."

"Yeah, sure," Buck said, and got up to peek into the kitchen.

Peyton had gone awfully quiet, and he had yet to shake the constant simmer of worry for her that had characterized his last several weeks.

She was only watching something on her phone, though, earbuds dangling from her ears as she stood at the counter patting lettuce dry with a dishtowel.

She jumped when she spotted him, then smiled and mouthed, "Sorry."

Buck winked and returned to the living room. "Seeing as we are rebels without a cause at the moment, your schedule's probably tighter than ours," he told Monroe. "Name the time and place, and we'll be there."

THEY MET THE head of Black Watch at a park near the marina, the bridge casting its shadow over the bay as it arched toward Coronado and the base Buck had once called home.

The sun was barely up and no one was around yet, so Buck and Joe sat on a bench near the end of the pier while Bennett and Wyatt leaned on the railing, to-go coffees steaming as they studied the view.

They'd left Peyton at UCSD a little while ago, in the care of Noah, who'd promised to take her on a tour of campus and to breakfast while this meeting took place.

Monroe didn't keep them waiting long. He strolled up with a dog on a leash five minutes before the appointed time, like it was his regular morning routine.

While the German shepherd sniffed the weeds sprouting near the base of a trash can, Tate stood off to the side, close enough to be heard by Buck and the others, but not so near that a casual bystander would assume they were together.

"Is that the same dog y'all had at the condo?" Bennett muttered, eyeing the sleek beast with frank appreciation.

"Yep," Monroe said. "Her name's Hera. Did two tours in Afghanistan before she retired with her handler."

"And you have her…why?"

"I like dogs," Tate shrugged, mildly affronted. "And Hera likes walks. Her mom let me borrow her so I wouldn't look like a drug dealer meeting you guys here."

Bennett looked dubious. "Right. Because war dogs definitely don't scream *threatening*."

Buck rolled his eyes. "Dude. Could we focus, please?"

Tate waved him off. "It's okay. I'll be quick. Our media campaign is bearing fruit, obviously. We've also found a shell company Doggett's been using to shield the contracts he's funneled to Landry Cox. Noah's going to do look for others, so I'll keep you apprised of what he finds." He nudged the dog away from a smashed beer can, and continued, "Last, but not least, now that Old Roy has lost the nomination, we've got a few former campaign staffers who might be willing to talk to us on the down-low about his antics."

Hera ambled up to Wyatt, so he let her sniff his hand while he shared a quick look with Joe. Bennett kept his gaze trained on the water, but his shoulders were tight and Buck could guess what he was thinking.

What they were all thinking, and counting on him to communicate.

"That's great," Buck said. "But…we need to talk about scope, here. This job is growing more legs than a fucking centipede, and now that we're out of jobs, we're a little concerned that, uh…"

Tate frowned at them each in turn. "You guys getting squeamish?"

Beside Buck, Joe huffed in irritation and cut right to the chase. "Dude, we're jobless and you don't come cheap. How the hell are we supposed to pay you now?"

Tate snorted. "I appreciate your concern, but let's get real. It was my old unit that got mowed down in Nabarut. I was going to have my fingers in this fucking pie one way or another. So stop worrying about my fee and write this off as me doing a solid for some friends, okay?"

"That's quite a business model," Wyatt muttered.

"Don't worry about my business model, Senior Chief," Monroe fired back. "Tackle what you're going to do if the Navy shoots down the appeal, instead. And they will—you know that, right?"

"Buzzkill," Joe complained darkly.

"Look, I've been sweet-talking your little Buckaroo for months now, but I'd rather have all four of you working for me," Tate said. "What's it going to take to make that happen?"

Bennett and Wyatt simultaneously gave up the pretense of disinterest, turning as a unit to give Buck identical glares of accusation.

He threw up his hands. "We had other shit going on, if you recall. I would never have made a decision without talking to you."

"Think about it," Monroe urged them. "I know you hoped to stay in, but you'll have a hell of a lot more leeway to pursue this thing as part of Black Watch Security. And it's not like I'm going to screw you over once I have you on board. You'll have my full support and the pay's damn good. So are the benefits."

Bennett looked the man over from stem to stern. "You gonna put all that in writing?"

"Of course. Say the word and I'll email you the packets as soon as we're done here."

Based on the pointed, stormy looks Buck was facing, there would be plenty of fireworks before those packets got read. He needed to shut this topic down before his brothers really started spiraling.

He told Monroe, "Appreciate that. We'll look everything over and see what's what. When do you need an answer?"

Monroe shrugged and crouched to pick up the stick Hera had dropped at his feet. "Take your time. Send me whatever questions you need to. For a complete team that functions like yours, I can wait."

PEYTON LISTENED QUIETLY as Buck told her about the job offer on the drive home, then commented, "Well, that didn't take long," once he was done. "I can't say I'm surprised, but…wow."

"I still have to go over the details," he assured her. "I suspect the money's going to be pretty decent, though, and I'm comfortable with Monroe's…you know. Moral compass."

She looked thoughtful. "That's helpful, but sometimes security companies operate in murky waters. How exposed would you be personally if something were to go wrong?"

"I'm going to look into that," Buck promised. "But I like the idea of getting to spend more time with you, and of having some flexibility about which jobs I take and when. That'd be a nice change for me."

"Buck," Peyton chided, "this is a big step. You need to do what's best for you."

"You are what's best for me. You're part of my life now, Peyton. Of course, I'm going to consider how this affects us."

"But I'm just—"

Buck pulled into their driveway and threw the truck in park. "Stop right there. Any sentence that begins with 'I'm just' is not heading in a direction I'll appreciate. You aren't *just* anything. You're a sunrise breaking over my life. You're the woman I love, and when I make any big decision going forward, I'm going to do it with your input."

Peyton scrunched up her face and crooned, "Awwww."

"Let's go inside," he told her.

They got out of his truck and headed into the house. Buck stopped Peyton in the kitchen and pulled her into his arms.

"I am never going to get tired of you saying stuff like that," she smiled up at him.

Buck dropped a brief kiss on her lips. "I love you. With every hair on my head and every bone in my body. Whole heart and whole soul."

Her pretty eyes welled up as she gazed at him. "I love you, too," she whispered.

"Excellent. Because job stuff aside, I have a question for you."

Peyton paused for a long moment—too long—in which he could feel every thump of his heart.

"Okay," she said carefully.

He took a deep breath. "You remember that list of attributes, the one you said I wanted in a woman?" When she nodded, he went on, "The thing is, I don't want those things with just any woman. I only want them with you. Because those things *are* you."

"Buck, that's so sweet." Peyton got flustered, turning pink and dipping her chin.

He decided to take it as a good sign and blazed ahead. "Peyton…seriously. I want it all. With you, I want everything there is to want."

"Okay, big talker," she murmured, "you've already got the job. Jeez." She was blinking fast and trying to find her footing, but she clearly had no idea where Buck was going yet.

"I beg your pardon," he said, "I am not blowing smoke. I am a man of my word and I fully intend to follow up this conversation with the actions necessary to turn goals into reality."

Peyton eyed him drily. "Now you're manifesting? That's not ominous."

"We'll see," Buck told her. "I think you just need a visual aid, so you can see what I'm talking about."

That salvo threw her off-balance again—which was right where he wanted her. If he let her get comfortable too soon, she was going to derail the plan with a whole lot of overthinking.

"I do?"

"Hopefully. But save that thought for later. Exhibit A will clarify things immensely."

Peyton squinted at him, completely stymied, and Buck tried not to laugh or give himself away.

He said, "Luckily, I know you very well and I have planned ahead. The thing I need is right…" He reached around her and rifled through the drawer where they kept takeout menus.

It was mostly for effect, though. Buck knew exactly what he was reaching for, and where he'd find it. When he faced Peyton again, it was with a small suede box in his palm.

"…here," he told her, getting down on one knee as the first shiver of nerves rippled through his gut. "Does this help?"

For an object so small, the box seemed to take up a lot of room between them. Peyton gaped down at it, and then at him, utterly speechless.

Buck smirked, but he was the farthest thing from cocky there was. "No?" he asked, clinging to his dumb playbook like grim death. "What if I do this?"

He flipped open the lid with his thumb and watched her eyes go as round as moons. Peyton took one look at the diamond ring glinting up from its bed of turquoise satin and started shaking. He watched it happen.

"Can you picture our future now?" Buck asked softly.

Her face glowed like a searchlight. Peyton *could* see it—he knew she could. But he hadn't asked her the most important thing yet, and too many expressions were passing over her face to get a solid read on how she felt.

Another hint of doubt swirled through Buck's stomach. Maybe he should have waited longer. Given Peyton a solid few months, at least, to get used to the idea.

But, no. Procrastination was for the weak. This was right for them, right now.

Peyton reached out with a trembling finger to touch the ring, so Buck got up and took her hand, hoping she'd let him put it on her. Her breath hitched at the contact.

Hell, Buck could relate. He was pretty sure he hadn't taken a breath for the last ten minutes.

"What do you say, Peyton Page? Will you marry me?"

If she'd been speechless before, she looked dumbstruck now.

The silence was unnerving. "Do you…" Buck hesitated. "Do you like it?"

The box felt like it weighed a ton, suspended in midair as he glanced between her face and the solitaire nestled in its pristine bed. He'd been so sure he'd picked well, but now he began to wonder if he'd made a mistake.

Several mistakes, perhaps.

Eventually, Peyton managed to smack him on the arm and squawk, "You bought a *ring*?"

"I might've mentioned how miserable I was without you. I needed to make sure that never happened again."

"What are you…are you sure about this?" she stammered.

"Never been more certain," Buck declared. "You want to try it on?"

Peyton held out her hand, but between her shaking and his nerves, he fumbled the thing. She yelped, launching herself at the floor and executing a panicked search of the kitchen linoleum.

Buck dropped down next to her and attempted to get her attention. "Peyton. Peyton," he laughed. "Babe, would you stop?"

She turned to glare at him, and he held out the ring. Just like that, she burst out crying, laughing and repeating, "Yes, yes, yes," as she launched herself at him.

Buck sat back and clung to her, burying his face in her hair and thanking his lucky stars that he'd made it to this moment in his life.

Whatever else happened, he'd always have this. It was more than enough.

When they were finally able to extract themselves and get the diamond on her finger, Peyton's grin was huge. She held it up to the sun and made stars flash across the far wall.

"I didn't expect you to be so shocked," Buck laughed, relieved and giddy with victory. "I warned you this was coming in very clear terms."

"Honestly, I didn't dare let myself hope for it so soon. If you'd changed your mind, I would've been crushed."

He laughed harder. "Peyton. Why would I hint if I didn't intend to follow through?"

"Because you're territorial?"

"Oh my god."

"It's not so far off the mark."

"Nevertheless," he huffed.

Peyton stared at that ring like it held the secrets of the universe. "People will think we're crazy. That we're rushing things."

"Screw them," Buck told her. "You're the one for me—what else is there to figure out? Besides, life's short. There's no point in waiting?"

Peyton took that in, her eyes bright. "You make it sound so easy."

The only easy day is yesterday. "It will be," he told her. "If I'm with you."

"And hearts just broke across the land." She smiled and leaned against him. "You're not worried about settling down?"

Buck pressed his lips against hers, and it was as electric as it'd been the very first time. "That will be a piece of cake. It's all part of the plan."

Epilogue

Buck

D INNER WAS ON the kitchen table, the platters of burgers and ribs crowding out the side dishes as their guests stuffed their faces in front of the baseball game on tv.

Peyton had been busy all afternoon, trying to feed people who were already stuffed—but Buck had finally managed to corner her in the kitchen when Joe interrupted, ambling over with what had to be a third helping of food piled on his plate.

"Tell you what," he said, "You fuck things up with Peyton again, and I'm rolling up in here, shooting my shot." He snapped his fingers. "Like that." Then Joe sent her a cocky smile completely at odds with his normally dour demeanor.

She snorted in amusement, but Buck wasn't having it. He muttered, "Language," like a prissy little schoolmarm, and gave Joe the finger behind her back.

Wyatt came over and shouldered Joe aside. "There's a line," he scoffed. "Why are you always, like, sixth to the party?"

Murmurs of agreement sounded from the family room, and Wyatt fixed Peyton with what was probably meant to be a charming grin. He looked like a damn joker.

Joe scowled. "What's that supposed to mean?"

Over on the couch, Bennett let out a howl—but it devolved into coughing as he promptly choked on his potato salad. Noah frowned beside him and whacked him on the back, showing more concern than the theatrics probably warranted.

The kid didn't know that yet, of course. He'd learn eventually.

"Let me ask you this," Wyatt was saying, "When was the last time you hooked up with someone?" He eyed Joe skeptically. "Because by my estimates you've been getting beaten at bat for a long fucking time. A *sixth-in-line* time."

At Buck's elbow, Peyton winced, "Low blow."

Buck looked between her and the two men squaring off next to the tub of ice on the counter, and held up his hands in what he hoped would be a calming gesture. "Let's not lose our shit, okay?" he began. "You want the nice lady to let you come back here, remember?"

"You know what, pretty boy?" Joe bellowed, blatantly ignoring Buck as he jabbed a finger at Wyatt's chest. "You can shove that line of crap right up your tailpipe. I wasn't aware I had to check in with you every time I got some, but I'll be sure to let you know now. So you can log it in your little book. That what you want?"

Buck clapped a hand on his shoulder and cleared his throat.

Joe glanced at Peyton sheepishly. "Sorry."

He handed him his plate and shoved him toward his chair, where Bennett was waiting to reach over and pat his back, murmuring, "Nice doggie. Down boy."

Buck glared at Wyatt until he backed away, then turned to Peyton—not sure whether he was annoyed by his friends' dubious manners or amused that they'd let their guard down with her. The entire exchange had proven that she was family, now, whether she liked it or not.

"This is so fun," she whispered, twinkling up at him. "We need to do this more often."

"Be careful what you wish for," he laughed. "We actually want them to leave sometimes." He intended to drop a chaste kiss on her lips, but shit happened—as it tended to do with her—and it got a bit out of hand.

Catcalls and kissing noises flooded the room. Apparently, everyone's attention hadn't been on Joe, Wyatt, and the flat screen in the corner, after all.

"All right, assholes, that's enough," Buck finally yelled over the ruckus.

"Don't worry," Peyton told him. "We'll get back to that later."

Buck pulled her close and kissed her lightly on the forehead. "Later seems very far away."

"You are correct," she agreed, peeking around him to check the tv. "It's only the second inning."

Buck winced, but at least there was an easy solution. "Party's over!" he hollered over her head. "Everybody out!"

A chorus of groans replaced the jeering, and a barrage of balled-up napkins and empty water bottles pelted them.

Peyton narrowed her eyes. "He who threw it, cleans it up," she declared, then pointed a particularly threatening finger at Ben.

Buck used the ensuing flurry of action as cover to crowd her toward the bedroom and their brand-new king-sized bed. "You come with me," he said.

Peyton took two steps and froze, grabbing his arm. "Wait." A news broadcast had cut into the game, the rapid-fire words of the anchor caroming around the room with keen-edged accuracy.

"While Texas senator Roy Doggett celebrates his reelection at an event in Austin tonight, questions about his connection to disgraced documentarian Joely Spitz continue to shadow him. The investigation into his stepson, Dan Cox, is intensifying, along with rumors that illicit arms dealing was taking place well before the Doggett family's involvement with Ms. Spitz began. News 4 spoke with several individuals familiar with the head of Landry Cox, including a former girlfriend with whom Cox cut ties only days before his first public appearance with Joely Spitz. Her name is Kim Sutherland, and she's the daughter of a prominent Texas surgeon outside of Dallas—"

Bennett shot up so fast, his plate clattered to the floor. When a photo of the woman appeared on the tv, all the color drained from his face.

"Shit," he breathed, as spooked as Buck had ever seen him.

"Dude, you know that chick?" Joe asked.

"Sutherland, seen here with associate Shannon Shaw, declined to comment when asked about the allegations, but she—"

Buck went over and picked up Ben's plate with a frown. "Hey. What's going on?" he asked.

Ben only had eyes for Ms. Sutherland, and he looked like the sight of her might make him toss his cookies all over Buck's sneakers.

"Kim is…my sister's best friend," he said eventually. "Since kindergarten. Longer, maybe."

Joe found the remote and paused the broadcast, freezing the image of two harried women at the center of a scrum of reporters on the screen. Even like that, it was obvious what a pretty pair they were, Sutherland blonde and willowy, and Shannon older and curvier than Buck remembered her.

"Wait," Wyatt yelped, *"That's* Shannon? As in, sister of Bennett?"

Bennett didn't tear his eyes off the tv, but he gave the barest nod.

"Holy smokes," Wyatt muttered, sharing a shocked look with Joe. "How have I never seen her before?"

Bennett wheeled around to fix wild, desperate eyes on Buck. "Oh god," he panted. "I've got to…uh…I have to, um…"

Buck grabbed him by the arms, holding him in place. "Deep breath. What needs to happen here?"

Bennett blinked rapidly, and his face went even paler. Then he spoke the most incomprehensible sentence Buck had ever heard him utter.

"I have to go home."

Up Next

Heat Seeking Missile

(Black Watch Security, Book Two)

When Bennett Shaw joined the Navy, he had every reason in the world to leave Texas behind, but the biggest one of all was Kim Sutherland, his little sister's best friend—the prom queen to his juvenile delinquent. The forbidden prize in the candy jar.

The girl he wanted most, but could never have.

The SEALs gave him the escape he needed, but now Bennett's been kicked out—and he's on a dangerous path to expose the people who ruined his one chance to make something better of himself.

Come hell or high water, he'll make them pay, but why has Kim turned up right in the thick of it?

Sneak peeks and release dates will be shared in my monthly newsletter soon! Are you signed up?

FREE BOOK

Get a glimpse of Morgan, Meg, Molly and Mina—*before* their happily ever afters take place!

Sign up for the author's Reader's List and get a free copy of the Lost & Found prequel novella "Girls Night Out."

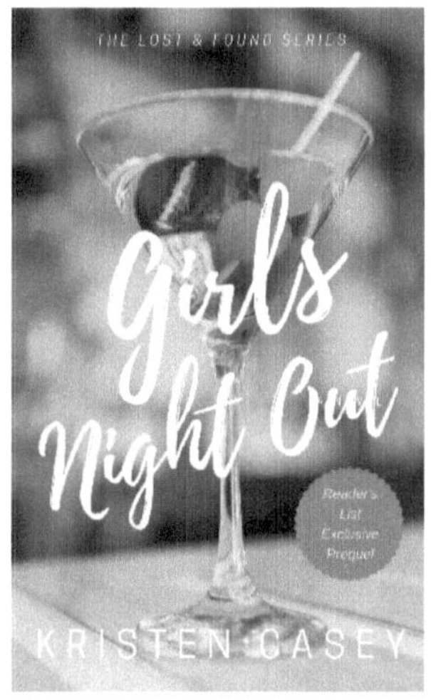

Visit Here to Get Started:

http://eepurl.com/ctGk1j

Also by Kristen Casey

The Triple Threat Series

The Titan Was Tall
The Doctor Was Dark
The Hero Was Handsome
The Triple Threat Box Set

The Lost & Found Series

Girls Night Out
Finding Home
Finding Love
Lost in Love
The Flynn Sisters Box Set
Finding a Husband
Finding Forever
Forever and a Day
The O'Connell Sisters Box Set

Acknowledgments

False Flag is my tenth romance novel and the first full-length book I've published since the COVID-19 pandemic began. The last few years have disrupted every writing routine I had in place, turning my publishing schedule upside-down and my ability to focus inside-out. I can not convey what a relief it is to have somehow, someway unearthed the flow of words that had been there for me before, and to have turned them into a story worth reading. There were several times in the writing of this book that current events coincidentally reflected the direction of my plot - which was both entertaining and not a little disconcerting, to say the least.

In any case, it helped me to know that I was on the right track. I hope you think so, too.

With that said, I'd like to extend a heartfelt thank you to Deborah Bradseth of Tugboat Design for *False Flag*'s gorgeous cover. Deborah has designed every one of my covers so far, and each one has turned out better than the last. I remain grateful for her knowledge and for her attention to detail, and for the way she puts up with my nitpicking about tiny things. She's a joy to work with.

Thanks also go to Helen Snay, whose sharp eye and helpful insight continue to make my books better. She's been asking for this title for a while now (semi-patiently), and I'm so happy that False Flag lived up to her expectations.

Finally, thank you from the bottom of my heart to my family, whose unwavering love and support makes all of this possible. You are my own happy-ever-after.

About the Author

Kristen Casey writes the kind of heartfelt, steamy books she loves to read—full of relatable characters and delicious dialogue. She lives in Maryland with her husband, two kids, and assorted cats, and in her free time enjoys all things crafty—especially projects she makes from yarn.

Sign up for her newsletter to receive exclusive content, sales, and new releases emailed right to your inbox.

Follow her on social media, for even more fun stuff!

Goodreads: Kristen_Casey

Facebook: AuthorKCasey

Twitter: AuthorKCasey

Pinterest: KristenCase0461

Instagram: Kristen.Casey.Books

BookBub: Kristen Casey

TikTok: KristenWritesRomance

Reading Order of Kristen's Books

The Lost & Found Series
Girls Night Out (Prequel exclusive to subscribers)
Finding Home (Book 1)
Finding Love (Book 2)
Lost in Love (Book 2.5 – Includes Lucky in Love)
The Flynn Sisters Box Set (Includes Christmas in Cambridge)
Finding a Husband (Book 3)
Finding Forever (Book 4)
Forever and a Day (Book 4.5 – Includes Forever Starts Now)
The O'Connell Sisters Box Set (Includes Heroes & Husbands)

The Triple Threat Series
The Titan Was Tall (Book 1)
The Doctor Was Dark (Book 2)
The Hero Was Handsome (Book 3)
The Triple Threat Box Set (Includes The Masquerade Was Magic and The Hero's Brother)

The Black Watch Security Series
False Flag (Book 1)
Heat Seeking Missile (Book 2)
Brothers in Arms (Book 3)
Fight or Flight (Book 4)
Search and Destroy (Book 5)
Squared Away (Book 6)